THE ONIONOLOGIST

The
ONIONOLOGIST

a novel by

M.J. Parfitt

Published by Phosphorus Press

Hardcover ISBN 978-1-7637001-2-3
Paperback ISBN 978-1-7637001-0-9
Ebook ISBN 978-1-7637001-1-6

For my first readers—Izzy, Liv, Maddy, Elli, Mum, and Ed.
Writing a book isn't so hard when people believe in you.
You carry my heart wherever you go.

Cotton Candy

The fluorescent ceiling lights flickered above my head, leading me into the airline office. Hesitating, I pressed the button to go up. In the past few years, I'd seen nothing in the building being repaired, but today, workers in blue overalls stood beside me. The unmistakable ding meant there was no going back, and I took a sharp intake of breath.

"Are you here to fix the lift?" I asked.

The maintenance worker smiled at me and shook her head.

"No, not the lift. There's a leak in the ceiling upstairs. Are you going up?"

"I guess I have to,"

"How bad is it up there?" she asked.

"You have no idea," I said.

Once we were in the lift, she pointed to my hair, and patting it, I retrieved a small twig wedged into a couple of escaping hairpins.

The journey to work had been challenging, and I felt like I'd competed in an episode of *The Amazing Race*. I waited for the rest of the day to unravel, expecting disaster in every step I took. I was in a downward spiral of doom and thought that perhaps I'd snag my stockings or be late and incur the wrath of the crew officer. A lead weight had lodged itself in my stomach since that morning.

When I opened the doors to the office, the familiar fragrance hit me: expensive perfumes, hairspray, and photocopy paper mingled, creating a signature airline scent. I stashed my bulky suitcase in a corner, along with a host of clones, and made my way into the crew office, shouting overzealous hellos.

I was relieved when I spotted Lucy talking to Claire; her dark, shiny ponytail with a minuscule orange clip made her recognisable even from behind. The clip was not an approved colour for our uniform, but she always wore it to work and never got pulled up for it.

"Lucy, you crack me up! I'm jealous. Sounds like a great night— Elle! Um, Lucy was telling me about your night out last week. You should invite me next time."

Claire's face was flushed; she squeezed my arm, pecked Lucy on the cheek and bolted off as soon as I joined them. I watched her open the door to the crew lounge; a chorus of chatting and laughing filtered out into the main office, juxtaposing with the severe and sterile atmosphere there.

There had yet to be an attempt to improve the aesthetic of anything, from the cold, grey metal office furniture to the dull paint on the walls. The dated accessories dotted around did nothing to make the space comfortable or welcoming; it needed dire renovation. Stained ceiling tiles and tired paintwork caught my eye at every turn. The faults all stood out today for the first time as if someone had just turned up the dreadful fluorescent strip lights to maximum brightness.

"Was it something I said?"

M. J. PARFITT

"Yeah, that was weird. Not like Claire," said Lucy.

Claire was one of those people you meet in life that everyone adores. If you invited her to your party, she would work the room and talk to everyone. By the night's end, she would acquaint herself with your mum, sister, and aunty and find out what your dog had for dinner—she was a sweetheart. Still, we weren't fond of her best friend Alex, and together, they were like a small box of chocolates; if you wanted the orange cream, you had to take all the flavours, and Alex was the Turkish Delight minus the delight.

I hugged Lucy and didn't want to let go. She was my living weighted blanket. I'd bought one from Amazon after buying into the hype. The weight and softness of it calmed me down whenever I was sad or exhausted. The downside was that it was heavy to lug around. If I ever got robbed in the night, I imagined popping it on the intruder, and he'd never be able to escape.

"God, I'm glad you're here! We have a lot to catch up on."

Lucy beamed at me as she fiddled with a loose thread hanging from my jacket. Whether it was my smeary sunglasses or re-packing my suitcase—she noticed the small things I didn't.

"You have the wrong shoes on, and you look sweaty, like you've been on a hike on your way here. Or did you meet some handsome stranger and go for a quickie somewhere?" she said, while we walked up to sign in for our flight.

"Hilarious. I've had the worst morning. I lost a shoe and—"

"Hey, Elle! Lucy!"

Spinning, I cricked my neck to greet the wide grin on Angus's face, and any remnants of the angst of my trip to work dissipated in a cloud of fairy floss and unicorns. He walked in with his jacket over one shoulder with panache. It reminded me of a 1960s Pan Am advertisement. All he needed was a gorgeous blonde on each arm, some Ray–Bans and Carly Simon's 'You're So Vain' accompanying his entrance. An outsider looking in might think him arrogant. Still, I knew he was being sarcastic and I loved every cynical inch of him. If Lucy was my weighted blanket, Angus was my Prozac.

"They called me out on standby! I can't believe I'm missing quiz night, but when I heard you two were on the flight, happy days! This is going to be epic! I've been trying to call you all weekend, Elle. Why didn't you call me back?"

"Sorry, I had car issues, and Hunter was in a weird mood. I'll explain later."

I spun to face Lucy, and we both looked at each other in confusion after hearing a loud creak. We looked up too late to react to part of the ceiling giving way. With no time to move, it tackled Lucy to the ground and missed me, apart from the cloud of white dust covering the lapels of my jacket. I froze as a large silver pipe hung in front of my face. Chaos in the office ensued, where everyone was confused.

"Elle, what was that?"

"Part of the ceiling. It fell on Lucy!"

Everyone moved in slow motion. There were hushed conversations behind the desk and gestures to the crew manager, Monty Blake. There was no immediate rush to offer first aid. Monty bustled out of his glass-walled office. He looked away when I squinted at him for a response.

"Lucy how are you feeling?" he asked.

He emphasised the word 'feeling,' paused and fidgeted with a form he was holding in his hand.

The egg on Lucy's head kept growing. I knelt beside her and shot a death stare at Monty.

"Can you at least bring some water and ice?"

Monty shot me a sideways glance, his face flushed, and he hurried off. He returned with a plastic cup of warm water and a withered smile.

Lucy tried to stand and stumbled like a scrawny newborn foal as we eased her into a chair.

"I think you'll be OK to fly, Lucy," said Monty. "It's just a bump. Please sign this. It's for workplace safety. We have to report any incidents on-site."

Confused, Lucy took the pen Monty was offering and stared at it. I looked up at him and then glanced farther out into the office. Monty's minions were still standing and gawking, but none came to help or enquire about Lucy. They fiddled with pens, looked down or pretended to be working on a super-urgent computer task.

They never had your back. Anytime I'd had a complaint from a passenger, they were quick to drag me in and grill me. It was impossible to recall a time when they had taken my side. Once, they chastised me because a passenger wanted to keep all her Harrods purchases by the emergency exit. She wrote a complaint letter after I insisted she put them in the overhead compartment. They told me that was not the way to handle it. That's when I had doubts about my chosen career path.

"She won't be signing the form, Monty; you might as well take it away." After I snatched the pen and paper from Lucy, I shoved them back at him.

"Well, it's company policy, Elle, I'm not sure—"

"Forget it, Monty. What is it? A liability waiver?"

He looked at me and backed into his office, muttering about me overreacting, and I turned to Lucy. She was pale and quiet. Angus returned with an ice pack, put his arm around her, and rolled his eyes at me.

"I don't think she should fly."

"No, I'm OK, I'm OK."

Lucy stood with stiff, awkward steps and rubbed at her head. Angus and I knew attempting to change her mind would be futile.

I thought back to her decision to have her beautiful hair cut short. Angus and I had tried to talk her out of it for a week. The pixie cut looked fabulous as she walked into the bar, surprising us on a night out. Lucy was right about most things; even when wrong, she was confident in her decisions.

Angus shrugged, and I returned a weak smile.

Earlier that morning, I'd drawn a smiley face in the condensation of my apartment window. Droplets running from the eyes resembled tears, and they were mine. I procrastinated about closing my suitcase, getting showered, putting on makeup, and racing around doing household chores I didn't have time for, such as folding washing that might have waited until I returned home. Brushing my teeth, the sparkler on my finger caught the light. I reminded myself about my engagement the day before, looking down at my hand and telling myself to be happy. My stomach fluttered with butterflies about the impending flight. It was always a lucky dip of workmates for the day; sometimes, the trip flew by and you didn't want it to end. Other times,

M. J. PARFITT

it meant working with the cast of *Mean Girls* and then going on a mini holiday with them.

As the lift doors opened, my upstairs neighbour was already inside.

"Morning, Elle. Off somewhere exotic today?"

He was carrying a bright green smoothie and his gym bag.

"Rather be you. Do you want to swap? I'd even drink that green potion. Think of me being imprisoned on a metal bird for eight hours as you're eating your dinner."

I wanted to be at home, spending the night with Hunter. I wanted to sit down with him, plan the wedding over a bottle of wine, not heat food carts, and deal with hand luggage and screaming kids for hours. These trips were frequent, and I'd be off somewhere else by the time I was over the jet lag.

I sat still in my car, which clung onto its new car fragrance, trying to check my complexion in the rearview mirror. It was smeary, and I rubbed at it, making it much worse. I might have been a blurred background on a Zoom meeting or someone who didn't want to be recognised in a TV report. My hair was in place with a neat bun at the back, a whole packet of hair pins hiding underneath, like a scaffolding job by a lousy builder. I'd sprayed my face with a finishing spray where it would sit, clogging my pores for the next eight hours or more. It was a mere mask, but it was all I had.

There was a time when this was the life I craved more than any-thing else. I'd have sold my soul for it or, at least, committed cold-blooded murder, and now I had an acute case of be careful what you wish for.

I was twenty-two years old and leaving for a trip to New York, and I knew there was something very wrong with me for taking my lucky life for granted like this.

At my last school reunion, everyone had been interested in what I did for work. Helen, whom I bonded with in maths class over our struggles with algebra and a shared love of Christian French—the nerd who sat in the first row—had lamented about her office job for a local solicitor. She might smack me round the head if she witnessed me like this.

It was a straightforward job, and I did it on autopilot and may well have been able to do it standing on my head or juggling plates. The opportunity to travel was exciting and fabulous, but you had to live the life to understand that the best thing about it wasn't the perks or the travel. It was the people. During my training course, I made my two best friends, and they were why I didn't leave.

The absolute truth was I envied people getting ready for their nine-to-five lives. If they were happy, then they were the lucky ones. Home every weekend, never missing a family get-together or dinner with friends. To be content in an ordinary life—why couldn't my heart and brain accept that as my lot? Taking a deep breath, I fooled myself into happiness once again.

M. J. PARFITT

Pressing the start button on the car and looking down at the battery indicator, it was clear I'd forgotten to charge it the day before.

"Fucking Tesla," I said, slicing the fragile Zen vibe up with a temper like a samurai sword. I sat sweating in my seat, expecting something magical to happen as if I were a heroine in a movie. A solution would present itself at any minute, and life would be perfect again. Perhaps James Bond would appear in a helicopter and whisk me off to Heathrow.

Hunter and I had made it back to my apartment by the skin of our teeth the day before for precisely the same reason—I hadn't fully charged the car. Angus had called several times, interrupting our argument, and Hunter kept ending the call.

"Perhaps it's important," I'd said.

"I doubt anything Angus wants is important. Jesus, Elle. Use regenerative braking, or we won't make it back."

We lurched into the car park, and he got out, slamming the door behind him. I chased after him, forgetting to put the car on charge again. It was a strange end to what should have been an incredible day after the engagement. I had ruined it with my lack of attention to detail, letting me down again. I'd spent hours afterwards trying to coax Hunter into a happier mood.

Tears built up, and I tried to blink them away. Tiny beads of sweat encroached on my upper lip. I got out, slammed the door hard, and kicked the tyre, hurting my toe. Elon Musk now had video footage of me attacking one of his beloved cars. A neighbour looked over at me with a bemused stare, and I recognised her from the day before when she'd also witnessed my argument with Hunter. I pulled myself together and waved, but she ignored me, got in her car, and sped off.

"Fuck you, we can't all be perfect."

There was no time to charge the car, even a smidge. My sole option was to Uber to the train station and jump on a train to Heathrow. There was no escaping that it would be a painful process with luggage and the uniform inviting gawking from fellow commuters, but there was no other choice. Calling my sister Holly wasn't on the table because she'd be busy with her toddler, Walter, and Dad might still be in bed. This left Hunter, and I'd be calling him over my dead body. I didn't want to give him more ammunition—he already thought I was an idiot for not charging the car the day before and would dine out on this for weeks at every opportunity he got, ridiculing me in front of his friends and family and saying I should never have bought the Tesla. It hadn't gone down well when I did it without his agreement. I backed down on most things, but now and then, I would break out and light a fire to prove I still had some autonomy left.

Shivering on the street in my thin uniform jacket, I stared at my phone, getting irritated as 'Jarrad,' the Uber dot, moved around on nearby roads, enticing me with an imminent arrival, then stopping or turning around. A sparse chestnut tree above my head rustled with a squawk and flapping, and I looked up just as a lone branch swung at me, and I ducked to avoid it. What I didn't avoid was the bird poop on my shoulder.

As soon as I got in the car, I took off my jacket and rubbed at the stain with a wet wipe. Through the car window, I stared at the gloomy sky, which was broken up by the bare sticks of trees lining the high street. The odd collection of shops with peeling paint and dirty windows was sad and unloved. They sped past my window in a depressing movie reel. I speculated on how many customers passed through the doors of Hockey Land or Spring's Mattresses. Later, it would bustle with people contented to live here with their ordinary lives. Something else had to be out there for me. I didn't know what that was, but I had to find it. If I didn't, I would die a slow, painful death towards my thirties.

"Where are you off to?"

"Oh, um, New York."

I hesitated at this question if I was in a taxi or Uber.

"Yeah, I won't be gone long. My dad is coming later to look after my cat."

The car's air con was distributing cheap aftershave, which wafted over me and made me gag. I wanted to jump out and walk.

I imagined Hunter's face if I had adopted a cat. He detested them. He'd thrown an empty beer can at his neighbour's small ginger cat when it had dared venture into the hallway outside his apartment door. Because of this, his neighbours kept a wide berth of him, and the cat had been missing from the hallway ever since. It had turned into a huge argument when I'd chastised him for being cruel. Hunter said it wasn't mean, just that the stink was abhorrent, and the cat had scratched his doormat. I was sticking up for the cat when he said I should have been sticking up for him, which made him detest the cat even more. The simple truth was I loved cats and would always protect a cat or any animal before a human, even Hunter.

We had a family cat when I was a child, and I adored him from his arrival as a tiny, fragile kitten to the big lump of fluff he'd morphed into in his later years. I missed having a pet, but being with Hunter Woods was worth the sacrifice. Sure, he was a little flashy, and there were other things I'd have to change about him, such as how he smiled at other women when he thought I wasn't looking or interrupted and corrected me every time I spoke. I told myself all men did this and thought I could fix him. After all, he'd asked me to spend the rest of my life with him.

"Guess you won't be away for long though, eh? It's not like a holiday, is it, your job? Must be annoying going all that way and not seeing a place."

I picked at the skin around my nail and bit my cheek. People always assumed I was flying to Costa Brava for the day and back with a planeload of tourists. They hated it when I disrupted their narrative to tell them I was going to Tokyo or New York for a few days.

"Yeah," I said. "You're right; we don't stay anywhere. We get there and turn right back."

The driver must have detected my sarcasm. I saw him glance at me in the mirror, and he didn't speak for the rest of the trip down the motorway.

I tried to appear composed at the station like I caught the train to work every day. Holding my head high, ignoring all the stares, I spun around and studied the departure sign. It was the wrong platform. With the most awkward twist of my ankle, I dashed past a stationary train and off came my shoe. It was under the train, sitting on the gravel between the tracks where it would live until someone thought to remove it.

It reminded me of those odd shoes you saw at the side of roads that caused you to ponder on what event had led them there. Now, I'd created a mystery for someone else. My hair escaped from the neat bun, my face flushed, and my deodorant was failing under my shirt. I wished I hadn't got sucked in by the advertising campaign for 'Primal Forest' natural deodorant with no chemicals. It had a realistic scent, like a pine forest or an old Christmas tree, but I needed a bucket load of chemicals right now to get me through this fiasco. I knew I would have to brave the station toilet and freshen up. This idea filled me with dread; public toilets were filthy enough, but I knew without venturing inside what awaited me in a train station toilet.

I looked from side to side. Tears welled in my eyes for the second time in an hour. I bent down, unzipped the flight bag, and took out the flat shoes I wore onboard. My feet sighed as I changed into these comfortable granny shoes. Walking past a grotty bin, I hurled the matching shoe into it, turned and stuck a middle finger up to the lone shoe on track two, and headed to the correct platform, forgetting to freshen-up in the station toilet.

As the train pulled in, I was sure it had some enormous black eyelashes attached to the front, but I decided I was hallucinating and put it down to stress.

There were no seats. It was jam-packed with people going to work at the airport or off on a trip somewhere. Holding onto the rail, I avoided eye contact with creepy men who reeked of dirty hair and clothes, and my body folded into uncomfortable angles, not connecting with anyone, trying to recycle air. Many eyes turned towards me, finding it impossible not to look at the uniform.

A lady in a trench coat was staring at me; it was a subliminal message, and I was once again a wind-up doll, ready for work: the forced warmth, the fake smile. Little did she know I'd prefer to hop off the train and go around to Hunter's apartment to check that everything was OK after our argument instead of flying to New York. It would niggle away at me now until I came home.

A seat opened as a man jumped off the train and made a beeline. As I looked out the window, I noticed a poster with a giant mascara wand curved over the track, and I realised the train actually did have eyelashes. It was probably one of the most hilarious adverts I had ever seen. I googled 'Train Your Lashes Mascara' to see where to buy it.

Then I texted Hunter:

"Hey, sorry about yesterday. I'm an airhead. Just looking at my beautiful ring. Can't wait to get married. Wish I wasn't going away. Love you."

I stared at the screen, expecting an immediate response. In return, I received a lacklustre, lone smiley face emoji.

M. J. PARFITT

Monty had collected himself after I'd told him off, and he was his brash self again, singing out orders and marching around the office.

"Elle, why are you not wearing the correct shoes?"

"Oh, sorry, Monty, I twisted my ankle yesterday at Pilates."

I stared into his eyes and dared him to carry on. He strolled off to his office with a huff. His trademark dyed-red bouffant was sprayed into perfection, but the grey roots poked through, contrasting with his impeccable dogtooth pants with a precise crease down each leg.

He had flaws as a human and a manager, but he always looked immaculate apart from his hair, which confounded me. His office also didn't reflect this personal presentation, and I noticed the piles and piles of paperwork spilling out from folders on every surface. A half-dead spider plant sat unloved atop a metal filing cabinet and faded posters of island locations which would have once been bright and enticing gave vibes of dreams long since given up on. I imagined other discarded items under his desk, such as a week-old Chinese takeaway, coffee cups, and beaten-up driving shoes.

"Come on, Lucy, let's help you up."

"Oh, thanks for looking after me, you two. That was a lot!"

The three of us walked off into our final crew briefing together. If I had been aware of it, I'd have bottled it up and stored the moment in a little time capsule in my brain, along with all the unforgettable moments in the job over the years. Instead, I stood there, hands in my jacket pocket, turning my new engagement ring round and round on my finger and watching Lucy to ensure she didn't keel over. Dust caked the sterile white plastic clock on the wall. I wished it backwards instead of listening to the captain's briefing on the flight path, cruising altitude or time of arrival. I need not have worried because Angus was writing it all in his yellow notebook.

Vitis Riparia

*O*nboard, Angus and I watched Lucy head to the upper deck, where she was working to make sure she navigated the stairs OK. We strolled down the aisle to our business class galley as soon as she had disappeared.

"Do you think she'll be OK?"

"It was quite a bump. I'm worried. It all seems odd to me. I still can't get my head around any of it. Who in their right mind would let someone fly after that accident?"

"Yeah, but you know why. Monty would have had to call someone out on standby, and it was late, and the flight would have been late. I'll bet there's some snobby VIP onboard."

"You think they'd do that? Put the flight before a human? Jeez, that's hard for me to understand."

My wish for a quiet flight came true as Angus showed me the passenger numbers. There were a lot of spare seats. I knew there would be a game of musical chairs where passengers tried to snag an entire row before anyone else. I had every intention of letting them fight it out for themselves. Angus was familiar with my lack of attention to detail and had written all the flight details out three times, once for himself, once for me and once for Lucy. He had even nudged me when the manager asked a safety question at the briefing. He was my work husband; it was a shame I couldn't work every flight with him, as I'd have enjoyed the job much more.

In the galley, I reached up to put my handbag away in a small compartment, closed it with a satisfying click, opened another, and took out the plastic cups. I could find anything in any galley with a blindfold at this stage. Angus let out a squeal.

"What the fuck, Angus?"

"Never mind me, what is that rock on your hand? Are you engaged? To Hunter?" he said, grabbing my hand and turning the ring over to inspect it.

"Well, yes, who else? Sorry, it was such a surprise yesterday. I haven't even told my dad or Holly yet."

"Where was the Instagram post?"

"Sorry. I should have called you. Who'd have thought when we met in Barbados on that trip that we'd get married? I hadn't even noticed him before. That was two years ago next week. I fell hook, line, and sinker on that trip."

"You sure did."

We ventured out of the galley and helped passengers as they boarded with endless luggage. Angus and I liked to play a game of who was wearing the most ridiculous outfit as the passengers boarded. I made mental notes of a man who looked like Prince, wearing a pearl necklace with a gold cross at the centre, and a lady with a Christmas T-shirt even though it was October, which read: 'I'm here for the presents,' with a picture of the Grinch underneath. One round man had three pairs of glasses dangling from his shirt; another was wearing multiple items of clothing depicting fish. I was excited to reveal my list, but when I opened my mouth to tell him, he walked off and busied himself with a passenger who couldn't read seat numbers.

Hunter had been acting strange for a few days after a recent trip with Angus to San Francisco. He kept pacing around and couldn't sit still.

"Elle let's go to the pub for lunch," he'd said.

"Oh, OK, sure, just let me get changed."

He looked impatient as if he'd prefer I hopped into his car in my Marmite jar–emblazoned PJs, with no makeup on my face. With his appearance, he took things seriously. Each season, he would take himself into Harvey Nicks and get the assistants to deck him out in a whole new wardrobe that cost thousands. I thought this was over the top, but I reconciled it with what I would prefer. A guy that took me to the pub in a hi-vis vest didn't hold much appeal.

We pulled up in his silver Porsche outside the Duck and Goose. First, he dropped his car keys in the footwell; then, he fumbled with the greasy iron handle on the door to the pub.

"Is everything all right, Hunter? Are you tired?"

I reached for his hand, but he marched to the beer garden, expecting me to follow. We sat on a picnic bench, and he had trouble looking me in the eye.

"Hunter, what's wrong? Are you breaking up with me?"

He ignored me and stumbled around on the grass—I thought he'd lost his contacts and bent down to help him. We cracked heads, and I stood up, rubbing mine, but he stayed on one knee and opened a duck-egg blue velvet box.

"Elle, will you marry me?"

I paused. There were no telltale signs leading up to this event, no moments when I'd suspected an impending proposal. I'd thought the opposite might happen. It was as if we had missed out on a stage, cheating me out of one of life's most memorable events.

"Um. Wow. Y—yes. Of course."

I looked down at the diamond ring I'd seen before at Tiffany's and feigned a big smile. It was out of place on my small hand, and I wouldn't have chosen it for myself. The central stone was a clear, square-cut diamond and smaller diamonds sat around its entire band, which I assumed was platinum. This grand gesture would have cost him a few months' salary. People on a neighbouring table cheered, and I blushed, turned, and smiled at them, and he slid the ring on my finger. He had beads of sweat on his forehead, even though it wasn't a warm day. I hadn't had time to digest any of it. Hunter looked as relieved as if he had just completed the London Marathon, and I had the misplaced sensation I had just passed the start line.

Leaving me mid-sentence, mouth half open, unsure what was going on, Angus swished out of the galley without even looking at me. It wasn't like him. Twisting the ring on my finger, I questioned why Hunter wanted to marry me, a person who wasn't brilliant, funny, beautiful, or accomplished, just plain awkward most of the time. I looked down at my shoe and spied a small square of toilet paper stuck to the heel, confirming my ineptness on cue.

I left the galley for the prolonged period of carry-on luggage wars and glanced at Angus, who was now laughing with some young guys. As the emergency video played, we converged again in the galley and shared another awkward silence. I couldn't recall ever having an awkward silence with Angus.

"OK, let's go do the crotch walk," he said.

"Oh, my fave."

Angus sat beside me on the jump seat as we prepared for take-off. I looked at the grey Heathrow fog, unsure if I'd miss it deep down. I hated this bit. I wanted to get on with the meal service and get the entire flight over with. A passenger tried to stand up and open the overhead bin and I signalled to him to sit back down. As I pulled out my small dog-eared notebook, which I found crumpled in my pocket, several hairpins fell out, and Angus shook his head at me.

"What's the plan, Angus? Bloody Marys and Eggs Benny at The King? They open at eleven. We could dump our bags and go straight there."

He didn't reply but studied the white, fluffy clouds out of the window.

"Look at that one, Elle. It looks like a bum."

The clouds always resembled something rude. It was never, 'Look at this one; it looks like a chair.' Angus could tell you about every kind of cloud, from cumulus to stratocumulus.

"You're a genuine mystery to me, Angus. You're in the wrong job. What about training as a meteorologist or something?"

He took an insane amount of cloud photos and filled his Insta feed with them every day.

"Have you signed up for TikTok yet? You need to follow my account."

"Argh, not getting on the bandwagon of another social media platform."

I smiled at the passenger opposite the jump seat, who stared at us. We were like caged animals on display in an airline zoo.

"Late night last night?"

Moving my gaze from the passenger, I turned to watch Angus.

"Might have an early one and watch a movie in my room."

"You? Stay in your room. Are you serious? What's going on? We should celebrate my engagement."

The passenger opposite gave me a disdainful sneer, and the plane lurched as the captain announced we were passing through turbulence.

"No shit, Sherlock," I said.

Some overhead bins clattered open, and a cart escaped from the galley. Unclipping my belt, I nipped in, secured it, and slid back onto the jump seat.

"Are you sick of this job, Angus? I mean, it's not challenging. We're not doing anything noteworthy, are we? I think I'm over it all."

I was fortunate that I hadn't had an onboard emergency. Nothing memorable except that once a passenger drank an entire bottle of duty-free whisky and pooped his pants, which was more of a dilemma than an emergency. Or, another time, someone choked on a banana.

I'd never had to say, 'Brace for impact' or 'Is there a doctor on board?'
I'd never slid down an emergency slide except in training once a year
in a faded blue jumpsuit. I knew this was a good thing—it meant I was
working in a safe industry where the standards worked—but I wanted
more out of life.

"Exactly why I like it," said Angus.

The seat belt sign came off, and the service began. People were awake
and demanding. It was an impossible Tetris puzzle of who wanted
which meal and navigation of passengers who thought it was a great
time to go to the toilet just as we had the cart in the middle of the
aisle.

In seat Twelve C sat a well-dressed lady with a casual, chic appearance. It was how I wished I looked—tall and lean like she could wear
a bikini or an Afghan coat walking down the King's Road any day of
the week. She kept getting up and removing things from the bag she'd
stowed in the overhead compartment. It baffled me why passengers
didn't keep everything in a small bag under their seats.

"Can you bring me a glass of Champagne? Not your cheap
sparkling stuff," she said.

I paused and leaned into her seat. "Oh, I'm sorry, that's only
available in first class. Business class does have a lovely sparkling."

"Are you kidding me? You're just a glorified waitress, but you
should educate yourself on the Champagne you serve; it's your job. It's
not too much to ask. We're paying a fortune to sit here, run along,
read your wine list, and bring me my Champagne."

She picked up a glossy magazine and feigned boredom. I caught the scent of the new magazine aroma wafting towards me and wished I could kick back with a glass of Champagne and a copy of *Vogue* instead of walking up and down the aisle with a tray.

As I slumped away with pitying or perhaps condescending glances from fellow passengers, I balled up my fists and bit my lip. There would be no more crying today.

Back in the galley, I shoved the cart in, kicked it, and gave the passenger the finger through the wall dividing the galley from the cabin. I was used to being treated like a dumb blonde. On the last flight I'd operated to Tokyo, a girl band seated in business class had asked me to hold up a blanket as they got changed into loungewear as if I was their assistant. I suggested they get changed in the bath-room, and it didn't go down too well. They'd pressed the call button for the rest of the flight just to prove a point.

The ironic thing about the misconception we were all dumb was that I had worked with countless people who had since done great things that required a brain. Some were now even pilots. Long-haul flying attracted adventurous people, not dumb people.

The main point that most passengers like this didn't seem to consider was that our glorified presence was an insurance policy you never wanted to use. We were there to enforce safety standards, get them off safely in an emergency, and administer first aid when required. It wasn't a joke. We trained for it intensively, and we would all be able to get them onto the wing of an aircraft if it was floating in the ocean, tie a life raft and swim if need be.

M. J. PARFITT

I brushed it off once I'd calmed down; I reached for a warm Champagne glass, and filled it with some cheap sparkling wine. Angus popped his head around the pleated curtain.

"What's up? You look like death. Are we being hijacked?"

"Oh, it's this 'Philip' in Twelve C; she's being a real bitch about her drink. She wants Champagne, and I explained it's not in business, but she's demanding it, anyway."

He tapped his pockets, produced some eye drops, plopped in a giant slug, and whisked the drink away. He was famous among the crew for these pranks. Plastic poo on a toilet seat was his signature move.

I could have stopped him. The passenger deserved a touch of diarrhoea, but I struggled with the retribution side of life. Once again, Angus was doing my dirty work for me.

The chief purser, Leanne, walked into the galley and overheard Angus as he was joking about the eye drop dosing.

"You have got to be kidding me! Did you poison a passenger? What if she sues us or becomes unwell on the flight? There will be consequences for you both. How could you be this stupid? Especially you, Elle."

It wasn't like me to be this cavalier with my job. I'd lost the will to care about any of it. This was a shitty day in a long run of shitty days, and perhaps I wanted the trouble that might follow. Leanne backed out of the galley, tutting. I knew she'd be completing an incident report as soon as she returned to first class. I wished I hadn't told Angus anything about the 'Philip.' We were both in hot water, and he liked the job; he wasn't at the same stage I was at yet. I knew he'd get there, but right now, he was content. I imagined we might get a slap on the wrist when we got back to London, which would go on our files.

We peered around the galley curtain as the passenger knocked back the cheap bubbles like Lilly Bollinger.

"She wouldn't know her arse from her elbow! What a stupid old cow. Telling me I don't understand wine. I understand I wouldn't drink that shite."

After the meal service, Lucy turned up in our cabin as Angus and I were rubbing lemon and sugar into our hands. It was one of our onboard rituals; it made our hands soft and filled in the downtime. The galley now had the pleasing bouquet of Bombay Sapphire and fresh lemons.

"How is it in the upper echelons? I'm jealous of you. You always seem to work up there. Do you bribe Monty or something? Do you bake him secret cakes? Nothing bad ever seems to happen up there. You look pale. How are you feeling?"

"Sick, Elle. I'm going to faint."

"Lucy, a ceiling fell on your head three hours ago. I told you not to fly, and when they tried to make you sign the form!"

"What form?"

She rocked from one side to the other, and I used my body weight to stop her from falling and eased her down to the rubber floor. She was like a dead weight.

"Bloody hell," said Angus. "What's going on now?"

He sat beside her, holding her hand, and I grabbed a cold face towel and placed it on her forehead. Then, for the first time, I asked if there was a doctor onboard over the PA.

A Scottish junior doctor called Dr Kelly approached the galley.

"What do we have here, then?" she said, crouching before Lucy. She looked at her head and checked her pupils.

"Look, I think she'll be OK. She may have had a minor concussion. Can she lie down somewhere for the rest of the flight?"

"Oh yeah," said Angus, "We have bunks."

"Oh, I don't think she should be up high."

"There are lower ones, too," I said.

"What happened to her head?"

"Oh my god, you wouldn't believe it; part of the office ceiling fell on her before we left," said Angus.

"I meant to tell you this, Angus, but when I was waiting for the lift to the office, some workers mentioned a leak in the ceiling they were fixing."

"Hmm," he said. "Interesting."

"And they still let her fly? That's a lawsuit waiting to happen. What's the beautiful lemon smell?" asked the doctor.

"Here," said Angus, "Rub this sugar in with the lemon. It's our secret recipe. I am going to bottle it up one day. Stops your hands feeling dry."

We guided Lucy to the small bunk area, tucked her into a crew bunk and drew up a roster to sit with her for the rest of the flight. I took the first turn watching; she was quiet, and my mind raced.

"Lucy, are you asleep?"

"No. My head hurts. When can I have some more painkillers?"

I looked at the glowing face of my watch.

"Not for a bit. Hang in there. Shall we chat? I don't want you falling asleep."

"Sure, if you like, but you can do all the talking. I can't think straight."

"What am I going to do with my life? I have 'A Levels,' but that's it. I've got a mortgage on the apartment and bills to pay. How can I change careers now? And Hunter would never agree to it, of course."

A familiar lump formed in my throat, and I loosened my scarf. I looked around the tiny space. There were six beds. Pistachio-coloured, itchy blankets sat on top of crisp white sheets. They had a weird stench, like dry cleaning chemicals.

"What's the point of these bunks? I mean, when do we ever have time to sleep in them? I can't say I've slept in them much. Do they ever change the sheets, do you think?"

There was no reply. Leaning over Lucy, I looked at her mouth. She opened her eyes with fright.

"What the fuck, Elle? What are you doing?"

"Just checking you were still breathing!"

"Not dead yet. The bunk bed monologue was a little much for me."

Hopping back into the opposite bunk, I let out a gigantic sigh.

"God, I can't do this anymore, and I understand about fucking wine."

"Are you sure the ceiling fell on me, not you? As for wine, you understand how to drink it."

As we neared the end of the flight, Lucy said she was feeling a little better, and we helped her upstairs. Angus and I had already done most of the work in our galley to prepare for landing, and I headed upstairs to give her a hand.

"Oh god, Jess has done most of the work. You're amazing, Jess," I said as Lucy's galley partner walked back with a tray in the upper-deck galley.

"How are you doing, Lucy?" Jess asked. "At least you've got some colour in your face now."

"OK, well, I better go back down and help Angus. Don't do too much, Lucy. Try to sit. I'll come back up after the passengers disembark and help you with your bags, OK?"

"How was she?" asked Angus.

He was stuffing mini–Grey Goose bottles into his cabin bag, and he took mine out of the compartment outside the galley and loaded it up, too, plus a nifty corkscrew I'd been admiring.

"Why have you got a jar of Marmite in here, Elle? We're going to New York, not Antarctica. It's waffles and bagels all the way, baby!"

"Hey, I can't live without my Marmite, and I'm not your mule!"

He laughed. "Let me get this straight. You're not going to drink these?"

"Haha, funny. Thanks for the corkscrew. I can use it to open all the bottles of wine I don't understand. How's the 'Philip' been? Any more trouble?"

"Well, she's been in the loo a lot. She doesn't look as polished now."

I peered out and watched her reach up for her bag again. Her hair was sticking up at all angles, her clothes no longer chic—they could have been from Primark—and her face was pale and blotchy.

"Payback's a bitch, isn't it?"

Moon Balls

*a*ngus changed his mind about a movie in his room. All it had taken were a few highlights in the taxi, like the Empire State Building and Brooklyn Bridge, and he was putty in my hands. He could never miss a night out in New York. Our conversation was fast-paced, loud, and a little manic. It was like this after every flight; a euphoria crept over you like you had just taken illegal drugs. I could see the taxi driver rolling his eyes.

"I think I've just gone past the point of no return," I said. "You know when you're so tired you stop being tired, and everything seems like a dream? Once, I stayed awake for thirty-six hours."

"I know, I was there! You just have to keep going. We can have a lie-in tomorrow," said Angus.

Lucy was quiet while she tried to apply eyeliner and mascara. Angus nudged her hand.

"Hey, watch it, you!" she said.

"Why are you making so much effort, anyway?" asked Angus.

"Angus, you never know who will be in this bar. I could meet the man that changes my life or I might get noticed by a model scout."

"Lucy, you are five foot five. You're not Kate Moss."

The drinks were going down fast, and we forgot all about the Eggs Benedict.

"How many have we had, Angus?"

"Shit, we haven't eaten," he said.

We scanned the menu and agreed on clam chowder in a cob bun because it seemed 'so New York.'

"Should we wait for Lucy? Why don't we order her some fries? She wouldn't eat chowder, anyway. Where is she? Should I send out a search party?"

The steaming chowder arrived, and the enticing aroma of spices and warm bread wafted under my nose.

"This is probably not the best choice of dinner when we've had a shit load of alcohol, is it?" asked Angus.

"I think we could have ordered one between us. I thought it said it was in a bun. This looks like a whole loaf."

To this day, I could never eat it again.

I watched as the bar filled with a swarm of after-work drink parties. We were well on the way to being too drunk, and the bar got louder and louder, and we had to shout to hear each other.

"Who's Lucy talking to?" I said.

"Mr Gorgeous. I clocked him as he walked in."

Tall and tanned with his white linen shirtsleeves rolled up, I wasn't picking up on any native New Yorker vibes; they were much more L.A. The dark jeans and boots gave him a self-assured, casual appearance, and my mind raced with thoughts of a sublime, younger version of Brad Pitt or Ryan Reynolds.

"Elle, are you listening to me?"

"What's up, Angus? What is it? You look like death. Are you

having a stroke, old chap?"

I feared he was about to announce a terminal illness or a move to Guatemala.

"Fuck, I'm going to say it now. I'm drunk enough. Look, Elle, you can't marry Hunter. He doesn't deserve you. I've been putting this off since San Fran. The number of times I tried to call you. I was ready to tell you yesterday, but you didn't answer the phone. He's a total wanker. God only knows why he proposed to you after everything he's done. He's making a fool of you, and I can't keep quiet and watch it anymore, especially after—"

He waved at my ring and gulped his beer.

"I knew it!" I said, banging my hand on the table. "I fucking knew it! He wouldn't let me answer the phone yesterday, Angus."

I cradled my hand on my lap, not wanting to ruin the moment of rebellion.

"It was Alex. She threw herself at him. Fucking blonde bob swinging from side to side, and she had on this tight little top that looked like any minute she was going to get a nip-slip. She went in for the jugular, taking the mic at a karaoke bar, and he was all over her like a rash. Even though I was there, he couldn't help himself. And even if he didn't do any of this, you still couldn't marry him. There is no way I can let my best friend change her name to Elle Woods. Every time you wore pink you'd the butt of *Legally Blonde* jokes."

My world collapsed. Alex was a talented singer; I'd heard it myself because I'd worked several flights with her, and instead of talking, sometimes she would sing in everyday conversation. It was like working with an overly dramatic cabaret singer; her voice appealed to everyone she met. Hell, I'd have kissed her myself. She could have been a professional; there must have been a backstory somewhere.

"Fuck, this is embarrassing. Who else was on the trip? Oh, hang on, let me guess. Claire? She was weird with me today at the office. I thought we were friends. Why did she stand by and let it happen? Oh my god, who else knows about this? Angus, we'll have to go to San Fran again. Let's do Napa and catch the ferry over from Vallejo. I need to, to—smudge it."

He guffawed.

"You're insane! You want to smudge San Francisco?"

"Right now, I hate San Francisco, and it's unfair. I can't let them ruin an entire city for me. They are not taking away my painted ladies!"

"Anyway, let me finish. Hunter and Alex were drunk and carried on to another bar after everyone else had gone home. I tried to persuade him to come back with me, but he wasn't having any of it. I tried, Elle.

"She made it clear what had happened the next morning on the crew bus, rubbing it in and talking loudly for my benefit. Before we took off, I confronted him and told him to eat a bag of dicks, but he said, 'Look, these things happen. I love Elle; Alex pursued it. It was all her.'

"She's vile, but come on, it takes two. Then to propose to you. What did Hunter think I was going to do? I'm sorry, when I saw the ring today. Oh my god, I wanted to die. How fucking *dare* he do this to you. All I could think about was pushing him out of the emergency exit on the flight home."

"Get in line. Hunter Woods thinks I'm pathetic and desperate, and I'll forgive him because who could live without him?"

Tears wouldn't come. A rage ran over my entire body, and I knocked back several straight vodkas alternating with sips from my Prosecco.

"Slow down, Elle. Pace yourself, or you'll see that chowder again soon, and it won't appear much different. Except there will be carrots."

Lucy came back giggling with her new friend.

"What's going on here, a fucking wake? I've spent half an hour building you up to Jude here!"

She kept looking at us both until I spoke up.

"Hunter's a motherfucker, and I'm unengaged," I said, ripping the Tiffany ring off and dropping it into my Prosecco with a plop.

Everyone looked at me. There was a chasm between us, filled with an awkward silence.

"Fuck Hunter Woods," I said.

"Yeah, fuck him!" shouted the guys on a neighbouring table.

I picked up my drink and necked it back in one gulp, forgetting about the sparkling ring at the bottom of the glass. They stared at me in astonishment as I wiped my mouth with my hand.

"What? Oh, shit, I drank it!"

"You're engaged?" said Lucy. "I didn't even get to see the bling! And now I never want to see it!"

We all cracked up, and Jude looked confused about what he'd stumbled into, but he couldn't help but get caught up in Angus's infectious laugh.

"You know what you have now, Elle, don't you?" he said.

"No, what?"

"Champagne problems!"

I was dizzy. Mixing grape and grain was coming to bite me. I crossed my arms on the sticky wooden table and dropped my head. 'Piece of My Heart' played in the background, and I wasn't so drunk I didn't pick up on the irony.

"Oh, my life sucks now. Fuck my life! I need to change everything, and I do understand wine."

"Why do you keep talking about wine? She was like this in the crew bunk earlier," said Lucy.

"Oh, she had a Philip in her aisle today who told her to read up on wine," said Angus.

"Philip?" asked Jude.

"It's crew code for 'passenger I'd like to punch' aka PILP, which morphed into Philip over the years," said Lucy.

"That's pretty funny, and glad my name's not Philip," said Jude.

I stood up, wobbling from side to side, and put my arms up in the air.

"I'm going to be a fucking oncologist."

The entire bar looked over.

"You're terrible at maths; that will never happen."

"No, no, but Angus, listen! I understand about wine, and I have a corkscrew!"

"Elle, while I'm sure doctors drink a fair amount of piss, I don't this it's a prerequisite."

"Doctors? What? Not a doctor, a wine person, a what's it—it was in the inflight magazine."

"I think what you meant to say was an oenologist," said Jude.

"Yes, that's what I said, guys, an Onionologist. I'm going to make

Champagne. My name is going to be on a label; that passenger will drink her words."

"Oh my, sit down before I break my ribs," said Angus, now curling into the side of the green leather booth. "Please stop. I can't breathe."

"Do it now!" said Lucy. "Let's find a course and enrol you!"

"This is kind of my area," said Jude. "I live in Sonoma. My family's had a vineyard there my whole life."

My speech had become slurry, and I tried to correct it.

"What kind of wine do you make? Oh, tell me it's Prosecco! Let's go there right now!"

"Haha. No, sorry, I'm mostly in the chardonnay business. I'd love to make Champagne one day, though. I'm in town trying to get new customers in bars like this."

"Oh no, Jude, I hate chardonnay. It's dry and tastes funny."

"Elle! Stop being rude," said Lucy.

"Oh, no, it's OK. You might like mine. You should come sometime and try it."

"Oh, I think I might like yours," I said.

Angus poked me in the ribs.

Jude smiled at me, and I could feel a magnetic pull to him, even in my drunken state. He emanated calmness and safety like he'd fight dragons for you or, at least, slay a cheating twat from London.

"It's a pretty fantastic career choice. If you have a degree in oenology, I mean, you can basically oversee the entire winemaking process."

I wasn't listening to him; all four eyes mesmerised me.

We embarked on a drunken rabbit warren of internet searches.

"Oh, this Pendleton place looks interesting, but I can't apply now, can I? It says I need all this information, and I don't have it; it's all at my dad's. I'll sort it when I'm back home."

"You won't," said Angus.

"He's right, you won't," said Lucy.

Angus dialled my dad and handed me the phone.

"Hello? Angus?"

"Hi, Dad, it's me. This is Angus's phone. Can you do me a favour?"

"Aren't you in New York, Elle?"

"Yes, Dad, we are, but I need you to scan some paperwork for me."

"Is everything OK? Are you in trouble?"

"Everything's fine. I just need this stuff for something. I'll explain when I get back. Do you know how to scan a document?"

"Elle, you can move in with me and rent out your place. This Pendleton's near to Brighton," said Angus, looking down at Google Maps.

Jude sat, not saying a word, with a shocked expression, and watched us apply for the degree as if we did things like this every day.

"You English people are weirdly decisive. Now I completely understand how you colonised the world."

"Whoa, I'm not English, thank you very much," said Angus.

We all squeezed into the back of a yellow cab. The city lights drew me in, and I had the urge to open the cab door, bolt off, and find a bar to drown my sorrows alone as if I were in a movie. I'd never been in a bar on my own without meeting anyone else. I considered adding it to my 'Itch List.'

"I was thinking," said Lucy. "Don't you think it's weird—all of us in this car right now are single? We're all attractive people with things going on in our lives. I mean, what's wrong with us? It's unbelievable, right? It's given me a brilliant idea. Don't take this the wrong way, Elle, but take you—you'd chosen who you thought was the perfect guy, good job, fairly good-looking, smart, not a serial killer, that we know of—"

"Oh my god, where is this going?" said Angus.

"No, hear me out! Imagine a dating app, but instead of matching you with a similar person with shared interests, it took everything you said you wanted in a partner and then gave you the exact opposite. You might meet a person you'd never consider in a million years. A bit like letting a fashion consultant choose your clothes because that shit works! I can tell you I've got a MaxMara coat I'd never have bought unless an assistant at Liberty had talked me into it."

Angus got a fit of giggles.

"I'll bet she talked you into it, all right! Who do you think you are, Meghan Markle? So, Elle should date a plumber from Watford? Or perhaps a rocket scientist from NASA?"

"Hey! What are you trying to say?" I said.

"That's your brilliant idea, in a nutshell?" asked Angus.

"Well, yeah. I think it is, and when I'm rich, don't come knocking for a handout, Angus, because I'll remind you of this moment!"

We pulled outside the Somewhere Nowhere club on West Twenty-fifth Street. I fell out of the cab.

Jude got us straight in, bypassing the queue outside. I stood at the entrance, mesmerised by some massive garden-like design installations. The centrepiece perched above the DJ was an enormous jungle plant. Angus pulled me inside the club.

"Wow!" I said.

"It's something, isn't it? I know the owner; he's one of the few people in New York who buys wine from us," said Jude.

"Jude, you need a drink. You're too sober."

I smiled at him and backed away onto the dance floor. I wanted to dance and forget everything for a night. He followed me but got caught up behind the group, and I lost him; then, I was alone in a vast crowd of strangers. I could have been anywhere—Hï in Ibiza, Green Valley in Brazil, or Pryzm in Brighton. It didn't matter; I needed to get lost in the dance music. The events from that night blurred in the hazy lights and sweaty bodies around me, and it took me some time to switch off and clear my head.

"Oh, my god! We've been looking for you for over an hour!" said Angus. They pushed through the crowd to me, and we danced to a remix of Miley Cyrus's 'Malibu.'

"I love this song," I said.

Waving my arms, I pulled Jude to dance. When the song finished, sweaty as though I'd fallen in a pool entirely clothed, the consuming tidal wave of emotion flooded back. I looked down at my Apple watch, a gift from Hunter, with its ridiculous sports strap.

'You need to keep up with technology,' he had told me. He didn't even use the automated windscreen wipers or headlights on his car. He loved to lecture me about anything. I ripped off the watch and stomped on it.

"What the fuck, Elle?" said Angus. "You could have given me the watch!"

They led me over to a small table at the side of the dance floor.

"Shall we go back to the hotel now?" I asked. The hair at the back of my neck was wet with sweat, and I rubbed underneath my eyes, knowing I had a panda face. My white silk blouse was fit for the bin at this stage, covered as it was in sweat and liquids of unknown origin. Jude made a sad face. He appeared drunk now and didn't want to break up the party.

"I'll come back with you," said Angus.

"You go ahead without me; catch you tomorrow," said Lucy.

"Make sure she gets home safely, Jude, won't you?" said Angus.

"Well, great to meet you, Jude. Sorry, I've been a basket case all night. I'm not usually like this. I promise. Maybe we'll meet again one day, and I can try some of your wine. Lucy, don't drink any more, though, will you? Remember, you hit your head."

"Ok, Mum, will do."

We hugged, and Angus and I fought against the crowd and escaped into the balmy New York air.

"Angus, I'm starving."

We stood on the sidewalk and devoured hot dogs. I laughed when yellow mustard dripped all over Angus's hand, and he lurched his whole body back, trying to avoid it dripping onto his clothes.

"This is fantastic," he said.

"It's probably not; you're just pissed. Hey, Jude's lovely, isn't he? I think Lucy might get lucky tonight," I said.

"I'm not sure it was Lucy he was into. Come on, let's go back. It's been a big night."

We sat in the backseat of the taxi, and I put my head on his shoulder.

"Everything will be OK, Elle. I promise."

I wasn't so sure. I could taste bile in my throat, and I really wanted to throw up the hot dog.

Vitis Mustangensis

T he light poked through the curtains in my hotel room, and I reached out and turned over my phone, which I'd forgotten to charge and was now on fifteen per cent. There were five missed calls from Angus and ten missed Facetime calls from Hunter. It appeared I had sent him a picture of us all sitting in the bar the previous night, each with a middle finger up; he'd seen I was with Angus. And I had no memory of sending it. So much of the night was blank.

Thinking hurt my brain, so I rolled out of bed and surveyed the absolute chaos in the room. In my haste, I had strewn the suitcase's contents all around the place. My head thumped, and I drank from the bathroom tap when it appeared I'd forgotten to buy any water.

When I reached reception, Angus looked bored in a pale blue velvet chair, scrolling on his phone.

"Looking for a date nearby?"

"Haha, funny. You're lucky I am still here. The assistant manager has walked by here three times. I think it was going to be lucky fourth."

"Where's Luce?"

"She stayed at Jude's hotel. She's gonna meet us there."

"Really? Well, good for her. Hunter tried to call me like ten times. Guess he's scared you've filled me in on his dirty deeds."

"Twat. Why doesn't he fuck off? Hey, what did you mean about him not letting you take my call at the weekend?"

"You know, when I think of it, he's quite controlling. I've been going along with it all, not questioning some of his behaviour. He never liked me being friends with you and Lucy. He thinks you're a bad influence. I don't think he even likes my family. I can tell Holly hates him."

"Oh my god, it's all coming out now. Luce and I were saying we were seeing less and less of you. He's been swallowing you up. I hate the way he speaks to you. He's condescending, and I've been biting my tongue for so long. Lucy was going to say something, but I told her not to. We've been trying to figure out how to broach the subject."

"Well, I wish you'd said something. It's humiliating. I was kind of thinking Hunter was a good catch, you know. Good job, handsome. I've been thinking about this all wrong."

We linked arms and hopped in a taxi to the West Village, and Angus rubbed in the blush on one side of my face.

"There's this thing called a mirror, Elle," he said.

"Oh, I couldn't face myself, honestly. I chucked on some blush and lip stain and got out of there. Do I look awful?"

"Nah, you look like you'd fit right in on Canal Street. We could find you a new man if you want to pop down later. If you're lucky, you could score a date at McDonald's tonight."

M. J. PARFITT

"I've never been this hungry or desperate for a coffee in my whole life," I said.

Angus and I ordered a second cup. The aroma was too enticing; I wanted to hook it up to a drip.

"Oh, what do we have here?"

Angus whistled as Lucy sat down.

She blushed and looked down at the table.

"I'm guessing you're over your brain damage?" I said.

"Shut up, you two. I am single. Oh, I'm sorry, Elle. I didn't mean—are you OK today? Jude's a good guy, and we talked most of the night, and then he said I could sleep on the couch in his room."

"Shall we have a proper drink now?" I said.

"Hell yeah!"

"Well," I said, picking up my dirty martini, "here's to being single with the both of you. Couldn't be in better company!"

A loud squeal escaped my mouth as the cocktail stick from my martini lodged in my eyeball, as I knocked back the drink. and everyone in the café turned to stare.

"Fuck, fuck, oh my god. I hate eyes. I hate eyes—get that thing away from me—fuck, fuck, fuck," said Angus.

He pushed back his chair, making it screech, and darted off to one side of the table, causing the other diners to stop eating their baked eggs.

"Shit, this is going to hurt, Elle. I'm sorry in advance," said Lucy, closing her eyes and whipping the stick out with the flick of her wrist. She replaced it with a clean napkin and told Angus to pay as she ushered me to a cab she was hailing. Angus trailed behind, and the other diners sat in stunned silence.

Lower Manhattan Hospital wasn't where we had envisaged spending an evening in New York.

I kept nodding off and hoping my friends had returned each time I woke up. The room was bare, and nothing was remarkable enough to keep my attention. Fake wood furniture paired with nylon curtains in this transient space; the singular thing in the room of interest was a black and white print of nurses at work in the fifties or sixties. Their starched white uniforms stood out in the grainy photo. Here I was with an embarrassing, self-inflicted injury. These women had forged the way, and women like me were still getting trapped in misogynistic relationships and ambling through life with no direction.

"Elle, we've called the office and sorted out the insurance paperwork with the hospital; sorry it took so long. Are you bored?" said Angus as he walked into the room with Lucy, throwing a Hershey's bar at me.

"I'm sorry, guys. I've ruined this trip. The doctor was here, and she said my eye is fine; I'll have to wear this patch for a while."

Then I whispered, "And the other thing will come out from you know where in its own good time."

"Oh, ew. I don't want to know about either end!" said Angus.

They sat by my bed, laughing at my new eye patch.

"Pirate Darkling. I think it's time you gave up the booze. Two mishaps in two days," he said.

"Thanks for looking out for me, team. You were amazing, Lucy. I was lying here wondering why you aren't at the helm of some enormous company. You handled the toothpick situation calmly like you could handle almost anything."

"Thanks for the vote of confidence, but I'm trapped like you. I was listening to you in the crew bunk. We're on the hamster wheel. I can't deny you've set something off in my head about the future. I wasn't thinking about it, but now I can't stop. When we were downstairs, I was reading about this hospital on a wall in the foyer. The first female American doctor, Elizabeth Blackwell she was called, founded it, and all female doctors ran it. She was twenty-four when she became a doctor and started this hospital eight years later. It made me think about some life choices I've made. I mean, I've achieved nothing, and I'm twenty-six, and she didn't even have Google! What are we going to do?"

"Wow. Yeah, you're right. We're real low achievers," I said.

"Bet she never got a cocktail stick in her eye either," said Angus.

"Yeah, but if she did, she could sort it herself without the help of a man," I said.

"My idea for the dating app. It's happening. I'm not sure how to raise the cash for it yet, but there will be a way. There's always a way," said Lucy.

I exchanged looks with Angus.

"I saw that, you two! Tell me when I've been wrong about something. Come on, tell me. You can't even think of a time, can you?"

"Well, you have a point, but I've never heard you say you wanted to be an entrepreneur. I mean, all we have to go on is once you said you wanted a pixie cut, and you didn't listen to us then either. Although thinking about it, you were the first to jump on apps like TikTok," said Angus.

"And she bought a ton of toilet paper before COVID, Angus. She has an eye for detail."

"True," he said. "You saved my life when I got gastro."

"We'll support you. If you're serious, let us know if we can help. I know you—you'll research the shit out of it; if there's an idea there, you'll make it work," I said.

"Oh my god, look at that cloud. It looks like two dogs humping."

"Angus! Ew, gross!" said Lucy.

"Oh, come on, you two," said Angus.

He turned from the window after snapping the cloud and uploading it to his Instagram account. He took one of me in my hospital bed with my eye patch on, and I poked out my tongue.

"Let's get out of here. I don't want to think any more about my dead-end future," said Angus.

⚬\⊙/⚬

Discharged with an itchy eyepatch in place and fresh assurances the Tiffany ring would turn up in good time, we eked out the rest of our time in New York.

Angus wanted to go to a comedy club in the village, and all I could think about was Mrs Maisel when a young woman popped up on stage.

The room was dark except for the stage lights. Deep velvet curtains hung at the sides of the stage. A double row of light bulbs surrounded it, which made me think of a giant makeup mirror. We sat in the front row on velvet chairs; Angus ordered us Pornstar Martinis with shots of chilled Prosecco, and it stirred up some of my PTSD from the previous night. I put my hand over my glass, but he was insistent.

Comedy clubs were not my thing. I found so few comics funny; most these days had political or social slants. It was as if they wanted to use the microphone to tell the audience what they were doing wrong instead of just making them laugh.

This lady looked nothing like a comic. Her appearance was too shiny and clean-cut with her black, skinny mom jeans and a denim shirt that looked like she had just been to GAP. I imagined she had dropped off the kids after school and popped out for a quick set.

"Hey, ma'am," she shouted.

I smiled and laughed with everyone else, unsure what I was laughing at.

"Oh my god, Elle, she's talking to you," said Lucy.

Angus was sinking into his seat. I looked up at her like a nocturnal animal caught in a torchlight.

"Yeah, you. That's right. I see you brought two eyewitnesses with you tonight. Sorry, let me focus." She put her hand to her forehead in mock thought.

The room erupted in laughter, and my face burned up as everyone looked over at me.

"Where was I? Yeah, you know, I could tell you a joke about an optical illusion, but I'm not sure you'd see the funny side of it."

Again, the audience laughed. Even my so-called friends laughed.

"Reminds me of a joke. Not planned; bear with me. Lady pirate walks into a bar and sits down. The bartender sees she has a peg for a leg, a hook for a hand, and an eye patch. She orders a beer, and while pouring it, the bartender says, 'What happened to your leg, if you don't mind me asking?' 'Well, many years ago,' says the pirate, 'I was sailing the high seas with me pirate boyfriend. We anchored near some tropical islands. I was on the deck, and before I knew it, an enormous wave had swept me overboard. A shark swam up and bit it clean off. I swam to the island and got a pegleg fitted.' 'Oh, that's awful,' says the bartender. 'But why didn't your boyfriend row you ashore?' 'Ah, well, I forbade him to go to the island, you see. It was inhabited with beautiful seamstress maidens who were making me a fantastic new pirate outfit in the finest silk, and he always had a roving eye. I told him if he laid a hand on one of them, I would chop it right off.' 'And what about your hook hand?' 'Well, the very next day,' says the pirate. 'I were walkin' on the deck o' me ship, and I'll be damned me if a wave didn't sweep me overboard again. Up came a whale this time and bit me hand right off. I swam ashore to the island and was fitted with this hook. Yep, all this cost me an arm and a leg, alright.'"

The room erupted in laughter.

"'Wow, that was such bad luck,' says the bartender. 'So, what about your eye?' 'Well, it was the very next day,' says the pirate. 'I were walkin' on the deck o' me ship, and I were looking out for rogue waves this time, mind you, and a seagull flew over and shit right in me eye!' 'Oh man,' says the bartender. 'And that blinded you?' 'Well, no,' says the pirate. 'But it was me first day with me hook, you see, so I asked my boyfriend to wipe me eye with his new silk handkerchief, and I forgot he'd had a hook hand fitted the day before.'"

I had to laugh; I mean, it was funny.

"Thanks for being a good sport, ma'am. What's your name?"

"Elle," said Angus.

"Well, Elle. I hope your eye gets better real soon; give her a round of applause, everybody."

"Oh my god, I want to die," I said, giving Angus a death stare. "For all she knows, I have a bona fide glass eye. I won't be able to go out in public like this, will I? How am I going to go back on the flight? I'm having heart palpitations."

❧

"We have to go to Central Park. It's such a sunny day," I said as we assembled outside our hotel the next morning.

We bought coffees served up in quintessential 'We are happy to serve you' blue paper cups from the deli next door and walked down the street.

"I'm sorry about last night," said Angus. "It was funny, but perhaps it was a little much after what you've been through."

"It's OK. I mean, that's the worst it'll be, right? I woke up this morning and thought, what can I do? It looks even more hideous if I take this thing off."

"You know why these cups are everywhere?" asked Angus. "The guy who designed them was this Czech Holocaust survivor. He wanted to pay respects to the local Greek restaurant owners, which is why they're blue and white, like the Greek flag."

"No way? I've always thought it was weird that every place has the same cups!" said Lucy.

"See! Everywhere we look, people are doing shit and leaving their mark in the world, and here we three are soaking everything up but not doing much to make our own marks and like you said Luce, we have the whole internet at our fingertips," I said.

"Well, I don't know about you; I'm helping people have pleasant, safe flights," said Angus. "Someone has to do that too."

"Yeah, but we have been doing it for long enough," I said. "Let someone else take a turn."

We lounged around the fountain in Washington Gardens like we were in an episode of *Friends*.

"You're Phoebe, Elle. The stupid things you get up to every day. I mean, come on!" said Angus.

"I'd prefer to be in *Sex and the City*," said Lucy. "I'll take Samantha. She gets all the action."

"Well, you can be Samantha, Lucy, but you'll also have a copious amount of STDs," said Angus.

"Oh my god, you're right," said Lucy. "She must have had every STD known to man. I love this part of our job. Sat here talking shite with you two and getting to hang out in places like this. Travel is so expensive; without the job and perks, it wouldn't happen as often. Can you see me stuck in some office?"

"Not really, I guess," I said. "What's the answer, though? Everything takes too long, and studying again fills me with dread."

I caught Lucy and Angus looking at each other, puzzled.

"What?" I said. "You two are acting weird."

"How much did you drink the other night?" Lucy said.

Angus pulled his chin down with his lips as Lucy started to say something, and she stopped herself.

"Let's each throw a coin in the fountain and make a wish for a new life by this time next year," I said.

"That's a big wish," said Angus. "But you never know."

I tossed a dime into the water, hitting a small child on the forehead. Angus put a hand over his mouth.

"Mommy, a pirate attacked me," said the child.

"Oh my god, is he OK?" I asked, running over to the mother.

"He's OK. You'll live, won't you?" She ruffled his hair. "Are you a Brit?"

"Oh, how could you tell?" I joked. "Did my accent give me away?"

"Well yeah, and this."

She waved at my body or clothes. I couldn't tell which. I smiled and walked away, bemused.

"What's wrong with my clothes?" I asked, walking back up to my friends.

"Um, well, you could do with a makeover, I guess," said Angus.

"Shut up, Angus! Now's not the time to bring her down. She's going through enough," said Lucy.

I looked down at my clothes. Blue jeans, white sneakers, and a blazer over a striped knit top.

"I guess you could do with a freshen-up," said Lucy. "I'll take you shopping. You always wear the same thing. It's your go-to look."

"Well, don't take her to Liberty. She'll leave with a MaxMara coat and a huge credit card bill."

"Shut up!" said Lucy.

"Come on," said Angus. "Let's go before you're arrested for assault. You know how litigious it is here; Mum is probably over there with the calculator, working out how much she can sue you to cover her kid's college tuition. Carrie Bradshaw's apartment is near here. Let's go before you maim another child. We can sit on the steps and take some selfies."

❧⁓❧

I was a passenger in business class on the flight home. However, I didn't enjoy the perks because I spent much of the trip imagining how Hunter might react to my eye patch and how I could confront him. I stared out the window, contemplating our non-existent wedding. The engagement was so recent it didn't count. In the absence of wedding plans and considering the actual length of the engagement, not to mention the deception, I didn't think I could even tell someone I used to be engaged. It was like an annulled marriage.

"It's a wonderful view, isn't it?" asked the man beside me.

He looked like a banker, with a deep red tie and an expensive striped black pin-stripe suit. I thought he had kind eyes and reminded me of a younger version of Bill Nighy.

"What were you doing in New York? And what happened to your eye?"

"Long story!"

"Well, we have a minute or two."

Angus walked up as I recounted the events leading up to my eye patch.

"I thought we'd have a perfect life, you know. I'd be a stay-at-home mum. We'd have a terraced home in town with crinkled linen everywhere. I'd wander on our floorboards barefoot, dressed head to toe in Lululemon, holding the baby and preparing a teriyaki salmon bowl. Pathetic, I know. So, Alex has stuck a massive spanner in my life. Although come to think of it, he'd never have agreed to the linen. Way too many wrinkles for his OCD."

"Elle, this man is flat-out cold—who are you talking to? Perhaps you should record an audiobook to send people off to sleep. You'd make a fortune."

I swiped him away, and he left me with a pile of mini–Grey Goose bottles. I drifted into a troubled sleep, dreaming of everything that had happened, muddled into one epic story like I was on acid.

When I woke up, empty mini bottles and strange glitter on my tray table surrounded me as though a fairy godmother had visited me while I slept. Gerald, my neighbour, pointed to my eye patch. I touched my head and found it had edged up onto my forehead. I could feel the long dent it had made and rubbed at it. Gerald looked at the array of mini bottles and smiled at me. He offered me a Polo, and I took one, embarrassed because I knew I stank of booze.

"Look. Here's my card," Gerald said. "I'm a lawyer. Call me if you ever need one, and don't worry about this Hunter chap. He's a bit part."

"How do you mean?"

"In the grand scheme of your life, he's a supporting actor. He's a miniscule moment. You strike me as someone who will go out into the world and see the crescent of the moon. He's going to see the whole thing from his Weybridge apartment."

"Gerald, are you quoting song lyrics to me right now? You don't strike me as a Waterboys fan."

Sauvignon Blanc

J said my goodbyes to Angus and Lucy before disembarking, not wanting to leave them. Lucy grabbed my hand and told me not to worry. She kept staring at my eye patch.

"Does it look bad? Do I look like an idiot?"

"Oh, Elle, it's fine. Sorry, I wish I could come with you into the office, but I've got this family thing with Mum."

"It's OK. I can handle the ridicule; after all, I was the subject of a comedy act in front of hundreds of people. Sweet of you, though. Thanks for a fantastic trip, and sorry for all the hassle. I'll call you guys later."

I looked down and brushed off more of the mysterious metallic dust I could now see on my jacket.

When I reached the office, my hair was a frizzy mess. I stood outside; my bravery badge was wearing off. I squinted in the daylight as if I'd escaped a Mexican prison. It was like the day after *The Hangover*, albeit I was missing a tattoo and a tiger, although I had an eye patch.

"Hi Elle, how was the trip?" Claire said as she left the main doors to the building.

"Here again?"

"Oh, I was helping with interviews, but I need some air. Some of these people, it's like they've never had a job interview. One guy interrupted every time we spoke; he even winked at me once. He didn't make it past round one. There's also a girl in a purple suit. I can't let that slide, either. Look, I wanted to talk to you about something."

"Alex and Hunter? Yeah, I know all about it. You could have stopped them, Claire. I thought we were friends."

"Angus and I tried. It seems it's been going on for a while. She's not all bad; she's misunderstood. There are a lot of layers."

"Yeah, well, onions have a lot of layers, and they stink, and they make me cry; you might be onto something. I'd like to understand why he gave me a massive Tiffany ring while he was having it off with her and god knows who else."

"Wait, what, you're engaged?"

"For a day, I was, yeah."

"Where's the ring?"

She looked at my hand.

"Um. Well, I'm not engaged now, am I? He can have it back for all I care."

"What happened on the flight? There are so many rumours going around about you and Angus."

"Oh, nothing much, a Philip issue. We'll probably get a slap on the wrist or something. Fuck, I don't want to go in. Does everyone know about Hunter and Alex?"

"Yeah, I'm afraid so. You know what it's like, any whiff of gossip, and it's round like wildfire. Let me come in with you."

Claire wheeled my suitcase into a corner and touched my shoulder.

"Right, time to go back in. Call you tomorrow to check you're doing OK."

Monty's office door was open, and I knocked on it lightly. He looked me up and down.

"Well, you've had an eventful trip, haven't you?"

He passed me an accident form to complete.

"Do you have a problem with *this* form?"

I half smiled, took the form, placed it on a notepad, and sat on one of the uncomfortable sofas. Filling in forms for me was right up there with ironing or making phone calls. I scribbled fast so I could escape the office and go home.

Out of the corner of my eye, I saw the blonde flick of a good hair-cut and knew it was Alex. I could detect the copious cloud of Chloé before I even saw her. I panicked. My heart raced. Alex stood right in front of me. Her straight bob was hot ironed into a helmet, and her uniform fit her body so well I thought she might have had it tailored. She looked into my eye and gave a smug smile.

"Elle, interesting look."

"Uh, well, Alex, my eye will get better. What's harder, if not impossible, to reverse is your black heart."

She spun around and continued talking to a group of friends. I was back in the school playground with whispers, secret looks, and an in-joke I wasn't party to. All these moments were stuck to me like glue. I pulled out the notepad I'd been using, tapped at the biro, trying to force the ink out, and drew a picture of a hand with one finger sticking up. It looked more like a dick and balls, and I tried to draw a ring on one finger to clarify, but it just made it look like a deformed dick. I studied it a bit and turned it this way and that; either way, it was befitting. After looking behind me to check for spies, I popped it into Alex's pigeonhole. Mission accomplished, I rushed to escape into the fresh air, relieved to be away from the passive-aggressive office, which now strangled every positive emotion in my body.

Daydreaming, walking towards the bus for the staff car park, I realised I had no car and had to lug my suitcase back to the terminal to catch the train. I consoled myself with the extra daily steps.

On the train, people stared and smiled. I stuck in my air pods and played RY X Essentials on Apple Music as loud as my eardrums would allow. 'Live Like This' summed up my relationship woes with Hunter. 'If this is what you want, take it from my bones, write your name in blood'—my song choice symbolised the decision I'd already made about Hunter Woods. Then I recalled we had tickets to an RY X concert at St Paul's Cathedral; Hunter had the tickets, and now I hated him even more. He wasn't even a fan; the tickets were my birthday present. My air pods died, and I yanked them out in frustration, snapping my Oreo cookie air pod case shut.

The only reason Hunter and I first spoke was because of that air pod case. I was lying by the pool listening to RY X, eyes closed, enjoying the novelty of the warm sun on my pale English skin. The memory smelled of coconut suntan lotion and watermelon margaritas when I sensed a shadow blocking the sun through my eyelids. I'd put a hand over my eyes and looked up to see him with a huge cheesy grin and a glint in his eye.

"Oh, hi."

"Hey, do you mind if I join you?" he said. "What's this Oreo cookie doing here?"

I'd placed a few of my belongings on the adjoining sunbed, and the air pod case's realistic appearance amused him. It was as if he'd never owned something for the fun of it. He ridiculed me, asking me how old I was, and instead of defending my love of Oreos and the fact the case had been a present from Angus, I blushed and considered whether it was time to grow up. I should have taken that first impression and thought harder about what it gave away about Hunter because it summed up everything from where I was standing now.

As I sat on the train. I couldn't help attacking one man with a Manchester United shirt on because that was Hunter's team.

"Look, it's a fucking eye patch. Have you never seen one before?"

He turned away, pretending he hadn't heard me. Then, regretting my outburst, I said, "Look, I'm sorry. I'm not having the best day. I shouldn't take it out on you."

"Don't worry," he said. "I shouldn't have stared. You do children's parties?"

I squinted at him and asked what he meant, but the train pulled up at my station, and I smiled and jumped off.

I stopped at Whimsical Wontons to buy some greasy Chinese food I hoped might soak up at least some of my depression. It usually worked on less dramatic things, like losing my purse or arriving at the dry cleaners to find them closed. I hadn't had a Chinese for ages because Hunter didn't like Chinese food. He always wanted an Indian, so that's what we ate. I wouldn't be able to face chicken tikka ever again. He was such a dick about it, too. He rarely let me order what I wanted. We always had to share his choice of dishes. Sometimes, I wanted an onion bhaji for a change, but that was never on Hunter's strict menu choice.

"Oh, Elle, I thought you'd moved. What you done now? You go to a fancy-dress party?" asked Cherry, the takeaway owner.

Cherry laughed, holding her stomach and putting her hand on her mouth. She popped some extra prawn crackers into the bag.

I shuffled out with my suitcase over the blue and white linoleum tiles. My life was a constant amusement for her, like when I got highlights and they turned pink, or emptied my bag to find some change when I'd lost my purse and had tipped out several pairs of knickers I'd left at Hunter's. I laughed with her and shrugged.

"Cherry, I'm not sure you'd believe me if I told you! Let's say it was an eventful trip and you may see more of me."

I turned the key in my front door, relieved to see no lights or signs of life. The stale air hit me, and I loaded the diffuser with fresh peppermint oil, hoping it might give me a lift and cleanse the air of 'Hunter vibes.' I leaned in and took a big sniff, but recoiled and gasped.

Turning the label round on the small bottle, I read 'clove oil.' My apartment now stank like baked ham, reminding me of the Christmas I would spend alone. What greeted me in the bathroom mirror when I checked my eye patch was the Elton John version on steroids, not the standard hospital eye patch I envisioned. *Angus.*

Flopping onto my newish sofa, the 'Cloud Couch,' reminded me of Hunter again. I spent many flights imagining jumping onto a cloud during meal service, which was the deciding factor in its purchase. Angus had come around as soon as it arrived and launched himself onto it. We tested it out by watching a marathon of Adam Sandler movies one Friday night.

Between *Happy Gilmour* and *The Wedding Singer*, Angus lay on it, curled up on it, sat, pretended to read a book, and finally declared it a successful purchase. Hunter hated it. He said it was too messy and would be hard to keep clean. He finally shut up when I told him about an interior design show where they had explained white was a good colour because you could wash it to death. Well, they said you could bleach it. I'm not sure I'd go that far, but it pushed me to go for white.

His apartment was generic grey and spotless. He had no imagination and got swept along with the colour du jour. Like the scene in *The Devil Wears Prada*—if the current Pantone had been cerulean blue, Hunter would live in an apartment resembling the local swimming pool. I had done little to my apartment, but at least it had a soul. I had an eclectic style juxtaposed with his sterile and bland one.

Hunter was right about the couch. It did always look like shit because I could never make it look unwrinkled, but boy was it comfy. I had long since given up the pointless task of smoothing it out each day, and something in the way it wound him up gave me a secret pleasure.

I listened to the silence and knew it would take some getting used to. On the flipside, life without Hunter, the controller, meant I could do whatever I liked, such as getting a pet. But I was still away a lot. My life had changed, and yet it was still the same.

Hunter might have been in my apartment when I arrived home on an ordinary night, making me an authentic carbonara. I'd half expected him to be there when I opened the front door, but I was relieved when I didn't see his car outside.

His presence had been the skeleton supporting my life. The question was: Who was I without him? Would I turn into a pile of jelly, unable to function independently?

Pulling a Corona out from the fridge and finding a lime that had seen better days, I put a slice in the bottle and slammed the fridge door. It had been concerning me lately if this affected the recycling process. Still, tonight, I had more on my mind than recycling. I ate the takeaway too fast, giving myself heartburn or a panic attack—I couldn't be sure which at this stage.

My mobile rang, and I ignored it. It rang again, and I flicked off the side button. I saw all the notifications of missed calls from Hunter. It hurt to see his name right now, let alone speak to him. I wanted to change it to something more appropriate, and my eyes caught a book of Emily Dickinson poems I had been reading before the trip, and 'Zero' was born. I laughed at my comedic spin on the 'Zeros Taught Us Phosphorus' poem. Now, it was like seeing the name of a stranger.

I imagined him running his slender hands through his dark, wavy hair. Was he sitting at home brooding in front of a Netflix show? Or was he at the pub with a couple of mates laughing and joking like a serial killer with no remorse, as though he hadn't just ripped the heart and lungs from a corpse in Woking?

Resolving to remove his presence for good, I darted around, slamming his things into a box, removing any trace of him, hoping this would enable me to move on and forget about the lying prick for good. There weren't many things to fill a box with. The Corona box, which was not a big box anyway, looked pathetic. All it held was a pair of red socks, a toothbrush, *Giggs: The Autobiography*, some Man United boxers, and sunglasses. There weren't even any toiletries to speak of. It was going to be impossible to make a dramatic gesture with a half-empty Corona box. Where were the trappings of a life we had shared for the past two years? I racked my brains for anything else, and the only other thing I could come up with was the Tiffany ring, which still had yet to be retrieved.

Peering into the wardrobe, I thought back to cleaning out a drawer for him and pushing my clothes along the rail to give him space—it was bare. So why was he insistent about it if he never intended to use it?

He'd been nagging me to move into his place for at least a year. Every time I slept over there and woke up after he'd left for an early flight, I would look around his dark bedroom at the plain walls and popcorn ceiling. I might as well have been waking up in Alcatraz. There was nothing so much as a succulent in it, fake or real. It could have been a serviced apartment. I didn't back down on my refusal to move in, which drove Zero nuts.

My apartment had gigantic windows, and the morning light streamed through. Even if you were having the worst day of your life, it gently picked you up and coaxed you into your day. I'd suggested he move in here instead, but he'd laughed and said he had a better address in Weybridge. I was grateful I didn't give in and move in with him. This whole situation would have been far more complex. All I had to do now was go cold turkey and cut him off for good.

Rustling around in the bedside drawer among the dust and abandoned hair-ties, I found a dried flower he had given me one day at the park as we lay in the summer grass, talking about our future. It was ironic. I had always thought I was in a rom-com, but it turned out I was in a fucking film noir.

My impulse to run to the loo was too much to bear. "Yes!" I shouted, fishing out the ring with my toilet brush. *Oh my god, you are a fucking ridiculous mess, Elle Darkling. I mean, who does this? Not Alex, not the Philip on the flight to New York.* Reaching for the bleach, I scrubbed at the ring till it sparkled with Zero's electric toothbrush. Then, I washed it with toothpaste to remove all traces of bleach.

I took the small box from inside the wardrobe and replaced the now sparkling ring, launching it and the toothbrush into the Corona box. I dashed into the kitchen, retrieved the ground chilli, and rubbed it into Zero's boxers. To be a fly on the wall when he put these on! But then I considered the safety of the passengers, given that he was a first officer, and I rushed to pop them in the wash.

I wiped at my tired eye. The burn was palpable and relentless as the specks of chilli dissected my one good eye. After I had quieted the sting and given my hands a thorough wash, I peeked under the patch. I replaced it when I saw a hint of red in the white of my eye and decided it would have to stay on.

The phone rang and ruptured the oppressive silence. I knew it was going to be Zero. My painful eyes, my pet-free apartment, and my social ridicule at the office. It was all Hunter's doing.

"Yes?"

"Elle, how was the trip? I've missed you. Shall we go for dinner, or do you want to stay in? I've been calling you. Why didn't you answer?"

"Are you fucking kidding me? That's what you have to say to me? After what you've done? Do you want to stay in and have a cosy dinner at home? Oh yeah, what movie shall we watch? *Fatal Attraction*?"

"Look, here's the thing—" he started; I hung up on the word 'thing.'

I threw myself onto the couch and wailed into the cushions. 'Look, here's the thing.' This was something Hunter always said when he was about to be a total prick. I wouldn't miss hearing it. Why did this hurt this bloody much? How hard would it be to hear him out? But something had changed. It was as if he had flipped a switch inside me, and I knew this wasn't what I wanted anymore. There had to be more. I'd had my share of cheating boyfriends. They were all archetypal, always chasing the next conquest to boost their needy, pathetic egos. I blamed their mothers. Raised to be self-important by their first female role model, they expected the same adoration from a girlfriend or wife. I wanted more from now on, and if the perfect love story never happened to me, I'd opt to become an old spinster with multiple cats. I'd take them to Zero's front door and let them pee on his doormat.

The cloud couch cocooned me until a loud noise disturbed my sleep— Zero was buzzing my apartment with Waitrose's best flowers.

Lilies—not my favourite, all that dusty brown stuff falling off the stamens. They were an overrated flower, and they were poisonous to cats. He was a cat hater, after all. Then I made a mental note to make 'cats—love 'em or hate 'em?' the first question for prospective new boyfriends after rising from the ashes in about a million years. Watching him loitering outside—ostensibly dishevelled but still full of his pompous self-assurance—I hated him more than I thought possible.

"Please answer the door, Elle. Let me explain."

"Save it, loser! Go see your new girlfriend. Oh, wait, she's on a trip. Fuck off, Zero. I never want to see you again; you need therapy for your fucking ego. Oh, and by the way, I hate those flowers as much as I hate you and your small penis. You cat-hating asshole. Go find another idiot to eat all your favourite Indian dishes."

It was hard not to open the door and ask him why, but I saw little point. I already knew every answer he could ever give because, in one form or another, I had heard them all before. *It was a mistake; it's you I love. I hate myself. I don't know why I did it. She kept chasing after me; I knew it was wrong. I am so sorry. Please give me a second chance. A third chance. Marry me. Forgive me.* I could never trust him again, and I couldn't settle and be poor old Elle 'in the dark' Darkling—it was too demeaning. I had to put aside the worry of perhaps never meeting the man of my dreams. The Disney ideal of the fairy-tale wedding was ebbing away. My continual disappointment in human nature confounded me. I had four people in my life who were rock solid: Angus, Lucy, my sister Holly, and my dad. That was it.

I still watched him from the window, standing for a time in equidistance with my apartment building and his ostentatious car, unsure what to do. I was a pushover; he had gotten his way at every juncture over the last two years, so this was a novel experience for him. He turned and slumped back to his car, looking at my window like a lost puppy with pleading eyes, but it was a half-hearted attempt, and I breathed a sigh of relief when I heard him screech away. I'd finally beaten him at something. I imagined him seething because he loved to win anything: Monopoly, Scrabble, Mario Cart, arguments—life.

"Fuck you, Zero, you twat," I said.

I stared at his rear lights disappear and his number plate fade like a dodgy eye test and thought I might never see it again: IE88 5HYT. I never had the heart to tell him it looked like 'I eat shit.' He had turned up one day with this new silver Porsche, and I had been fit to burst but didn't say a thing—even to Angus and Lucy; my loyalty had known no bounds, even with the comedy gold that Angus would have lapped up.

Grabbing my phone, I sent him a text: "Thank fuck you've finally got the message. Just saw you driving away, and it reminded me—I keep forgetting to tell you your number plate reads 'I eat shit;' so maybe go do that."

I summoned all my courage to call my dad and sister Holly. Once I did this, it was final. There was no coming back from imparting this news. It was a pivotal moment to tell your friends and family. It was game over once they knew Zero for who he was, and I knew it.

"Don't worry, Elle," said Dad. "We'll sort all this out. Get some

M. J. PARFITT

sleep if you can tonight, and we'll sort it all out tomorrow."

"Fucking asshole!" Holly shouted into the phone, and it woke her sleeping toddler. "Gosh, Elle, I better go. See you tomorrow. Love you."

I sighed and fought back more tears. My head throbbed with the exhaustion of the analysis and introspection I'd been at since I'd found out the truth. Scrolling through photos on my phone, I marvelled at the man who could live this life with me, throw it away for a quick roll in the hay, and then offer me a misplaced marriage proposal.

My phone beeped again, and it was another message from 'Zero.'

"Baby, call me. We need to talk about this. I need to explain everything. You owe me that. We can't throw all this away. It meant nothing. Sorry. You know I love you, please, Elle."

I sent a text: "Go eat a bag of dicks," but the phone auto-corrected dicks to ducks, and it was too late to change it.

The three dots under the text appeared, disappeared, reappeared three times, and stopped altogether.

I retreated to the fridge, scouring it for junk. The shelves scattered with crumbs and pools of dried milk added to my dour mood. My latest attempt at being healthy involved me purging anything with over two grams of carbs, and the fridge was bare. I opted for a mug of hot chocolate, which had escaped my cull. I collapsed, exhausted, on my bed with a giant chocolate milk moustache.

Trebbiano Toscano

ap, tap, tap. My bedroom window was being pelted with stones—either someone had died, or my apartment was mid-blaze. The pillow over my ears wasn't doing the trick. When I sniffed it, it was like Zero was in the room, so I stumbled over to the window, still making out the faint outline of the smiley face from a few days before, and traced my finger over, giving it a sad mouth, then heaved up the sash, and looked out under my crusted, sleepy eye. It was Angus, waving below, all fresh-faced and loud, pissing off all my neighbours with his merriment.

❦

He wafted in as always, like a clean load of laundry in contrast to me, who stood mouth open, half asleep, dazed and confused. He was holding a brown paper bag with warm chocolate croissants, making me hungry and desperate for tea.

"Why are you tearing up? What's happened?"

"Oh, it's you. I'm just grateful for a friend who cares like this and never disappoints me. You're the best. I mean, you could have left it for a couple of hours. I could use more beauty sleep, but we can't have everything. These earn you brownie points, too. Come to me," I said.

"Anyway, what the hell are you up to now?"

He looked me up and down with disdain.

"What do you mean?" I said, patting my hair on one side and pulling at the white towelling robe.

I leaned past Angus to look in the mirror behind him. The bling from the eye patch was now dotted over my entire face, and the chocolate moustache stretched across my mouth as if I was auditioning for the Joker in the next Batman movie. We both howled as he snapped a picture of me on his phone before I could object, and I rushed into the bathroom to wash away the evidence. I'd have been mad at him for documenting my silly predicaments if it were anyone else. Still, it was fun between us; he was like a brother to me.

"I popped in to check you were OK," he said. "Apparently, you are not!"

"No, no. I'm OK, I guess. It's a lot to process, but what can I do? Alex was in the office yesterday, looking smug, and she said this wasn't a good look. Zero kept calling me and even called round here, and I told him to eat some ducks."

"You've lost me—who's Zero? And why is he eating duck?"

"Oh, sorry, yeah, I renamed him Zero in my phone after a Dickinson poem, and the duck thing was a mistake. It auto-corrected dick on my phone."

"God, I'm glad we cleared that up."

I hit him on the arm.

"Look at this box."

"Did you drink an entire box of beer last night?"

"Well, you know I didn't. You saw my chocolate moustache."

He peered in and spied the familiar duck egg blue box.

"Ah! So, you retrieved the bling! Ew, gross. You should keep it and sell it on Marketplace. Getting some compensation from Zero would only be fair. I don't know why you're giving it back to him."

"I don't want it! It's not even my taste. It's ostentatious. You know me, I'd prefer something quirkier. He didn't even know me, did he? Yesterday, he turned up here with lilies! I hate lilies. Look at the box; there's nothing of his here. He was determined that I move into his place, wasn't he? He thought I would do whatever he wanted."

"Did you talk to Zero, then?"

"Yeah, to say fuck-off. I was peeking from up here."

"I never thought he was good enough for you, Elle. It wasn't something I'd have ever told you while you had the rose-tinted glasses on, but I thought he was a real flirt and a controlling asshole."

"Don't hold back, Angus; no, really, say what you think."

Biting my cheek, I looked out onto the road, watching a petite lady hunched over with a kyphotic spine, limp across the zebra-crossing with her shopping in a wheelie bag, stretching her frail arms.

"Oh, I'm going to be a sad old lady like her," I said, gesturing for Angus to look, "but with cats. One in each colour."

He shook his head and looked down, wiping away some invisible crumb from the bench top.

"No! We are not doing this, Elle Darkling. Zero wasn't the one. Be pickier. If you'd just put as much effort into meeting the love of your life as meeting a new pair of shoes!"

"Fair," I said.

"Hey! So, there's another reason I came around. Any missed calls from the office?"

"No, why?"

Picking up my phone, I saw a missed call, which gave me further anxiety. Life was spiralling out of control in every direction. When you had cracked the secret happiness code, something cropped up, sinking you into another melodrama.

"Lucy got one, too," said Angus.

We turned on the bar stools and looked at each other.

"What do you suppose about? The Philip?"

I walked over to put the kettle on.

"Fuck, I don't know. Monty tortures us with psychological warfare every time we set foot in there. I used to love it, but now, it all seems so passive-aggressive."

He put his face into his hands and screamed into them.

"Life sucks."

"Yep, sucks balls," I said, taking a massive gulp of tea and burning my tongue. I jumped up and stuck it under the cold tap. I knew I'd pay for it and wouldn't enjoy food for days, which was a double blow when I was going to Dad's for one of Holly's meals.

"Oh god, you're a walking disaster. I can't leave you alone for five minutes. Do I need to childproof your entire kitchen?"

He was joking, but deep down, I knew he thought I was a flake.

"OK, I've gotta go," he said, checking his watch. "I met this guy online, and I'm catching up for a coffee with him soon. He didn't suggest Greggs, so there's a small win. Shall we catch up later for drinks? I'll call Lucy, too. Wimbledon, OK? Tequila Mockingbird? I know it's loud in there, but it's dark, and you can hide the patch! You are going to your dad's, anyway, right?"

"Yeah, sure, I'll be there—me and my eye patch. I looked underneath, and it's still all red and blotchy. I'll have to wear it or look even more hideous."

"You'll look mysterious with it on. Trust me."

Angus blew a kiss and departed in a cloud of Casswell-Massey Number Six. It reminded me of a shower gel I had used in a hotel with Zero on a winter's weekend in Paris. Once again, my chest tightened as I remembered what I was dealing with. I took a slow, deep breath and stepped onto the balcony to find air, knocking over a wicker chair and plant pot on my way out.

"Shit. Oh, for fuck's sake!"

"Elle?" Grey called from the apartment above.

"Yeah, Grey, it's clumsy me. Not a burglar! How's life?"

"Yeah, good. Is everything OK with you? I saw Hunter looking flustered out the front last night," he said, peering over the railing even though he couldn't have seen me from the angle of his balcony unless he dangled himself on a rope.

"Err, not really. Long story. Well, not long. Oh, I'm sick of it. I won't bore you."

"Well, I'm here if you need to vent. I'm off to the gym now. Catch you later."

Grey at the gym was something I didn't have trouble imagining at all. He was easy on the eyes, as well as being an adorable human—a winning combination. I was pretty sure he'd be more interested in Angus, and it gave me an idea that if the Greggs guy was a loser, perhaps I should introduce them.

Between Candy Crush and an intense social media stalking of Alex and Zero, several hours passed, making me dizzy from staring at the screen.

I called Lucy and put her on loudspeaker, so the phone wasn't near me.

"Hey, Luce. How's the head today?"

"Oh, it's fine. I'm sitting here writing a business plan for my dating app. I need to pull a spec together to get a quote for developing it."

"So, you're serious about it, then? To be honest, I thought you'd change your mind."

"No, it will work. I'm sure of it. You set my brain off. I need a side-hustle I can slide into and eventually move away from flying."

"Well, hats off to you. I wish I knew what to do myself. I could work for you!"

"But—" said Lucy.

Looking at the kitchen clock, it appeared I'd lost the day doing nothing productive.

"Shit, I have to go. I have dinner at Dad's. See you later at the bar!"

The phone rang as I was driving to Dad's.

"Hello, is this Elle Darkling?"

"Yes, speaking."

"I'm calling about your application to Pendleton. It was a little late, but your application letter was enthusiastic, and we'd like to offer you a place."

"Um, that's—"

I stuttered and faltered into an awkward silence.

"Hello, Elle, are you still there? We have an application here for a degree in Viticulture and Oenology, with your name and phone number on it. This is the right degree, isn't it?"

"Um, can I call you back later? Sorry, I'm driving now, and it's not a great signal; I didn't catch your name."

Red lights slowed me down, and I brushed the dust off the screen in my car.

"My name's Jane Foster. Well, you have a week to accept the offer, Elle. Looking forward to hearing from you."

I knew we had discussed my applying for a degree, but had I actually done it? Everything was blank. It made little sense why Angus and Lucy had mentioned nothing about it.

"Hey, Siri."

"Uh, huh?"

"What's viticulture?"

"I can't show you that information right now."

"What! Hey Siri, come on."

"Uh, huh?"

"Hey Siri, I see a little silhouetto of a man."

"Scaramouche, Scaramouche, will you do the Fandango? Thunderbolt and lightning very, very frightening me—Galileo, Galileo, Galileo, Galileo, Galileo, Figaro magnifico. But I'm a poor assistant; nobody loves me—"

"Hey Siri, shut up! So, you can sing fucking 'Bohemian Rapsody,' but you can't read me Google? What the fuck!"

"Hey Siri, take a note: look up viticulture and oenology."

The call moved to the back of the queue in my head because, arriving at Dad's, I saw my nephew Walter in the distance, holding up a toy giraffe in one hand and a threadbare blanket in the other. Scooping him up, I breathed in his sweet baby aroma and kissed his soft cheeks.

M. J. PARFITT

He was the cure for all modes of depression and anxiety; I was sure of it.

"Hi, Dad!" I said, reaching for a hug with my free arm.

Holly came up behind me and put her head on my shoulder, smiling at Walter.

"What has Aunty Elle been up to now?" she asked, cocking her head towards the eye patch, now a mottled patch of dried glue spots with one lone gold star in the centre, which Walter fixated on, like a kitten with a feather on a stick, following my head as I moved around; never losing sight of the star. He reminded me of one of those bendy, elastic animals you pressed up from the bottom. I swung a shopping bag in front of his little face.

"I've got a surprise for you, Walt!"

"Is it a kitten?"

"Oh god, no. We don't keep kittens in plastic bags."

He opened the bag, removed the Thor figure, and forgot about the kitten. The trip to FAO Schwarz had been worth the effort when his round face glowed, and his eyes twinkled like perfect little blue stars. Head to toe in GAP Kids with tiny shoes—he was always well-dressed. Holly was a good mum, and it made me proud.

"Oh my god, so much has happened since I saw you guys."

I reached over, scooped up Walter again for a second cuddle, and grabbed a glass of red wine.

Holly brought in three steaming plates of sand crab lasagne and a small bowl for Walt. The table fell silent. There was something about the food Holly prepared. It filled you with joy, and it felt sacred. The delicate flavours danced in your mouth, forcing you into sublime silence. I looked up at her.

"Wow. Holly, how do you do this?"

She blushed, but I could tell it had made her day. I wanted to fill them in on the trip but wasn't prepared to let Holly's food go cold.

"Poor Angus had been trying to tell me, and he finally plucked up the courage. I mean, what was Hunter—I mean, Zero—thinking?"

Holly and Dad looked puzzled.

"Is Zero in the new Marvel film, Aunty Elle?" asked Walter.

"Oh no, this is an evil villain I know, Walt. Although come to think of it, he is an excellent actor."

"Zero?" asked Holly.

"I had to change his name on my phone. It was messing me up to keep seeing it. This way, I'll never forget what an absolute you-know-what he is. I guess he hoped Angus wouldn't have the balls to tell me. He must have lost the plot. I know people have affairs, but then to turn up as if nothing happened and expect everything to be OK, like he'd forgotten his front door key or something. The worst thing is I've wasted two years of my life and have nothing to show for it except an eye patch."

"You poor girl," Dad said, putting his hand over mine across the table and shaking his head. "Zero doesn't deserve you. Good job, you found out now. What's still confusing me is why you called from New York and asked me to scan all those bloody documents. It took me hours to find them."

"What documents? Wait—a—minute. In the car, there was a weird phone call from a lady. She offered me a place at Pendleton College or something. There's a week to decide. I know we discussed it at the bar. Still, I don't remember actually applying, and weird that Angus and Lucy have mentioned nothing."

"So, what was the course?" asked Holly.

"Viticulture and Oenology—don't even know what it is, something to do with wine."

"Let's look it up after dinner. Who were you with?"

"Angus and Lucy."

"Might have guessed Angus was involved in all this drama. The little shit," said Holly.

Holly always had a problem with Angus. Every time I mentioned him, she made a pinched expression and changed the subject. My usual way of dealing with it was to pretend I hadn't noticed.

Mum's roses were visible through the conservatory window; their beautiful colours were still apparent even in the diminishing light of the day. There was a space left in the house where the warmth of her hugs and her ability to solve all the world's problems in the blink of an eye used to live. Right now, she'd know what to say to boil everything down, making it appear trivial. She would have popped open a bottle of bubbles as soon as I'd walked in. Over two years had passed, and living without her was still hard. She died not long before I met Zero, so she never got to meet him. That had made me regretful until recently, but now I was thankful.

Dad caught my eye, and then he teared up as we looked at the roses. The peachy-coloured ones with pink-tinged petals were our favourite; they wafted divine incense, like fresh lavender in a summer's breeze. If you closed your eyes, you could transport yourself to the beautiful market in Aix-en-Provence on a summer's day, with its abundance of lavender, rows and rows of fresh spices and hand-made leather bags. The fragrance mingled in the dry summer heat to create a perfect essence of Provence.

Sensing the change in vibe, Holly stood, rattled plates and glasses, and busied off into the kitchen. I never talked about Mum with Holly. Holly was kind but not great at the 'emotional shit,' as she liked to call it. She split from her husband Nick after he admitted to an affair at work, and it was clinical. She cut him off overnight, and I hadn't seen him since. Holly never mentioned him, either. I stared after her and then turned to Dad.

"How are you, Dad? Did you go for the check-up we talked about? You know, after the dizzy spell?"

"Oh, I'm fine. Fit as a fiddle. Always out there in the garden, you know me."

"But Dad, I want you to go for me. Promise? Will you call them and make an appointment?"

I knew he wouldn't. The only way to force him to the doctor was to orchestrate a kidnapping. It was also impossible to see a doctor these days. I wondered if the government had some sort of master plan to put as many people off as possible, hoping they would die, and they wouldn't have to pay out as many state pensions.

"Yes, yes, I will. Now, what about you? What's the plan with this college thing?"

His words papered over his thoughts and cut off any chance for an honest conversation about himself. This was how it had always been, and I struggled against it. He never let me in. At least when Mum was alive, she had been the mediator, connecting us all and forcing Dad to communicate.

There was a boy in my final year at school that I fell in love with—everything in the world hinging on his adoration. Losing time or sleep over a pimpled teenage boy seemed absurd looking back. Mum had

M. J. PARFITT

been a rock. If I saw the guy now, I knew he was likely balding with a crappy life, working in a mattress shop in Woking."

Mum had made soup and toast and endless cups of sweet tea. She took me out shopping or to a movie, and slowly, I got over it. She was another weighted blanket of a person who swooped in and sorted out your life as well, if not better, than any Knightsbridge life coach.

"Seriously, how do I pay for it? There's the mortgage and my car payments, and let's be honest, being brave and smart isn't something I'm known for. Then there's the studying, which would be hard, and how would I live? I've got no savings left, and going back to living like a student—how could it work?"

"You could do it if you put your mind to it," he said, looking up at me as he spoke, taking each word like he was hopping onto stepping stones. "Perhaps you subconsciously want to change your life. I know you've enjoyed flying, but isn't it time to think about what's next? I'm trying to imagine what your mum might say now."

He looked at the roses, heaved in and out with an audible sigh and ran his old, age-spotted hands over the polished wooden, mid-century table. I thought I caught a whiff of the Mr Sheen polish Mum used. I didn't know if you could even still buy it in the age of the microfiber cloth. Perhaps I imagined the scent, which wasn't even there. Maybe I imagined I couldn't change anything when all that stood between me and a new life were a few phone calls.

"Your mum would tell you to find a way, Elle, and like I said, you've had a wonderful few years flying and everything, but you could do anything you wanted now. Don't leave it too late."

In walked an oven-gloved Holly, plonking an apple crumble on the table with a jug of thick, clotted cream. It was a gesture that paired well with the wild, uncontrollable, strawberry-blonde mop and the smattering of chestnut freckles across her nose. She reminded me of an advert for a farm shop, wheat swaying in the background and a spotty apron around her waist, holding out a pie crust. She was as blunt as they came, but I loved that the most about her.

"Jesus, Holly, I'll explode!" I said, puffing my cheeks to Walter, enticing another infectious giggle.

Holly had been a well-regarded sous chef at a top restaurant in London when she got pregnant with Walter. Her wedding ring was missing, which I noticed as she reached to push a stray hair from her face.

"Well, Dad, she won't be an eye surgeon," laughed Holly, tapping the eye patch.

"Stop it, you!" I said. "Walter, what would your mum do for laughs if I wasn't around?"

He beamed at being included, popped a chubby hand into his mushed apple crumble and stuck a big lump on his eye.

"I think we know who he takes after, don't we?" said Holly.

Petite Verdot

My week off work was not much fun. I knew I'd soon regret wasting it moping around my apartment. Shopping with nothing in particular to buy was mind-numbing. There was no need for another shade of blue nail polish, and I'd already purchased the mascara I'd been obsessed with after seeing the fabulous eyelashes on the train.

Now I knew the characters in *Selling Sunset* by name and had moved on to *Selling the OC.* If Zero was here, there was no way he'd have agreed to watch reality TV. We had to watch *Game of Thrones* or anything with spies in it. I was an expert on any James Bond movie, from Connery to Craig.

I came to a stark realisation I'd let my whole life revolve around him. He was like the sun; I was planet Earth, wholly dependent on this controlling star. One day, I gave in over a takeaway dinner decision. The next was where we would go on holiday, until it got to the big life decisions like where we would marry, and even though I loathed to say it, which engagement ring I'd receive.

We'd been into Tiffany's before to look around, and he'd pointed out the ring he ended up giving me. He raved about it, and if he'd paid attention to me, he would have picked up on the fact that I was not as enthusiastic. It wasn't me. I wanted something smaller and less showy.

It was all about his friends, too; if we went to dinner or a party, it was never with Angus and Lucy, and we rarely visited my dad's or sister's. We even spent the last Christmas with his family. His hobbies dictated my hobbies; we hiked or took ski holidays. He'd forced me to buy a mountain bike. It wasn't me. I needed to scrape back the layers of control and attempt to figure out who I was before I ever met Zero. He had mummified the real me for so long that I struggled to unearth it.

To break the monotony of being stuck inside, I took the stairs to the row of metal mailboxes and searched inside mine. There were no letters, but my hand touched something cold, and I dragged it out to see that I held the spare key I had given Zero. I stood on the spot, dumbfounded. He was now not the one grovelling for forgiveness. In typical Zero style, he wanted the last word, as if he had been the one to break it off. He couldn't even let me have the parting shot. I doubled over and screamed into my hands. Unable to take any more humiliation, I pulled it together when Grey came up to me, put his arm around me, and took me up to his apartment.

I spun around and studied his home. I'd never been inside before, despite being invited several times. Zero always had some other activity planned.

His apartment was breathtaking. The cool blonde floorboards gave the open-plan room an impression of space my apartment didn't have. There were pots of succulents, giant fig trees, and hanging plants in every shade of green I could imagine around the room. A chunky, fringed, woollen throw lay on the end of a sleek dark blue velvet ottoman, on which some considerable coffee table books and a Jo Malone candle also sat. I wanted to watch a movie and snuggle in front of the sleek fireplace. Massive Slim Aarons's prints in thick white frames adorned the living room walls. He had chosen all the prints of 'The Desert House Party' in the Palm Springs series. I'd had a similar plan before Zero talked me out of it, saying it was 'too much.'

The kitchen was sleek and uncluttered with an ice-white stone bench top and dark cabinetry. Vibrant plants trailed from a bookshelf which contained Grey's cookery books. The earthy accent tones were calm, and I could have stayed there forever. The whole place had an inbuilt aroma like the Liberty fragrance room, and I had apartment envy.

"Your place is amazing, Grey. You have a real eye. Love all the plants and the colours and textures."

I walked up to the wall behind the flat-screen TV, and I ran my hand over the cold Venetian plaster, recognising it immediately from my addiction to many DIY shows. "You're in the wrong job!"

"Really? I love interiors. The personal training pays the bills. I could help you with yours if you like," he said, holding up both palms.

He refilled my teacup; even his tableware was in the same earthy shades to blend in with all the natural elements that filled the space. This was a person who knew who he was. He wouldn't let someone control his choices. The pièce de résistance of his masterpiece was him. His cashmere sweatpants and ecru top made me imagine him on the cover of *Homes & Gardens*, showing off his abode. He was a striking man with a firm jawline that wouldn't look out of place on a Hollywood star or at least a contestant on *The Bachelor*, and his dark eyes communicated so many things without him even opening his mouth.

"I don't know if I'll stay in the apartment. It's up in the air. I'm in the middle of a huge life shift. Hunter, or Zero, as we will now refer to him—long story—has been controlling me. God, I'm stupid. I've had my blinkers on, believing we were compromising, but all the time, I was surrendering. When other women do this, I don't understand why they put up with it. It turns out I'm one of them.

"God, Grey, I'm sorry I'm venting about all this Zero crap, and I've barely asked you anything. You must think I'm a real bore. I promise this isn't what I'm usually like. Tell me what's going on with you."

"Elle, don't worry about it at all. You're not stupid. It's not a crime to fall for the wrong person. You're vibrant and fun and deserve so much more. But it's great you found out before it was too late. Forget about Zero and consider yourself lucky it happened like this."

When I left a couple of hours later with a new Chinese money plant, I was angry that Zero had stopped me from getting to know Grey sooner. It was item number 'I've lost count' on my 'reasons Zero is a total wanker' list.

After a few late nights reading *Slaughterhouse-Five*, I convinced myself to travel to Dresden for a mini-break, so I called Angus, hoping he would talk me out of it.

"Why do you read a book and try to impersonate the protagonist? You always do this, and now you want to go there?"

"But I don't want to go to Tralfamadore," I said.

"Did your neighbour give you some funny tea along with the plant? I'm not familiar with the airport code for that one."

"It's an alien planet in the book."

"It sounds like a weird fucking book," he said. "Read something funny like *Bridget Jones's Diary*, and maybe you can get laid by a sexy publisher."

"I'm educating myself, Angus; I get a mini-life lesson from each book."

"Really? What lesson did you learn from *Slaughterhouse-Five?*"

"Hmmm, well, um, it's like time is linear. So, everything has already happened; you can't change anything."

"Ah, like your situation with Zero. Not fate, not bad luck. Who knows? This strange book might help you move on."

"And so it goes," I said.

"So *what* goes?"

"The narrator says it every time someone dies in the book. Weird, I guess."

"Sounds odd to me. I'm not rushing out to buy this book. I'm worried about you, but I'm going on a trip tonight. Do not, I repeat, do not go to Dresden. I'll call you later. Are you going to meet up with Lucy?"

"I'm rotten company right now. I'm at the wallowing in self-pity stage, I don't want to inflict it on anyone else."

"Please try to stay out of trouble!"

"Oh, Angus, before you go, I almost forgot; how did the date go?

You didn't mention it the other night."

"Oh, not good at all! He brought along a small pug dog called 'The Captain,' spent the whole time talking to it in a stupid voice, and even kissed it on the lips. You know I'm not a dog person—cats all the way. The only reason he didn't want to go to Greggs was because he couldn't take The Captain. Honestly, I give up on this dating game. It's demoralising. I swear there are no decent guys out there anymore."

"Grey would be right up your street. You should check out his place. I mean, wow! It blew me away. Why don't I try to set you guys up?"

"Oh, I thought he was straight," said Angus. "Interesting, but you know I'm not into those macho bodybuilders. Although I do like the sound of being blown away!"

"Angus! Stop! He's into interior design. It's his passion. I mean, he likes Slim Aarons prints," I said. Letting it hang there.

"Hmm, why don't you have a dinner party and invite him down when I'm back?"

I sat on my balcony, opened a bottle of expensive pinot noir, and poured a large glass. The full moon hung in the silent sky as if it might drop any second. There were no stars, but I knew they were there like I knew my new life, good or bad, was waiting for me somewhere in the linear universe. I picked up my glass and looked at its dark red contents. *Well, you might be the answer to my problems, after all.*

My locker in the car park was full of junk. I pulled out several boxes, and dust flew everywhere. Eventually, after unearthing a rowing machine and an elliptical trainer, I found the mountain bike Zero had made me buy. The tyres were flat, and it took half an hour for me to figure out how to pump them up. Zero had always managed everything to do with the bike when we were mountain biking for the day in the New Forest or some other location he had planned.

I pedalled off down the road, merging in with traffic, not considering a trial run on a quieter road might have been the sensible option. Before long, I was in some deep shit as I approached a roundabout and couldn't bring myself to go over it. I panicked and took the first exit, perhaps a touch too fast, and clipped the back tyre of another cyclist. Profanities were slung backwards over the traffic noise, and I died inside.

I wished I hadn't had this brilliant idea and deliberated about how I would cycle home.

Suddenly, I was dreaming, outside my body, flying over the bonnet of a car and then laying still, curious if this was what it was like to die. "And so it goes," I heard myself mutter.

I stood up and looked around. People were staring. The world slowed down, and all I could hear was my internal voice. The driver put both arms on my shoulders and asked if I was OK. I stood like a mute rag doll. Someone had called an ambulance, and I climbed into it, insisting I was OK. I drifted again into the safe place inside my head, grateful I wouldn't have to ride my bike home. I wanted to stay in my head and forget everything else for as long as possible.

Holly and Dad rushed into the emergency department, looking like the world's weight balanced on their shoulders. They breathed a sigh of relief to find me awake and unbroken.

"Oh, thank god," said Holly, holding her chest and sitting beside me on the blue pleather recliner.

"The stress. Oh, my god. Dad, come and sit here."

He was sobbing, and I had to reassure him I was OK.

"But why were you on a bike?" he asked. "You shouldn't ride a bike. You're not safe on them. I didn't even know you owned one."

I laughed and coughed at the same time.

"Dad, you make me sound like I'm mentally ill. Thanks for the vote of confidence!"

"Are you OK, though, Elle?" asked Holly. "You know, after the Zero thing."

"Holly, if I were going to top myself, I wouldn't do it on a bike, on a roundabout in Woking! I've had a lucky escape. I've been doing some soul-searching over the last few days, and Zero was over-bearing."

"Ya think?" said Holly.

Then we laughed, and we couldn't stop. It was a kind of hysterical ecstasy.

They took me home, and I picked up the mail on the way in and flung it on the table. My dad put the kettle on as he tackled the washing-up. Holly sat at the table and studied the letters.

M. J. PARFITT

"Hey, there's a letter here from the airline."

"Really? Weird. A physical letter?"

I eased myself up, looked at the envelope, and ripped it open.

Elle,

Please attend a formal interview to discuss events on flight AA431 on the 6th of July 2019. We permit you to bring along a support person on the day. Please note they must be present as support only and cannot be directly involved in our discussions.

Kind Regards,
Monty Blake

"Short and sweet," said Holly. "What's it about?"

"Hmm, we don't know. We all got a phone message, too. We guessed it was about this rude passenger or Lucy passing out. There was an incident in the office just as we were signing in; the ceiling collapsed and landed on her."

"That's awful," said Holly. "Is Lucy OK?"

"Well, I've been checking in with her. She seems fine. She doesn't have much of a memory of it at all."

Dad sat down, placed our tea on the table and coughed.

"Well, it can't be about Lucy because they've said you might need a support person."

"Oh, shit, you're right, Dad. But what have I done?"

"OK," said Holly, "go through everything that happened on the flight."

"Hmm. Not much. Except. Oh. Angus put eye drops in a lady's drink, and the manager thought it was both of us—oh. I guess it's that;

when I say it out loud, it sounds bad."

Sitting down, deflated, I put my face in my hands and noticed a Post-it note sticking out from under the empty fruit bowl. On it, Zero had written: 'I found this cornflake and thought of you' and stuck on the note was a perfect heart-shaped cornflake.

I picked it up and lifted it to show Holly and Dad.

"But I don't even buy cornflakes."

My sadness at losing everything and my utter confusion at the contradictions Zero was throwing at me reduced me to a howling baby. I pulled myself together and slammed my fist down on the cornflake.

"Calm down, Elle. It's just a cornflake," said Dad.

"Oh my god, they are going to fire me."

"Well, tell them the truth, Elle. Say it was Angus," said Holly.

I looked from Dad to Holly and wanted one of them to solve this. I eased myself up again, grabbed my mobile, and texted Lucy and Angus. Both replied, saying they'd had letters.

"This seems like an impossible situation where I lose, no matter what I do."

They were both quiet, and Dad grabbed my hand.

"Yesterday, we were talking about you doing a degree. Why don't you? Walk away from this. Look how sad you are."

Holly said nothing. There was a long, silent pause in the conversation.

"Why did Angus do it?"

"He did it for me. The passenger was a rude bitch. That's how this whole me applying for the degree came about."

"Hmm, he is a shit, but I knew it would be for you. As much as he infuriates me, he always has your back, no matter what. I'm with Dad. Go in there, tell them to go fuck themselves and reinvent yourself."

"That's—not what I expected you to say. I've never understood why you don't seem to like Angus, Hol. He's like a brother to me."

"Honestly, that's why. It's hard to admit, but I'm jealous. I'm jealous because you're my sister, and I don't want to share you, and I guess I'd like a friend like him too. You know, Elle, life's short. Find some joy in it. This airline doesn't give two shits about you, and you have a fantastic opportunity to try something amazing. I want you to be happy. Do you want me or Dad to come with you to the office?"

"Jeez, did you hit your head or something, Hol? That's a lot of talk about feelings for you. Nah, I'll be OK; thanks for offering, though. I've got a lawyer."

The thought of Holly going in with me was frightening. She wouldn't be able to keep quiet. It made me chuckle despite my bleak mood.

"A lawyer? Why do you have a lawyer, and why does it stink of baked ham in here?" asked Holly.

They settled me on the cloud couch with more tea and said their goodbyes, and I dozed off into a deep sleep.

At three a.m., a sore back woke me up because I'd been sleeping on the large volume of Emily Dickinson and couldn't get up from the couch. I rolled myself onto the floor by easing the top half of my body down first, laying there paralysed, then trying to do some exercises to release my back and hips. I pushed myself up like an awful breakdancer, too scared to sit down again.

My pride was still hurting from finding the key in my letter box, and I took my laptop into the kitchen, stood by the counter, and emailed Zero.

Dear Zero,

Thanks for the key. Dumping you was the best decision I ever made. Never come here again, you pathetic twat.

Look, so here's the things I hate about you:

1. Small penis.

2. Rude and obnoxious.

3. Finishes all my sentences.

4. Never empties the dishwasher.

5. Doesn't straighten the cushions.

6. Has never replaced a toilet roll.

7. Flirts with other women.

8. Oversized ego.

9. Can't change a tyre.

10. Hates cats.

Oh, and fuck you.

I didn't send it. I left it in drafts and vowed I'd never see Zero again. Was he meeting Alex at the airport right now? Was he relieved it was all over between us? He would get over it quickly. All men did, or they put on an outstanding show of it.

I funnelled the pent-up frustration into sorting out all the kitchen cupboards and fridge and jumped for joy when I found a long-lost

Snickers bar wedged in the back of the refrigerator. And when I had used up all of my aggression, I sat down in front of my computer again and vowed to sort out my shit.

I searched for the email from Pendleton College, clicked on the link to their website, and navigated to their wine degree section. They had a professional-looking wine centre with their own vineyards and had won a medal for a sparkling white wine they made on-site. What appealed most was that it was a practical degree where you put your knowledge into practice. The website drew me into the idea of a new and exciting life. Before I knew it, I could imagine myself turning up on day one, and it scared the shit out of me.

I had to be sure it wasn't a reaction to the split with Zero. It had to be a deliberate plan of action; otherwise, he was still pulling my puppet strings from afar.

After a three-hour internet search on everything I could find out about working in the wine industry, which veered off on many tangents, I had to admit it fascinated me. It wasn't something I'd ever thought about doing. I'd seen the movie *A Good Year* with Russell Crowe and enjoyed it. I just had nothing real to compare it to.

I opened another tab, filled my Amazon cart with books about wine and clicked on the 'Buy Now' button. Then I found an adult colouring book titled *Shove It Up Your Fucking Arse*, selected Zero's address and sent him the gift. Next, I found a gnome riding a dachshund and sent it to Angus with a card reading, 'This should exasperate your neighbours!' I found Lucy a book called *Is This Love or Dopamine?*—a book looking at online dating—and sent it to her.

I fell asleep again on the cloud couch and woke to find I had drunk an entire bottle of pinot. My head banged, and I drank straight from the kitchen tap, and I realised I did this way too often. Breakfast was yesterday's takeaway pepperoni pizza. Looking at my apartment, I gave myself a pep talk, straightened up the cloud couch as best I could and vowed this was a new me.

I looked around the room. Grey and I had the exact apartment configuration, yet my place looked unlived. The paintwork was tired, and the carpet had seen better days. I had no artwork.

The first day I moved in, I had collected the keys from the estate agent and was full of plans to decorate and improve the place. None of which I'd done as Zero talked me out of a new kitchen, new flooring, upgrading the bathroom, and yet he was hardly here. Even my apartment suffered from his control over me, and I hadn't noticed a thing.

My front door buzzed.

"Hey, Elle, it's me."

Lucy arrived at the door with an overstuffed tote bag, a laptop case, and a bunch of vibrant peonies.

"Oh, Lucy! I forgot you were coming. Sorry, I've been a bit rubbish this week. I didn't want to bring you down, too."

"Oh, never mind about that. Can you help me? I have all these mock-ups for the app, and I need you to be a beta tester. This is for you," she said, handing me a bottle of tequila.

"A what now?"

"Don't worry about it. Just grab some glasses. I need a drink."

I sat and pored over the contents of her tote bag. She had written a business plan and had swathes of research and data to support her vision. I handed her a shot.

"Have you had any sleep since I saw you last?"

"I have to get this up and running before someone else does it. I have a trip in a few days, and I want it done before then."

"So, I never asked you the other day, but what's the opposite man for you then? I mean if you join this app?"

"Oh, I'll be joining the app, Elle, and so will you. We'll be the founding members. But to answer your question, I'm always drawn to these moody men in boring, nondescript jobs, and you go for the brash types, and Angus—I haven't figured out his preference yet. I'm working on it."

"Well, he didn't have a wonderful experience with that Greggs guy that had the dog, so perhaps your app can hook him up with a dog lover from Somerset."

When Lucy had gone, some of her energy and optimism had rubbed off on me. I headed to the gym, but as soon as I arrived, I had second thoughts. I'd joined over a year ago, and then Zero had repeatedly talked me out of going and had worn me down. The direct debit got sucked out of my account each month, but I hadn't been for at least six. Mulling it over in the car and eating most of a packet of Fruit Pastilles, I admitted defeat, turned the car back on and drove home. I wasn't a gym girl.

As I pulled into the car park of my building, I saw Grey waiting for me and waving. Panicking, I squirted water from my drink bottle over my face as if I had been working out.

He waited for me while I parked my car.

"Hey, Grey! How's your day going?"

"Great, thanks. How are you doing today? Good idea to get back to the gym!" he said, smiling and looking at my feet.

He caught the lift as I pretended to check my non-existent mail, and I looked down and saw I was still wearing my pink UGG boots.

Albarino

$\mathcal{T}$oday, Heathrow overwhelmed me. It didn't care about the looming day of reckoning for me, Angus, and Lucy. It carried on regardless. Buses merged, and cars honked, oblivious to the stress we shared. I looked around. Would some of these people get fired today? Were they the lucky ones, satisfied with their lot? They moved like streams of independent ants, impervious to each other's movement, and I was one of them.

I had an ominous sense of how the day might unfold. At home, I'd considered calling in sick. Angus and Lucy came up behind me just as I was getting ready to bolt.

"What are you doing out here?" asked Angus.

"I don't want to go in, but also, I'm waiting for Gerald."

"Gerald?" said Angus.

"You know, my lawyer. I was sitting next to him on the plane on the way home. You said I bored him to death."

"Oh, of course! Your lawyer Gerald. How could I forget Gerald? Seriously, you think you need a lawyer?"

"Well, it can't hurt. Work said we can have a support person, and he's mine and yours."

"Come on, how bad can it be?" said Lucy, grabbing me by the arm.

Gerald walked up, still in a pin-striped suit, but this time with a blue and white polka-dot tie.

"What the absolute fuck?" whispered Lucy as he walked towards us. "Your lawyer is Gerald King?"

"You know him?"

"Yeah, how do you know him?" asked Angus.

"You two astound me. Don't you watch the news? Having Gerald King at a workplace dispute is the English equivalent of having Robert Kardashian here. He got Charlie Kane off for the first-degree murder of his wife."

We looked at her in stunned silence as Gerald bounced up. He was like Tigger on steroids.

"Hello, troops," he said.

"Um, hello Gerald. This is Lucy and Angus. Look, are you sure you have time for this? I had no fucking idea you were a famous lawyer. I'm so embarrassed I could die."

"Elle, you do not know how boring my work is day to day. I wouldn't have given you the card if I didn't mean it."

We were all ushered into a room with a carpet like a worn-out Brillo pad and lighting that would make Michelle Pfeiffer look like she was having a bad day. In the corner sat several Resusci Annes and some first-aid kits, and I recognised the room where we had our first-aid training. I looked for the model some rebel had drawn a love heart tattoo on and spotted it on a protruding arm. Angus and I had named her Lola. I caught his eye, looking at the same thing, and we smiled.

After I introduced Gerald, the room fell silent. It was apparent the management also watched the news. I sat at the large, bland faux-wood conference table with Angus and Lucy, and Gerald sat in a chair off one side. He had a yellow legal pad and a Montblanc pen in one hand and the other hand propped up his chin.

We waited for Monty, his boss, and the flight manager to sit down and sort out their paper files. I looked down at the service road below, watching people come and go and wishing I was down there and not up here facing who knew what.

The room was hot, my head thumped with an impending headache, and I had an urge to laugh. I looked at Monty's paper file and wondered what drivel it could contain. Perhaps a series of minor misdemeanours stretching back over the last four years? I guessed it was empty. Two things that became obvious to me were: A. I didn't want to end up like them, and B. This was not where I belonged.

"Thank you for coming in," Monty said, turning to Angus first.

"As you know, we pride ourselves on passengers' care, service, and safety. There are some serious allegations against you all relating to the poisoning of a passenger's drink with an eye drop solution on the last flight you operated together to New York."

Angus turned red, stammered, and looked out the window. His foot was tapping under the table, and I could see his bright yellow socks poking out of his shiny shoes. Lucy looked shell-shocked. It confused me why she was involved in any of it, as she had been working the upper-deck, anyway.

A surge of adrenaline rushed through me as though my whole body was being dragged down a drain hole at breakneck speed. My heart pumped to keep up, and I wanted to vomit. I looked over at Angus and Lucy, my ride-or-die best friends, and glanced at Monty and Leanne, the manager from the flight and Monty's boss, whom I didn't know from Adam. I heard my mum's voice. 'Nothing is as awful as it seems right now. You'll look back and laugh. These people don't care about you. When life sends you lemons…'But the last one was, 'Look after your friends; good ones are hard to find.' There was one option here for me to be true to myself, and it scared me. I glanced at Gerald, wrote him a quick note on the back of a dry-cleaning token and passed it to him. He nodded.

Monty looked irritated and spoke up again.

"We also have a disgusting note left for a fellow crew member with a diagram of male genitalia. We can't tolerate this type of behaviour," he said.

I thought I detected a look in his eyes. Perhaps even one of appreciation for the prank, but here he was, sitting with the file in front of him and a condescending tone directed at us all, and I dismissed the thought.

I stared Monty straight in the eyes. He was wearing an expensive suit and an immaculate orangey-red silk tie, ironically in the colour of the Golden Gate Bridge. I couldn't suppress a giggle, tried to cover it up with a cough, and Lucy and Angus glared at me. Again, I noticed the white roots of his hairline, the white poking through the red like unstoppable grass growing into flowerbeds, now much more of them visible than when I'd seen him a week before.

I stood up, grabbed my trusty Longchamp, deliberately pushed in my chair, and faced the three bosses.

"It was me. These guys had absolutely nothing to do with it. You'll have my resignation by the end of today. Now, if that's all? This meeting is over."

Angus and Lucy sat open-mouthed, and I turned to walk out into the sun-filled hallway, which now held the appeal of a tropical paradise. Halfway out the door, I changed my mind, slowly turned back, and spoke directly to Monty.

"Looking at the ceiling here, Monty, it also seems in a state of disrepair. Have you had it checked for safety recently? And regarding the one in the crew office falling on Lucy's head before the flight, which knocked her out. I did witness you bringing out the waiver for her to sign when she was practically comatose, offering her no first aid. You barely even asked her how she was. Lucy was sick on the flight, and I had to call for a doctor. So, when she goes to court to sue your ass, I'm giving you notice that I'm right there by her side as a firsthand witness. I think you've met our lawyer—Gerald. By the way, your hair looks fucking ridiculous; get your roots done, for god's sake. I'm not sure you are setting the right example here for personal grooming standards."

I hissed the last bit, making Monty look down self-consciously. He blushed and looked rattled. I'd bet good money he'd be straight out to light a cigarette as soon as this meeting was done. I dropped the enormous grenade and walked out, elated and disappointed, all at the same time. It didn't seem right, attacking his hair, but he didn't look after my friend, and I couldn't forget that.

I grabbed all my stuff, everything I had with me anyway, dumped it onto the front desk and walked out a free woman. No one said goodbye. No one said anything. It was as if I had never worked there at all.

"See ya!" I shouted over my shoulder.

It was wild, blowing up my whole life, but damn, it was exciting. I headed to a coffee shop in the terminal and rustled in my bag for my phone. It was always a mammoth challenge locating anything in it.

"Hello, is this Janet? It's Elle Darkling here. Sorry, I couldn't chat the other day. Had some life stuff to sort through. So, about the place you offered me. I'd love to take it."

My heart raced out of my chest like a stallion breaking a gate. This wasn't just blowing up my life. This was blowing it up, then getting on a rollercoaster.

My hand shook as I sipped the crappy Heathrow coffee, which looked like two different liquids unhappy in the same cup.

I could see Angus marching toward me, and I held his gaze.

"What in the fuck? I didn't ask you to do that, Elle. Come back with me now. We can sort it all. You can't do this. It's insane."

"No. Those people are awful. It's too late, anyway; I'm going to uni. I'm doing a degree at Pendleton. But you will have a new lodger. I'll rent out my place or sell it. It's done. My one regret is I didn't keep my wings for memories. I was so mad I bundled everything up and left it there."

I looked at him for a reaction when I mentioned Pendleton. He shifted slightly in his seat.

"This is all my fault, and now you have no job, and I get to keep mine?" he said. "It's not fair."

"Yeah, but seriously, as your friend, consider leaving too. Not in such a dramatic way as this but think about studying photography or something. Life is too short. Can we agree? This time next year, you won't be here fake smiling and delivering plastic food to 'Philips'?"

Angus nodded between sobs and held my hand.

"You're like a sister to me; you know what you did. I mean, no one has ever stood up for me before."

Lucy walked up with her arms linked in Gerald's, wagging her finger at me.

"Jeez, you have put the cat among the pigeons, my friend."

"Sorry, I couldn't resist. Did work offer a payout?"

"Gerald was amazing. It's pretty big. I'm taking it, so it looks like we are both unemployed, and I'm giving part of the cash to you."

"No way. I'll be OK. I called and confirmed my place at Pendleton. You could have given me the heads up I'd applied, guys! Even when I told you they called me, you said nothing!"

I looked from Lucy to Angus, and they both laughed.

"This meeting is over," said Angus.

He laughed and nearly fell off the chair.

"You were like Alan Sugar in *The Apprentice*."

"So, let me get this right—you are studying winemaking? I was sure it would be 'The Fundamentals in Spirit Production' given your penchant for the old goose!" said Gerald.

Angus burst out laughing.

"Gerald, I fucking love you!" he said.

After a mock pause, we all shrieked, and everyone in the vicinity stared at us. We beamed at each other, wide-eyed, like rabbits caught in the headlights. The adrenalin was pumping through our veins.

We were all caught up in our thoughts when the blonde helmet bob walked towards us. She looked over with a trademark sneer and whispered to her group. I didn't know who some of these people were. It was as if she employed a cast of actors to play her friends. They approached the table, and Angus stretched back in his chair and crossed his arms. A large meat cleaver entered my heart again, and Lucy looked on at the scene with mild amusement.

"You need to give Hunter the ring back, Elle. When are you going to return it?" Alex said in a croaky voice, like an old fishwife, as though she smoked as many fags as Monty. All she had going for her was a trim figure and neat hair. She'd age like an old piece of leather and I took comfort in that.

Tapping the table, I heard the quiver in my voice but banished it.

"Sorry, what now? What's it got to do with you?"

"He made a huge mistake with you, and it's a twenty-grand ring. You can't keep it," said Alex, smirking at her friends, who stood like mutes.

"I'm trying to understand what's going on here. You want the ring for yourself, don't you?" said Angus.

"Well, duh, it's expensive. Elle only had it for a day." Alex said.

"Oh, but she loved it from the bottom of her heart. I think it would be a real strain for her to part with it," Angus said.

All three of us were struggling to hold in the laughter.

"Not that it's any of your business, you total fucking bitch, but I plan to give it back. Not my taste, anyway, and pretty shitty of you to fuck my fiancé and then come over and speak to me like this. At least have some class. Choke on it. I know I didn't."

Alex looked at me, confused. She muttered some incoherent throwaway remark, then tottered off towards the office. I'd seen a teeny chink appear in the made-up face as I watched her fade away with her wheeled suitcase. I imagined the gossip which would last for months in the crew office. When Ivana Stevens had shared all her airline secrets on her TikTok account, sometimes wearing her uniform and sometimes her pyjamas, they eventually fired her, and that was two years ago. People still spoke of it as if it was yesterday. Everyone I knew would be there now with nothing else to discuss but the ménage à trois in which I had become embroiled. It was mortifying but also out of my control.

"He's not seriously giving her the same ring. It's fucking weird, and weird she'd want it," said Angus. "And why are they getting engaged? He was engaged to you a few days ago. I mean, they hardly know each other. You couldn't make this shit up."

"God knows, but she's all show, and he's a tight arse. You lose so much on second-hand rings compared with what you paid, even a Tiffany one. He wouldn't want to lose a pound on it."

"Shut up," said Lucy. "This is comedy gold. We can make them look like total fools. It will be the highlight of my year; Alex will want a big engagement party, won't she?"

Angus was a little too excited to find out all the details of an impending engagement party as the social butterfly of our trio. They both looked a little too enthusiastic about this potential takedown.

"Hang on a minute, was that *the* Alex?" asked Gerald. "She with massive spanner and disrupter of townhouse acquisition in London with crinkled linen?"

"See, Angus? He was listening!"

Then they all left, with Angus saying he needed to slide into some DMs and find out as much as he could about an engagement party and Lucy rushing for an appointment at the bank to secure the funding for her app, which Gerald was now also attending.

She was on a mission to make a go of her business venture, which we still thought was bananas, but if Gerald thought there was something in it, maybe she was onto something.

Sitting back for once, I looked around the terminal. I'd never paid it much attention before, always rushing to check in for a flight or get home. People from all walks of life were busy, heads down, and for perhaps the first time in my life, I was the one who had nowhere to be, so I called Holly.

"Hey, Holly. I did it. I'm officially unemployed."

"Oh wow, well done! Come over, and we'll open a bottle of Champagne, and you can tell me all about it. I'm so proud of you."

Turning sideways in the wardrobe mirror, I studied my appearance. My chosen outfit was a royal blue knit dress. The goal was not to look like we were gate-crashing the party, but like we were out for drinks on a casual night out. When I pulled up my hair into a messy bun and saw a thread hanging at the neck of the dress and tugged on it, like a failed knitting attempt, it carried on and on in an unravelling continuum. Soon, there was less and less of the dress's neckline left. Choosing the outfit in the first place had taken me ages, and it was a perfect balance between casual and smart. There was no way I was about to start the entire process over again. I snatched up a thin black suit jacket and covered up my cleavage.

My Uber arrived at the same time as Angus's, and we hugged excitedly outside the bar.

"This is going to be fun!"

M. J. PARFITT

I wasn't super keen on confrontations, and there was no telling how this might unfold. It was weeks since I'd seen Zero, and I didn't want to face him at all, really. A nervousness buzzed in my stomach, and I would have preferred to be at home watching anything on Netflix.

Lucy walked up behind us as we were ordering the first round. She had Gerald and his wife Valerie with her.

"Hey, my gorgeous friends! You already know Gerald, and this is his wife, Valerie. They are my new investors. I booked a table," she said, pointing to a brown leather booth near the large bay window.

Valerie had the porcelain complexion and height of an ex-model. She fit right in at The Ivy with her expensive shoes and dress.

"Oh wow! That's incredible," I said. "Valerie, I'm sorry about hijacking Gerald for the dispute the other week."

"Oh no, I told him to do it. He told me all about you when he got home after the flight, and I said you sounded hilarious and interesting. Now look at what's happened! Because of you, we met Lucy, and it's exciting. You were courageous to quit your job, Elle, by the way."

Lucy ordered a bottle of Veuve, and we arranged ourselves in the booth.

"To Madame Clicquot!" said Lucy, raising her glass. "And may our friend here follow in her footsteps and fill the world with beautiful Champagne!"

"And a toast to my friend here. Let's hope she matches many unlikely lovers!" I said.

The bar was loud and buzzing with no discernible language except a merry hum. Laughter carried itself over the music, and glasses clinked.

"Now, Elle, no martinis tonight, OK? I ban you from a drink requiring a cocktail stick," said Lucy. "I'm going to order some Aperol Spritz for us all."

I was pretty sure she drank it because she loved the colour.

Then her eye caught something behind us, and Angus and I turned to see Alex and Zero and their groupies shouting in drinks at the bar.

"Oh, we are on! Been waiting for this all week," said Angus. "I barely slept last night. I was playing all this out in my head."

⋰⊙⋱

Angus and I headed to the bathroom, bumping into Claire.

"Angus! Elle! I haven't seen you guys in ages. I didn't know you were coming?"

"Coming to what? We're here with some friends," he said, pointing over at Lucy, Gerald, and Val.

"Oh—right," she said. "It's Alex and Hunter's engagement drinks. Oh god, this is awkward! I'm sorry, Elle."

"Awkward? Who for? Oh, that's all water under the bridge. Look, I'm busting. Must go. Great to see you, Claire!" I said.

⋰⊙⋱

We joined the others back at the table.

"Alex won't be able to resist the urge to come over. You know that, right?" Angus said.

"Oh my god, Elle, why are your breasts practically sitting on the table?"

I looked down; a button on the jacket had popped off, and the plunging neckline was on full display. The heat rose to my cheeks, and I clasped my hands over my chest.

"I wondered why guys kept looking over here," said Lucy.

"I thought we looked fucking gorgeous," I said. "When, in fact, everyone in the bar has been copping an eyeful all night."

Val handed me a pashmina from her bag. I could tell it wasn't her first fashion emergency. It was as if I was slowly collecting mentors and well-meaning friends like tumbleweed rolling through my life since I'd loosened myself from the grip of Zero.

We were having so much fun we started to forget why we were there, and the night turned into one of sharing stories and anecdotes. Gerald had so many from all his high-profile court cases. Occasionally, someone would come up to the table and ask if he was Gerald King, and he'd pretend to be Russian or say he was someone else.

When I told everyone about the eyelashes on the train and the heart-shaped cornflake on a Post-it, we got into a fit of giggles.

"You are making this up!" said Gerald.

"Well, if you're not, I want that mascara," said Val.

When Alex approached with a group of friends about an hour later, I had forgotten all about her. She was wearing a flashy gold dress. I could see Val looking at it with a bewildered expression. The fabric had poorly creased. It reminded me of one of the round, chewy toffees in a Quality Street tin that was always left at the end, along with the nougat ones.

"I don't recall sending out an invitation," Alex said in a voice one or two decibels higher than needed.

"To what?" I asked, pulling the pashmina a little tighter. "A Quality Street fancy dress party?"

Val snorted and placed a hand on Gerald's arm.

Alex deserved a little of what she dished out, even though I felt like a complete bitch.

Lucy and Angus were finding it hard to breathe.

"Don't play dumb, Elle," Alex said, as she patted her dress.

"Well, this is a public bar, Alex, unless you booked out the whole place. We've had this night arranged for some time. Now I'm single; the world is my oyster."

Alex squirmed and searched for a witty reply but came up short. Zero loomed nervously over the crowd and spotted Alex and her friends talking to us. He pushed his way through, and my heart sank when I saw his floppy hair, and he caught my gaze.

"Hi, Elle. Look, so—" he said.

"Here's the thing—" the three of us sang. We laughed so loud that everyone stared over at our table. Clearly, Alex hadn't had enough time to be sick of his favourite phrase yet; she looked at us, confused.

Zero looked down, embarrassed at the ridicule, struggling for words.

Alex broke the silence and whipped out her ring finger, sticking the diamond squarely in the middle of our booth, making it glint in the overhead lights. She reminded me of a mean child I had encountered in the primary school playground after a cruel teacher's aide ousted me from the school dance show because I had no sense of rhythm. The girl had proudly shown me a bright red lipstick that they would all get to wear for the performance without me. I had since seen that unremarkable girl working in the local Iceland, and I hoped Alex would get her lifetime achievement award in the same fashion one of these days.

"Looks better on me, don't you think?"

A final humiliating blow. This twisted bitch wouldn't let it rest. It was unfathomable why Alex wanted to hurt me. People had affairs all the time, but most had the decency to be a little embarrassed about them or, at least, to show some sensitivity to the wounded party. But not Alex.

"Yeah, it suits you, and I think it's apt that it's now on your finger. Every time you look at it, you can think of my butthole."

Everyone in the group looked at me. They had expected me to be quiet and slope off, even sobbing a little. This new version of me had finally broken through the ice. This was what had been niggling away at me; I had been playing the part of the clumsy drip. Not anymore. Zero stared at me.

"Oh, poor Elle. Jobless and ringless. Poor, poor Elle," said Alex, she was partly singing. It was like she had a singing form of Tourette's.

"To coin a phrase, see, here's the thing, Alex, there was a good reason it took Elle a while to give Hunter—aka Zero—back the ring," said Angus, projecting his voice so the whole bar couldn't help but listen.

The bar was hushed.

There was a lengthy pause, where Angus smiled like a Cheshire cat and gave his phone to a nearby table; they had promised to capture the whole thing on video. Lucy and I looked down at the table, smirking and kicking each other in the leg.

"We were on a night out in New York, of all places, and Elle accidentally swallowed your new engagement ring while sipping a glass of prosecco. To give it back to Zero so that he could re-gift it to you, she had to poop it out! And now, as you say, you're right; that shit looks better on you.

"And Zero, I imagine you cleaned your teeth before you came here tonight? I hope you didn't use the electric brush you left at Elle's. It did such a good job of cleaning the thing up. Oh, and one more thing—do you have any cornflakes at your place, Alex?"

Zero was white. Alex was red, and the surrounding group became even more silent, then erupted into the most hysterical laughter. Alex turned and tried to rush out, but her dress was too tight, and she could only make pigeon steps.

"Elle, this isn't you. This is exactly why I tried to get you away from these two. To be this pathetic, even for you, it's scraping the barrel. You wanted me to move on, and I did. You don't have a life without me, do you?" said Zero. "When will you grow up and see you will never amount to anything without me? I wanted to look after you. I wanted to marry you. You called it off. You said you never wanted to see me again, yet here you are."

I bit my cheek and fought back tears.

Angus attempted to speak, but I spoke over him. I tried hard to project my voice.

"Are you joking? You're not exactly Timothée Chalamet. The trouble with you is you have this colossal ego that no one woman can satisfy. You know nothing about me; you never asked. Why don't you piss off and kick another cat or something? Yes, that's right, everyone, this boy likes to hurt poor, defenceless animals. You know what they say about that, don't you, Zero—you're probably a psychopath? The scary thing is he's a pilot."

Zero stormed out, turning to give Angus and me a glare. The bar erupted, and we were being bought drinks left, right and centre, with people coming up and congratulating us on our successful prank.

We watched the arguing couple under the streetlight. Alex waved her arms about and shouted, and Zero looked like he would welcome a massive sinkhole in the street outside The Ivy. The pair's gestures resembled a *Carry On* scene. Alex eventually stormed off, and Zero followed as we hummed the *Carry On* theme song.

"The people in this bar don't believe this happened. You know—me swallowing the ring."

"Elle, if we told these people what happens to you daily, they wouldn't believe any of it!" said Angus.

"You know, Alex 'shit ring' is right about one thing. You are ringless and jobless, and I couldn't be prouder of you," said Lucy.

Viognier

Driving up to the front of Pendleton for freshers' week in my crappy new-old Volkswagen Polo, I pinched myself. I couldn't quite acknowledge that I was going through with the accidental plan to change my life. The majestic red brick building with neat walled gardens and pea-shingle pathways that greeted me housed Pendleton's plethora of courses. It held so much of my future in its hands it scared me, and I struggled to understand how I would find enough courage for step one: climb out of the car.

As I entered the car park, a guy dashed out in front of me. I slammed the brakes and sat resting my head on the lambswool steering wheel cover, which I had yet to remove, and I jerked back, thinking of the previous owner's germs.

"Hello. Sorry about that. I was talking to my mum on the phone and wasn't looking where I was going. It's my first day, and I'm a little nervous. She was talking me off the ledge."

"Jeez, being run over would have been a terrible first day. It's mine, too," I said.

"What degree are you taking?" he asked.

"Oenology."

"You park, and I'll wait for you. I'm doing the same degree. We are going to be great friends. I can feel it in my bones, and our first story will be the one where you nearly killed me with your terrible driving."

"Hey, you stepped out of nowhere!"

"Haha. I'm Vinjay—call me Vin."

He did a little bow, and I laughed. He wore tan corduroy pants that I had seen no one wear except my dad and a navy wool vest with a purple diamond pattern down the front as if he'd just had a quick nine holes. His company took the sting out of my trepidation. He was a weird little guy, but I thought I liked him, and now I had a bounce in my step.

"Hi, everyone. My name's Guy, and this is my second year of a viticulture and oenology degree. I'll be taking you on the guided tour today, and then we can finish at the wine centre, where you can sample our wine and ask all your burning questions. You're going to love this place. Everyone does."

He had a casual appearance—a checked flannel shirt, skinny turned-up jeans with brown leather boots—and looked down at my own clothes, my signature look of blazer and striped top. There had been no time to go shopping, and I had no money to buy anything after buying textbooks and a laptop bag. All I'd done the week before was add clothes to an online cart and remove them individually until I was happy with the total bill. All I could afford was a leather belt from New Look. Even though I'd rented out my apartment, there had been a lot of hidden costs in getting it ready.

Lucy had promised access to her wardrobe, but she was pitching to investors in California with Gerald and Val. I would have to wait a few weeks or raid Holly's wardrobe instead. Even Holly's wardrobe had some items in it that were more up-to-date than mine.

Guy looked about seventeen; I was De Niro in *The Intern* without the confidence and lifetime of experience. I breathed an audible sigh of relief when I saw a few students who looked older than me or at least the same age. Everyone in the group turned to look at me, and my face burned a scarlet red.

Another student, Heidi, smiled at me. She had a pierced nose and several earrings and was younger, but I didn't think she was a school leaver; she had a worldly air and knew far more about wine than I did.

The one experience that counted here was winemaking; knowing how to heat a meal cart or open an emergency exit did not equip me for this world. My small amount of knowledge currently extended to the pile of Amazon books I'd worked my way through and a wine trip in France.

We bonded at the wine centre over a bottle of pinot grigio. Some students were already being a bit wanky about the wine, talking about it as though it were a Châteauneuf-Du-Pape. I would avoid them at all costs. A man with a blue argyle cardigan called Howard was the most irritating, and he seemed to be the self-appointed leader of this emerging pack. The others sat enthralled with his tales of working in Tuscany or how the invasion of the ancient Greeks had instituted viticulture in Italy. He acted like he didn't need the degree. I already knew he would not be popular with any of the lecturers. I sought the misfits without an agenda, and our trio was born.

M. J. PARFITT

Heidi had travelled around Europe, hence her confidence and piercings. She had fallen in love with Burgundy and dreamed of moving to France and working in a vineyard. She had been to Beaune, a town I had visited near the hills of Côte d'Or. It was a stunning town with sandstone buildings and a little market square on the Route Des Grand Crus tourist trail, which I had taken with Holly and Mum. I could always picture it because it was there that I tried my first snail. Our shared experience gave us some common ground. It was my one interesting wine story, apart from the Philip in twelve C, but it was a start.

Vin was an international student from Goa who wanted to buck family traditions and become a winemaker. In the car park, overcome by nerves, he told me his mum had tried to talk him off the ledge by suggesting he fly home.

He'd been working at a company in Goa, which made a gin called Greater Than. I choked on my pinot when he told us they made it with crowdsourced cricket bats—used chipped and bashed ones. At first, I thought he meant they made the lids out of bats, but he explained they used them for distilling the gin.

"I have some with me. I want you both to taste it. It has notes of leather and toasted wood. You can't buy it outside Goa, which started me dreaming about making wine as a career. Well, with a twist. I'm not sure what the twist is yet."

I took a shine to this unusual person. He wasn't discussing a topic we could look up in a book, like the Greek influence on Italian viticulture. He was current and excited. Not that I didn't respect the culture of wine, but we didn't yet have the authority to talk about it like Howard did. That's what I found irritating. He hadn't done his time, and yet, on the first day of a degree we hadn't even started, he was acting like he knew it all.

I fell in love with Vin's mission to create wine in unorthodox ways. The conformists in the other group smirked at his stories, but Heidi and I thought him a disrupter.

They all talked in notes and flavours—even Heidi and Vin. They were already ten steps ahead of me, and imposter syndrome lingered over me for months.

I had lost all hope of being popular with my fellow students because I wasn't cool, didn't dress well, knew little about wine, and, of course, my family didn't own a vineyard in Bordeaux. This changed when they learned I lived off-campus at Angus's house. They had a student sixth sense for free food and alcohol, and from then onwards, it appeared I had made some silent pact to host these new friends for any social gathering beyond the wine centre.

"Are you coming to the pub tonight, Elle?" asked Heidi several times over the first month at Pendleton.

"Not right now. I must catch up with you all and get used to learning again, or I'll get left behind. Don't stop asking me, though, will you? Promise I'll get my head around this soon."

In this first month, Angus would knock on my bedroom door and tell me he'd found me lying in bed, laptop open, with all the lights on. I woke up to find all my things put away like a child.

When Angus was away on a trip, I would forget to eat and did no housework, continually scrambling to clear everything up before he got home. I constantly texted him to ask when he'd be back, and he thought I couldn't live without him, but I was checking to see how much time I had to make his house presentable.

Despite the pure exhaustion, I had forgotten work could be fun, and I barely had time to consider my old life.

"You know, Vin, I keep imagining the bottles and bottles of wine I've bought over the years and served to all those passengers. I didn't even know how many grape varieties there were. I sometimes question whether I can do this and be good at it."

We were in the library late afternoon, and I had hit a wall. I would have spurts of 'I can do this' and bouts of 'Why do I think I can do this?'

"Elle, you're so hard on yourself. You don't need to come out of this with a hundred per cent in your exams; you need to get a job, and people like you always get jobs."

For a minute, I thought he meant because I was a generic white person.

"You're a lovely person. I could tell that from the moment I met you. It shines out from your smile. That other group sees it, too. That's why they don't give you the time of day. They know you will conquer the wine industry and leave us all for dust."

"Oh, Vin. I'm so glad I nearly killed you with my car that day. But you're the one to watch. You are like my friend Lucy. You think about the world differently than the rest of us."

When I calmed down and stopped studying as much, Angus and I frequented the local pub whenever he was home from a trip. We would catch up before a log fire in the winter or the beer garden on a sunny day, and I'd tell him about my course. I knew I was driving him to distraction. Still, if I was, he was making a real go out of pretending to be super interested. I felt like a two-year-old telling my dad about my exciting day at school.

"Angus, did you know grapes don't ripen once you pick them? You have to pick them at exactly the right time for the variety of wine you're making."

"So, what grapes do you use for sparkling wine?"

"If the grapes are slightly less ripe, the wine is way more acidic. So, these are used in sparkling or white. Some grapes are picked late; they're sweeter for dessert wine. Today, I found out how much the weather impacts vintages. The vintage might be much different if the weather is off one year, and the grapes don't ripen properly. And do you know they don't wash them? It ruins the concentration of the wine."

"Really? What about chemicals?"

"I know. It makes you think, doesn't it?"

"You seem to love this, Elle. I've never seen you interested in a subject. I think you were just going through the motions before you started this. What do you think you'll do when you finish?"

I reached over and dunked a beefy chip in his aioli. It was hot and burned my mouth.

"Fuck! Hmm, I don't know yet. Is it bad that I haven't even thought about it? I have to do a placement first, and I haven't even thought about that either."

I knew I wanted to be an expert. There were so many variations in every step of wine production, and I had to see as many of them as I could, which meant much travelling. I'd given no thought to this part of it all. Learning all this and not applying it to different terroirs would make no sense. I knew I had to expose myself to other countries and various wines to become the winemaker I wanted to be.

Bacchus

*H*alfway through the first two years of my degree, being a relatively poor student had become second nature. The Tesla was long gone, and my VW had a dent in one door and hair embedded in the carpets from the previous owner's wire-haired dog. I'd rented my apartment out to a nurse Holly knew from her pottery class.

Even though I detested him with a passion I'd usually direct at corrupt politicians, I often daydreamed about what Zero would think of the new me.

It surprised Angus and Lucy when I embraced the cheaper lifestyle: shopping at Aldi, borrowing library books, not buying new clothes. Lucy kept gifting me hers; some still had the price tags on. I suspected she was even buying me clothes, as some were in my size, not hers. Lucy had always been naturally thin, and I was curvier.

We were having a lazy Saturday watching *New Girl* from the beginning for probably the seventh time since we'd been friends.

"Luce, I'm getting the hint you're ashamed to be seen with me in the same Levi's and faded Zara sweatshirt!" I said as I got up to microwave the popcorn.

"I know you're doing this outdoorsy thing, Elle, but you don't have to dress like you work on a farm. Develop a style for when you're working at Moët!"

"Love that you think I could land a job at Moët. You're the friend every girl needs. I wouldn't stand a chance. Some of these people have got way more experience than me. I need to adjust my expectations."

"Rubbish. That's the exact opposite of what you should be doing. Forget about everyone else. Walk your own path. It's not all about experience. Angus said you are doing well at uni, anyway."

"It's going OK now. It took a while for me to get back in the groove of learning."

Lucy hugged me.

"Aw, I'm so proud of you, Elle."

"You're proud of me? I'm proud of you, Zuckerberg! Anyway, enough of this sentimental stuff. You said you'd show me pics of your new house."

Lucy looked through her phone, scrolled fast, and blushed when I glimpsed a guy in one photo.

"Who was that?"

"Oh, just an investor."

"You take pics of all your investors with no shirt on, looking buff? Oh my god, is this your house? Holy shit, it's massive. When can I move to California and squat in your pool house?"

"It's a huge reno. I think knocking the old one down would have been easier."

"Wow. And what are Gerald and Val up to? Have they got a place there, too, now?"

"I prefer being closer to LA, um, it's a pivotal time for the company, but they're looking for somewhere in the Bay Area."

She fiddled with her ring and her necklace.

Lucy had hit the big time with her app and website, Ignite. She was one of those rare, brilliant people who could see things others couldn't, a Mary Perkins or Whitney Wolfe. She was now in the upper echelons of the über-wealthy and was a billionaire. It was unfathomable to Angus and me after originally ridiculing her idea.

Here I was, hanging out with her on a Saturday, with microwave popcorn in Angus's tiny house, watching re-runs as if she worked down the road at the local chip shop. It spoke volumes of who she was; I knew she would never change. The only giveaways to her changed status were the orange Birkin slung on the chair by the kitchen table or the Cartier watch that poked out from the sleeve of her light grey cashmere sweater.

Her Chinese heritage had given her strength of character, but with a Chinese mother and white father, it had been hard for her to know where she fit in. Now, there was no need for her to fit in anywhere.

She split her time between London, where she had a beautiful Chelsea apartment, and California. Nowadays, she even had her own Wikipedia entry:

> *Lucy Ng (born July 5, 1995) is a UK entrepreneur. She is the founder and CEO of publicly traded Ignite, Inc., an alternative online dating platform launched in 2020.*
>
> *Ng was named as one of 2020's and 2021's* Forbes *30 Under 30; in 2022, she was named in the* Time *100 List. In February 2022, Ng became the world's youngest female self-made billionaire, when she took Ignite public. She is the youngest woman to have taken a company public in the United States, at age 30.*

The number of times I'd googled Lucy was excessive. I guessed at work she was a badass boss, but with us, nothing changed except that we benefited from the rewards of her success. She took us to glamorous parties and spoiled us. Many evenings, we hung out on the rooftop of her Chelsea apartment, making a dent in her exquisite wine cellar with its glass doors and subtle lighting. I often thought about letting myself into her house on a rare hot summer's day when she was away and curling up inside it with a good book.

I had helped her acquire some fabulous collectable wines. Through this, my knowledge became more comprehensive because, unlike most of my fellow students, I had the luxury of tasting a host of expensive wines.

Once Lucy bought the most expensive wine in the world, one of the three hundred bottles of a 2011 AurumRed Gold tempranillo. After all, twenty-five thousand euros for a bottle was nothing to her.

Vin was envious because the winemaker Hilario García had implemented ozone therapy in cultivating his vines—his secret to producing this incredible wine. I had never seen him jealous or angry, but he barely spoke to me for a week after I told him I'd tasted it. I hadn't even thought about him when we'd opened the bottle, and I was eternally cross with myself for my blithe disregard of his feelings by drinking it without him.

"Luce—Did you remember Vin and Heidi are coming for dinner? They wanted to meet you, and you've been away so much. You don't mind, do you?"

"Of course, I remembered!"

I don't know why I asked. Lucy wasn't in the habit of forgetting anything. She was insane with the calendar on her phone and managed it with military precision. If I looked at her phone, there would be an entry that said Vin and Heidi, and if I clicked on the notes section, she would have written *War and Peace* on everything I'd ever told her about them.

Lodging with Angus was like living every day in an episode of *New Girl*. We were close. Partly because he helped me through the worst times and mainly because we shared a bathroom. There was not much in the way of secrets anymore. He had seen it all: the blunt razor blades, the cup I used for my periods, the corn cutter I used on the dead skin of my feet.

Having dinner without him in his house seemed wrong, but he was away often, and I had to find a window when Lucy was in the country.

The doorbell dinged at exactly seven p.m. I smiled to myself because Vin was always punctual. Lucy jumped up to answer the door. I stood behind her and watched the easy way she hugged Vin and Heidi and talked to them as though they had known each other for years.

I'd called Holly for her lasagne recipe and produced the steaming dish, wincing from the poker heat even through the oven gloves. Lucy put the salad she had made on the table and then disappeared out into the hallway.

"Elle, this smells amazing," said Heidi.

My tastebuds salivated over the aroma of garlic, oregano, and basil, and I was desperate to sit down and eat it. I spun around and grabbed the garlic bread, catching it before it burnt.

"Garlic bread, too?" said Vin. "I brought you some pinot noir."

He stood to grab his Waitrose bag just as Lucy walked back in.

"You can put that away, Vin," she said. "I've got the wine covered."

On the table, she placed a lacquered black box and said nothing.

"Is that?—" I said.

"You can do the honours, Vin," she said.

"No, it can't be! But Lucy, we can't drink this; you must save it," he said.

Vin sat back down and stared at the box.

"Go on—open it up. It's a thank you for looking after my friend here. You and Heidi have been so supportive, and I can't be here much. To be honest, I probably owe you ten of these."

"But it's so expensive, Lucy. I know how much that cost. I don't even know how you got it."

"Never you mind. What does it mean if I don't share it? Come on, open it up, Vin."

He stood and opened the wooden box as if it held the holy grail, which it did. I half expected a brilliant ray to escape when he opened the lid. Inside the box was a bright red felt cushioning the dark bottle; we all got up and crowded around Vin as he eased the bottle out of the box. He ran his fingers over the embossed section at the bottle-neck and Hilario García's golden signature. Lucy handed him my stolen corkscrew. I noticed the logo of Asana Air was now worn off. He looked at us all as if he was a tribute in the *Hunger Games*, about to test his footing for a landmine.

"May the odds be ever in your favour," I said.

He eased out the cork, and I picked it up and sniffed at it.

"You can leave this open for two years, and it will still be drinkable," he said.

"Come on, Vin," I said. "I want to eat that lasagne. Oh my god, I just realised you have the most appropriate first name for what we do."

He laughed and poured us all a glass. I listened to it pouring into each glass like molten gold.

"You are just realising that now?"

It sat, inviting us to try it.

"If you drink from either side of the glass, it's supposed to taste different," Heidi said. "It brings out new flavours, aromas and texture."

The table fell silent under the spell of the wine's remarkable palate. I detected the blackcurrant first, then slowly, notes crept up on me like caramel, toast, and coffee, all supported by an oaky under-tone.

"It does taste different on each side of the glass, doesn't it?" I said. "Lucky I cooked the lasagne to a nuclear level. It's probably just right by now."

"We need to add this bottle to your notebook," Vin said.

Angus and I had been compiling a notebook called 'The Good Stuff' with each wine we had tried, as he never returned from a trip without a new one.

"He'll be back in a few hours. Let's save him a glass," I said.

I served some tiramisu for dessert, and we sat around laughing and joking until we heard the key turn in the lock.

"Angus, you're early!"

I rushed up, grabbed his bag, ushered him into the kitchen, and practically pushed him into my seat. We only had four chairs. I placed the warm lasagne in front of him, heaped some salad on the side, and Vin poured out the last small glass of wine as if it were the last water on Earth.

He took a sip.

"Why the hell are you all staring at me? And I'm not early, I'm late. Do you listen to anything I tell you, Elle?"

"Bad day?" asked Lucy.

"Yeah, let's not go there. I'll tell you later."

He took a sip of wine, and we all waited, barely breathing until he declared his verdict.

"Hmm. Like that. Made of squash rackets or something, is it Vin?"

"Sacrilege!" said Heidi. "Lucy bought it. It's the AurumRed, squillion pounds a bottle stuff."

Angus's eyes grew wide, and he spat out the wine in shock as he was mid-sip.

"Well, I can't waste this," he said, licking it off the table.

We had already drunk two more bottles of pinot noir when Angus got home, so we were all quite drunk. Vin rolled around on the floor, and Heidi and Lucy put their hands in front of their eyes.

"Angus, do you have any more of those tiny bottles of Grey Goose?" asked Vinjay.

"Jesus, Vin. I'm going to end up sacked if I keep supporting your alcoholism! Look in the suitcase."

Angus took centre stage many nights, enthralling them with tales of his last trip at the local pub. There was always a Philip involved and sometimes a plastic poo but never a bottle of 'Blink and you'll miss it' eye drops.

Vin and Heidi always treated us like grown-ups. When our younger friends drifted home, we often joked about it. That anyone could think we were mature was beyond hysterical. Lucy was the adult in our trio, and Angus and I agreed every trio needed one. If we were the friends from *Harry Potter*, she'd be Hermione.

Vin and Heidi stumbled to their Uber. Lucy was the last to leave.

"Right, you two try to stay out of trouble. I'll be back," Lucy said in her best Terminator voice.

We waved her off, watching her tail-lights disappear.

"Does this make you teary, or is it just me? I'm not sure if it's the wine, but every time she goes off, it breaks my heart a little," I said.

"Same. The flight home was so shite. There were these two newbies, and one was called Lucy, and this sadness came over me. Because I realised, you two don't work there anymore. Not sure I can do it much longer, either."

Angus pulled me in for a hug, and I rested my head on his shoulder.

"You know, Angus, we make the perfect couple."

"Damn that X chromosome getting in the way," he said.

Passerina

My mobile rang as I washed up after another messy student house party. I was nursing the mother of all hangovers. The previous evening, we had finally sampled two bottles of the Cricket Bat Gin. My head still pounded after scouring my room and Angus's for paracetamol. All I had found was one lonely Advil, and it hadn't touched the pain.

It was Holly. I pressed a bubble-covered wet hand onto the loudspeaker button.

"Elle? Dad's in hospital."

I dropped a plate, which smashed into the sink, cutting my finger. It stung in the soapy water, and I kept my hand there, willing the pain to wash over me and balance out the pain in my heart. The tight choke of anxiety crept from my chest to my throat. This was the first time it had returned since the drama with Zero. Grabbing my jacket and keys, I hopped into my car, praying it wouldn't let me down.

I made the drive to the hospital in a red haze. I'd have been none the wiser if I had run a thousand red lights or taken out a lollipop lady. The shitty icing on the cake was not being able to find a parking spot and swearing at people who got to one first. I drove around with tears streaming down my face and thought for a second about turning around and going home, and then I could pretend this wasn't happening at all.

As soon as I saw Holly's face, I knew it was desperate. Dad had had a stroke. I spoke to an obtuse, balding man with little doctor syndrome. He blurted facts and figures at me with no compassion. 'How do you sleep at night?' I considered saying as I looked into his dead eyes.

"He's my dad. Can't you tell me what's wrong in plain English? Is he going to be OK or not?"

The doctor looked down at his scuffed shoes like I was wasting his time. He caught my gaze and shuffled his feet. Then he drummed his fingers on his cheap plastic clipboard. I was about to give him the motherlode of abuse when Holly walked over, mouthed a sorry over my shoulder, and steered me away.

"Come on, you," Holly said. "He's a twat, though, I agree. The nurses fucking hate him. They told me everyone hates him, even his kids. They all joke he stole his doctor's coat from their dress-up box!"

Holly wrapped me in a big bear hug and stroked my hair; I could smell her Chanel No. 5. I pulled away, caught between the warm cocoon of my sister's love and the yearning for my mum. Lost for words, panic set in.

A familiar depressive cloud landed on my head, and I struggled for air in the sterile hospital corridor; I pushed through the swing doors into the foyer and raced outside.

I held my chest as I breathed in and sobbed, and that's when I saw Zero slouching in through the foyer with an expensive-looking bunch of flowers with no lilies in sight, and I did a double take.

"Oh, Elle. Um—hi, how are you?"

He looked at me, and I looked at the flowers.

"How did you find out?"

"Umm, they called me," he said.

"Well, it's sweet of you to come. I don't know what I'm going to do," I said, burying my face in Zero's chest.

He pulled away.

"He might die. What will I do? I want someone to tell me what to do."

"Oh god, Elle, your dad? Look, here's the thing, Alex, um, she had a baby. Sorry."

Zero stared at me in horror, but I detected a slight hint of a sarcastic smile touching his lips and a glint of ridicule in his eyes. Then he was gone with a patronising squeeze of my hand. His hand was damp and cold, and I wiped mine on my jeans as he walked away.

Freshly humiliated. Even after this long, it still stung. I wanted to curl up and die. I watched Zero walk away in the clothes I had never seen before, probably from his latest seasonal wardrobe purchase. He didn't exude excitement. There were no new-father vibes when I'd seen him walk in. His step had no bounce, and he was ambling as if putting off a painful business meeting. Not how I would want the father of my child to react when I'd been in labour for god knows how long. All this confirmed what I already knew: I'd had a fortunate escape.

Despite knowing this, it bothered me that I was getting left behind in life stages. Alex and Zero had their first child, and I was still in the middle of a degree. My bank account was empty, and I was working a part-time job in a local farm shop. It was hard not to question my choices. Rumour had it they had bought a lovely house in Richmond. And now my dad. Who knew, he might wake up and be right as rain? He had to be.

"Fuck this life."

"Talking to yourself again?"

Angus and Lucy walked up to me with outstretched arms.

"Why is Zero the dickhead here?" said Lucy.

"Oh yeah, I made a real dick of myself. I thought he was here because of Dad, but he just became one."

"Oh god, Frankenstein's baby. Can you imagine what a terrible mother she'll be? The poor child will never do a thing right. It'll feel like it's in the army," said Angus.

"If it's a girl, she's kind of screwed on the genetics front. Alex seems well put together, but if you look closer, it's a high-maintenance job on the wrinkles and grey hairs."

Lucy was always up to date on the latest trends and treatments, but I was never sure why. Her skin was youthful and blemish-free; she would never need them herself.

"Yeah, she has a forehead like a Shar-Pei between doses!" said Angus.

"Oh, stop it. It's a small baby!" I said. "He didn't look ecstatic about the whole thing. He's such an arsehole. Why is it still hard for me to see him? I know he's a dick, but it all comes flooding back when I see him."

"Here," said Angus, handing me a miniature Grey Goose from his pocket. "Take a swig of this, to calm your nerves."

"Are you still stealing minis, Angus?" said Lucy.

"Yeah, we need them for all of Elle's student friends, especially Vin."

They held me tightly on the way to Dad's room, and Holly sat beside him, sobbing. His paper-thin skin was grey, like he'd gone somewhere else even before his heart stopped beating. The tubes and machines made little sense to me. If he was going to die, I didn't want it to be this way. I didn't want him to pass on in this sad room with its sterility and mock, rubber-duck-yellow painted walls, the view of the trees below rubbing salt into open wounds.

I put my arms around Holly; then Dad spoke and broke the silence with such clarity it stunned us all.

"Holly, your mum's here. She said to tell you she saw you in the vineyard, and you looked happy—Nick's one of the good ones. Forgive him. Elle, I know you love Pear Drops. Look out for them; it's a sign," he said.

The patient monitor beeped in a long, silent tone. We looked at each other, unsure what to do or say. The words hung in the room. I wanted to scoop them up, capture them forever, and replay them when I needed Dad again. Still, they were gone out into the ether with Dad—all his last thoughts mingling into one weird commentary that reminded me of a computer malfunction. We sat stunned, not wanting to make the last steps to say goodbye and not knowing how to leave without him.

I walked out to the foyer with Angus and Lucy and said goodbye, promising to see them later.

"I'm going to buy us fish and chips, so don't eat here," Angus said. "It will be nasty stale shite anyway, like plane food."

I wasn't the least bit hungry, just nauseous, but I nodded in agreement.

I was just about to walk through the hospital's automatic doors and saw Walter in my peripheral vision.

"Aunty Elle!"

Nick loosened his hand, and Walter ran to me. I breathed in his cuddles like they were hard drugs for my broken soul and looked up at Nick. He was gaunt, and his clothes looked creased and seemed to hang from his body.

"Long time no see, stranger. Where have you been? I know you did the dirty on Holly, but you didn't have to ditch our whole family."

"Elle, it was a mistake. I kissed someone from work once, and it's been the worst mistake of my life. Holly can't forgive me."

"You kissed someone once? She said you'd had an affair. Oh, for god's sake, I understand why she never wants to discuss it now. Come on; we're going inside. Well, come on then!"

M. J. PARFITT

We walked into the room, and Holly fell to pieces as soon as she saw Nick. It's funny how the love of your life lets you be fragile. Alone, you must be stoic, but when you have crutches, you can let go.

I took Walter to the vending machine for a Kit Kat, and we sat on the uncomfortable burgundy plastic seats in the corridor. He told me about his trip to the park with his dad. He asked why his grandad had died, and I had no answer for him. I stuttered and eventually gave up the futile attempt to explain something I didn't understand.

"Will he have any friends to play with in heaven?"

"Gosh, I hope so, and he'll have Grandma. Do you remember her?"

He nodded and then moved on to questions like who put the chocolate in the machine. Then he circled back to the tricky questions. He wanted to know why Mummy was crying, which made me cry, too.

Nick left the room and gestured to Walter to put his little arms in the small puffer jacket he was holding.

"Everything OK?"

"I hope it will be. I miss you, sis," he said.

We kissed Dad on his forehead, and I held my hand on the side of his face, trying to find him in that body somewhere. I closed my eyes and thought he'd take an unexpected breath and sit up. My hand grew colder, and I pulled it away. We collected his things and walked down to the coffee shop. I floated out of the room, not consciously deciding to leave, but Holly's hand on my shoulder guiding me away.

Having no parent alive was unimaginable. I hadn't ever considered it a possibility. An icy shiver ran up my spine and lodged itself in my jaw. I didn't want to acquaint myself with this void. We were helpless, like leaves falling from an autumn tree, leaving the branch they'd never know again. We wouldn't forget Dad, but we knew our memories might become distorted, fade, and diminish like they had with Mum.

"What Dad said, Holly. It was strange about Nick and the vineyard slash Pear Drops thing. I know you struggle with him kissing someone else, but divorce isn't the answer when you have a great kid like Walter. It was just a kiss, and he regrets it like hell. I'm sorry, I think you are making a big mistake, that's all. Try to work it out, like Dad said. You made me think he'd slept with someone else, for god's sake."

Holly nodded. She stirred some sugar into her coffee despite never taking it with sugar.

"I'm not sure it was about the kiss. You know, I never got over losing Mum. I never thought she'd not be there, you know? And then it happened so soon after, and somehow it all got jumbled into one thing, or I projected my sadness into it. I guess I'd been too angry for a long time, and then I didn't know how to get our marriage back after everything I'd said. In my mind, forgiving him made me a pathetic loser. I'd already flushed my career down the toilet for him. It was a way of hanging onto the last threads of my dignity."

"So, what now? Why don't you think about moving into Dad's? It might be good for you as a family, and there's all that space. You could do a reno or something."

"But what about you? It's half yours."

"Well, I'll be OK. I don't even have a job. We'll cross that bridge when we get to it, OK?"

A shadow loomed over our table, and Zero looked down at us.

"I'm sorry."

"Oh, fuck off, Zero," we both said.

He gave us an empty glare and walked away, red-faced.

"What an absolute prick," said Holly. "You know I never liked him. Such an arrogant twat. What the hell did you ever see in him?"

We held each other outside the hospital. The car park was empty, and rain pooled in pockets on the road, sparkling under the street-lights. The air smelled earthy, and I had never felt so cold.

"You know, Holly, that feels like a hug from Mum."

We held each other's hands until we let go at our fingertips and took our separate ways into the car park. I watched her walk to her car. She was different somehow.

When I arrived home, I found Angus and Lucy sat in the tiny back garden with a full-sized bottle of vodka in front of the fire pit, passing it between them. They'd added some new logs to the fire, which were smoking out the entire street. As soon as I opened the car door, smoke filled my nostrils; I could hear the neighbours slamming their windows.

"Wow, a grown-up size bottle of Grey Goose. I haven't seen one of those forever. The neighbours seem pissed. They haven't got over the gnome on the dachshund yet."

Lucy stood up and dragged me over to a chair by the fire. She smelt like smoke; I didn't want to wash my hair. Angus wrapped me in a granny blanket and forced the bottle into my hand. I took a huge swig, burning my throat on the way down.

"To your dad!"

The fire sizzled like a gust of wind had given it more fuel, sending shivers down our spines.

"Hey, I know this might not be the first thing you're thinking of right now, Elle, but I might have a vintage placement for your final year. Remember Jude, who we met in New York on our fateful trip? We kept in touch, and he's got an incredible vineyard in Sonoma. He said you could do it there. He's a good friend of mine these days," said Lucy.

"Wow! Really? Are you serious?"

"I'll text you his details, and you can email him and sort it all out from there."

"So, kept in touch, huh? Anything we should know?" asked Angus.

"No! He has a friend I'm interested in, but it's complicated. I don't know, relationships are hard."

"That's all we're getting?" I asked. "You meet a mysterious guy, and that's it?"

"Elle, it's not that simple. There's a lot to it, and I can't tell you anything."

"Is this guy a spy?" asked Angus.

"Does he have a beard?" I said.

"Does he wear glasses?" said Angus.

"I know exactly what you two are doing. It's not 'Guess Who'!"

Silently, I said goodbye to dear old Dad. If these two were by my side in the trenches, making me smile even today on the worst day, I would survive.

Semillon

The business class seat beckoned, pristine, waiting for me to destroy it with crumbs and rogue peanuts.

Angus, Lucy, and I had a Californian road trip planned up the Pacific Coast Highway. Our last stop was to be Jude's vineyard in Sonoma, ready for me to start my internship.

I opened the calendar app on my phone and looked at the following day's agenda: My birthday, Van Morrison, at The Greek. Then I opened my notes and found my list entitled 'Itch List'—aptly titled for the things I wanted to scratch off in life—and ticked off Greek Theatre and Pacific Coast Highway.

Clinking Champagne flutes and the welcoming smiles of the United Crew made me sink back farther into the leather seat.

Flying in luxury made me think about the many flights I'd taken in economy over the years. Trapped in a confined space with the other passengers in rigid seats with rough, unwelcoming fabric covers. The passengers always had some quirk or another which irritated the hell out of me, like once on a trip to Rome where the old lady next to me coughed the whole way—I spent most of the flight with my face wrapped in a silk scarf—or a large man on the way to Dubai who could barely fit into his seat and had no choice but to let his arms infringe on my seat. I didn't blame him, but I still had the most uncomfortable flight I could recall. But the worst neighbours were always those who stank. I couldn't stand it and would furtively spray perfume around me, pretending to retrieve something from my bag.

The seats in economy always reminded me of the bus trips Holly and I had been on with our grandparents. Over the years, they took us to various tourist spots in London, such as Madame Tussaud's or places like Stratford-upon-Avon, to see Shakespeare's old school. They had done so much for us when we were kids. It saddened me they never got to fly anywhere. Even after all these years, I thought of them often.

My grandma had made flasks of hot coffee, which were still burning hot after a whole day out. Her corned beef and pickle sandwiches on the way home were a thing of legend. When the lights came on inside the bus as the night drew in, we would have a picnic. I couldn't fathom how she had made food taste so incredible. It was like she was some food magician, and in my whole life, eating all over the world, I'd swap it all for one more curry or spaghetti Bolognese made by this mystical chef. If someone asked me who I'd invite to dinner, alive or dead, she'd be first on the list on the condition she cooked the meal.

Grandma was the most hysterical woman I had ever met. When she and my grandpa had wanted to get married, she'd jumped out of a window, and they had run off together. I recounted this story to Lucy and Angus, who sat enthralled by the real-life love story.

"Oh, I'd have liked your grandma," said Angus.

"I think that's why we're friends. You're like her, and she'd have adored you both."

"Except she had way more luck in the love department than me. Lucy, Elle promised I'd get blown by her old neighbour, then dared to move!"

I swiped him with my Decanter magazine and flicked through the channels on the screen to plan my viewing schedule for the flight.

"I could get used to this, Lucy," I said as I stretched out. "One day, when I'm a famous winemaker, I can pay for our tickets! Thanks for this trip and everything you do for us daily."

"Oh, stop! Seriously stop. I was lucky, and I'm sharing it with you two. If I didn't, where'd be the fun in that?"

I could sense the plane gradually speeding up before we took off, and the odour from the metal food carts heating told me we were on our way. I was heading towards the bottom rung on the ladder of my new career as a winemaker.

⸙

I woke up, peeped out from under my eye mask, and lifted the window shade. The slightest tangerine glow was building under the clouds. This view always made me smile, no matter how many flights I took. The promise of a new day and all the possibilities that might unfold captivated me. I carefully closed the blind again and turned to Angus and Lucy.

"I'm nervous about this internship."

"Oh, don't worry, it's a week away," said Angus. "We have a holiday to enjoy first."

I ordered a Napa cab sav, held up the glass, studied the deep violet contents, and then took a sip. I would have knocked it back two years ago without a second thought. Today, from this one dainty sip, I detected a smoky tobacco, spicy yet herby aromatic. It bombarded my palate with berries, dark plums, and a hint of vanilla and spice.

"Come on then, aficionado. What's the verdict?" asked Angus.

"Hmm, what we have here is a concentrated wine. It's fresh and young but balanced with the seamless finesse of a supple tannin structure. It's got great potential to be an exceptional wine, which will evolve over the next decade."

"Holy shit, did you read that on the label? I mean, can you tell all this from one sip?"

"Oh gosh, sorry. I didn't mean to sound like a wine snob. I've gotten used to thinking like this about wine. It's like second nature now."

"Well, let's not dwell on the internship, Jancis. I think you'll be OK," said Lucy, looking up from her laptop.

"Who's Jancis?" asked Angus.

"Jancis Robinson, she's a wine expert on TV. Lucy is a smart arse," I said.

I waved my arm towards Lucy, spilling the wine over the tray table.

"Oh, and there we have it, back in the gutter," said Angus, taking a snap on his phone as the wine pooled into a deep purple stain.

"So, Angus, did you bring your new camera?"

Whenever I did stupid things, Angus recorded me non-stop on his phone.

"Stop biting your nails, and yes, I brought it. I'm excited about using it on the trip. Can we stop at the *Big Little Lies* bridge? It looks so cool on my Mac screensaver."

Collapsing in hysterics, I avoided eye contact with a passenger across the aisle who gave me a reproachful glare.

"You can laugh, Elle, but the background in the screensaver is the exact road we'll be driving on."

"The correct name, Angus, is the Bixby Bridge. I read locals are sick of people going to take pictures of it since the TV show. But we can stop wherever you want, so long as I'm in Sonoma by next Friday."

Lucy was still busy tapping the keys on her laptop. She barely looked up from it lately. She'd been trying to persuade me to join Ignite, but I was still off the idea of a man after the embarrassing gaffe with Zero. I turned a deep crimson, thinking about the hospital misunderstanding. He had a family now, and it was all water under the Bixby Bridge for him, but it was still quite raw for me. I hadn't had a relationship since. I'd had a couple of one-night stands with younger guys at uni. They were like puppy dogs eager to please, and I always regretted it the following day, wanting to sneak out and pretend it hadn't happened at all.

We hopped on a shuttle to the Hertz office, and all agreed on Lucy driving, as she had been living here on and off for the last couple of years. We were finally on the freeway after a few errant laps of the concourse in front of LAX. Twice, I told Lucy she was going the wrong way, but it was always too late to change lanes.

The Greek Theatre was buzzing. We'd taken a Lyft from the ivy-covered Airbnb, and the bass and crowd cacophony was audible before we opened the car door. We walked through the ever-increasing crowd to the ticket booths, and a stench of rotten food emanated from somewhere.

"I'm glad we ate already," said Lucy. "That does not look good."

She peered into someone's polystyrene takeaway box. A brown blob of something trying to pass for guacamole made me gag as I saw it pass by. Angus retched.

"How hard can it be?" asked Lucy. "I mean, it's avo, lime and pepper. How does that brown shit happen?"

We'd already made an obligatory trip to Whole Foods for some fresh salads before checking into the Airbnb, which was lucky because none of us were eating what was on offer here.

Grabbing two beers each, Lucy searched the rows for numbers and found our seats. We had an eagle-eye view of the whole theatre. The Greek was a moderately sized amphitheatre with red plastic seating, perfectly nestled in a rocky backdrop. It looked like an album cover, and I got goosebumps at being somewhere so iconic.

Watching the venue as it filled mesmerised me. Angus was in his element, people-watching, and all three of us picked out the groupies.

"They're dressed like prostitutes. And look at that one with the bob. She has a backstage pass," said Angus.

I looked down at her. She was so thin her skin had a blue tinge to it, as though all her veins were just underneath the first layer. She was wearing a faded denim mini-skirt and a crochet top with no bra that would have looked great at Coachella, but here it seemed like she was trying too hard; there was a look about her like she smoked crack and was allergic to water and soap. I was still jealous of how thin she was.

"How do you know, Angus?"

"I heard her bragging about it to her friends."

"I bet the acoustics will be amazing!" said Lucy. "You know, from her pole position."

"Lucy!" I said.

"Jeez, they rock up late here, don't they?" said Angus.

Some groups turned up when Taj Mahal was finishing his set.

Soon, we were singing our hearts out to 'Bright Side of the Road,' and my Itch list was a little shorter. I looked sideways at my friends; it was one of the happiest moments of my life. As soon as he played 'Brown-Eyed Girl' in the encore, I couldn't stop the tears from trickling down my cheek. I attributed it to many things: being lucky enough to see the world, having the most brilliant friends, grabbing a new life, and finally doing something I loved. I was kind of free, and it was priceless.

Towards the end of the concert, we saw the groupie leave her friends and make her way down to the side of the stage. Angus laughed, and her friends turned to look at us.

"Hmm, we better get out of here," said Lucy. "We don't need to get into a fight at the start of this trip, do we?"

"Hey, that's our Uber!" shouted Lucy at a laughing group who poked out their tongues as they climbed into our car.

"What the fuck!" Lucy said.

"Lucy. Hey, Lucy," someone shouted.

We spun around, and Lucy's face flushed.

A group of good-looking people hugged Lucy, and she introduced us. The cloud of expensive fragrances surrounding them starkly contrasted with the foul-smelling junk food nearby. They looked familiar, and I was sure I'd seen one of them on *SNL*. I heard someone ask Lucy how Mark was, and Lucy was evasive.

"Hey, I've got a great idea," said a tall, loud guy wearing sunglasses despite the late hour. "Come with us. We're going to a party in the hills."

We followed their car through the winding roads, the headlights illuminating the dry, scorched grass and steep rocks. I could see the LA skyline in the side mirrors from the backseat, and I was in a scene from *La La Land*. I expected Ryan Gosling to step out on the road and break into song.

"Hey, Lucy, who is this guy you are seeing? Someone called Mark. You're being so weird about it," said Angus.

"Yeah! I agree," I said.

It appeared Lucy was about to elaborate, but we pulled up to some substantial wooden gates that opened slowly and followed the car in front up the driveway, and she trailed off.

We finally arrived at a house I'm sure I'd seen featured on *Selling Sunset*. The walls were mostly glass. An impressive Art Deco chandelier hung in the foyer. Everything inside was custom-made. Huge luxurious rugs, enormous bowls of moss, and elaborate flower arrangements dispersed a divine, exotic fragrance in each room.

"Grey would love this place," I said to Angus. I made a mental note to text him because I hadn't been in touch for a few months.

M. J. PARFITT

Lucy's friend Wilder told us it was a film producer's house. Angus and I were silent. The large main room swarmed with wall-to-wall celebrities and servers offering chilled Champagne and fresh sashimi, which melted in my mouth. I'd never tasted fish as fresh, even in Japan.

We had to leave our mobiles at the door on the way in. Angus was stunned into silence again. I had rarely witnessed this in our long friendship.

And then, one minute, he was standing behind me, and the next, he'd disappeared. They both left me alone as a real estate agent ambushed Lucy, trying to persuade her to buy in The Hills.

The buzz of conversation and the glow of the azure blue pool drew outside me. It was a stunning and expansive infinity pool, and the backdrop of the LA skyline took my breath away. I stood looking at it for the longest time, trying to build up the courage to chat with random strangers until I found a bar serving martinis. I downed several French Raspberry and Lemon Drop flavours.

"Which do you recommend? I see you've worked your way through most of them!" said a guy about my age, wearing skinny jeans and a baggy-fitting shirt with a black waistcoat thrown over the top. He'd forgotten to do up most of the shirt buttons, and I could see his collection of boho chains dangling underneath. I turned to see if he was talking to someone behind me, and I didn't have the words to say no after seven martinis when he asked me to take a dip in the pool. We stripped to our underwear and hopped in after carefully placing our drinks beside the pool. He explained he was an out-of-work actor from Arizona.

"Interesting undies, Elle! So why are you here alone?"

Shrugging and too drunk to care if my undies weren't sexy

enough, I laughed. By that stage, we were in the water. I'd just picked up every pair out of the drawer when I packed.

"Maybe it's the undies! I'm not here alone. My friends ditched me, but they're around here somewhere."

"So, who are your friends?"

"Oh, I'm friends with Lucy; not sure if you know her. She's the mastermind behind Ignite, and Angus; he's a mastermind with a camera."

"You're friends with Lucy Ng? Oh wow, friends in high places. I'm actually on her app, look!" he said as he swam back to the side of the pool, hopped out and grabbed his phone. He sat on the side with his legs dangling and showed me his Ignite profile. Liam Golding. Then it hit home how big of a deal Lucy was. She'd opened the door to a world we would never have seen without her, and her name was now so ubiquitous that random strangers didn't need to hear her surname to know who she was.

"Hey, could you ask her to introduce me to Mark?"

Staring at him blankly because the question confused me, I stuttered. Lucy still hadn't given us any information about this mysterious Mark. Still, by then, we were getting dive-bombed by other revellers, and the moment passed.

Angus was walking around looking for Lucy and me; he wasn't expecting to find me in the pool, so I called out to him, but every time I cried, "Angus," Liam shouted "Polo."

Eventually, Angus saw me after I waved frantically at him, and Liam joined in, shouting, "Angus, Angus!"

"What are you doing? I leave you for five minutes!"

"You have been gone for so fucking long!" I said. "Look, I made some new friends. Everyone, this is Angus. Find my clothes, will you, Angus?"

"Where did you put them?"

He searched under the pool lounges, behind the tables and mammoth plant pots but couldn't find them anywhere.

It was like the million times I'd showered at the gym but forgotten my towel and had to dry on my sweaty gym top. Once, I had taken an olive-green blouse to change into after a workout but I owned two similar ones. One had shrunk in the wash, but I'd held onto it in case I ever lost a lot of weight. The arms were too tight and trying to get into it was like stuffing sausages. So, I went to lunch with Angus and Lucy, with two olive green sausages at my sides. Angus would never let me forget it. He always called it my dysentery top and mocked me, asking if I also kept some long jeans in case I suddenly developed a growth disorder.

Angus grabbed a pool towel, and I shivered. Liam jumped out, grabbed his clothes, and handed me the waistcoat.

"Here you go, Elle. Put this on."

Lucy walked towards us, and I thought she'd be mad at me for embarrassing her.

She had her arm linked with a short man.

And that was how I met 'Van the Man' in Liam Golding's waistcoat and a movie producer's pool towel.

Angus stood by, shaking his head.

"Excuse Elle. She doesn't normally dress like this!" said Lucy as I reached to shake his hand. The striped fluffy towel fell to the floor, leaving me in knickers and Liam's waistcoat, which might not have been so terrible. Still, I looked down as they all stared at my crotch, specifically at my knickers printed with slices of salami that read 'Pizza Slut' across the front with a familiar knock-off logo. A stocking filler from Zero. He was the gift that kept giving.

Paseante Noir

"OK. First stop, Santa Monica Pier!" said Angus.

We parked in the strange wooden-planked car park, which felt very wrong, and made our way onto the pier. It was much like a pier in San Francisco—pre-requisite candy floss, the big wheel, synonymous with Santa Monica, and a wonderful pale, deep sandy beach. Angus took a million snaps—on the big wheel, as we ate strawberry ice cream, and perused the little stores selling souvenirs from China on either side of the boardwalk. Eventually, we collapsed on the beach, jet-lagged and a little hungover but exuberant with holiday energy. I wanted a long hot shower and to change my clothes.

"This is going to be pretty full on, stopping everywhere like this," said Lucy. "But I don't want to miss bits. We may never do this again in our lives. We should make the most of it—of all of it."

Lying back on the soft sand, I closed my eyes and let my mind go blank.

After a while, brushing the sand off my jeans, I got up and suggested we head to Venice. Angus and Lucy stared at me in horror, and I looked back at them, squinting against the sun.

"What? We have to make a move if we want to do all this stuff."

"It's—um, your hair," said Angus.

I grabbed a section from the side in a pony, and my hand caught something sticky. There was gum stuck through one side of my hair.

"Oh, my god. What the fuck?"

I apologised to a passing couple with small children.

"What am I supposed to do about this? Stop filming me, Angus. I know I'm a disaster; you don't have to keep reminding me, OK?"

I tried to storm off, but my feet were moving at a reduced speed in the icing sugar sand, and I looked ridiculous. Back at the car, they hugged me.

"Look, it will be OK. We can go to a hairdresser in Venice," said Lucy. "I'm sure it's not that bad. They'll be able to sort it."

"You're not selling this to me, Luce. Have you seen how bad it is? It's even on my jacket," I pointed to a sticky patch on the shoulder of my favourite denim jacket. I found it in Camden Market on a shopping trip with Holly, and it was my reliable old friend.

We merged into the traffic; Lucy, still unused to driving on the wrong side of the road after being in the UK for a couple of weeks, swiped every traffic cone outside Santa Monica Pier—Angus and I sunk into our seats. We had rented a Range Rover, and driving around like a learner distorted the impression we wanted to give to the Santa Monica locals.

"Oh, oh!" said Lucy. "Should I stop and pick them up?"

"No! Keep going. You're holding up the traffic!" said Angus.

"Oh, I think we should have gone to Venice first. Looking at the map, it's below Santa Monica," I said.

We navigated along a narrow road, and Lucy had to turn left across traffic to get to the beach. We came up to a red light, and Angus shouted.

"Turn! Turn!"

"Wait, what? It's red."

"No here, trust me, it's turn on red if it's safe."

"Oh, this is crazy. Are you sure? Are you sure? I know more about driving here than you do, Angus, and I don't know this rule!"

She turned slowly, and people honked. Eventually, we parked up and looked around, underwhelmed by Venice. Driving on the wrong side of the road was stressful. Poor Lucy. I couldn't have done it. She was always so brave.

"Pongs a bit here," said Angus.

"Like an economy toilet!" we said at the same time.

"I thought Pink lived here. We must be in the wrong bit," said Angus. "Surely this isn't it?"

The small hairdresser was tucked away a few streets from the beach.

"Look at the sign!" said Angus.

Lucy and I looked up and read 'Locksmiths.'

"Oh, that's funny," said Lucy.

The salon was cosy and warm from the hairdryer heat. The blend of coffee and expensive hair products mingled through the air of the light-filled room.

Lucy and Angus sat twisting in the white plastic chairs, sipping on sodas as Demi, the Cali local, attempted to work some magic on the gum in my hair.

"I'm sorry! It won't come out."

Demi made a sad face.

"Let's chop into it and give you a blunt bob. You can pull it off!"

I had many flaws, but I loved my hair; it was always the one thing I could count on. I looked at my friends as they came up behind me.

"It will grow back," said Lucy.

"And we think it will look amazing on you," said Angus.

"Yeah, right," I said. "Never mind the fact I just paid a small fortune to get it highlighted before we left."

Bursting out of the salon, arms linked with my new, wavy bob bouncing along the street, we approached the car park.

"Not really like Brighton, is it?"

"Oh, I don't know. It can get pretty sketchy on a Saturday night," said Angus.

I dropped my sunglasses when a dodgy-looking man with a brown paper bag walked by too close. They fell under the car, and I rummaged under the wheel, not wanting to touch anything. The whole place was dripping in grime. A small grill we had parked in front of caught my eye—it had two tiny lights sparkling against the sunlight, and I peered closer, gagging at the stench, "Lucy, can you back the car up?"

Angus and Lucy stared at me, and I made my way to the grill and peered in. Rifling for a pen from my bag, I eased it off the wall. Looking inside again, I heard the faintest mew. Carefully scooping my hand into the blackness, I gently picked up a tiny grey kitten. It was a featherweight and covered in sticky cobwebs and dirt, and I tried to brush it off. It was all alone and shivering. Angus passed me a torch, but there were no signs of more kittens or a mother. I put my sleeve over my mouth.

"Oh, what! It's so tiny. Are you sure there's no more?" asked Angus as he snapped more photos.

We all checked, and when we were confident we were not stealing a kitten from its mother, I wrapped it up in a sweater, puzzled over what to do, and fell in love.

"We have to take it to a vet or something," said Lucy. "What else can we do?"

I cried. The tears poured out of me.

"Aw don't cry. It's OK. Well, look, let's stop at a pet store and grab some supplies because we don't want it peeing in the car, and then we can think about what to do."

Angus nodded over my head to Lucy.

It mewed its tiny mews until it finally fell asleep in the crook of my arm.

We continued up the Pacific Coast Highway and pulled into Malibu Seafoods. Angus rolled his eyes at us, and I stumbled over what to order as the lady shot me death stares. I whispered to Angus to order the steamed shrimp salad and said I was going outside before the kitten cried.

I pinched my thigh under the table to test that this wasn't some crazed dream as I looked out at the Pacific. The salt air kissed my skin and enveloped me in a holiday cloud.

We sat famished, waiting for our buzzer to go off. We didn't need to talk, we just smiled at each other, understanding we all felt the same way, relaxed and happy at not having to work or study and just be together.

Finally, laden with too much food in little plastic baskets, we perched on the shabby picnic table, sat, and devoured as much of the feast as our stomachs would allow. The kitten woke, ate shrimp from my salad, and sat on the table. We laughed as he sat there, his baby head bobbing from side to side, watching a tiny ant.

"He could be a movie cat. It's like someone's already trained him. We should have dropped him off at Warner Bros, on the way," said Angus.

❧

We made a few pit stops in places Angus had on his list, like one town called Solvang with mock Tudor façades, cute cafes, and some tasting rooms where I picked up wine for that night. The kitten let out tiny meows from my leather bag as we strolled around buying ice cream dots and mini-doughnuts. Lucy spotted a tasting room in town, and a metal sign outside advertised the wine as 'Garagiste' style.

"I'm rusty with my school French, but I know that means mechanic, and I'm not gonna lie—I've got some concerns about this wine," said Angus, as we left the tasting room loaded with two boxes. Lucy walked behind with her face up close to her phone.

"I know, right?" I said. "It started in Bordeaux in the nineties with small-batch wine being produced by people at home or in their garages. It was a kind of movement that stopped wine production being so exclusive that you needed inherited vines or stacks of cash. You don't need to own a vine or a cellar. Some people even rent a couple of rows from other cellars. People can be a little snobby about it, but there are some good ones out there. Let's hope these are, anyway."

"I should have a bash at it when I get home and charge sixty-nine pounds a bottle,"

"Oh, my god, Angus, you are so cheeky. What will you call it?"

"Hmm. How about 'Garbige'? You see what I've done there?"

"Hey, do you think Lucy is OK? She seems distant, and she's been stuck to that phone like glue. I feel like throwing it out the car window."

Angus had booked a hotel for the night at Pismo Beach. Lucy was yawning and rubbing her neck when we arrived after stopping briefly in Santa Barbara for a Starbucks. On the map, places had looked so close together, but by the time you factored in a few wrong turns, parking, pulling off the highway and getting back on the highway, it was time-consuming, and we all realised we should have given ourselves way more time to make the trip up to Sonoma.

As we pulled under the bridge to crossover into the road for the hotel, Lucy, thinking it was one way, drove on the wrong side. We all shrieked, the wine clanged in the box by my feet, and I closed my eyes, but luckily nothing was coming the other way.

"We live to fight another day," said Angus.

Lucy hit him on the arm.

As I waited in the car with the kitten, Lucy and Angus checked in, and I scrolled through Instagram and saw a post from Claire, who was at Zero and Alex's house in their back garden, holding their small child. The knot in my throat tightened, and I zoomed in, studying the face to see if the little boy resembled Zero. It wasn't as if I could block

Claire, but I hated that there seemed to be no way of shielding myself from ever seeing Zero again.

"What's wrong?" said Angus.

He jumped back in the car before Lucy, who had gone to make a phone call.

"Oh, nothing. I'm being an idiot. Wouldn't it be great if you could put a block on pictures of people you didn't want to see? You know, if artificial intelligence recognised a picture of Zero, it would skip my feed. I just saw Claire's Instagram, and she was at Zero's place holding their kid."

"Come on, stop letting this affect you so much. Time to move on. It's almost like you need a Zero colonic. You should probably join Ignite. I joined, not that I've had much luck with it, but loads of people have—well, clearly," he said. He waved towards Lucy.

"Let's go find the shop before Lucy comes back. The lady at reception said it was up the road. We can walk and get some fresh air."

We walked across the brick-paved courtyard and I noticed weeds between most of the pavers and then looked up at the rooms, which were arranged in a U shape around it. The doors were dirty and in disrepair, and I knew it hadn't been cheap. I got worried about what was behind the doors.

We walked up the hill to the local shop. Angus loaded Ben and Jerry's 'Phish Food' flavoured ice cream, Lays chips and some bread rolls with an enormous pot of shrimp and Crab Louie salad into our cart.

"Don't you want to go out for dinner?" I asked. "It's like you're in a competition to load the trolley with as much as possible in five minutes."

"No, I'd rather hang around on those sand dunes, drink all your garbage wine and talk shit with you two. Look, I'm a tad worried about the rooms. You didn't see the reception area. My hair felt like it was sticking up on end when I got outside. There was that much polyester and shiny pine on every surface. Good job, I got these."

He rustled in his pocket and produced some weed gummies.

"Got them from a dispensary in Loz Feliz before the concert, and I completely forgot until just now."

"Where the heck have you two been? I nearly called the cops," said Lucy.

She was leaning on the car bonnet, still on her phone. Angus held up each arm with the plastic bags.

"Cops!" I said. "You are so American."

"We have carbs," Angus said.

The main bedroom was tiny and windowless, and the bedcovers were a headache-inducing patterned nylon from the eighties. There were two interconnecting rooms, and one had an ensuite.

"Ew—gross," exclaimed Angus as he dumped his bag at the end of the bed.

"But look out here, Angus!" I said, opening the French doors.

The hotel nestled into soft mounds of grass, and fluffy white rabbits bounced around, popping up and darting throughout the dunes.

"Did I fall down a rabbit hole?" Angus said. "Why are there magician bunnies?"

Lucy opened a bottle of the rosé we'd bought in Solvang. We

rinsed out some glasses and sat outside, enjoying the majestic sunset.

"The old bag at reception gave us this," said Angus, holding up what looked like marshmallows and biscuits. "There are some fire pits you can make s'mores on over there."

We settled the kitten in the bath with a towel and litter tray, and I fed him more shrimp I'd saved from lunch.

"You're getting far too attached," Angus said from the doorway. "She's cute, but you can't keep a kitten. You know that, don't you?"

I picked up the kitten and peered underneath.

"I think she's a he. Your Y chromosome has a friend."

Lucy was chatting with some surfy guys who had stopped as they returned to their rooms. I watched them run their fingers through their surf-waxed hair, transfixed by Lucy. They explained how they were in Pismo Beach to go sand boarding, and she feigned interest. She was a magnet for men. Lucy was beautiful, but it was something in her warm face which made people want to stop and talk to her and her beauty was like a cherry on top. I would have been jealous of her if she weren't my best friend.

"God, so much has happened since we were all in the US together. Life really can change on a dime," said Angus. "You two have done such impressive things, but I'm still doing the same old thing. I think I'm getting left behind."

"We'd never leave you behind, Angus, my love," said Lucy. "It would be like losing a limb, and to be fair, how many times have I offered you a job at Ignite?"

It was true she had asked him so many times I had lost count. I understood why he wanted to do something for himself, but it was stupid, and I had told him as much. I'd given up arguing with him about it.

It got late, and we ate s'mores and gummies until I felt sick. We swapped stories for hours with the sand surfers next door. Lucy got them all to join Ignite and even persuaded me to join.

"What? Lucy, it's matched me with a brewer from Greenville in North Carolina!"

"Give it here, you liar!" Lucy said.

She chased me for my phone until we collapsed in a heap on the damp dune.

She grabbed the phone and stuck it in front of my face, and opened the app.

"Ahh. It's matched you with Kyle—a barista from the Bouchon Bakery in Yountville! You can meet up with him when you get to Sonoma. See, my work here is done!"

Angus and Lucy stayed up till six a.m., but I was exhausted. I didn't know how they kept going.

The next day, I woke in the bathtub; the kitten sat under my chin, licking marshmallow and biscuit crumbs off my shirt, and a rank shower curtain was draped over my head. I opened the corner of one eye, and Angus snapped away as Lucy nudged him.

"Angus, stop!"

I sat up with a crick in my neck, rubbed it and picked up the purring kitten. He had a warm fragrance, like a cat version of Walter.

"Good job, I didn't want a bath," said Angus.

He was already packing his toiletries. He'd showered and changed in the ensuite, and Lucy was drying her hair as best she could with a tiny hairdryer that sounded and stunk like it might explode any minute.

"Haha, sorry, I'll go get ready too."

On the way to San Luis Obispo, the car was quiet. The wine had slowed me down, and my head thumped. I drank all the water in my Yeti bottle.

"I'd love some Marmite on toast now," I said.

"You and your Marmite. Vegemite all the way," said Lucy.

"Traitor," I said. "Next, you'll prefer Dilmar to PG Tips."

Beautiful scenery bombarded us from every angle, and California drew me in bit by bit.

Trees lined the quiet town street as we walked towards Angus's next stop on his mystery tour. He'd wanted to stay here for the night because there was a hotel called The Madonna Hotel with elaborate rooms in quirky colours. Lucy and I said we thought it looked weird and vetoed the idea.

Angus said we had to see a wall covered in gum. He wasn't exaggerating. The gum ran up both sides, right to the top, in every shade of pastel I could imagine. It was like a giant art installation. He handed us both a stick of juicy fruit, and I looked for a spot where I wouldn't have to touch any other gum, but I couldn't bring myself to do it.

"They clean it all off sometimes," said Angus. "You stay away from the walls, Elle. We don't want another trip to a hairdresser. You'll end up like *GI Jane* by the time we leave."

I pulled out the kitten and said, "I christen you, Luis."

Angus snapped away as I held Luis aloft.

"Oh, love the name," said Lucy. "But you are not keeping him! You're only here for a short time, OK?"

"OK, I know, but I want to find him a wonderful home. I don't want to drop him at some random vet's. He's been through enough."

We pulled off the highway to stop at Hearst Castle when we reached San Simeon.

"Angus, you are an amazing tour guide! Researching all these places. We never would have done this much." I hugged him as we stood on the hill after a whistle-stop tour around the massive estate.

"La Cuesta Encantada," said Angus.

"What's that now?" asked Lucy.

"It's the name of this place—Enchanted Hill," said Angus as he snapped more photos.

"I can see where the name comes from," I said, looking towards the Pacific. "I'm enchanted."

"It's easy to understand why so many songs about California exist. I mean, look at it. It sort of grabs your soul, doesn't it? I'm not sure I ever want to leave."

"I can see where this is going," said Angus.

"Member number twenty of the Silicon Valley billionaires club, and now you. I'll be stuck in Brighton with no friends, still in the same job. Even Vin and Heidi will leave."

The further we drove, the more the invisible roots of the olive groves in Sonoma pulled me in. We drove on through the winding, majestic Big Sur with its picture-perfect backdrops. The endless Pacific hugged expansive cliff-topped bays.

"Oh, is this it?" asked Angus as we pulled up to the Bixby Bridge. "It looks rubbish. I can't even be arsed taking a photo of it—Apple must have touched up the Mac screensaver photo!"

"Oh, wait a minute!" said Lucy, looking down at Google Maps. "This isn't the right bridge."

After several more twists and turns in the road, we saw the real bridge shrouded in a delicate Californian mist. We stood at the edge to take a selfie with a group of other pathetic tourists on a tiny patch of dirt, and I wanted it to be over and climb back in the car. I loved seeing spots from TV shows or movies but standing there seemed wrong and I would have been happy to see it from the car and experience driving over it.

Driving farther, we passed one beach where sleeping seals slouched like giant breathing rocks, camouflaged on the shallow shorelines, and all around us still hung a light, magical mist.

Lucy made a last-minute decision to drive to Pebble Beach, and the traffic snaked past the opulent homes. We were trying to guess which house used to be owned by Doris Day and then stopped for lunch in

Carmel at a quiet little bistro with white napkins, snooty waiters and fifteen-dollar bottles of sparkling water. I was half expecting Clint Eastwood to walk in, as I'd read he lived there. One upside to working as cabin crew was lots of downtime to read every gossip magazine, and my head was still full of useless information. That afternoon, we made our way to Monterey.

Lucy was half asleep when we pulled into the wide circle before the Portola Resort and Spa.

"Reese Witherspoon stayed here when they were filming *Big Little Lies*," said Angus.

"How do you know that?" I asked. "I mean, they probably make it up to entice guests!"

He even asked at reception, and when they verified the fact, he turned to us with a smug look.

"You are an idiot," Lucy joked. "But you're our idiot."

Angus had thought we might need space at this point on the road trip. We had separate rooms, and despite loving them dearly, I was grateful.

I jumped onto the comfy-looking bed, bursting with plump starched pillows and striped navy nautical bed linen. The room was low down, below street level, but I didn't care because it was spotless, and all I wanted was to fall into a coma for ten hours. Luis snuggled into a big cat basket I'd picked up in Carmel, and he looked so cute I wondered how I'd cope with giving him away.

The sound of someone banging a hammer cut my dream short, and I stirred in my sleep, angry that the hotel was doing renovations.

Coming round, I heard Angus and Lucy and stumbled up to open the door.

"You have a chocolate mint stuck on your cheek. I will repeat, you need constant supervision," said Angus, barging in and heading for a cuddle with Luis. "OK, freshen up. We are going out for drinks. We've been calling you. Seriously, when you fall asleep, nothing can wake you. One day, Luce, she had an exam and even set her alarm. I knew she'd oversleep, so I set one too. I had to shake her to wake her up. She slept through the whole thing. You'll owe it all to me when you are a real 'Onionologist.' I want free wine for life, and I want the good stuff, none of that garbage."

Lucy took Luis from Angus and snuggled into him.

"Talk about me getting too attached to him. You two are hypocrites."

I tousled my hair, put on the bare minimum of makeup, and finished it with a rub of my new Jo Malone solid perfume, which I'd now replaced from its liquid form to trim my diminishing student budget. We kissed Luis goodbye and promised him a treat when we returned.

We didn't return for seven hours.

Angus had found a whiskey bar. Lucy drank more than I had ever seen her drink.

"One more drink, Elle, then we can go," she said.

"I'm tired, Lucy, and I'm worried you'll get alcohol poisoning."

"But I want to make the most of every moment, seize the day."

"Well, we can carpe diem the fuck out of tomorrow," I said, putting my arms around her.

As I leaned into her, I got a face full of whiskey fumes. She pulled me down to kiss my cheek, and we both fell off the chair and toppled over the table.

We waited outside on the street for Angus.

"You got thrown out of a bar?" he said. "Oh my god, you two are embarrassing. I was getting lucky in there. He could have been the man of my dreams. Did you see him? He looked like a young James Dean."

"More like James Corden! Angus, I don't want you to find the man of your dreams in a Monterey bar on a Tuesday night. Come on, let's go. We need to take Lucy back. She's a little pissed in case you didn't notice!"

It was a foggy six a.m. in Monterey as we headed off on the last big leg of the trip. I felt sure Lucy was still drunk.

"Jeez, why are these people fucking beeping at us?" I said. "I mean, it's foggy. How can we go faster?"

"I know, right?" said Angus. "So rude."

"Oh," said Lucy as she turned on the wipers. Angus had been chatting so much he'd steamed up the car windows. We laughed hard, and Lucy was struggling to drive; we were all hyperventilating, and

Angus looked out of the back window and waved at the truck driver behind.

❧

"Is it me? Or is this a scary road system?" asked Lucy as we travelled farther up. "Why are these people driving so bloody fast? I've seen no cops. It's like they all drive as fast as their cars will go."

She breathed a tremendous sigh, and I could tell her shoulders were slumping.

"Luce, you're amazing to drive like this. I couldn't have done it," I said, squeezing her on the arm through the two front seats, and Lucy jumped and braked hard.

"Jeez, Elle, don't fucking do that when someone's driving!"

Angus turned to look at me, and I stuck my hand in Luis's basket. She'd never shouted at me before. I pushed back my tears, bit my lip, and stared out the window.

"You see, the bar on the truck in front of us?" he said.

I loved him for trying to change the subject.

"Where do you mean?"

"The bar at the bottom there. It's called the Mansfield Bar. After Jayne Mansfield, the actress. She was in an accident, and her car went straight under a truck, and it killed her."

"Oh god, that's awful. Pick that gem up from a pub quiz?"

"You guessed it."

"Go on *The Chase* or something, Angus; your head is brimming with these useful bits of information," I said.

Zinfandel

The roads into Napa were potholed as if Napa locals had fought some violent battles before our arrival. Angus and I remarked it hadn't been what we expected. I'd seen better roads in a village in the middle of the Cotswolds than the primary thoroughfare into Napa. As we approached, I was expecting long rows of vines on either side of the road, and I knew they existed somewhere.

"We're driving through the Croydon of Napa right now, guys," I said.

"I know, right?" said Angus. "What's with these roads?"

As if Angus had invited chaos, the car lurched to one side, and we skidded into the gravel edge of the unfinished road.

We stood looking at the shredded tyre, and it was clear none of us knew how to change it.

"We could wave someone down," said Angus.

"Do you know what, though, Angus? There are like three of us here, and we have a phone. Can't we google it? I know we need a jack."

"Here's the jack," said Lucy, appearing behind the car.

Between us, we jacked up the car. We even removed the old tyre with much grunting and swearing and a look at some guy swilling beer and explaining how to remove the nuts on a YouTube video.

"I'm trying to get his spare fucking tyre out, you two, and it won't budge," said Angus.

"Really? Fuck," said Lucy. "it's too hot for this. I can't do it. I'm sorry."

And she disappeared. She ran into some trees, and I couldn't see her. I didn't know what to do with the car jacked-up and the kitten sleeping on the back seat.

"Angus, go find her and see what's wrong, and I'll try to figure this out."

I tried everything to get the spare out, but there was no manual in the car, typical of a hire car, and it wasn't straightforward. I was hanging out the back, wiggling away, trying to make it move when a truck pulled up.

"Hi. Having problems?"

The man was tall and tanned and had a friendly smile and fabulous American teeth. He was looking at me as though he found something amusing.

"Uh, not really, changing the tyre."

"Oh, I didn't mean you were a poor, helpless female, or anything; I can help. My dad has this car, and I changed one on his just the other day."

I stood aside, and he got the tyre out with no fuss and had better tools in his truck to tighten everything up.

"This will sound weird, but have we met before?" I said, as he lowered the car.

"Uh yeah. Sorry I wasn't memorable, Elle, but you were."

"Oh, my god, Jude? How embarrassing! Well, in my defence, I was pretty wasted when we met."

"I'm looking forward to working with sober Elle!"

"I'm pretty excited too, Jude, and thanks so much for the

opportunity. Googling you so I knew what you looked like would have been a good idea. I knew you looked good. Uh, I mean—"

"Haha. Thanks. So where are Lucy and Angus?"

He stared at me and smiled, and I blushed, looking away.

"Oh. Yeah, Lucy was having a bit of a meltdown, and Angus went after her."

"Not like her. Is everything OK?"

"Yeah, I mean, I'm sure she's fine. I think the driving's been a lot."

"Well, I have to get back. Lucy has plans for us all to go out before your first day and I'm having a party, so I'll see you a couple of times before you start."

He kissed me on the cheek, and I breathed in an intoxicating mix of bergamot and sandalwood.

I leaned against the car and told myself to get it together. After all, he was going to be my boss.

Angus and Lucy ran over to me, and Angus howled.

"Hahaha!"

He was nearly hyperventilating.

"You—you look like a cat!"

I peered into the side mirror and saw my nose was black from car grease, and indeed, I was a couple of whiskers away from a cat. No wonder Jude was so amused.

Lucy grabbed a wipe and cleared it off, but not before Angus had snapped me doing a pose from *Cats the Musical.*

"You fixed the tyre? What the fuck! How?" said Angus.

"Well—" I said.

"Sorry, Elle. I'm tired and hangry. Can we get going?" said Lucy.

"What was the hilarious movie set in Napa?" asked Lucy.

"Ooh, I know *Wine Country*," said Angus. "Elle and I watched it a few weeks ago, didn't we? It confused me on the way in here because it didn't look like that in the movie."

"Yes! Oh my god, so funny. I loved it, that actress from *Bridesmaids*, she's hilarious! Let's watch it again. We might see somewhere we've driven by."

"This doesn't look right, though. Did we come a back way?" asked Angus.

"I don't think so. Do you want to drive?" said Lucy.

"Should we stop for a rest now?" I said.

"If you see anywhere, I'm all ears," snapped Lucy. "But I haven't seen a place I want to stop at. Let's get into Napa and find somewhere there, OK?"

The car was silent. All the camaraderie and happiness of the past few days diluted into awkwardness, and a depressing black cloud hung over the last bit of our journey into Napa. It was unusual. I couldn't think of a time when we'd snapped at each other, even when Angus and I lived together in the small house. We had a silent code, no bad blood over any petty shit. The bond and the trust were so strong nothing could come between us. I always thought our friendship was invincible, and this new side to Lucy was unnerving.

Angus pulled up Google Maps and directed Lucy to Oxbow Market in Napa. Downtown Napa, to be honest, was a bit of a dump, but here, in the middle of it, was this gem of a place. Angus and I didn't dare comment on our disappointment with the town. Lucy let her head hang as soon as she turned the ignition off.

The Oxbow was a collection of separate artisan food shops under one roof. Towards the back of the building, through the aroma of antipasto and strong cheese, laughter and a clinking of glasses drew us into a whitewashed wood-fired pizza restaurant. A cloud of roasted tomatoes and garlic wafted over us.

"Oh, this is what we all need!" I said, putting an arm around Lucy and raising an enormous glass of cab sav, salivating over the thought of a pear and walnut salad.

When I had no reply, I saw Lucy burst into tears. Fat tears rolled down her flushed cheeks. Her eyelashes were wet, and she wiped her tears with the sleeve of her linen shirt. Her dark eyes looked misty and tired, without their usual sparkle, and she looked out of the window as if she couldn't bear to look us in the eye.

"What's wrong?" asked Angus. "Oh, I wish we'd all taken a turn at driving; it was too much for you."

"Is it work?" I asked, sticking a piece of prosciutto into my bag for Luis. "You've been on the computer or your phone a lot. You need a proper break."

"Oh no, it's not that. I had a mammogram before we left the UK. It's not the best news, but I'm trying to be positive and not ruin the holiday. Sorry, I've been googling everything on WebMD—big mistake. I'm scared shitless now. This trip—it's been the best time, but I'm struggling to keep it all inside, you know? I'd planned to tell you guys on the last day. I'm so sorry to do it like this."

Angus was crying. I put my hand over my mouth, stopping my face from contorting, and I cursed the gods for dealing this hand to my wonderful friend. This shocking news took me to dark places like losing Mum and Dad; losing my friend would be too much to bear. My stomach lurched, and I caught my breath and pushed it all back inside to show Lucy a crisp outer shell. "OK, OK, how bad are we talking?"

I tried to speak even though my palms sweated, and I glugged the wine like I was drinking lemonade, which burned my throat.

"If they take one, they may as well take the other," said Lucy. "I want to cut the odds of getting it on the other side."

The pause in conversation hung in the air.

"Hmm, OK, thinking out loud here, but as money is no object, why don't you have the op here? You can do it quickly; I'll be here for you. I'm sure Angus would stay. Wouldn't you, Angus?"

He nodded through tears, reached under the table, and grabbed my hand.

"Thanks, Elle, but I need my mum. Anyway, I'll see you when you come back to the UK; promise we won't dwell on it over the next few days. It's been eating me alive. What a weight off my mind. I've told Mum, and obviously Gerald and Val know."

Angus was hyperventilating. I tipped out a Danish pastry I'd had in my bag for two days—much to the delight of Luis, who licked the custard—and handed Angus the paper bag. "Breathe," I said, not even looking his way.

Life was callous. When it was coming together, another thread worked loose and unravelled.

I looked at my friend, who filled every room with her presence. Her dark hair shone in the sunlight, and her tanned, toned arms made her look athletic even though she never exercised. She was always our rock. Anyone who met her walked away with the impression that they had met a truly remarkable person. It was inconceivable that these tiny, errant cells could be her kryptonite.

The pizza sat cold and congealed in the middle of the table, along with the unfinished wine. Angus looked at me for reassurance, but I looked away. I wanted to punch something, smash stuff and scream out loud.

"Thanks to you two, my life is amazing, and this has been the absolute best road trip. I mean it. You're both incredible. I'll find my way through this, I promise. Think about planning the next trip, Angus, when you get home. I'll even drive, but no more stray animals, OK?"

She dried her eyes, straightened her shirt, and put her smile back together like an impossible puzzle.

We bought food from the markets on the way out. Even though we had no appetite, we all knew food would be the answer later. Angus and I loaded cheeses, wine, cupcakes with thick, pink icing, and sourdough bread into oversized paper bags.

We didn't make it back to the car in one hit. There were many stops for cries and hugs; we were oblivious to the passing stares as Luis got braver and poked his head out of my bag.

"I think he likes it here," I said.

"If anyone asks, say he's a therapy cat like those people at the airport," said Angus. "You can get away with anything over here if you say that."

"Well, he is kinda my therapy cat," I said. "I think he's sniffing the food; he keeps popping up. Where are we staying this time, Angus? I forgot to ask."

"Oh, I didn't book this one; it's all Lucy."

"You'll see," said Lucy as she tapped the side of her nose.

We drove out to Sonoma, and I grew more curious. Lucy stopped in front of a white wooden house with a roughly painted olive-green front door and a big brass sign welcoming us to Twenty-Nine Cedar Lane.

As we stepped inside, a perfect spread from *Vogue Living* unfolded before us. Straw hats, baskets arranged on the walls, and other thoughtful accents drew my attention. From the tasteful oak-leafed wallpapered sections, worn wooden floorboards, and a beautiful wood-burning stove to the Belfast sink in the kitchen, I fell in love with it all. The home was a simple but welcoming cocoon.

"Lucy! This must have cost a fortune," I said, peering into the bedrooms.

"Well, I know you thought you were staying in an apartment in the vineyard, but I arranged this instead. You can stay here till you finish your placement. Technically, Jude arranged the whole thing, not me. He's an amazing guy."

"He did? You shouldn't have done this. How will I ever repay you?"

"Are you kidding me? I have what I have because of you," said Lucy, choking up. "You stood up for me. I wouldn't have done any-thing about it myself. I wouldn't have got my business off the ground.

You even introduced me to Gerald and Val, and he's been a godsend. Although we won't mention you two mocking my original idea in the cab on the way to that club!"

"You built a successful company with no help from me; you'd have done it anyway," I said.

"No, Elle, I wouldn't have. It wasn't just the money; it was the lecture you gave me about the future. All that soul searching in the crew bunk."

"She's right, Elle. I know I take the piss out of you. Still, you always encourage us to follow our dreams and now look at you, you're following your own," said Angus, sticking his head around the corner. "And I can tell you it will be crap without you. It's like you're the glue. You go through all these situations but always make something worthwhile out of them. An expert with pig's ears and silk purses, so to speak."

"You two give me way too much credit. Mostly, my life is one big accidental mess, and you guys encourage me. Wow, just wow. You've been going through heaps of shit and found time to pull this off. I don't deserve you," I said, crying.

Luis jumped out of the bag, and I dashed for the door.

"Oh, someone's getting cheeky!" said Lucy.

We sat around the fire pit, exchanging funny stories for hours that night, and laughed at Luis as he looked out at us from inside the patio door, lifting a paw like a dog.

"I wish I could keep him," I said. "I am kind of in love, guys!"

"Yeah, we can see that," said Angus.

"Jude is picking us up tomorrow for a Napa wine tour," said Lucy. "Not early or anything, about eleven, OK?"

"So, what's going on with you two? It seems like you have been spending some time here," said Angus.

"Oh, nothing. It's not like that at all with Jude. He has a girlfriend now. It was never like that with him; we liked each other as friends and kept in touch. I've been out to dinner twice with them, and I've been to his vineyard, too, with some friends from LA for parties. I thought he had a soft spot for you, Elle, when we met him in New York, and he's always asking about you. He was excited when I told him you needed a placement, but he's got this girlfriend now, although I am not a fan. Shame he's off the market because you would have made a good couple. He has a lot of friends, and some are pretty great."

"So, are we talking about this mysterious spy?" I said.

"Well, yeah, not a spy, but sooo awkward, and I don't live here full time, do I? So, it's hard to know how to approach it. And now I have to go back and sort out this medical stuff—get surgery and chemo, probably; it's all going on the back burner. Anyway, it's not exactly something I want people to know."

Angus and I looked at her in amazement. She was still into this guy, and we knew nothing about him.

"What about me? Are there any eligible bachelors here I should know about?" Angus said.

My thoughts turned to Angus. Since I had lived with him, he'd had no whirlwind romances I knew of. One time, I'd arrived home from uni to find a man lying on his bed, but it turned out he was a mattress tester. Angus had bought a new one, and it had sagged in the middle after a matter of weeks. A man was there to test it, and I'd seen him while he was lying on a sheet he had laid on the bed. I just thought he was a friend of Angus who had a touch of OCD and had brought his own sheets with him. Angus seemed offended that I thought he was having a fling with a middle-aged man called Derek, who had a paunch and receding hairline. Perhaps I was cramping his style. It might do him good with me away for a while.

"Hey, shall we go in and watch *Wine Country*?" I asked. "Poor Luis is in there all alone."

In the kitchen, Angus opened another bottle of wine.

"What's that one?" I asked.

Angus looked at the label. "Black Chicken Zinfandel."

"Ooh," I said, "The heritage grape."

"Oh, stop with your wine nonsense, young lady, and just drink it," Angus said, pushing a glass towards me. "I read an article the other day that said they put all these wine buffs in a room blindfolded and dead set; they could not tell a cheap one from a top-shelf one."

"Well, I probably couldn't, that's for sure," I said.

We settled in to watch the movie and drank all the Zinfandel.

"Your teeth are sooo red," said Angus, taking another photo and video of me.

"Stop it!" I said.

Lucy was asleep, and we covered her with a blanket.

"Is she going to be OK?" asked Angus.

"She is. I'm sure of it. She has to be, doesn't she? Or I don't know what we'll do; she's the strong one. So, what's happening with you, Angus? Getting through this degree has taken up all of my time. I haven't asked about you and how you're doing for ages. Sorry, I've been a terrible friend—not a narcissist, I promise; it's just I always think you have life under control. Are you going to quit flying and make a go of the photography or something?"

"I don't know. You know me. I muddle along. Perhaps it's all I can do, and I should be happy with it."

I studied him. He was more than a person who should muddle through. He was larger than life, a fully formed persona, idling along when he should have been out there grabbing life.

"So, what happens when you graduate? We haven't talked about that either. I'm scared you'll leave me."

"Well, I don't know. It's hard because of Holly, Walter, you, and Lucy, although you and her are away a lot, anyway. I guess I'll have to travel. If I want to be an expert I think it's the only way."

Luis let out a half yawn meow, toppled over on one side, and Angus captured it perfectly.

"He's like a kitten version of you!"

"Do you think anyone will notice if I smuggle him in my luggage?" I said. "Oh my god, the time when we were on the tarmac in Milan on that Alitalia flight, an old lady had a tiny spaniel in her bag, it was stinking hot, and we were stuck for an hour while they got off and unloaded her luggage."

"I forgot all about that!" he said. "No, the best one was when you sat behind that ex-US president, and he stared at your boobs when he boarded the plane."

"Oh gosh, we should write a memoir—but Angus, that's it! You write it! Reach out to everyone we know, collect everyone's stories, and include photos you have taken. You must! So tempted to wake Lucy up. She'd agree. Imagine the cover—one of your lovely cloud photos."

"Really? Do you think?"

He was quiet. Knowing him, he was going through a list of reasons he couldn't do it.

"You know, Angus, when you do something or create something, forget anyone you ever knew may read it, see it, or judge it. Do it without that barrier, or none of us would ever do anything new," I said.

"But how do I do it? I don't have the first clue."

"You just take one step, then the next. You collect the stories, and the rest will fall into place. And look—" I said, nodding towards Lucy. "You have one of the foremost business minds in Silicon Valley for a best friend. Give it a few weeks before asking for her help. But it might be good to take her mind off it all when she's had the op."

He looked down, bashful. He was quick to change the topic.

"You know I'm thinking about Luis. I hope Jude likes cats because you'll have to persuade him to adopt him."

"Hmmm, good idea; I was thinking there's bound to be someone at the vineyard I can charm. Perhaps it's Jude."

The next day, at ten fifty-five, Jude arrived for our day of wine tasting. He appeared to have gotten more handsome since changing our tyre, but I was also mindful that he had a girlfriend and was now my boss.

He acted like he didn't know he was drop-dead gorgeous, making him even more appealing.

Angus nudged me as we got in the back seat of his truck and made a wide-eyed expression like he had a thyroid issue.

"Ahh," he said. "This is what I thought Napa looked like! Jude, getting here was a nightmare. We had a flat tyre, and Elle changed it."

"Um, well, I didn't change it. Jude did. I tried to tell you two, but it wasn't the right time, with what happened. Jude was driving by, and he stopped to help."

"When what happened?" asked Jude.

"Oh, nothing," said Lucy. "We had a fight."

Jude looked at me in the rear-view mirror with a puzzled expression.

Yountville was the first stop, and we paused for wine tastings all the way to Calistoga.

"Elle, do you want to stop at The Bouchon and see if Kyle's on?"

"Who's Kyle?" asked Jude.

"Elle matched with a barista from there on the app," said Lucy.

"Oh, right," said Jude.

He looked out of the side window, and there was an awkward silence.

At first, I stared out at all the picture-perfect buildings and endless green vines, but as I got drunker and drunker, I cared less and less about the scenery. We were all drunk except Jude.

"This is a bit of a habit, Jude. Us being drunk and you being sober," said Angus, recounting the night of the Tiffany ring saga.

"That was so long ago, wasn't it?" said Jude.

"Who'd have thought we'd be here with you now? I appreciate you letting me do my internship here. My classmates were pretty jealous, I can tell you. We have this one friend who used to work at this gin distillery in Goa that uses crowd-sourced cricket bats in the gin-making process. How mad is that?" I said.

"Yeah. Jude, you would like Vin. He wants to make wine in quirky ways, too. His parents sound like a complete nightmare. Poor guy cops it every time he calls home. They keep trying to get him to go home to Goa and ditch the degree. First, they said his granny was sick, and then the family dog was pining for him. The latest thing is that they can't afford to stay in their house unless he goes back and helps them," said Angus.

"That's tough for him. Do they really use cricket bats in this gin, or is that a joke? I'd love to have a go at something wacky like that. It would be cool to do something unique. You know? Winemaking is the same year in and year out unless something goes wrong, and that's not very cool at all."

At Calistoga, we followed Jude and Lucy into a restaurant they had been to before. We walked through a stunning courtyard, and diners were chatting and laughing. Everyone we met that day was happy, and it wasn't hard to understand why with the fabulous wines on tap. The restaurant was one of those places where the outside didn't give away what you'd find on the inside, like cutting into a pomegranate. Casually scattered white, oversized floor lamps filled the area, and lights twinkled from every tree.

The gigantic chandelier that hung from an enormous, twisted oak tree drew you in like an enchanted garden or a child's bedroom display at Ikea, trapping you in never-ending circles around the store.

One lady grabbed me by the arm as we walked through the other diners' tables. She stank of garlic and wine; we were at different stages of drunk and she had a head start.

"Oh, my god, you're her! Can I take my picture with you?"

Angus pulled me away and suggested she'd mixed me up with someone else.

"That was weird. I don't think I've ever been mistaken for someone famous," I said.

"Yeah, weird," said Angus. "She seems pretty drunk."

We walked out to the pool area, arriving at a bar serving upmarket homemade tacos.

"This guacamole is next level," said Angus.

The bartender explained they used whipped avocado, pistachios, and kale when he heard him raving about the taste. I took out my phone and texted Holly the recipe. Then, I looked at the time and hoped I hadn't woken her up.

"These are the best tacos I have ever tasted," said Angus, with his mouth full. "Sure, beats a kebab at Mac Doner in Brighton. Elle and I have been living off them lately."

Then he fell off the bar stool and landed on his butt in a grassy area where he stayed. I spat out my margarita all over Jude's linen shirt, and Lucy dropped her head onto her folded arms.

"Jesus, you two, do you have to make a bloody scene every time we catch up with Jude? I'm sorry, Jude. I wish I could say this is unlike them, but you know I'd be lying!"

Cinsault

I sat outside on the rickety porch with my first coffee. Today would be awful; there was no getting away from it. I wanted to beat the dawn to its deliverance of terrible memories in the making, and deal with goodbyes on my terms.

Lucy stumbled out, stole my coffee, and took a big slurp. She approached the handrail on the deck fence, pulled herself onto the ledge, and swung her feet. Her toenails shone with gel in a vibrant orange.

"So, my friend, today's the day!" She grabbed both boobs and said, "This is the last time you will see these babies."

"Oh, stop," I said. "Maybe the doctors won't have to remove them both."

"No, I want them to. I want to be rid of this cancer and make sure it's all gone for good. So, looking forward to your semester here?"

She waved her hand at the beautiful backdrop.

"If it weren't for you, I'd probably have been stuck in a crew room in Narita heating a katsu curry, but I'm lucky enough to be here with my two best friends in this beautiful place."

"Well, we're here because of you, Lucy. I wish I were coming back with you. I'm sure Jude would understand."

She looked down and rubbed at the bleached wood railing.

"Yes, well, that's why I didn't tell you. You've worked hard. Finish

M. J. PARFITT

this, FaceTime, and show me what you're doing; it will distract me. And don't tell Jude. I don't want everyone to know. He'll worry. What are you going to do today?"

"Loads of studying. I'm so nervous about tomorrow at La Vallée."

Toast cooking in the kitchen wafted outside as Angus made breakfast, and he arrived with a tray of mimosas.

"Angus, just when I think you're the best friend a girl could have, you take it up another level."

I hugged him. He wasn't coping well with Lucy's diagnosis, and it worried me he'd be back in his house alone until I returned. He was looking pale and dark circles hung under his eyes. I would have given anything to gift him a perfect night's sleep.

Lucy and Angus jammed their bags back into the car, and before I knew it, I was hugging my two best friends, not knowing if I'd see one of them again. I held onto them with physical pain in my heart. I couldn't keep them here forever, and I couldn't magic all their problems away and protect them from this unrelenting battle of life.

Finally, the car trailed off into the distant vines until it was a speck carrying precious cargo. I wanted to run after them and jump in, but life had other plans. I staggered back inside, snuggled up to Luis, and poured over my books to prepare for my first day at Jude's vineyard.

As the sun set, tyres on gravel stirred me from a deep sleep. I peeped over the top of the couch as headlights illuminated the front porch and I could see the midges buzzing around in the night air. Perhaps I was about to get caught with a kitten in a rented holiday house, or I was in the wrong house, like Goldilocks. A face emerged from the dusk and pressed itself against the glass. I was so shocked I knocked over a bottle of Zinfandel, and it fell on the Moroccan cream rug.

"Oh, shit!" I said. Throwing paper over the mess, unable to choose whether to check who was peeping in the window or save the rug. The door opened, and a familiar face peeked around the frame.

"Hey, I'm looking for Lucy. Sorry to disturb you. I'm not an axe murderer or anything."

"Oh well, that's good. Who are you? You look familiar, but I can't place it. Norman Bates?"

"Haha, I'm Mark. I'm—um, a friend of Lucy's. Did I miss her? I was going to come to Jude's party last weekend, but I had to work."

"Oh, you're the mysterious Mark. You did. She left this morning. I'm Elle," I said, offering him my hand. Then I started hunting for soda water and opened every cupboard in the kitchen until I found some, grabbed a cloth, and approached the rug. The lid was tight, and it exploded in my face, all over my shirt and leggings.

"Oh, for fuck's sake!" My hair was now plastered every which way over my face. I brushed it off and tipped some more soda water on the rug. "Sorry, this is a rental, and I'm worried I won't be able to get this stain out."

"Here, let me help."

Mark looked like he'd walked out of a spa. He was the perfect amount of sun-kissed, had light brown hair which looked like he had just been to the hairdressers for a blow dry, muscled forearms, and a few beaded bracelets near his Patek Philippe watch. Thanks to years of reading inflight magazines, I was pretty good at recognizing a good watch. He rolled up his expensive shirt sleeves to help, and I saw a small tattoo on his wrist of the letter L in Times New Roman and he saw me looking at it and pulled down his sleeve. I wished Angus was here.

He had an essence about him I couldn't relate to any of the aftershaves we'd had over the years on Asana Air. When he smiled, he had a charisma which lit up the entire room. I became conscious I was staring at him and looked down at the rug.

"Who's this little fellow?" said Mark, picking up the kitten in one hand and pressing his nose up to his face.

I wanted to get on my phone right then, take some photos for Angus and text Lucy to demand to know why she'd neglected to mention that on this planet of eight billion people, she had met an incredibly perfect guy and let him go. I ticked the list of his attributes off in my head.

1. He liked cats.

2. He didn't mind a bit of cleaning.

3. He looked good.

4. He smelled good.

5. He looked amazing.

We did our best with the rug but gave up when it became clear the pink hue wasn't budging.

"Look, this is all on me," said Mark. "Give me your number. I'll have my assistant call you and arrange a rug cleaner, OK?"

6. He had a good job.

"That's kind of you. I'm a poor student, and that would be helpful, if you're sure."

"Oh, I know all about you, Darkling. Lucy has told me so much I feel like I know you. I helped Jude find this place for you—it belongs to someone I know. Please don't sweat about the rug. Plus, you're quite famous on TikTok. I'd have recognised you anywhere."

7. He's kind.

"Sorry, what? Oh, not me. I'm not much of a social media gal."

He fumbled in his jeans pocket and took out his iPhone, and he showed me a video of me getting gum stuck in my hair, and there I was having my hair cut, and there I was sleeping in a bath, and there I was with grease on my nose pretending to be a cat. From what I could tell, the pictures were as far back as when I split with Zero. I couldn't look any more; it was all too embarrassing.

"Wait, what? I don't understand. Who posted this stuff?"

I slunk onto the sofa and grasped with profound disappointment that it was Angus. There was no other explanation.

"Omg, I can't go outside. Everyone will think I'm some idiot!" I said, grabbing my glass and heading into the kitchen. "Do you want some?"

"Uh yeah, great. Thanks. Look, I'm sorry. I thought it was a joke you were in on," Mark said.

8. He likes wine.

"Does Lucy know about it?"

"Oh, I don't think so; it wasn't her who showed me, it was someone at work, and I knew it was you from Lucy's Instagram but I keep forgetting to ask her."

"Well, at least I have one friend left then."

I poured Mark a large glass. He looked at me, clearly panicked that he'd caused trouble between friends.

"Lucy is going to kill me. Where is she, anyway? She hasn't returned my calls, and I need to see her."

9. He loves Lucy.

"She left for the UK today. You should chat with her."

"So, she hasn't told you anything about me?" he said with a confused expression.

"Well, she said she had met someone but was cagey, and she's got a lot on her plate right now."

"You mean like work?"

"Look, Mark, I can't talk to you about this. She'd kill me. Just call her."

"I have tried; I don't know what else to do."

He looked at his watch.

"Gotta get going. Early call in LA tomorrow. My assistant will be in touch about the rug, OK?"

Then he was gone, and I never got to finish my list.

I picked up my phone and scrolled through the La Fille Maladroit TikTok account. It was all me looking like a complete fool for all the world to see.

I summoned Siri, who translated it into French for 'clumsy girl.'

"Oh, Luis, the boy will pay!"

I shrieked at the kitten, who peeked at me from his cosy spot on the couch, his grey fur bristling around his neck. Then he turned onto his back and stretched out his legs like he didn't give two shits about my tantrum.

The alarm blared out after an inadequate sleep. The noise woke Luis, and he lifted his head to see today's drama unfolding. Changing my outfit five times until there were no other options, I pulled on the navy pants and striped top I couldn't bring myself to stop wearing. At the last minute, I ducked back into the house and turned on the TV for Luis. Google said cats slept for fifteen hours daily, so I hoped he could do that while I was at work. I set off for my first day at Jude's vineyard in my small rental car. It was like my first day at uni, school and the airline all rolled into one anxiety-inducing journey.

As I pulled up in the paved driveway, Lara, Jude's girlfriend, pushed past me out from the old wooden doors of the tasting room. The place was majestic, like the cover of an oversized fairy tale book. A bright cerise bougainvillea trailed from one side of the sandstone wall in front of the main house. To the left sat a tasting room with a small car park for visitors, and beyond the rear of the property stretched row upon row of vines over undulating hills. It was immaculate, like a fine painting, and I took a mental snapshot. Jude had inherited the place from his dad, who was now too sick to take care of it.

"Oh Lara, um, hi."

Lara didn't even give me a look; she flounced off, threw her expensive leather bag into the passenger seat, hopped in her convertible Audi, and sped off.

"Something I said?"

"Elle! You're so early. Sorry about that. I guess we're going through a bit of a bad patch. You know how it is."

I shook his hand, smiling, not knowing how to respond, and clutching at words.

"OK, well, let's give you the official guided tour. You can put your stuff in the office through here."

I peeked into the room with its wood-panelled walls and the morning light from a sash window streaming in, making it warm and welcoming. There were papers and cream paper files neatly stacked on his desk, and behind it sat a green, worn leather desk chair that looked inviting. The air in the room was full of cedar and Jude's aftershave, and I thought I could detect cinnamon toast he might have had for breakfast, and it made my stomach rumble.

In the cellar, the oak barrels lined up in uniform, inviting us into the first tunnel, and then the complex, peppery aroma hit me. Pendleton was a working vineyard, but nothing had prepared me for La Vallée Estate. It had the worn grooves of repetition. Depressions from foot treads on the stone floor sat like age rings on an old fig tree. I could see the path of thousands upon thousands of bottles of wine.

"You sense it, don't you? The promise is those barrels. You're an addict like me. I can spot one a mile off," he said. "Lara doesn't get it."

"So, how'd you two meet, anyway?"

"You can thank Lucy for that; she got me onto her Ignite app, and the algorithm supposedly picked Lara. I know Lucy has made a ton of money, but I'm still unconvinced about the concept!"

"She's gorgeous. I think you did all right. Yeah, I'm still not sure whether to meet that guy it matched me with."

"No boyfriend since you ate the Tiffany ring for an appetiser? I saw the prank you played at the engagement party on TikTok."

"Come on, you too? I just learned about this bloody TikTok thing from your friend Mark yesterday."

"You saw Mark?"

"Oh, he was looking for Lucy. He said he came up from LA. Quite a journey only to find she'd left."

"He drove up from LA. Wow, he's got it bad. She should put him out of his misery."

I thought about the tattoo I had seen on his wrist but said nothing.

"I know, right? Angus is in some deep shit," I said, not wanting to talk about Lucy. "I'm waiting to confront him when I get home, but this might be the end of the road for us. He's made me look like a complete twat."

"No! Nothing can break up the three musketeers. I will lose all hope for humanity!" said Jude.

"You have a beautiful business here, Jude. The vines look fabulous, and these cellars are something else. Oh my god, it's so real compared to what we have at Pendleton."

"Haha, I've fooled you with the organisation of the whole place. It's my strength. What I'm not great at is making all this more profitable. My family isn't rich. Dad took a chance long ago when Sonoma wasn't what it is now, and we haven't kept up with how business works these days. Can you help?"

"Well, let me take it all in for a week, and then I'll chat to you again. All this is part of what I've been studying in my degree: how to generate multiple income streams. Perhaps I've learnt something you could apply here once I understand how your business works right now."

There was so much work in the vineyard. I was helping on the vines, in the cellar, tasting room and on the mountains of paperwork, which I loved because it gave me a good excuse to sit in Jude's chair. I imagined him spinning to look out the window over the vines, wrestling with why he was with Lara or chatting with his friend Mark about my friend Lucy.

Every night, I rushed home to Luis's cuddles and to study. I had an angry phone call with Angus, which ended like a train crash and culminated in me asking him to pack up all my stuff and put it in the garage for when I got home. He said he couldn't do that because he'd filled it with all the bottles for his Garbige boutique wine.

I FaceTimed Lucy to tell her about the visit from Mark.

"Oh, sorry I didn't tell you, but you know why now, I suppose?" she said.

"Not really. It's up to you; you don't have to tell me anything about it, but Mark seems like a great guy. I even made a list."

Lucy looked at me, puzzled, and we continued discussing other things. She tried to persuade me to forgive Angus, but I changed the subject. She was going through chemo and losing her beautiful hair, but she still looked amazing in her Saint Laurent silk scarf with its retro, orange flower pattern. I could see multiple vases behind her filled with peonies in every colour.

"I'm sorry I'm not there for you. I would come with you to every chemo session if I could. You know that don't you? Do you think you should tell Mark and Jude? Mark seems to be in love with you. I don't think this is fair, really."

"Cancer's not fair, Elle. This is the way I want to deal with it. I'm not asking you to understand."

"OK, OK, as long as you're sure. Promise I won't say anything."

❧

My rental car died one night after work, and I sat laughing at how different my life situation was today compared with the day I forgot to charge the Tesla. Jude was walking back from his truck and stopped to help.

"Not starting?"

"Nah, it's dead."

"Why are you laughing then?"

"Long story. I might tell you one day."

We tried to jump it, but it was dead, so Jude took me home. I breathed in the fragrance of his truck, which was infused with the familiar aftershave. He didn't need an air freshener. I loved the fact that he was so organised even in his car; if there was any debris, it was in the glove compartment. Then I glanced at the back set and saw one of Lara's designer jackets. The Chloe label poked from the navy wool as if to remind me she was always there in the background, staking a claim to her man, even if I couldn't see her.

I invited him in for a gin and tonic, and he walked around the small house surveying the rooms and picking up books on winemaking I had strewn around the place.

"This is a welcome change from wine," he said, positioning himself at the table on the front porch and pushing the twig of rosemary deeper into the glass. A scratching on his leg made him look down to see the gorgeous fluff ball, Luis.

"Oh, my, he's an angel, isn't he? Why do you have a kitten?"

I relayed the story, and I guessed by how he looked at me, he thought I was odd.

"So—cats. Love 'em or hate 'em?" I said.

"Oh, I could never hate an animal. My family never let me have a pet, but—" he reached down, gently lifted Luis, and looked him over. "Well, yeah, I kinda like this little one." Luis snuggled into his shoulder, and Jude looked besotted and snuggled back. I saw him sniff his warm fur and look into his little blue eyes.

Neither of us spoke again about the rental car, and I had the company come out and tow it. Jude became my taxi service each morning and night. He would usually bring gifts for Luis, like a toy collar or treat. It devastated him when we couldn't find him at all one afternoon until, after an hour, we spotted him neatly curled up in his tail behind a basket in the lounge.

"Luis! You are a sneaky little fellow." He picked him up and snuggled him, and my heart melted.

"You know, Jude. I was thinking, and you can say no, but I need to find Luis a permanent home when I go back to the UK. He loves you. Would you take him in?"

"Oh, I'd forgotten you would leave. I've got used to you being here. Um, of course, I'll take the tiny fellow. Slight confession here: Angus already asked me, and yes, you're mad at him about the social media prank, but you're his closest thing to a family. He didn't do it to hurt you."

"I don't see why he thought I'd find it funny. It was mean. It's not like I can help it. I'm clumsy, but I don't want the world to know that. Can we change the subject? It makes me too mad.

"Listen, I've been thinking about your business. I think there are some things you can do to increase profits by investigating some alternative income streams. You could sell into some other wine markets like France or Australia. You have some superb wines, Jude, and even though I hate to say it, social media is a necessary evil. My final, maybe a bit more of an 'out-there' idea, is to try a pop-up restaurant."

"Sell wine to France? Really? You think the French want Californian wine?"

"Well, if there is one thing the French know, it's wine. Once they taste yours, they will be in love. And about the restaurant idea—I know how you could try it out if you are game."

Urbane

I was a gigantic sponge, soaking up everything I was learning at La Vallée, which was so much more than I had learned at uni. It overflowed from my mind each night as I lay restless from the excitement.

It wasn't like working for a boss with Jude. There was no hierarchy with anyone in the vineyard. All his employees respected him because he was even-tempered and trusted them to do their jobs. When I made a mistake, he didn't chastise me or make me feel like an idiot. Once, I undercharged someone for some wine they ordered in the tasting room, and he said not to worry about it.

The atmosphere surprised me because it was so adult. I didn't know if he had thought much about it or if it was just who he was. Either way, it was another thing I adored about him. His only flaw was Lara—a big, immovable one.

Jude mentored me through each step of the production of what was, in many critics' eyes, the best chardonnay in the Russian Valley. He explained how he had taken time to learn the skills from his father, coming home from college each break to work and learn more.

His vineyard La Vallée Estate nestled into the Russian River Valley as if it had been there before humans discovered wine. Lush valleys banked with silver olive trees. Fruit orchards stretched up the undulating hills. Outbuildings and chocolate-box sandstone cottages dotted the estate, breaking up the vast greenery of the vines and trees and providing landmarks for anyone who got lost in this rambling place. If I lived here, leaving would be impossible. It was like an enchanted, secret garden which took hold of you and left you speechless—each day brought a different angle of appreciation. Usually, the ten-day mark anywhere had me itching to leave. Here, I wished the days were longer, or there was some way to stay forever. Sometimes, my mind thought up fanciful ideas of Jude begging me to stay on and work for him or him splitting up with Lara and declaring his undying love for me. Angus would have known what to say to talk me out of the stupid daydreams.

Before Sonoma or BS, as Jude and I had referred to it, I was a pinot noir drinker, and it was still my favourite wine. A pinot from Central Otago was at the top of my list. I had visited some cellar doors on a trip to New Zealand, and from that moment, I'd fallen in love. I wouldn't have ordered a chardonnay on a night out. Pendleton had widened my palate and I appreciated a good white, but it wasn't my first choice. Jude's chardonnay, however, changed my life forever.

"Now, Elle, I know you are a red wine drinker, but it's time to taste the chardonnay," Jude said one evening after work.

He poured a small amount to taste into a clean glass and looked into my eyes like a chef hanging on tenterhooks as you tried his latest culinary masterpiece. As I inhaled the jasmine-like fragrance, he nodded at me to take a sip, and magic danced into my mouth. Fresh lemon, apple, plum, and peach melded into a sublime fruit cocktail, leaving me with a zesty, sophisticated aftertaste. It was aptly called La Limonar.

"Not bad, huh? The breeze and fog from the Pacific give us the perfect growing conditions for chardonnay and pinot noir grapes here. That's why Napa vineyards buy our grapes."

I'd already tasted his excellent pinot noir, but I had a chamber in my heart for this chardonnay. He didn't use oak barrels, which gave it an unmistakable, crisp, untainted taste. Like a desperate love affair, I would never feel the same about chardonnay again. I questioned whether I would taste another wine like it as long as I lived.

I lived my days for these nights. There was an invisible tug on my heartstrings whenever Jude spoke to me or walked into a room. His blue eyes looked intensely into mine, and I knew every shade, from the bright cornflower blue to the green, dead at the centre. I found it unfathomable that Lara had the most incredible guy alive under her nose, yet hardly looked up from her tiny screen to stare into those eyes.

Lara cut each evening short, sulking until Jude took her out for dinner. Or she'd sit like a zombie on her phone. I'd given up on the attempts at friendship. She considered herself way too cool to converse with an intern.

"Don't you need to go feed that scrawny cat, Elle?" she said one night.

As she'd said it, she picked away at the arm of her wicker chair as if she'd been plucking up the courage to tell me to piss off.

After that, I'd make excuses each night and go home. Jude always looked disappointed, but the situation had become awkward, and it was easier not to sit through it. I'd already rented another car when she got a little testy about the time it took for Jude to drive me home. Thinking of them at dinner together drove me insane, so I studied each night, and that's all I did for weeks, apart from developing an addiction to Reese's Peanut Butter Cups.

On weekends, I'd go to either go into Napa or drive to Vallejo and catch the ferry across to San Francisco.

I found the bakery in Yountville called The Bouchon Bakery where Kyle, my match from the Ignite app, worked. Everyone else had discovered it, too, as the queue often trailed out onto the sidewalk. It quickly became something of a weekend ritual. Every weekend I'd walk past a giant ceramic fruit basket art installation. It reminded me of the tiny basket of blueberries I'd had in a doll's house as a child because both shone like the fruit on a French strawberry tart. Sometimes I wished I'd kept it to take it out and compare it with this mammoth one.

"Back again, beautiful?" asked Kyle.

We had been messaging over the Ignite app since I'd arrived in Sonoma, and we had been flirting like this every weekend, but I hadn't agreed to a date.

He handed me a coffee with a question mark. The week before, it had been a heart, and he'd asked me out for a drink, and that time, I'd made an excuse.

"So tonight? Are you going to make me beg?" he said.

"OK."

"OK? I'll pick you up at seven."

I wrote my address on the back of the receipt, and he tucked it in his denim apron pocket with a seductive smile.

I walked outside and sat on a stone wall, panicking about my first proper date with someone other than Zero for years. The façade of the café was pale green, and French-styled, golden-yellow signage hung above the old painted doors. I took a photo for Holly and Lucy, nearly including Angus in the text, but stopped myself. Then I snapped my flaky croissant and sent it to the group chat. We were always joking about croissants anywhere except France being awful or questioning why people heated them or stuffed them with odd ingredients like avocado. This was the most enormous croissant no-no as far as we were concerned. I missed texting Angus. I wanted to tell him I had a date and send him a photo of the giant fruit bowl and my croissant. He was still the first person I wanted to say anything to, but the trust was gone, and I didn't know how to go back. Breaking up with him was a million times worse than breaking up with Zero.

My phone beeped, and it was a text from Angus with an online news article. He didn't give up. He continued to text and call, even though I never replied or picked up. I clicked the link, and the face looked familiar. The title read: 'Dr Kelly's Magical Hands: Doctor turns an old family recipe into million-pound business.'

I zoomed in and squinted at the face. Then, a text arrived from Angus.

"Did you see who this is? And look at the ingredients. It's our lemon and sugar recipe with almond oil and sea salt instead of packet salt. It's the doctor from the last flight we worked together. She stole our secret recipe."

The aroma of Bombay Sapphire and lemons filled my memories. I had to smile, partly because Angus had sent the message and because it made me feel good to think of another woman succeeding and kicking goals in the world. I didn't reply, and it was like driving a knife into my heart to leave him hanging.

When I arrived home a few hours later, I saw Jude's truck parked in front. He got out and looked awkward.

"Hey, just popped in to see if you fancied lunch. Plus, I wanted to snuggle Luis. There's a kitten-shaped hole in my life since you got a new hire car."

"Haha. Um, yeah, I'm starving. Everything we need is right here. The markets were great today."

He helped me unload the fresh vegetables, herbs, fruit, and homemade sourdough bread and watched while I toasted pine nuts and blended the pesto into a pleasing green paste.

"Let me make you my favourite sandwich."

"Can I help?" said Jude.

He was sitting on the floor, making Luis dart around with a red light from a pointer he had in his pocket.

"You make some coffee once I have them in the sandwich press."

I cooked halloumi in a pan with the honey a worker from Jude's vineyard had given me and spread the pesto on the sourdough. Then, I loaded each sandwich with roasted pumpkin from the fridge and topped it off with sundried tomatoes and a big handful of spinach from the market. We sat out on the deck with our coffees, and I watched the steam from the coffee dissipate into the cooler autumn air. Jude bit into the sandwich, which was too hot, so he took a few breaths.

"Elle, this is so delicious. Easy to see why it's your favourite. This seems cheeky, considering I came here to take you out for lunch."

"Lies. You came to see a certain little pussy," I said.

Realising my faux pas, I turned a deep red and put my hand over my eyes. Jude laughed and threw back his head, and I put my head on my knees and kept it there until I stopped blushing.

"Uh, so where's Lara?"

"Lara is unsurprisingly at some influencer thing. Sounded tedious to me."

"So, you'll never guess what. I have a date tonight!" I said.

He blew his coffee and took a big gulp.

"Oh, right. Anyone I know?"

"Just a guy from a café. You know, the one I matched with on Ignite. He asked me last week, but I said no. Then I was texting with Gerald; I'm not sure if you've met him. He works with Lucy; he was her first investor. I sat next to him on the flight back from New York. Did she tell you about him? Anyway, he said go for it, girl. You're young and single, so today I said yes. Gerald's become a mentor to me. Anytime I don't know what to do, I text him. Usually, I'd text Angus about things like this, but well—you know."

"When are you going to forgive him?"

"I don't know if I can."

"Good luck with the date. It hasn't worked out that well for me, has it?"

I stood and headed back inside with the dishes, and Jude followed with the coffee cups. As I turned from the dishwasher, we bumped into each other, and I sensed he was thinking about kissing me. Then he coughed, picked up a cloth, and wiped the crumbs off the countertop.

"You don't waste your weekends, do you? Since you mentioned it, I've been trying to persuade Lara to get the ferry from Vallejo and catch a Giants game in Oracle Park. There's not enough reason for her to do it. It's always got to have an angle that she can exploit on her socials."

"Oh, that view of the Bay. It's magnificent. You must persuade her. I'm reading this series of books—*Tales of the City*; it takes place on a street called Barbary Lane in San Francisco. Have you read it? It's not an actual street—it's a pun about the Barbary Coast. Macondray Lane might be Barbary Lane, so I went there. It has these wooden steps you walk up from the road to get to the houses."

"*Tales of the City?* Not read that or anything for ages. At night, I'm practically unconscious; gotta find a balance somewhere in all this."

"Oh, read it, Jude. It's such a good book series; with you living here and knowing San Francisco like you do, you might enjoy it. It's set in the seventies; it follows people living in the same building and becoming friends. They all have a unique set of complications in life and become a weird little family. We could watch it on Netflix together when we finish it. It started as a serial in the *San Francisco Chronicle*. Honestly, it was ahead of its time."

"OK, OK, I will," he said. "You know they do a movie tour of San Francisco, don't you? It leaves from the pier; we should go before you leave."

'Leave' hung in the air like a knife waiting to fall. My throat tightened.

His eyes stayed on me long after the conversation had ended. We stood in silence like a stalled game of chess.

My date, Kyle, was driving in as Jude drove out of the driveway. I saw Jude glance over at him through the car window.

"Ready?" he shouted.

"Give me ten minutes. Come in and have a drink while I get ready."

"Who was that?"

"Oh, my boss."

"Your boss comes over at the weekend? He must be working you hard."

"Well, we're friends too."

Kyle swatted Luis away from his leg, and I concluded he didn't deserve a one-night stand. Then I noticed his suede shoes with odd buckles on them and metal tips, and I wanted to laugh and tell him to get out.

"Not a cat fan?"

"Yeah, not a fan. I think they are evil. It's the eyes—you know."

"Clearly, I don't know, or I wouldn't have one."

I threw on a pair of old Levi's and my Zara sweatshirt and rushed Kyle to the car.

I looked back at Luis, "Don't worry, poppet, you'll never see that cat hater again. Just let me get rid of him, and I'll be back soon."

Jude and I were on a lunch break. I was sitting in his kitchen next to the countertop. He was making me his favourite pastrami sandwich on rye. I watched him place the Russian dressing and sauerkraut on top of the pastrami, immersed, like when he made wine. Next to the oven, he had an impressive collection of old wooden chopping boards of varying thickness; some looked like antiques, and I imagined his mother giving them to him. Like everything else about him, his uncalculated interior style worked.

He took down some cornflower blue plates from the rack on the wall, and I grabbed a jug of lemonade out of the fridge. We had become a strange couple, perfectly in time with each other but not together. Then Lara would show up, and we'd go back to being boss and employee, and she would eye us both suspiciously.

"I started reading *Tales of the City*, Elle. I wish I could live there and have Mrs Madrigal as my landlady. Imagine the parties."

"Yeah, and the free weed," I said.

I noticed he didn't ask how the date went.

Lara walked in and made a face as she looked up from her phone screen.

'What would Mrs Madrigal say?' became our secret handshake.

"What are you guys even talking about?" asked Lara.

She rarely paid much attention, and we were both taken aback.

I still knew little about her, but from what Jude had told me, she wasn't an idiot. She scored fifteen hundred on her SAT, which Jude said gave her a significant chance at an Ivy League school. She'd lost interest and had been shopping and Instagramming the last few years away. When he told me this, I understood her on some level.

"Lara, you really must read these books! They're set in San Francisco. It's funny to me how all the old social rights issues are still the current issues. It makes you think things will never change. Maupin must have thought things would improve when he wrote them. Not to say they haven't. Just lately, it's been so damn disappointing."

"Blah blah blah," said Lara.

"I'm sorry, Lara, what?"

"You're such a book bore. God, this is boring," said Lara.

"If you read a book instead of looking at TikTok, you might be less bored. Try it sometime. You are a woman; don't you care about your rights? Sorry, Jude, I'm going to go back home now. I've suddenly got a headache. By the way, Lara, you are the rudest person I've ever met. You make no effort with Jude's friends. You have nothing to say, and you look fucking ridiculous in those outfits from the nineteen eighties, and while we are on the subject, no one cares you were in the semi-finals of a hip-hop dancing competition in 2015 when you were still at school."

Lara wasn't even listening. She had her phone up against the portable speaker.

"Are you seriously Shazam-ing Fleetwood Mac right now?" I asked.

"Well, I've never heard it before," she said.

"Oh, my god. Do you live in a cave? Now it's clear why you struggle to have a conversation. You have no reference points unless they originate on TikTok.

"Shazam-ing Fleetwood Mac," I muttered, stomping to my car.

I was sad about missing the sandwich, and I wanted to shout at him to come with me and listen to Fleetwood Mac, talk, and drink excellent wine, but he belonged to Lara, and I was leaving soon, and none of this would be my problem.

M. J. PARFITT

Garnacha Tinta

*H*olly, Nick, and Walter bounded through arrivals at San Francisco International Airport. Seeing them after so long, my
heart was ready to burst. Looking at them outside of home like this
was odd. They appeared more worldly than when I saw them in their
bubbles in the UK. Now, I saw them as a stranger might, and then,
when we caught each other's eyes, that split second was something I'd
never forget.

"Aunty Elle, Daddy doesn't have a job now," said Walter.

"Oh, Walter! Daddy got made redundant," said Holly.

"Yes, Daddy got made into a doughnut at work; now he takes me
to school."

I made a shocked face at Nick and bent down to snuggle Walter.

"We all love doughnuts, Walter!"

"We can talk about all it later," said Holly. "Oh, it's sooo good to
see you, tell us all about the trip so far!"

"Come on," I said. "It's an hour's drive from here, and we can chat
on the way."

I was eager to get them in the car and show them the sights.
Walter squealed as we drove over the Golden Gate Bridge. I told them
the story about the orangey-red colour not being the planned final
colour when it was first built, but people liked it, so they kept it.

"But why isn't it golden colour, Aunty Elle?"

"See the water down there, Walt? It's called the Golden Strait."

We pulled up in front of the perfect white house, and I rushed to jump out and show the place off.

"I have a surprise for you, Walter!"

"What is it? What is it?" he ran off inside, looking around.

"Well, I'll give you a clue. It's not in a plastic bag."

A squeaky mew, another, and a fluffy tail emerged from behind the couch. Walter yelped in surprise, and his entire face lit up.

"Now, this is Luis. I found him in Venice Beach. He had no mummy and I'm looking after him right now."

"What the hell, Elle? A cat? What will you do with him when you leave?" said Holly.

"Oh, it's OK. Jude is going to take him. He loves him."

Walter was rolling around on the now pristine rug. Mark's assistant had been super-efficient at sending a cleaner out.

We walked out to the porch, and I poured each of us a glass of Jude's La Limonar.

"Oh, this is good!" said Nick and Holly.

"I know. Hey, listen, I wanted to talk to you guys about something. Don't be mad, but the vineyard needs a boost. By Jude's admission, he doesn't have the entrepreneurial vision to take it to the next level. Not that I do either; it's all fresh in my head with uni. So, I came up with a few ideas, and one of them was trialling a restaurant. I instantly thought of you, Holly. I know I'm springing this on you, but I thought we could try a pop-up restaurant. He has all these barns and outbuildings, and he's nearly finished putting a kitchen into one."

Holly looked at me and Nick. Then, down into her glass of chardy.

"God, I don't think I could do it, Elle. He'd be better off getting in a professional. It's been so long."

She darted back inside to see what Walter was doing.

"It would be good for her, Nick."

"Yeah, you're right. She's lost her confidence, that's all. You know what she's like. Let her sit with it for a few hours."

While we were at the Napa farmers' market, the freshness of the food overcame Holly. The fragrant herbs in the sunshine and the fresh fruits and vegetables offered a striking contrast to her Sainsbury's shop in New Malden.

"Oh, I'm going to cook for you tonight!" Holly exclaimed and threw an assortment of goodies into her basket. "Invite Jude, too."

"Well, I can, but I'll have to invite his girlfriend, Lara. I'm not sure you'll like her; she's up herself. You know, Instagram zombie, 'look at my perfect life.' She's pretty but boring. We've had a bit of a falling out. She was being such a twat, and I was over it."

"Oh god, one of those. Why's Jude with her? He seems so normal. Still, invite them. I want to talk to him about this restaurant idea."

Nick smiled at me as Holly turned over apples and inspected shiitake mushrooms. I took Walter's hand and led him to a doughnut stall, and he chose the most chocolatey, gooey one on offer called 'Hot Mess.' I told him to eat it without licking his lips and videoed it for Holly. His little face struggled with extreme concentration.

"Oh, Aunty Elle, my tongue is working on its own. It won't do what I say," he said.

"Oh, thanks heaps, Aunty Elle!" said Holly, looking with disdain at Walter's sticky face. She dug in her magic bag for a wet wipe and scrubbed at him.

"Definitely not breaking any trade description laws. It's clearly a hot mess."

"Mum, stop; it tastes like soap."

I called Jude on the way back to the car and invited him and Lara for dinner.

"Oh wow, are you sure they don't have jet lag? I mean, we won't say no. From what you've told me, I am excited to try Holly's food."

It was a warm, still night for autumn. I set the table out on the back lawn, found some old tea lights left over from someone else's past soiree in a kitchen drawer, and set an enormous bunch of hydrangeas I had bought at the market in a cut crystal vase. Holly and Nick worked furiously in the kitchen.

"Oh my god, the aroma is incredible," said Jude as he walked in.

I introduced everyone. Walter was shy and ran behind me, and Luis chased him and grabbed onto the leg of my jeans, making me trip backwards. Lara rolled her eyes and smirked, and I blushed. I thought of Angus and the missed photo opportunity.

Jude coaxed Walter out with a disappearing coin trick, and Lara placed two bottles of wine on the countertop and sat on a bar stool surveying the tiny house. Holly shot a wide-eyed look at me.

"So, what do you do, Lara?" asked Holly.

"Do?"

"You know, for a job."

"Oh, not much—influencer stuff, a bit of modelling."

I coughed and offered her wine and hors d'oeuvres.

"You're pretty settled here, Elle, considering it's short-term," said Lara.

She stuffed another goat cheese and salami stuffed date in her mouth.

"Not really, I just have a suitcase!"

"Well, you gained a cat, which we are now going to be stuck with, I hear."

"Oh—um, sorry. I asked Jude, and he said he wanted to take him, but look, I can find someone else, I'm sure."

"No, I want him!" said Jude. "You don't even live with me, Lara. It won't affect you, will it?"

"But it does affect me. You can say goodbye to impromptu weekends away, that's for sure," said Lara.

My phone beeped, and it was a text from Angus with sad eyes, pleading for me to forgive him. Then, one from Zero asking how I was and whether I had time to catch up when he was in San Francisco.

"Sorry," I said, "it's Angus again."

Holly and Nick served a feast bursting with delicate flavours, using all of Holly's market finds. Creamy mushroom soup sat on two plates. The middle plate was more petite than the last, leaving a rim filled with tiny mushrooms, roasted parsnips, shredded beets, and dainty micro herbs. The principal attraction was a majestic roasted rack of lamb in a jus made using Jude's wine and a sumptuous platter of roasted vegetables. Finally, the dessert was a simple lemon tart with limoncello cream on a crisp white plate with tiny lilac flowers and a dusting of icing sugar. It was simple, hypnotic food.

There was lots of chatter between courses, but as soon as each dish was served, the group was silent, entirely entranced by the complex flavours. Even Lara was speechless as she snapped the stunning presentation for her Instagram feed and savoured each bite.

"Wow. Just wow!" said Jude. "I think it's the best meal I've ever eaten. Don't tell my mom!"

"See?" I said. "I knew you'd love Holly's food. She's amazing. She got the cooking genes from our grandma, but her food is way fancier. I'm not sure why I didn't get them."

"Oh, I don't know. That sandwich you made me the other day was something else."

The sentence dropped like a stone; Lara shot Jude a look across the table, and Holly tilted her head at me.

"So, when will you come and do this at the vineyard?" Jude asked.

"Well, we need to plan the menu. Work out budgets, advertise the event, and finish up with your renovations. We are here for a month. Let's do it before we leave?" said Holly.

I looked at Nick and Jude and smiled. I knew this would be good for Holly.

Finally, we all shuffled past a sleeping, angelic Walter spread out like a starfish on the couch, with Luis curled into his shoulder. They had made friends quickly as if they had been together since birth.

Goodbyes lingered on the front steps, and Jude rested his hand on my shoulder. I wanted it to stay there.

"Your sis is awesome, guys. She has been invaluable at the vineyard. I don't know what we will do without her when she leaves. And apologies about the Philip."

No one said anything because only I knew what he was referring to, and I coughed and changed the subject.

As we washed the dishes, Holly and Nick recounted how Lara was not the right fit for Jude, and I laughed.

"Yes, but she's pretty, and it's all guys want, no matter how much they say they don't."

"Who's this Philip, by the way? He lost me at that point. Is it someone you work with?"

"No. It's what we would call people we'd like to punch when I worked for the airline, and we told Jude about it when we first met him in New York. Can't believe he remembered it. I guess he was talking about Lara tonight. She was really rude."

"Such a shame," Holly said. "So, tell us all about this Angus saga, and how's Lucy doing? Angus wouldn't do anything to hurt you intentionally."

I explained that the friendship with Angus was over and that I meant it.

I'd have to face him soon to collect my stuff, which wouldn't be pleasant. Holly and Nick invited me to stay with them until I had a job. I hadn't given it much thought except a few daydreams about a

Champagne house in Épernay. California hadn't been on the cards, so anything was possible.

Nick carried Walter to bed, and Holly hugged me tight.

"So, what's the plan? I'm jealous of the life you are building for yourself. It's so exciting! I'm proud, too; whenever anyone asks what you are doing, it's a joy to tell them what you've done. You're quite brave," said Holly.

"Pah, not sure it was brave, definitely stupid. I don't miss flying, though. I was over it all, and now I've left, I feel quite nostalgic about it. Maybe Angus should have quit, too. Perhaps that's the problem with him; he's bored."

I looked down at my phone. More missed FaceTime calls from him. He wasn't giving up. I wiped down the countertops and dried dishes to distract myself from it, much to Holly's protests.

"Your food was amazing. I'm so happy you agreed to do the pop-up."

"Scary but exciting!" said Holly.

"What would you say if Jude offered it to you as a regular gig?"

"How would that work? I can't move my family to California, can I?"

"But why not, Hol? I mean, why not? Nick's out of a job. Walter's just started school. All I'm saying is keep an open mind."

Holly fell silent. She hadn't thought of this as an outcome in her wildest dreams. She imagined this would be a fun adventure to see me, not a trip to change her small family's lives forever. Then they had arrived at this perfect cottage, and I had seen the possibilities written all over her face.

"Gosh, I don't know, that's a lot. You're a lot. I mean, it's your thing, being brave and everything. I like to play it safe, and there's Mum and Dad's house."

"It's just a house without them, and something Dad said about you in a vineyard…I know it's stupid; he was probably getting us mixed up, but I don't know. The more I think about it and the time I've spent here, the more I want it for you guys. Imagine growing up here? And I've even got Walt a ready-made pet!"

I held out both palms to a sleeping Luis still on the couch.

"Look, probably pie in the sky, but I'm saying—if an opportunity pops up, take it or at the very least consider it."

When Holly had quit being a chef, I had thought nothing of it. It was what mums did. It's what women did. I was preparing to do the same thing when Zero shattered everything into a million pieces. Women put life on hold. It was ludicrous that Holly had missed out on six years of career progression, salary, and opportunities. It was a balancing act, like a great wine.

If only everything could be as simple as this Bordeaux, I pondered, holding it up to the light and pinching the stem of the glass. It was a Légende Pauillac 2015 Holly had brought with her, saying she thought I may have had enough of Californian chardy. Never. Never would I tire of the delectable nectar that was La Limonar.

The wine was dark, verging on purple. At my first sip, it hit me with sharp berries, like cranberry or cherry, then it left another earthy aftertaste, and I imagined it in oak barrels for months before it had travelled on this long journey to Napa. The last flourish was a minty overture.

"How's the wine?" asked Holly.

"Really, good! It has a minty overture."

"What the fuck?" said Holly. "Mint? Are you for real?"

"Holly, you're a chef. You know it's science, don't you?"

"I don't understand it. Could you explain it to me? You don't add flavours to wine, do you?"

"OK, but it's a lot."

"I'm getting a notepad," said Holly.

"So, let's talk about esters. No, before that, you need to know that there are three main wine flavours. Number one, think fruity, floral, and herbal. Number two spicy, and number three earthy. Oh, and wine gets its taste from the skin of the grape.

"So, back to esters. The wine esters come from acids. I thought you'd know this stuff 'cause they're used in sweets and essential oils. In wine they're the foundations of the fruity flavours like the apple in Jude's chardy or the raspberry in a grenache. Then you have herbaceous pyrazines, an organic compound which smells like veggies. You know it from coffee and chocolate, yeah? Examples would be bell pepper in cab franc or grass in a sav blanc. I can't believe you are writing this down!

"So, moving onto terpenes—oh my god, give me the book. I'm going to write it down for you."

I sat and wrote out the whole science behind the flavour of a wine. When I got to dessert wine, I had to look it up in another small notebook. Holly sat silently in disbelief.

Terpenes:

Rose & Lavender—Christmas trees, desert sage sweet and floral or resinous herbaceous (also used in beer!)

Lychee—Gewürztraminer

Rose—Muscat Blanc

Lavender—Grenache & Côtes du Rhône

Eucalyptus—Australian Shiraz

Thiols:

(Bittersweet Fruit)—organosulfur compound, earthy foundation fruity in tiny amounts, but in larger amounts, it smells like garlic = wine fault.

Grapefruit—Vermentino, Sauvignon Blanc, Colombard

Black Currant—Red Bordeaux and other Cabernet Sauvignon & Merlot

Sulphur Compounds:

(Rocks)—gives wine minerality. Some smell good—chalky aroma in Chablis.

Some bad—think wet wool—basically UV damage.

Chalk—Chablis & Champagne

Metallic—Young, Freshly Opened Red Wine

Volatile Acidity:

Bacteria = volatile acidity or acetic acid. High doses smell like acetone.

Adds complexity to very fine wine in low doses.

Balsamic—Chianti & Amarone Della Valpolicella

Pickles—Red Burgundy

Brettanomyces:

Phenols are like alcohols. Found in sesame seeds, peppers, and weed. In wine, a type of phenol is a wild yeast called Brettanomyces. If good = clove and bacon. If bad = horse poo!

Clove—Châteauneuf-du-Pape ($$$) & Côtes du Rhône

Bacon—Paso Robles/Central Coast Syrah, Barossa Valley Shiraz

(Notice there are no horse examples :)

Geosmin:

Think—Earthy Mushroom

An organic compound from bacteria. (Smells like Dad's potting mix.)

Common in old/new world wines

Spicy Flavours:

Rotundone = terpene oils of black pepper, marjoram, oregano, rosemary, thyme, and basil. Peppery taste to wine.

Peppercorn—Syrah, Grüner Veltliner, & Cabernet Sauvignon

Basil—Dry Riesling

Pink Peppercorn—Viognier, Gewürztraminer

Lactones:

Esters in honey wheat bread, peaches, coconut, roasted hazelnut, butter.

Vanilla & Coconut—Oak-aged red/white wine

Hazelnut—Mature Sparkling Wine

Thiols:

(smoke and chocolate)

Grapefruit pith and passion fruit

High dose= smoke, tar, choccy, coffee

Coffee—Sonoma Pinot Noir!

Chocolate—Argentine Malbec

Botrytis:

(Noble Rot) = Fungus eats ripe fruits and veggies when ripe.

Adds richness aromas to dessert wines.

Sotolon—Honey, Fenugreek, Curry

Furaneol—Caramel, Pineapple, Strawberry

Phenylacetaldehyde—Rose, Cinnamon, Ginger

Marmalade—Sauternes, Tokaji

Ginger—Spätlese Riesling

Holly grabbed the notepad.

"But Elle, I see nothing here which says mint."

"But looking at this list, what do you think is in those grapes?"

"Terpenes?"

"You're right because it would be the terpene oil from an herb like mint."

I tapped at the notebook with my pen.

"Some of this might be wrong. Let's get Jude to check it, but honestly, that was useful because lots of this will be in my exams."

"You really understand wine, don't you?" said Holly.

Pinot Blanc

*H*olly and I made indelible memories on their family holiday to California. We explored every corner of Sonoma and Napa, not wanting to waste a second of our time together before saying our goodbyes. We visited as many tasting rooms as possible, with Holly trying to guess the flavours and returning to the list I had compiled for her.

Artesa reminded us of a mini-Louvre. The entrance was triangular, and they had built the entire building into a wonderful green hill, like a billionaire's bunker between Napa and Sonoma.

I'd wanted to go there since reading about the Spanish company producing an Albariño. We invited Jude along with Lara. So far, we had kept them at arm's length after Lara was unbearable at the dinner party. There was no way I'd allow her to ruin my sister's holiday. On this occasion, we relented because Jude hadn't been to Artesa, and he'd overheard us talking about it.

A couple of hours passed quickly after we ordered several flights. We sat on the paved terrace with views across the rolling hills of patchwork patterns in three shades of green. The green vista would always remind me of Jude. Olive, sage, and emerald would linger in my memories of California for as long as I lived.

Walter soon became bored, along with Lara.

Jude told them about cab sauvignon being 'The King of Grapes.'

"Excuse me, Jude, who is the queen of grapes?" asked Walter.

"Oh," said Holly. "Mummy knows the answer to this one, Walter. It's your Aunty Elle."

She told them about the grape lesson I had given her.

Everyone laughed except Lara, who rolled her eyes. It was obvious she didn't like small children, I thought. Even if she didn't want them, it was a stony heart that didn't melt with virtually anything Walter said.

"So, Lara. How's life with you? I think we got off on the wrong foot. This is me extending an olive branch," I said.

I'd had at least three wines by this stage.

Jude choked on his wine.

"You think? Well, that's because you and Jude are always deep in conversation about something, right? You're always talking about some Mona or Marianne, I don't know," said Lara.

I had to look away when Jude smiled at me over the *Tales of the City* reference and Holly looked confused.

Whenever he smiled at me, I felt like I was standing on a stage, and every light in a theatre shone down on me and no one else.

"Oh, well, he is my boss. It might be hard to do the job without talking to him."

Holly and Nick deflected the confrontation by asking Walter what he was doing. Lara stuck her head back in front of the phone screen.

"Shall we try some more wine?" I said.

Jude followed me.

He grabbed my elbow at the bar.

"What was that?"

"Hey? I'm trying to connect with her; she's—look, Jude, why are you with her? She's such an asshole."

Jude looked shocked.

"Oh god, it's awful, isn't it?" he said. "Until you came here, I was going through the motions. Lara's pretty, and it was easy if I did whatever she wanted, but I think you are the polar opposite. You're beautiful too, but you're funny and open, and she's a—"

"Fucking child," I said.

Jude threw back his head and laughed.

"I'm sorry, maybe the drink talking, but what the fuck, Jude? She's not good enough for you. There, I've said it! Not sure how I'm going to come to work on Monday."

"I know you're right. But you're going home soon."

"This isn't about me, Jude. It's about you. It's better to be alone than with that idiot. OK, I'm going to stop now; I've gone too far."

Picking an invisible piece of fluff off my jacket sleeve, I lifted the tray and walked away. He leaned in and whispered into my ear. His voice was so close to me I could almost taste the sweet wine in his mouth. I wanted to pull him in towards me and for him to kiss my neck and tell me he was in love with me.

"Meet me tonight by the olive groves on the bench seat at eight. I'll bring some drinks. I need to see you. Please."

"Um, OK," I said.

I walked away with a dangerous, lightheaded excitement that coursed through my body that I knew too well.

"That looked cosy," said Holly.

I handed her a rosé, and she sniffed its bouquet.

"You have no idea."

The rest of the afternoon passed in a blur. I was feeling too shell-shocked and guilty about Lara.

Whenever Jude looked towards me, I looked away. It was intense, and I was mad at myself for starting this. If only Kyle had been a cat person.

My bedroom floor was strewn with every outfit I had, as I tried to balance looking fabulous and like I'd thrown something on without a care in the world. The outfit I'd chosen comprised some old torn jeans and a black linen shirt, and I hoped it gave the impression I wasn't desperate for Jude to kiss me and tell me he was in love with me. I also hoped the button I'd left undone on the top gave a conflicting impression. Disaster spelt itself out in a ten-foot sign. Several times, I picked up my phone to text and make some excuse, but I couldn't bring myself to type the words each time.

I tiptoed up the crunchy gravel to the sleeping olive grove. Jude was already sitting there. I could see his silhouette, his hand stretched and resting on his head. He turned to see me and relaxed, handing me a glass of his Midnight Serenade pinot noir, and I sat beside him, our legs slightly touching.

Like Russian Valley's signature home fragrance spray, the night air was clear and aromatic. I could taste it.

"So, where's Lara?"

"She's gone home. I said I was tired."

"Are you tired?"

"No, Elle, I'm not tired."

He leaned in towards me and kissed me deeply. I floated up above reality. The easiest thing in the world was to let this situation go where we both wanted it to go. To stay in Sonoma and love this man how he deserved to be loved.

"Jude, this is a mess. It isn't right doing this or even being with you like this when you are still with Lara."

"I'll sort it all out tomorrow, OK?"

"But you know I'm going home soon. Please don't break it off for me. Do it for you. We don't know where this is going with us, do we?"

He looked down at his boots.

"Let's find out."

I looked up, and the universe seemed endless in the night sky above us, full of possibilities. Yet, I was sitting with the most perfect guy I'd ever met, but there was no way I could stay and end up right back in the same place I was before. The old me was in a parallel universe, living someone else's life. This was my chance. I intended to grab it with both hands.

"We shouldn't do this, Jude. My heart is at odds with my brain, but it's time I listened to my brain. You're amazing, but you have a girlfriend, and I have stuff to do, so I can't stay here right now."

We sat quietly until I broke the silence.

"After the degree's finished, I'm considering France to travel and learn about wine in a different terroir. It will be hard to rest until I do it. A job at a Champagne house in Épernay would be the dream. It's a long shot, but who knows?"

He nodded. It was a catch twenty-two. The vineyard was his life, and there was no escaping it. He couldn't leave it and work this out with me for an extended period. We hardly knew each other, so neither had the agency to ask the other for anything.

Out of rational ideas, we both agreed to let fate work it out.

My stomach made a loud rumble, and Jude laughed.

"What? Jude, I'm starving. Do you have any food? I'm serious; I might pass out if I don't eat soon."

We trailed back to the house, and he made me a crispy omelette. I sat on the other side of the counter, watching him pad about in the kitchen.

"So, you cook too?"

"I don't have an exhaustive repertoire, but I can make anything with eggs, and you missed out on my signature pastrami sandwich."

"Soufflé?" I asked as I nearly fell off my bar stool.

"Are you OK there? Do you need a seatbelt?"

"Hey, you! Stop making fun of me! How are you not married already, Jude?"

"Ha! No exciting story there; never met the right girl at the right time."

"And the pattern continues," I said.

He dropped me home. We left each other with all the words still floating around in our heads but never reaching our lips. Despite knowing the romance was going nowhere, I still lay awake all night, thinking about how it could work. I had to be realistic and couldn't see how, even if he broke it off with Lara.

I had to concentrate on my goal. Becoming an exceptional winemaker.

After giving up on the futile attempt at sleep, I walked to the kitchen, stuck the coffee pot on, and walked out to the deck. Luis followed me and sat before me on the table, yawning and licking his lips. I stared into his green eyes and wished I was a cat. Life had no complications, just where the next meal and cuddle came from.

"Being a human is exhausting, Luis. Can we switch?"

"Aunty Elle," whispered Walter as he approached quietly, "Luis doesn't understand English."

"Oh, I know, Walter. Sometimes, you just need a good sounding board."

"What's a soundboard?"

"You know when you have an idea and want to check with someone else if it's good?"

"Well, it's not a good idea, Aunty Elle! I don't want you to be a cat. You couldn't get me cereal."

"Is that a massive hint, Walter?"

We avoided each other at work. The drink had made us both brave, but Jude would default to the easiest route like most guys. Nothing was hard about having a beautiful girlfriend on tap just up the road in

Napa.

Working out on the vines and helping to prune and cut out the older wood, I found the ritualistic nature of it therapeutic. My mind was clearer after a few hours in the fresh air. This thing with Jude, whatever it was, would soon be a fond memory.

At lunchtime, I escaped to the cellar for some silence. As I walked up the entrance path everything grew quiet. The cellar pulled me in like a cold magnet. Out of the corner of my eye, I saw a flash of lilac, and looked up to see Lara walking over a hill with a guy who worked for Jude at the vineyard. He was a quiet sort who kept to himself and had barely said two words to me since I'd arrived. They looked deep in conversation. She leaned into him, and I watched as they stopped on the brow of a hill, and she brushed back her gold hair and threw back her head as if she was laughing.

I pushed open the oak door, and the worn wood of it was soft against my palm. The ethereal cellar was a tonic, and the icy darkness enveloped me and slowed my heart rate as the silence washed over me like an alcoholic church.

As I turned into a tunnel, there stood Jude. I could hear my heartbeat and thought he could hear it, too.

We stood smiling at each other. There was no awkwardness in the silence, just an understanding that we were both doing the same thing simultaneously, like some karmic plan.

"Awkward," I said.

"Oh god, I've been avoiding you all day," he said. "Can I be honest?

I think I'm in love with you."

It didn't even surprise me; I was in the same boat. I sat on a stone bench and rubbed my neck. Jude walked behind me, massaging it, then bent down and kissed it. I turned and pulled him down to me.

"Did you break it off with Lara?"

"Not yet. I'm bad at this kind of stuff."

"She was outside before. I saw her talking to that quiet guy that works for you. I don't even know his name. Moody, silent, hair in a quiff at the front."

"Oh, yeah, they went to school together. Was Lara outside here?"

"No, no, a little way off and walking away. God, I wish I didn't feel like this."

"How do you feel?"

"I think you know. Do many people come in here?"

"Nah, there won't be anyone in here for a bit. I've got a place we can go," Jude said, leading me to a small dead end of one tunnel.

We had to squeeze into the space past a pile of supplies. Ordinarily, I would have felt claustrophobic. We kissed for longer than I had ever kissed anyone, and it was too late. My brain gave up trying to fight my heart.

"Do you want to do this?"

I didn't speak but grabbed for his belt and kissed him again; there was no doubt in his mind this was what I wanted, and I forgot every complication we faced. It was all white noise.

Outside the cellars, we sat on the wooden bench in silence. I was the

M. J. PARFITT

first to break it.

"I love you too, Jude, but I don't see how we can make this into what we both want it to be. The old me wouldn't go back to finish my degree. After all, it's not every day you meet the perfect man. But I have to go back, and I have to become a winemaker. I can't ask you to wait for me, but if, by some miracle, someone hasn't already snapped you up when all this is done. Shall we give it a go?"

"Well, let's promise each other that, then. Let me finish things with Lara. If you like, I could visit you in the UK, and France if that's where you end up, and you can come here for holidays. It'll be hard, but other people do it, so why can't we?"

Resting my head on his shoulder, I breathed in his cedar warmth and felt my life fall apart at the seams. Leaving was going to kill me. The pain of Zero cheating on me paled in the shade of this new emotion. I hadn't ever loved Zero. I might have grown to, but he'd damaged every nerve in my body when he cheated; he wiped it all out. I'd never loved a man until now and I finally understood the emotion behind every heartbreaking love song ever written.

Tempranillo

The day before the pop-up restaurant, I finally took one of Angus's FaceTime calls.

"Hi, Elle. How's it all going?"

"Fine, yeah, great. How about you? You must have some spare time now you're not filming me. You don't give up easy, do you?"

I could tell he was blushing as he dropped his head. He looked sad, but I reminded myself he had made me look like the complete twit. I fiddled with a biro and kept tapping it on a Post-it note.

"Look, I'm sorry. I was going to tell you all about it the night Lucy told us she had cancer, and then I couldn't; it was the wrong time. I want to explain. It's not what you think."

"Really? Strangers approach me in the tasting room, taking photos, asking if I'm the 'TikTok girl.' Can you imagine? Kill me now."

"Will you talk to me properly when you come back? Please don't move out."

"Not sure we can move past this, and never thought I'd say that to you. You've blindsided me. It'll take time for me to come to terms with what you've done. Sorry, loads going on here. I have to go. Bye, Angus."

My anger didn't stop me from worrying about him. He hadn't spoken to his family in years; all he had was me, Lucy, and a couple of friends he used to fly with on Ryanair. I took a big breath and wiped a stray tear from the corner of my eye. I headed off to the vineyard to meet Holly, Nick, and Jude for a run-through of the following night's dinner service.

Lara approached me in the cool air of the foyer of La Vallée and tilted her head to one side.

"Is this some new makeup trend I don't know about?"

Unable to understand what Lara was getting at, I rummaged in my bag for a mirror. It wasn't jumping out at me, and the harder I looked, the deeper it went into hiding. Tipping out the contents of the bag on the travertine-tiled floor—a cat toy, fifteen hair ties, a banana, a hotel room key, a fork, a pinecone, a Spanish dictionary, a torch, a cork, a leaf, a small marble—a theme emerged. I knew Walter must have been stuffing things into my bag when I found a squished-up Jaffa Cake. Jude walked towards me, bent to help me pick everything up, and laughed at the weird contents.

"What's all this?"

"Oh, stop! This is all Walter. Well, most of it is."

We looked up and laughed, and he laughed even more as he studied my face. He picked up a packet of pocket tissues from the debris left on the floor and tried to wipe something away from my eye.

"I think it's blue ink. It's not coming off. I miss you," said Jude.

"It's OK. I've got it."

I stuffed everything into the bag, rushed to the bathroom, leaned on the closed door, and held my breath. Lara was still here.

As Holly arrived, I walked out of the bathroom, and Jude was still holding a squished Jaffa Cake.

"You like Jaffa Cakes, Jude? They are my favourite too!" exclaimed Walter.

Holly looked puzzled, but there was no time to explain today.

Holly and Nick had staged the barn with rustic, bleached wooden farmhouse tables, crisp white linens, fresh wild flowers, big white pillar candles, and sparkling vintage cutlery with engraved handles. It took my breath away.

I absorbed the oaky warmth of the place. The sunlight hit the room, making subtle shadows here and there and fractions of rainbows as the light caught the cutlery. A team of chefs were busy prepping in the kitchen under Holly's expert supervision. She hadn't missed a beat.

"Wow, you've left me speechless, guys. Hey, this would make a great wedding venue, Jude. Put that on the list for next week. Call up some wedding planners and put the feelers out. There's another income stream for you—even a film location. I knew a girl who used to rent out her house for films and magazine shoots. It was quite lucrative."

"Elle, slow down, one thing at a time. I can't keep up with your ideas. I'm unsure what my dad will think when he sees all this. He's old school. It was always just about the wine when he ran it."

"Yeah, and it's a shame life can't be like that anymore, Jude, but you want this place to survive and compete, and it's how it has to be these days."

Holly stared at me like I was a stranger to her. She had never heard me talk about business or anything remotely professional. Then I saw her looking at the ink stain on my eyelid as she gave me a knowing smile.

We had sixty bookings, over two sittings, the following night. Jude had done a stellar job of promoting the event in Sonoma. It would be hard work but lucrative when we weighed up the potential wine sales. I had arranged for shuttle buses to transport people back to their accommodation to push the wine consumption up even further. We'd even opened a second barn and converted it into a temporary wine bar with a guitarist so the diners could stay longer after their meals. Nick had the idea of an ordering menu for home deliveries if someone wanted a case or two delivered. I was nervous. If this didn't work out, I had dragged Holly and Nick into it, and Jude's mum and dad would be coming. A lot was riding on it.

Holly had a horrendous headache. I dashed around to find Advil and Tylenol before it became a full-blown migraine. I couldn't afford for her to be off her game tonight. Plus, I wanted her to enjoy it. They would go home soon, back to normality, and I wanted her to savour the rush of all this and bottle it up for when her life was back to school drop-offs and packed lunches.

Jude and I welcomed the first guests, and one was George, Jude's dad. His eyes filled with tears, and he hugged Jude and said he was proud. Jude soaked it all up, and I could see relief flooding over him.

"It's all about evolution, Jude. I've been giving it a lot of thought lately. That's why we are all here, after all. And I hear we have you to thank for this, Elle? Amazing job. It sounds like you'll have a distinguished career in winemaking."

"Will you return to us when you've finished your degree?" asked his mum. I thought she winked at me, but I wasn't sure.

I blushed and brushed off the compliment, pushing everything back to Jude, who looked attractive in his chino jeans and white linen shirt. It was too much. I would die by a thousand cuts without his love and eternal admiration. Yet, I knew it was a lost cause when I had seen Lara leaving again only that morning.

"Oh, I don't know where I'll end up. But I'd love to come back one day."

I saw a dark shadow flash over Jude's face as he helped his dad and mum to a nearby table, and then he returned.

"Hey, did I tell you Mark's coming? How amazing is that?" said Jude.

"Mark, aka rug cleaning guy?" I asked.

"Err, well yeah," said Jude.

"Why is it amazing? I thought he was a close friend?"

"Yeah, but it was a lot to ask with his schedule."

We cut the conversation short as guests arrived and had to be shown to their tables, and the night raced ahead. It was frantic and noisy, and we barely spoke to each other all evening except to communicate something vital, like a forgotten order.

I bumped into Mark as he was returning from the bathroom.

"Oh, hi! Hey, Mark, thanks for sorting out the rug clean. I think it's better than when I moved in."

"No problem. So sorry about all that. How's Lucy? I gave up trying to call her. I think I broke her message bank. Is she here? My life means nothing without her. Elle. Can you give her a message or something? I've sent her a million peonies but nothing."

He looked like he'd lost weight, and his eyes seemed to be sunken in his face. He'd lost a little of his sparkle. I looked at his wrist tattoo as he ran his hand over it.

"Err, no. I can't believe I'm going to say this, but look, Lucy's been sick. That's why she's been avoiding your calls."

When I told him about the cancer diagnosis and double mastectomy, he cried, not a solitary tear but a waterfall. He sat on a wine crate in the corridor, not caring he was wearing white jeans and not giving a second thought to the beautiful lady peering over the crowd, trying to figure out where he had disappeared.

"But why didn't she tell me? I would have dropped everything for her. I could have been there. She didn't give me a chance. And why didn't you tell me, Darkling? Before, when I came over to the cottage?"

I hadn't known who Mark was to Lucy. I didn't know if it was my information to tell a stranger, but now, on reflection, perhaps I'd made a mistake. Maybe I should have ignored Lucy.

"Shit, I'm sorry; I didn't know what to say or if I should say anything. She didn't tell us about you and made it clear I wasn't to tell anyone."

"But why didn't Jude tell me?"

"Tell you what?" asked Jude as he walked past.

"About Lucy."

"What about Lucy?"

They both stared at me with hostility when Mark explained to Jude how sick Lucy was. I pushed away the urge to cry and ran outside into the chilled night air, gasping.

I stared at the inky sky, which looked like a giant stardust fork had pricked it and considered all my decisions. They were tiny compared with the great expanse of the universe above my head, but they weren't my choices, and I was now pissed at being stuck in the middle like this. Lucy would have been angry if I'd told them before; now, I had told them anyway, and she would lose it.

Storming back in, I found Jude and Mark shell-shocked in the hall-way.

"Look, you two, it wasn't my information to give. Lucy told me not to tell anyone. Now, she may never speak to me again, so that's net zero on the friends front, what with Angus betraying me."

The restaurant grew quieter as people drifted off home. I returned to say goodbye to guests and check that everything went smoothly as we prepared to wrap up the night. I gave a convincing performance as a composed host, even when Holly asked me what was wrong.

There were too many balls in the air: Lucy, Angus, me and Jude, and my uncertain future. It all overwhelmed me.

M. J. PARFITT

The car ride home was silent. Holly kept trying to discover what had happened, and I changed the subject each time. We paid the young babysitter and said awkward goodbyes. Holly made hot chocolate with whisky because she could tell I needed it. We put up our tired, aching feet on the ottoman.

Nick came in a bit later. He'd offered to clear up and let us go home. He threw the keys on the credenza and picked up Luis for a snuggle.

"Hot chocolate? Shouldn't that be a glass of Champagne? What a success! I'm so proud of both of you."

"Well, it does have whiskey in it," I said. "It's not as lame as it looks."

He had stepped up; he was the father figure of our small family now, and Dad had been right about him.

Sometime later, with a soft tap on the door, Jude appeared with a bottle of wine and an apologetic smile. Holly and Nick said their goodnights after briefly chatting about the night and agreeing on its success.

"Oh, before you go, guys. I wanted to ask if you'd like to make this permanent arrangement?"

I knew this was his plan all along. They said they needed to discuss it, but I could tell they'd already decided. I wondered if it was partly Jude's way of keeping me in his life.

After they had gone off to bed, Jude turned to me.

"You have a friend, Elle. You have me," he said.

"Oh, I'm sorry. You were both angry, and I was scared you wouldn't forgive me. I don't have many friends, and I want to keep the ones I have. It wasn't my news to share."

"You still should have told me, even if she said not to. She's one of my closest friends. I'm devastated. Will she be OK?"

"The doctors have said she will be. I've been FaceTiming her every day. I know she feels bad about not telling you, but I think she thought you'd tell Mark."

"Which I most definitely would have," said Jude. "I'm going back to the UK with you if that's OK. It's not right carrying on like normal when she's sick."

"What about Lara? I see you haven't broken up with her yet."

"Hmm, that's another problem. I was going to, like we talked about, but now. Oh, Elle, she says she's pregnant, and fuck, I don't know what to do. It's a mess. I was ready to end it, and then she dropped this on me," he said.

He flopped down on the couch. Of course, Lara was pregnant.

I had been gradually falling in love with Jude since the first day he took us to Napa, or even before in New York, like the pinot out in the oak barrels, soaking up all the intensity inside, bit by bit. It was something real, and now someone had punctured the barrel, and the wine had evaporated as though it had never existed. Any glimmer of hope for a future with him was gone, however remote it had been in the first place, but I knew the world wouldn't end. The complexities of life had hardened me. I wasn't a pessimist, but I'd become more of a realist slash optimist instead of a staunch optimist.

"Oh. I mean. Wow! That's—um..."

I looked away, not wanting him to see the tears.

He stood and held me close. I knew he had tears in his eyes, too. I felt his hot breath on my neck, and he tried to kiss me, but I pulled away and walked into the kitchen.

I poured him a glass of wine, and we sat for hours talking, laughing, and listening to Fleetwood Mac as though nothing had happened between us and were simply friends. We both accepted that we were soul mates, with a sad ending to our love story.

"I know this is a mess, but I enjoy hanging out with you, Elle. You always cheer me up," he said. "Do you wanna go to the movies tomorrow? We both deserve a day off after tonight. Please? It will help to take my mind off this Lara stuff," he said.

"Uh, sure."

When I thought this sounded like an odd date, he added, "Ask Holly and Nick, too. My mum can look after Walter."

I was happy to take the crumbs if they were all I could have from Jude. He was a good friend, and I wanted to be in his company. I even toyed with the idea that Lara had orchestrated the whole thing, perhaps sensing Jude pulling away from her. But it wasn't my problem anymore. Once again, I had complete freedom and intended to use it wisely.

After Jude left, I cried to myself. I wished I hadn't fallen for him. Life would have been so simple without the added complication. I snuggled up to Luis, and Holly stuck her head around the lounge room door.

"Everything OK?"

"No, everything is not OK, sis. I'm in love with Jude, and Lara is pregnant."

"Oh, yikes! Poor Jude. That's not good news. And poor you. I thought you had fallen for him and vice versa. What's he gonna do?"

"He'll do the right thing. You know that as well as me, and that's why I love him."

Mourvedre

We queued for tickets for a new blockbuster action movie, *Trident Star.* As was customary here, we bought popcorn and cokes in gigantic sizes. I was hanging on every word Jude said. He was handling the awkwardness a little easier than me. I was putting on a great show, but inside I was empty. Holly and I chatted, joked about the portion sizes, and compared everything to London. The opening credits came up on the screen, and Nick had to hush us.

I spat out my popcorn all over Jude.

"But it's thingy. I mean, it looks like Mark."

Jude laughed, and the people behind him told him to put a sock in it.

"How did you not know?" asked Jude.

"Oh my god, I feel like such a twat. Mark must think I'm an idiot."

"No, he said you are the most genuine person he's ever met, and I was a fool if I didn't ask you out."

I was glad he couldn't see the blush on my face in the dark theatre. Now it all made sense; why Lucy had been quiet about the whole thing. I watched as Mark acted his way through the blockbuster and filled the entire screen with his charisma. I was desperate to call Angus or turn to the people behind us and say, "I know him!"

As we walked out into the sunlight, Jude checked his phone and returned a missed call.

"Hey, you must have a sixth sense or something. Elle and I were talking about you. OK, OK, yeah, I'll ask her," he said, putting the phone beside him.

"Mark says he's going to fly out on his private jet tonight to London to see Lucy, and do we want to go along with him?"

"Wait, what, like today?" I said.

"I mean, yeah, I guess."

"What about the vineyard?"

"Well, I'm hoping," he said, turning to Holly and Nick, "these guys will manage everything. Holly has plenty to do if we want to make this restaurant permanent."

I looked on in amazement as my family's lives changed. Still, I couldn't help puzzling where I fit into all this, and I wasn't keen on watching Jude and Lara settle into marital bliss. But I had to forget all that for now.

❧

It was evening by the time we headed to the airport. Mark swung by and collected us in his movie-star black SUV.

"Hey Mark, I'm sorry I didn't recognise you. We watched your latest movie today, and I feel like an idiot."

"What? What do you mean? It was like a breath of fresh air. You made me think about a few things. I mean, the money, the lifestyle, it's amazing, but all the rest of the bullshit you can keep. You not recognising me made me miss the anonymity. That's the entire problem for Lucy. She hates it. Hates the lifestyle. I'll change a few things in my life if she'll have me."

Jude looked back at me with wide eyes.

"I saw that, man. I mean it. This sucks. If I meet a woman and fall in love, I can't let all this bullshit get in the way."

"Love? Wow, not a word I have ever heard you say," said Jude.

Mark's driver pulled into an airfield in Sonoma.

"Wait, what? We can go from here?" I asked.

"You betcha. We can pull up near the plane; there's virtually no crap like flying commercial," Mark said.

"Perhaps you should rethink your exit from fame and fortune, Mark," I said.

As I boarded the small flight of steps, trying to look as cool as I could manage, I lost the footing in my ballet flats, and Jude put a firm hand behind me to stop me from falling.

"So tempted to say something right now. How are you not the most proficient among us at walking up plane steps?" said Jude.

Onboard passport control merely entailed handing our passports to the captain.

I had spent so much time saying goodbye to Holly, Nick, and Walter that I had forgotten to say goodbye to Sonoma. My heart-strings pulled as we lifted off above the vines until they were thin green beanstalks below. I didn't know when I'd see them again.

"This is weird. I'm in a movie," I said, tucking into a bagel and washing it down with vintage Veuve.

Laying back in the plush leather recliner, I closed my eyes, and Jude covered me with a blanket.

"Darkling is cool," said Mark.

"Yeah, it's a problem," said Jude.

Keeping my eyes shut, I willed myself to sleep.

Dreaming of flights, movies, and California, I slept for eight hours and woke in confusion to find Jude and Mark playing cards.

"Sleep well?" asked Mark. "How do you do it?"

"Melatonin and Champagne always work for me. Old flying habits die hard."

Feeling a dribble at the corner of my mouth, I tried to wipe it away. In the bathroom, my mascara was sitting under both eyes like two black eyes, my hair had big knots and was sticking up at all angles.

The glass cabinet contained supplies such as cotton pads and small bottles of Chanel toiletries. Sitting on the toilet seat, I rubbed some hand cream in. It was a million miles away from Angus and my lemon and sugar trick. He would be at Lucy's if he wasn't on a trip and I didn't know what to say to him or how to say it.

Mark and Jude were still playing cards.

"Don't you know this game, Elle?" asked Mark. "Did you never go backpacking? Thought all you Brits did, like a rite of passage or something."

"Oh, missed that one; when I started flying, there was no point. I'm not really into slumming it."

"OK, I give up, card hustler," said Jude after I beat them at Shithead for several rounds.

We spent the rest of the flight sampling some expensive Napa wines Mark had gotten loaded.

"You know I envy your life, Jude," he said. "When I was at the vineyard the other night, I thought, this is cool, man. If I wanted to buy a vineyard in Sonoma, would you help me find one?"

"Help create more competition. Hey, I don't know about that! No, yeah, of course I will. I know of a couple, but you're probably looking at twenty million for a good one."

"Yeah, I figured," said Mark. "I was hoping to convince a business partner to come in on it with me."

He winked as he said this, confusing me and Jude.

We landed in London after lunchtime. It had a distinct scent from California, it was more industrial and metallic. Being home after this long was surreal, and I was excited to see Lucy. A car awaited us on the tarmac, and we headed into London to surprise her. Mark handed us both chilled sparkling water, but I wanted something stronger to give me Dutch courage to face Angus.

Jude and Mark kept asking me where we were in London and asking for the names of buildings we drove past. It was Jude's first time in the UK, and he was taking it all in. I tried to imagine what I would think if I lived in Sonoma all my life in a fairy-tale vineyard and I saw London for the first time. I couldn't imagine it, but I guessed seeing all the statues and palatial buildings was strange. Mark had the driver go right through London so Jude could see the hustle and bustle.

"How do you cope with all this traffic?" he said.

"Well, I don't cope with it, Jude. I live in Brighton, and before that, I lived in Surrey. It's busier than Sonoma, but not as bad as this."

"Do you think you will live here, though, one day?"

"I don't think so. And now you've stolen my family, so I guess I'm going to have to move to California at some point, aren't I?"

"Yeah, that was my master plan."

"Maybe you could manage my vineyard, Elle. I won't have a fucking clue," said Mark.

"Yeah, and I can babysit for Jude in the evenings."

The car was deadly silent, and I regretted the words as soon as they slipped from my mouth.

"What? Babysit?" said Mark.

"I haven't told him yet, Elle."

"Oh, god, sorry."

"Lara's pregnant."

"Lara? Oh man, I thought you two—oh," said Mark.

Lucy lived in a beautiful penthouse in SW10. We pulled outside the light brick Georgian façade and buzzed a few times, but there was no reply.

"You think she's out?" asked Mark.

"Hmm. Hold on, I have a key," I said, rummaging in my large sack.

"Oh, here we go," said Jude. "Watch out for flying Jaffa Cakes!"

"What's a fucking Jaffa Cake?" asked Mark.

After rifling and pulling out countless keys, I found Lucy's.

"What the hell are all these keys, Elle?" asked Jude.

"Mostly, I don't know."

"You look like you live in Windsor Castle or something," said Mark.

We unlocked the door with one key, and Mark called out.

"Sssh, Mark, it's the apartment on the top floor; Lucy doesn't own the whole thing. There's a cranky bitch neighbour down here who will fuck you up if you make any noise at all. No life—one of those. When Lucy moved in here and the movers were going up and down, they used the door mat to keep the door open. She kept coming out and moving it back," I said, loud enough that Mrs Thomas could overhear if she were being her usual nosey self.

"Where's the lift?" he asked.

"It's a listed building; there is no lift; get ready to lug this lot up four flights," I said.

Winded and red-faced, we finally made it after a few stops to lean on the waxed wooden bannisters. I unlocked the door to the apartment.

"I see how she keeps so fit now," said Mark.

"Wow," said Jude. "You would never think a place like this was inside such an old building."

"Well, she does have deep pockets!" I said.

We called out, but everything was silent. I could hear the faintest buzz of music.

"Come on," I said, "I think I know where she is."

We walked up another flight of stairs.

"I'm not sure we should go into her bedroom," said Jude.

"No, we're not; follow me."

We climbed one final set of stairs into a glass opening, which led us to a rooftop garden, and there, curled up under a blanket, next to Angus lounging on a nearby chair, was Lucy. She stopped talking mid-sentence and, mouth agape, looked at us in disbelief.

"What the absolute fuck?" said Lucy.

Angus made a jerky movement in his chair.

"For fuck's sake, Angus, you're always falling off a chair," I said.

"Elle why is Mark Trevino on the roof?" he said.

"Why don't you ask our friend here," I said, patting Lucy's legs under the blanket. "Seems like you're not the only one here who's been economical with the truth."

He ignored me and looked at Lucy for an explanation. With tears in his eyes, he got one when Mark rushed to Lucy, cradled her hands, and buried his face in her hair, crying with the raw emotion of everything he hadn't let go of until now.

"Come on, you two, let's go to the kitchen and leave these lovebirds. I need some wine," I said. "It's been at least two hours since we've had a glass."

We recounted the whole escapade to Angus, who sat in silence.

"Pinch me, will you? I mean, even that you're here in the flesh is too much for me to deal with, but you bring a movie star with you?"

I laughed and then reminded myself I was mad at him.

"Guys, I'm hungry. Do you think if I get some takeout, everyone will eat?" said Jude.

"I think there's a high chance of that, Jude. You want me to come with you?" I said.

"Nah, you two need to sort some stuff out. I'm getting out of your hair for a bit. If I don't return in an hour, send out a search party. Don't kill each other! Do I need to hide the kitchen knives?"

We stared at each other in a standoff. Neither wanted to say the wrong thing, but knew if we didn't say something, we would destroy our entire relationship for good.

"So, let's have it then," I said.

"I'm sorry, but listen, OK? I can't lose you like this. It's tearing me apart. I was so bloody angry when Zero did all that to you, and I was partly responsible because I was on the trip. We didn't know he was already seeing Alex on the side."

"Alright, you don't need to rub it in," I said.

"Sorry. You're like my sister. I wanted to make him pay; when we planned the prank at The Ivy, I filmed it; well, I got the other table to film it and uploaded it to TikTok. It got a lot of views. I mean a lot. I've been using this hashtag, LXIX. It's Roman numerals for—"

"Oh, gross! I know what number that is, Angus."

"Well, it worked. The Chinese obviously have a good sense of humour. You were such a popular heroine. I think it's because social media sets everyone up to feel like crap. No one is perfect like all these inane influencers would have you think, and then along you came, and people thought, oh well, there's someone else making a complete tit out of themselves. They could relate to you. I was angry because you gave up your job for me and you had to rent out your place. It was all so unfair, and let's be honest, you do some funny things. I was making a compilation of your awkward moments just for us. Then I started sharing them, and #La Fille Maladroit was born out of a trip to Paris. The sponsors came knocking, and it made so much money I kept going. I did it so you could pay off your apartment."

"You did it so I could pay off my what?" I said. "With a TikTok account, or do you have me on Only Fans too?"

"I know you're hopeless with checking your bank account; guessing you haven't checked it lately?" he said.

"What are you on about? Now things are less liquid, I have to be on top of my finances."

"Check it now, Elle. Just to be sure."

"Oh, for fuck's sake, why are we going through this performance? Say sorry, Angus, and we can move on."

"Sorry for not telling you, but I'm not sorry for the money. You're free now. Do whatever you want," Angus said.

Clicking on my banking app, my eyes had trouble focusing on the figures: two hundred and sixty-eight thousand pounds. My eyes continued to blur, and I strained them and then looked at Angus quizzically.

"Is this for real? Well, fuck me," I said, falling back into the couch. "Who knew, fucking TikTok! Two hundred and sixty grand. Are you shitting me? But I can't keep it. You have it. I want you to leave that job. And I'm sorry for ever doubting you. You should have told me. I feel so bad now."

"Well, I tried to, to be fair. No, it's yours now. It was all about you. You think you are a clumsy fool, but people love you. They love authenticity. It's why it worked."

"Well, if you are sure, but there's one condition, OK? You're putting together the book we discussed, and we are self-publishing it if we have to. No arguing. It's happening, or I won't take a penny."

We hugged, and he held me so tight it made me tear up.

"How am I going to repay you for everything? Not just for the money but thinking you could ever want to hurt me. It was so stupid."

"Oh god, I've missed you," we both said together.

Jude let himself back in with my key, and we unpacked the Chinese food.

"So, what did I miss? I don't see any black eyes. Can I assume we are all friends?"

"Angus is a fucking social media mastermind and has paid off my mortgage, Jude. You know, normal friend stuff. Oh, and he's publishing a book."

"No friggin way?" asked Jude. "For real? Wow."

"Yep. Angus is my guardian angel," I said.

Then I cried for the rescued friendship, missing family, and sick friend, not to mention losing the love of my life to an Instagram-influencing twat. I was inconsolable, and there was nothing Angus or Jude could do to stop the tears.

"Sorry," I said, drying my wet eyes. "I don't know what's happening. It's been a lot."

"Why do I feel like I'm missing something?" said Angus.

He kept asking questions about Mark and the private jet. He didn't understand why I didn't know what Mark Trevino looked like. It was never-ending; my head was about to explode. Angus kept looking from me to Jude with an intrigued look. Ultimately, Jude was unnerved and suggested we go to a pub down the street. There was no sign of Lucy and Mark.

It was quiz night, and we rocked up in time to enter a team. We were not great because none of us knew the answers to the sports questions. Still, whenever we had a correct answer, Angus would shout it out instead of writing it down, frustrating, and amusing Jude and me.

We ordered tequila shots, and Angus loosened up enough to ask what he'd been dying to ask all night.

"So, spill. What's going on between you two?

I kicked him under the table, but he ignored me and carried on.

"Angus, we're star-crossed lovers," said Jude.

"We are not lovers, Angus. I want to make that clear. It was one time!"

"Lara's pregnant," said Jude.

"Oh," said Angus, seeing the deflation in Jude's face, "that's, um, whatever you want it to be, I guess."

"I want to be with Elle, but the universe is malevolent."

"Fuck the universe!" said Angus, holding up his glass. He squeezed my hand under the table.

Thinking I'd like to remember this night, I stopped drinking after the tequila. A headache wouldn't be a welcome visitor the next morning with jet lag, too. Jude and Angus chatting together had been fun to watch. Together, my two favourite men were a sight that warmed my heart. It was a memorable and impromptu night; despite the pub's sticky tables and stale beer fetidness, I digested every detail for when I was sad and needed it again.

We could still have an affair, but to put another person through what I'd experienced was not something I could ever do. It was scary to be alone, but worse, to die of a broken heart. Complications like an ex-wife or kids would never interest me. Many people could handle the extra dimension it added to a relationship, but not me.

When I had been flying, sometimes the thought of dying in a plane crash would come out of nowhere. That hopeless desperation of something being entirely out of my control came over me now when thinking about Jude. Distance was the great healer of heartbreak, so I hoped the Pacific Ocean would suffice.

"Come on, you two. I'm tired, and I think we've given the love-birds enough time alone," I said.

We walked up the road, arms linked, laughing and joking, with Angus singing the *Friends* theme song at the top of his voice down the road to Lucy's apartment.

Mrs Thomas, walking her immaculate Bichon Frise, tutted at him; even the dog seemed to look at Angus with disdain, and he bowed and said, "Apologies, madam."

He reminded me of the chimney sweep from *Mary Poppins*.

"I've missed you so much, Angus. Life is not the same without you."

Ambulo Blanc

Two weeks later, Angus and I waved goodbye to our friends as they left for San Francisco. Lucy and Mark were going back to find a vineyard. She would sell most of her shares in Ignite and step down as CEO, hoping Gerald might take on the role. Mark wanted to dial back on the acting and concentrate on producing, writing, and the new vineyard. Jude was returning to face Lara and whatever life he would try to make with her and their child.

Jude and I struggled to say goodbye. The pain was physical. It ripped into our throats and our hearts. It was brutal, and Angus, Lucy, and Mark saw it. They looked away, and I could see Angus grabbing his cheeks and looking down at the floor when I caught his eye.

We hadn't so much as kissed since he'd found out about Lara, but that didn't stop me from wanting him to try. I wasn't sure I had the willpower in me to say no.

He embraced me and whispered in my ear.

"It will always be you."

He placed a small box in my pocket, and I looked into his eyes, and we said nothing else. He walked through security and didn't look back.

"Well, it's just you and me, kid," said Angus.

He squeezed my hand and pulled me out from the terminal, and we headed off to catch a train back to Lucy's.

"I wish we could buy a ticket and get on that plane, too," I said.

"Why are they flying commercial? I don't think I could be arsed to walk around like Mark in the dark glasses and cap all the time," said Angus.

"Good question. I didn't think about it. I know Mark booked first class. Could be the bed—he's so thoughtful he probably wants Lucy to get lots of sleep."

"You'll be OK, Elle."

"I know that. Fucking life, though. Just so hard. He offered me a job at Vallée Estate after I graduate. How awful would that be, seeing them together every day?"

I stuck my hand in my pocket for the box and pulled it out.

Inside was a delicate gold necklace with a tiny gold wine glass and bottle hanging from it.

"He must have brought that with him," said Angus. "That says a lot, doesn't it? Here, let me put it on for you."

I looked down at it and touched the small glass as if rubbing Aladdin's lamp, willing Jude to return to me.

With the car loaded for the trip back to Brighton, Angus and I locked up Lucy's apartment. She had said we could stay there, but we both wanted to go home to all our stuff and chill out. I'd missed Vin and Heidi, and we both agreed this wasn't our life.

As we were leaving, I tripped on a clay pot, and it shattered near

Mrs Thomas's door, which opened so quickly the old bat must have been hiding behind it. She was angry as usual, but Angus rattled off in French before she spoke.

"Nous sommes désolés mais nous ne vous comprenons pas. Cette fille est vraiment maladroit," he said with a flourish.

The old lady turned red from the neck up and gave Angus and me an evil glare.

"Home at last," said Angus.

We had both been staying at Lucy's, and I hadn't returned to Brighton yet.

"So, you didn't pack me up?"

"You won't escape my friendship, Elle Darkling."

He threw a cushion at my head, which missed and knocked off a small plant on the side table.

"And she's back!" said Angus.

"There's a rather fine bottle of wine here for you to try," he called from the kitchen. "Claire and I went to a vineyard on our day off in Queenstown. It was called Muselet Wines—Ken, the owner, was a lovely bloke with a bloody good pinot. Light-bodied and delicate and full of complex flavours like cherry and raspberry, balanced by an earthy, mushroomy flavour and a touch of vanilla spice. But you're the expert. Let me know what you think."

"Angus, what have we done to you?"

M. J. PARFITT

Things returned to how they had been before California. I went to uni, Angus was frequently away on trips, and sometimes we had nights out with my uni friends or old flying pals.

I FaceTimed Lucy and Holly each week, got my head down and worked day and night, studying for my degree, and revising for exams.

"Jesus, Holly, what the heck are you feeding that child—he's a giant. I keep meaning to ask you—how's Jude?"

She was in the kitchen at Vallée. She looked over her shoulder and whispered.

"Um, yeah, OK. Jude's doing OK, I think."

And that was all I got. I hadn't been in touch with Jude except to thank him via text for the necklace, and he had just sent a heart emoji back, but that was the end of any communication we had.

"Did you get our flight details? Don't meet us at the airport, it's too far. We'll see you at the graduation ceremony, OK? I booked us all lunch after, and there's a spot for Angus."

"I feel bad; you coming all this way."

"Well, don't."

"We have to sort out the stuff in storage and the car. I owe you and Angus for packing it and dropping the car at Nick's dad's, so lunch is on us."

"It was nothing. You would have done the same."

I returned from uni one afternoon to find Angus waiting with a letter.

"So, when were you going to tell me?"

I felt the familiar motif of Châteaux Marguerite indented on the thick envelope.

"When there was something concrete to tell you, you know you'd be the first to know. It might be a 'Non, merci.'"

"We both know it won't be," he said as he wiped his tears. "Go on, open it."

It was like opening exam results.

"For god's sake, Elle, will you open it already?"

"OK, looks like I'm leaving in September. It's not far, it's why I chose France. You can visit whenever you like; it's close to Paris."

"I'm an orphan," he wailed.

"Oh, shut up. You are always away! And now you get to hightail it to Épernay for a Kir Royale with moi whenever you fancy. Imagine the events I can get you into. It will be so much fun. And honestly, Angus, you never know what might happen. You might land a fabulous job you can't turn down, and you might move away yourself."

I stood at the side of the stage with Vin and Heidi by my side. I was hot under my gown and fanned my face with the programme. This was it. Now, we had to go out and put everything into practice. Heidi was off to Tuscany, and Vin would head to La Mancha, where he would work for none other than Hilario Garcia. Lucy had put a good word in for him, and he'd gone to meet the man himself. He tapped his fingers on the side of his leg, and I knew, like me, he was eager to begin his career. Heidi's eyes were full of tears, but mine and Vin's were dry, and we couldn't wipe the smiles off our faces.

My name was called, and I approached the stage but became

distracted when I heard Walter call out my name as they handed over my certificate; it fluttered in slow motion to the first row of the audience. I held up my hands in defeat. Angus caught the whole thing on video by accident this time. There was no way this one would end up on TikTok.

Standing up, I tapped my glass.

"So, I've got something to tell you all. I've got a spot at a Champagne house in Épernay."

The table was silent except for Angus cheering. He stopped when no one else joined in.

"Oh, I'm sorry!" Holly said. "I'm happy for you. We just selfishly thought you'd come to Sonoma once you finished. I planned out the whole thing in my head."

My head slumped, and I sat back down, staring at the table.

"If it weren't for Lara, that would have been perfect. I think you know that. So, how is Jude? You barely mention him, and Lucy has been equally evasive."

I took a big gulp of Champagne.

"Oh god, we wanted to tell you the whole thing, but he insisted you had to finish the degree without burdening you," said Holly.

"What the fuck? Knowing what?" I said a little loudly.

"Oh my god, keep your voice down; people are staring," said Holly.

"Aunty Elle, why are you all grumpy now? Is it 'cause you lost that piece of paper?" said Walter.

We all laughed. Angus was in stitches.

"Oh my god, I love your family."

"Oh, come on, Angus, you are part of it. Let's stop the pretence. This is your family, too," said Holly.

Angus brushed away a tear, and I squeezed his hand.

"So, I'll tell you the whole shitty story. Don't fucking interrupt me, you two? Lara was—what would you say, Nick? Three months pregnant, and they were organising the wedding. She was being her usual ass of a self, a pathetic narcissist. Watching the guy get kicked to the curb each day was hard. It was all planned, and a week before the big day, Jude's dad had another stroke. He wanted him to be there; he said let's put it off for a few weeks until he's better. She throws a massive fit right in the foyer. She calls him pathetic and says he doesn't love her, blah, blah, blah. It carried on for so long that it was like an episode of *Days of Our Lives*. Then she says, I should have run away with Mark when I had the chance, and he's like—what the fuck? He gets in his car, goes to Mark and Lucy's place, and punches Mark in the face. Then Mark's like, What the fuck, man? And when he's calmed down, Mark says, what are you on about? I mean, no way! You're my best friend, and I can't stand Lara; she's everything I hate. So, Jude returns, and Miss Instagram is crying outside now, saying, where have you been? Can you imagine? We are all watching this from the barn—and he's like, to Mark's, and he said he wasn't ever with you and, she says, not that Mark. Mark, who works for you, and he goes quiet and says, is this baby even mine? And she says, no, it isn't. I don't think you have it in you! She gets in her car and fucks off. And that's it, except Jude has some mental health issues now. He's moody and angry all the time. I think partly because he lost you in the crossfire."

"You don't know that, Holly," said Nick. "I'm scared to broach any of this with him. He seems quite fragile right now."

"Oh, my god," said Angus. "This is unbelievable. You are right, it's so *Days of our Lives.*"

We all fell silent; even people at the adjacent table were listening in.

"Well, at least he's rid of the idiot, but why hasn't he contacted me? I was secretly hoping he'd come with you. I know it's stupid. We had something, you know?"

My phone beeped.

"Is it Zero again?" asked Angus.

"Zero?" said Holly. "What the hell does he want?"

"He's not giving up. I should see what he wants at some stage," I said.

"Why would you bother? He caused you so much pain. Block his number, Elle," said Holly.

I didn't want to block his number and wasn't sure why. He was giving off wounded animal vibes, and I had a whiff of a cheap ego boost or an easy revenge. I couldn't explain that to any of my family. It was such a complicated, emotion-fuelled situation. I knew they would never understand that it wasn't black and white.

"Elle, Nick and I need to thank you, and we don't think we've done that properly yet. You've changed our lives. You gifted us the opportunity of a lifetime with what you've done for Walter and us. It's hard to put it into words," said Holly.

"Well," I said, nodding at Angus. "We just need to sort this one, and I'll be happy."

Angus blushed and played with his beer mat.

"Elle told us what you did with the TikTok account. She's lucky to have you as a friend, Angus. There's something I wanted to talk to you about. Jude and I were chatting with Lucy last week, and there's a job for you in Sonoma if you want it. Both vineyards could share you as the social media slash marketing manager. What do you think?" said Holly, tilting her head to one side. "There's a house as part of the job at Lucy and Mark's vineyard—Castello di Amanté."

Angus's jaw dropped to the floor. He looked from Holly to me and back.

"Elle?"

It was a stroke of genius. Angus was bloody good at all the stuff the rest of us lacked the skills in. It was the perfect way to get him to move.

He jumped up, climbed onto the table, and danced on the spot.

"Aunty Elle," said Walter, "Why is Angus acting like a lunatic man?"

"You know, Walter. He feels chipper because he doesn't have to push the cart anymore or talk to Philips ever again!" I said, beaming at my friend.

My phone beeped again, and I replied to Zero this time. I texted under the table to avoid the inquisition I would get from everyone.

As Holly and Nick returned to their hotel and Angus headed back to Brighton, I told them I was meeting up with uni friends and headed off to meet Zero in Covent Garden.

I pushed through the crowd at the bar and saw him instantly. Something about him irritated me without even speaking to him. He was flirting with the bartender, and I could see it from the other side of the room. Nothing about him had changed. He was still wearing loafers with no socks, which I had always thought looked absurd in London. Yes, if you were a suave Italian zipping around Milan, you could carry it off, but it looked like you were trying too hard here. I turned around and went to walk away, but something made me turn back.

So here I was in this alien situation, caught betwixt meeting a stranger and someone I was once close to. There should be an actual word for it. Something like 'proximated.' He leaned over and kissed me on the cheek. He reeked of wine and 'Carolina Herrera Bad Boy.'

"So, Z—Hunter, how's Alex and the kids?"

He looked taken aback.

"Not good. We split up. The whole thing was a bloody big mistake. I had to see you. I've missed you so much. You look great."

"Come on, you're joking, right? What's this about?"

I took a gulp of wine and missed my mouth slightly.

"Elle, you don't change."

I wiped my mouth on a napkin and looked straight at him, trying to read his thoughts like I had done many times when we were together. I wasn't sure there were many thoughts in his head at all. He was like an automated machine devoid of emotion.

He looked astonished when I told him I had a spot at a Champagne house in Épernay.

"It's all so strange to me. You were never interested in wine when we were together."

"Um, well, I didn't think you were interested in fucking two people, but it turns out you were pretty good at it."

"Touché."

We chatted about my degree, the internship in Sonoma, and Holly moving there, and he was silent. The conversation was all one way.

Every time I asked about the kids or Alex, he changed the subject and talked about work or acquaintances we had in common. When he'd gone to order a bottle of wine, I purposely changed the order and asked for a Rhône Valley syrah.

"Don't worry, I'll pay for it," I said.

I held the glass by the stem, turned it towards the light, inhaled the bouquet, tasted it slowly, and half closed my eyes. He stared with his mouth wide open.

Outside the bar, as people pushed by us, he made a clumsy attempt at a kiss on the cheek lingering a second too long, and I agreed to meet him in Paris in October.

Nebbiolo

We had moving boxes in every room. Neither of us could find either of the tape guns we had bought.

"Damn it," I said, "I don't want to go down to the shop again."

"Found it!" shouted Angus. "One was in the fridge."

We collapsed in giggles and looked around at all our stuff. It was all going into storage. Angus had yet to learn how his job would work out, and I had no fixed abode.

"Look at us with our lives in boxes," I said. "Should we even be keeping it all? Will we even want it when we have somewhere to keep it?"

"Let's go down to the pub. I'm thirsty!" said Angus.

We sat in the Fox and Hounds beer garden and ate fish and chips, which tasted so good after the hard work of packing. The sun broke through the chill in the air as we pulled up some chairs to a mildewy wooden table.

"I am going to miss fish and chips."

"Oh, for god's sake, Angus! You're not going on an expedition to Antarctica."

"OK. You know what I mean. I'm nervous about the job, and it's not like someone there doing it already can guide me—I'll have to make it up. Hey, and anyway, Miss 'I can't leave home without a jar of marmite.' Talk about pot and kettle."

"You'll be OK. I know you will. We know you are a maestro with social media, don't we? And your photography skills are second to none."

He punched me in the arm.

"What did Monty say at work when you quit? You never mentioned it."

"Yeah, that's because he said nothing, like I had only been there a week, not seven years. They handed me a letter about how many miles I had flown."

"Wow? Can't say as I ever got one of those."

"I have something for you," said Angus, digging into his pocket.

He pulled out some shiny wings.

"Because you didn't keep yours, and all you got was a bottle opener!"

"And I still have the bottle opener, Angus. You have to admit, it's a damn good one. I'm taking it to Épernay."

I turned the wings over in my hands.

"Angus, are you sure? Don't you want to keep them?"

"Nah, I want you to have them to remember to fly back to us in California."

I grabbed him by the neck and kissed him on the cheek.

"What time is the truck arriving tomorrow?" I asked.

"Have you noticed how you never know what's happening, and I make all the arrangements?"

"Sorry. You know I'm not organised enough to sort this out, and you are so good at it!"

It was four fifty-five a.m. when I woke up. It was too early, but my body clock was out of whack. I didn't go to bed early enough to justify waking up at what was ostensibly still night-time and yet every day come four fifty-five, I was awake and there was no going back to sleep.

Angus was already in the kitchen. He had his head in the oven, and the room smelled toxic.

"Don't do it! There's hope for you yet. You have a whole life ahead of you."

"Funny. Some of us have to clean this place."

"The worst thing about moving out is all the last-minute stuff and cleaning."

"I don't see you doing much cleaning," he said.

I laughed and left for a shower.

"Hey, I'll clean the shower after I've finished in it. So, you can scratch that off the list. What shall I do with your leg razor?"

I ducked when he threw a Tower of London tea towel at me.

"Just nipping into London for a bit to see Mum and Dad's graves and say goodbye. Won't be long."

The door slammed behind me, and I looked around the street, trying to take photos in my head of the memory. I knew we wouldn't be back here again.

I picked up the gnome on the dachshund, put it in my front seat in case Angus forgot it, and secured it with a seatbelt.

Sitting near both graves, I was wishing we'd gone for the cremation option. I walked around the side of the church and found the caretaker.

"Oh, hi, um, excuse me. Can you come and see these headstones? I want to ask your advice. I'm going away, and I don't want to leave them like this, you see? Can I plant it out with some roses if I pop and get them?"

"Oh yes, you can do that, no problem at all. See you later, then."

I drove to Mum and Dad's and knocked on the door. It was eight a.m., which I thought was an acceptable time to turn up unannounced. I peeped in the front window, but no one was home. I walked around the back. It all looked unloved since we'd rented it out. The grass on the lawn was dead, and weeds ran rampant over the garden beds. Someone had already hung out their washing, and towels and sheets I had never seen before hung on my dad's washing line.

Hunting in the shed, I found a spade and gloves. I picked up a red bucket and made my way to the peachy roses, pulling up a Google video on how to transplant them. It said to water them well; I filled the bucket with the squeaky garden tap, which made me smile. The day Mum had planted the roses, Holly and I tried to help with mini watering cans, and here I was about eighteen years later, digging them up. It symbolised new beginnings; these roses didn't belong here anymore, like none of us did.

The video suggested pruning them, but I didn't have time, so I dug the spade into the deep mud puddle and it splashed into my face. I wiped it on my sleeve and carried on despite the mess. I thought I had enough of the root to pull them up. Struggling to find a section to hold on to that wasn't thorny, I fell backwards as they gave way, and the thorns scratched my face down on one side, but I kept going until they were all dug up and popped the spade back into the shed.

When I returned to the graveyard, the caretaker looked at my face with concern.

"What happened to you, miss? Have you been in an accident?"

I touched my face.

"Oh, I had a bit of trouble with these bad boys," I said, swinging the bag.

He nodded and walked away, shaking his head.

I straightened up my back, marvelled at my handiwork, and watered the roses before leaving. I said goodbye, touching a kiss on each headstone, looking over my shoulder as I left the graveyard, feeling like I was leaving them behind. At least they had each other.

I opened my phone.

"Hey, Siri. Take a note: Tell Holly never to put me in a graveyard."

When I returned to Angus's, I surveyed the space. Everything was gone and all that remained were tumbleweeds of dust, hair and a few metal caps from mini spirit bottles.

"Where the hell have you been?" he said.

He came out from the bathroom, and I knew he'd been re-cleaning the shower.

"I've been calling you—" He stopped as he saw my face. "Oh my god, Elle, what's happened? Were you attacked in the graveyard? Shall I call the police? Here, sit down. Oh, you're muddy. Elle, why are your clothes muddy? You're scaring me."

"I'm fine; just been doing a bit of gardening."

"Gardening?"

"You know, the roses from Mum and Dad's. I got them and put them on their graves, but I got into a fight with the roses and hence this."

"You are quite insane."

Angus took many snaps from different angles, and I posed for all of them.

"Just for us, though," he said.

As I returned to my room to grab some clothes from my bag, a removal man pulled me to one side.

"You know, miss, you don't have to deal with domestic violence these days. There's a hotline and everything you can call."

I laughed.

"I'm OK. Just clumsy."

The man nodded as though he had heard it all before, and carried on shifting boxes.

"So, we are done!" I said.

M. J. PARFITT

I leaned on the mop as we surveyed our tiny home. Neither of us had qualms about leaving the place, just sadness at leaving each other—the floor mopping our last tie as housemates.

Angus was selling his car, and the guy was collecting it. He rang the front doorbell, interrupting our sad moment.

I hadn't sold Dad's car; I was leaving it back at my apartment building. Grey didn't have one and said I could leave it in his spot. I promised to pick it up as soon as I returned. I was reluctant to sell it. Dad's convertible mini had been such a fun car to drive, especially after driving the beaten-up one I had bought after selling the Tesla. And how could I sell his car? I still had all his old stuff in the glove-box, and occasionally, I was sure I could smell Cool Davidoff.

"Hey, I've been thinking," said Grey as he brewed us a pot of tea. "Why don't I buy the car from you? I could use one, and it solves your problem."

"I'm not ready to sell it yet, Grey. Drive it all you want, and we can sort the details out when I'm back again. Look after it, won't you? It's—it was my dad's."

Grey hugged me and whispered in my ear. "I'll take good care of it. Don't worry, Elle."

Angus wasn't listening; he was looking around Grey's apartment. "Elle said you had good taste, Grey, but this place is something else."

Grey blushed a deep crimson and bit his lip.

"Well," said Angus, "I wish we could stay longer, but we both have flights. It was great to meet you finally; shame our friend moved before she could get that dinner party arranged!"

"Another lifetime," said Grey.

"Bloody hell. You could have told me how gorgeous he was."

"Well, I told you, but you brushed it off and said you didn't like muscles," I said, squeezing his bicep.

The cab stopped at terminal two first and dropped me off first. Angus got out and hugged me as tight as he could.

"Thanks for giving me an exciting new life," he said.

"I'm a facilitator, that's all. Oh, I bought you a book," I said, passing him the brown paper bag.

"Tell me it's not *Slaughterhouse-Five?*"

"No, no, it's not, I promise," I said, giving him one last peck before I darted inside the terminal, where I fell into a fit of inconsolable crying. Angus came running after me.

"You forgot your phone! My god, why are you ugly crying? Stop it right now," he said, holding me by the shoulders. "You go get on that plane and make some fucking Champagne and then come and live in California with me. We can laugh all about this when we are in rocking chairs drinking the finest Napa cab sav we can buy."

I sat in my aisle seat. I always chose it. A controversial choice, one might say, but a window seat made me feel hemmed in; as soon as there was something to see, loads of eyes were on you as everyone

M. J. PARFITT

looked out of the window, not the middle seat, also yuck to that—the chance of sitting next to more weird people increased. With the aisle seat, you could leave faster and only had one seat companion.

Standing up, I let a petite French-looking lady take the middle seat. I helped her pop her bags up in the luggage compartment, watching as she pushed her handbag under the seat in front. The bag moved several times, and the woman looked at me for a pledge of allegiance. Smiling and pretending to read, I tried to keep out of it. All I wanted was to start my new life. If they detected a pet onboard, all hell would break loose, and we'd turn around and taxi back into the terminal like the plane version of the Walk of Shame. Panicking and texting Angus, who was still in the lounge, my anxiety returned.

"So, we have a pet situation here."

"No way. Like that day we were flying to Milan?"

"Yep—sat right next to me. I'm not telling—you know how much I love being delayed! What do you think?"

"Well, you're an accomplice now—what could go wrong? How the hell did she get that through security?"

"We have both seen it before!"

My phone beeped with a text from Grey and a photo of the gnome and the dachshund sitting in the front seat of Dad's car.

"You forgot to take your friends with you. Do I have to adopt them now? Not sure they go with my aesthetic."

"Haha. That's Monty and Vinny—they're Angus's friends. Can you pop it in your lock-up?"

I closed my eyes. Soon, I was floating into a deep sleep. Worn out from the emotional exhaustion of saying goodbye to my family, then Angus, and even seeing Zero. It was a lot in a short time, and I needed to reset and compartmentalise that side of my life to focus on this new chapter. I dreamt of Jude and woke myself up, angry he was seeping into my dreams when he didn't take the time to call me up and say hello or tell me about Lara.

As I woke, the lady next to me was popping bits of biscuit into her handbag slash pet carrier. I saw the man in the window seat look-ing at the bag. I gestured to the lady by nodding sideways, pretending to brush some stray hair back into my ponytail. The lady darted her eyes sideways and zipped the bag up a smidge more.

"So where are you going, young lady, and what happened to your face?"

"Oh!" I said, taken aback by the thick French accent. "I'm going to Épernay. I've got an internship at a Champagne house—Châteaux Marguerite—and the face, well, I had a fight with a rosebush."

"Non? C'est pas possible! I live in Épernay. My family owned one of the French Champagne houses for many years. You must come and visit me. So how are you getting from Charles de Gaulle?"

She handed me some Cetavlon, which I hoped was the same as Savlon cream, for my face, and I took a blob and rubbed it into my cuts.

I explained I was taking a train, and the lady, who introduced herself as Françoise Lavigne, offered me a lift. She insisted.

Françoise gave me the dog bag to carry off the plane like I was her assistant, and I didn't feel I could say no. As we walked past the flight attendants, the bag gave a small bark, and they all looked at each other, not wanting the headache of paperwork or delays but tutting at me. Then I looked down and saw a drip on my leather boots; the poor pup had had an accident.

I wiped at my tan ankle boot with a tissue as I waited at the luggage carousel, but the stain wouldn't budge.

"What size do you have?" asked Françoise as we entered the terminal.

"Oh, thirty-seven, but don't worry about it at all. I'm sure it will dry."

Françoise marched off to collect her suitcase off the belt. She had that indescribable French confidence about her. Then we waited until no one remained except stragglers who were probably waiting at the wrong baggage carousel. I told Françoise she should go on without me, but she refused. So, we marched over to the desk, and Françoise seemed to roast them.

"They will send your suitcase to your address. Can you give it to them? Ils sont idiots."

The shuttle bus pulled into the car park, and Françoise marched off to what I assumed was a small Renault Clio. Just as I thought it was a good job my luggage was missing, she walked past the Clio to a convertible Jag.

"Oh, your car, it's beautiful! My dad would have loved this!" I said. "He had a convertible mini, but I think he would have loved something like this."

I sat in the front seat and smoothed my hands over the chestnut leather seats.

"It was my husband's, and I couldn't sell it after he died. My daughter keeps trying to make me, but I don't want to," said Françoise. "And I do what I want these days."

She had sadness in her eyes, and even though she smiled, she looked empty.

The fluffy Pomeranian was now bouncing around on my lap and looking at the scenery. Françoise said his name was Gatsby and explained she'd got him from a rescue centre when her husband died, and her daughter Juliette had moved to Paris. As soon as she had brought him home to her opulent residence in Épernay, he had walked around like he was lord of the manor, and she immediately knew he was Gatsby!

"So let me get this straight—you have taken Gatsby to and from London and no one has stopped you?"

She laughed and waved her hand in the air.

I relayed the finding of the kitten in Venice Beach. Françoise seemed captivated by my adventure but bemused by the bubble-gum wall, which led to the naming of the kitten. Soon, the topic turned to Jude.

"So why are you here, Elle? It sounds like you found the love of your life but are running away from him!"

"Not running away, just doing me," I said. "The old me wouldn't have hesitated to drop everything in my life and mould myself into someone else's."

Françoise nodded in agreement and conceded that most women did this, and maybe it was something we should stop.

"I want to live my life on my terms now. I've wasted so much time trying to live on other people's," I said.

We pulled up outside the iron gates of Châteaux Marguerite.

"So, this is your new home!"

The impressive building and its sturdy iron gates filled me with nervous excitement for the first day at work.

She dropped me off outside the modest French apartment which would be my home for the next few months. It was in stark juxtaposition to the impressive Champagne house but was close enough to walk to work.

Sitting on my small bed, I called the airline twenty times, chasing my bags. A knock at the door broke the monotony.

A middle-aged lady who spoke in French held out a teal peacock leather suitcase with outstretched arms.

"Madame Lavigne envoyé ces articles pour vous."

"Oh. Merci, Madame. Merci," I said, and the lady turned and left.

I unzipped the case. Françoise had filled it with a bag of toiletries, sweaters, jeans, ballet flats with two entwined 'Cs' adorned on the top, and a tailored pantsuit with a cream silk blouse. I studied the labels, none of which I had been able to afford in my life. I tipped out the toiletries and sniffed the French almond shower gel. This was a world away from my 'Boots the Chemist' offerings. It was one of the kindest things anyone had ever done for me. I sat down on the bed, transfixed by the luxury of the clothes and at the kindness of Françoise.

Françoise's beautiful home became my second home. Her daughter Juliette worked for a fashion house in Paris, and she became obsessed with me losing my luggage. Even though it had long since turned up, she made it her mission to come home laden with clothing, which she had to alter to my size. In return, I would turn up with a bottle of Champagne and cakes from a patisserie in my street.

I was soon the best-dressed intern the Champagne house had ever seen. Gone were the blazers and striped tops. People in the office complimented my wardrobe daily.

My new clothes became an obsession. They gave me joy, and I cared for them, knowing I was fortunate and privileged to wear them. I worried about how to finance this new me when I left here. It wasn't a pretentious desire. I had worked with plenty of girls who ran up credit card bills a mile high to dress like this. This was the last seal of my new identity. The clothes gave me extra confidence, which had been missing my whole life.

Pinot Meunier

Épernay was close to perfect; if my friends and family had been there too, it would have been everything I never knew I wanted in life.

One Saturday when I first arrived; Françoise gave me a guided tour of the town.

"Epernay has a lot of battle scars, Elle. They have burnt it to the ground over twenty times throughout history yet see how magnificent she is. She is like a grand old dame with true French grit."

Françoise gestured to the buildings with a flamboyant wave of her arms. She was wearing a Christian Dior silk headscarf that matched her dark sunglasses. I thought she looked much younger than her age as I watched her stare at Épernay from our vantage point in the town square.

"The Nazis stole millions of bottles of Champagne during the Second World War, but they didn't ruin us. Under these cobbled streets run one hundred kilometres of subterranean cellars containing over two hundred million bottles of Champagne."

I could relate to Épernay on many levels—we were like soul mates.

Françoise sipped at her expresso.

"We'll make a French mademoiselle out of you yet," she said.

I told her about the TikTok account, and she asked to see it, but when we looked for it, Angus had closed it down.

"Friends are the greatest gift life can give you," she said, "and they come in many forms. My husband was one of mine, and Juliette is another. I had a friend like Angus when I was your age. We argued and haven't spoken since. He might be dead for all I know."

She fiddled with the ends of her scarf and checked her lipstick in a small gold compact.

My mentor at the Châteaux Marguerite was Monsieur Beaufoy. He expertly guided me through each stage of the Champagne-making process. I had never met a man with so much knowledge about a subject. He lived and breathed Champagne and Épernay.

First, I learned about growing and harvesting grapes. There were strict rules from the governing body—from the grape variety, to farming methods such as pruning, the height of plants and harvesting, and how far apart each vine had to be planted.

I was there for harvesting this year. Châteaux Marguerite didn't own vineyards. This was something which surprised me the most. They sourced the grapes from many growers, some small, some large.

My first French purchase had been a soft leather notebook from a small stationery shop in Épernay on my day out with Françoise. I contemplated the purchase for too long, at last choosing one that spoke to me like a red grape. I'd written 'Champagne—Méthode Traditionnelle' on the front page. The book gradually filled up with each production stage as I chatted with the vineyard growers, cellar hands, and oenologists. I covered every angle to suck everything out of as many brains as possible.

"Your notebook is a wonderful idea," said Monsieur Beaufoy.

"It was my friend Françoise's idea."

"I used to have a friend called Françoise many years ago. Make sure you both hang onto each other; young people live in a Champagne bubble these days."

"Oh, she's not young," I said.

He stared at me, and then his assistant interrupted with a delivery he had to sign for and the moment was gone.

I had a daily routine of walking past the green bottles lining the cool dark cellars with my AirPods in, listening to the same Taylor Swift song about Champagne problems—two words that should never be in the same sentence, I thought. I no longer needed a mantra to go to work. Work was my new life.

I touched a bottle; it was cold and sturdy. I wished I could watch this one bottle for its whole life. To track its every move and see how it ended its days—perhaps in a dusty cellar or onboard a yacht in the Maldives. I made a note in my book: 'Speak to Lucy about tracking Champagne bottles.' I began flicking through it, holding it under a wall light.

Méthode Traditionnelle

Harvesting:
Once harvested, the grapes are pressed, and juice is extracted from the grape skins. Controlled by the AOC—how much pressed. Huge effect on the

resulting Champagne.

Yeast:
Yeast is added—consuming the juice's sugar, leading to fermentation.
Produces 'Vin Clair' (regular wine) non-sparkling, acidic—11% alcohol.

First fermentation:
(Base)
Aged for months in steel tanks: Oak not good for clean taste. Fermentation finished in 2 weeks, but Champagne aged till April. 'Lees' left over from the yeast after the first fermentation gives the wine a more developed flavour/texture.

Malolactic fermentation:
'Malo'—addition of bacteria react with the malic acid = less acidic and more buttery flavour.

Blending of Bases:
'Assemblage' is the correct ratio to achieve a balanced flavour profile. Blending = consistent taste year to year. Lots of bases are stored for future use.

Initial Bottling and Second Fermentation:
'Tirage' gives sparkle to wine as old yeast dies in each bottle. Bottle cap used like beer cap 'crown cap'—pressure builds inside. Carbon dioxide forms at two weeks—3 months. Ends when the sugar from the liqueur di tirage is consumed.
Ageing on the Lees:

Yeast dies when sugar is gone and forms sediment 'Lees.' Lees ageing = time wine spends in contact with dead yeast cells. Develops Champagne. Autolysis = cells split open when destroyed by their own enzymes + amino acids. Champagne develops more character the longer it's aged on Lees. It is at least 15 months, but most are two years of non-vintage cuvees. Vintage 4–5 years. Excellent vintage can age for 20 years or more.

Riddling:

'Remuage' Bottles kept on the side are slowly turned as sediment settles on the side of the bottle. The neck ends up pointed down; lees concentrated at the bottleneck—it takes six weeks. By hand on wooden racks or using gyropallete = 1 week.

Disgorgement:

By hand, Open the bottle and remove sediment using CO_2. Quickly tilt bottle upright to avoid losing the wine.

'La glace' bottleneck in refrigerated ice-salt bath, Plastic in the lid freezes sediment. When the cap is removed, the plug comes out. How did someone figure this out?

Dosage:

'Liqueur d'expedition'—Champagne and cane sugar are added to replace lost liquid during Disgorgement.

Brut = (no sugar added), Extra Brut = (very little sugar), Doux = (most sugar). Less sugar drier.

Bottling and Corking:

Strong cork. Softened by heat and hammered into the bottle to seal.
'Muselet' holds into place—metal cap protects cork—done by machine.
Bottles must be strong to avoid explosion.
Champagne was the first wine region in the world to use cork to seal bottles!

Cellar Ageing:
Aged in a cool cellar. Amino acids left over from dead yeast cells react with
the leftover sugar in wine = Maillard reaction. Like browning bread
during baking = toast/yeast flavour.

Since meeting Juliette and Françoise, I wore a handful of key pieces and mixed and matched them with a chicness I hadn't had in the UK. My hair had grown long since the impromptu haircut in Venice Beach. I laughed, thinking back to the memory of our road trip; I grew so nostalgic I FaceTimed Lucy, forgetting the time in California.

"Elle, it's seven a.m. Are you trying to give me a heart attack? Is everything OK there?"

Mark looked down at the screen and placed a cup of tea next to Lucy.

"How sweet!" I said. "Hi Mark, how's the vines?"

"Great! Yeah, all good. When are you coming to see them?"

"Hey—is there a guy in the background?" said Lucy, interrupting and propping herself up on her pillows.

"Err, no, I'm alone," I said.

"Well, it's funny you called; you must have a sixth sense because we have something to tell you! We're getting married! It's in May. So, you have come back then for bridesmaid duties!"

"What? Wow, congrats, you two. I'm so happy for you. I'll be back. Try and stop me!"

I looked down at my phone as I ended the call. I would miss all the good bits like wedding dress shopping and choosing a cake. It was like flying all over again. I was nostalgic for lunch catch-ups with Angus and Lucy. I was missing Holly and snuggles with Walter—and missing Jude. The problem with wanting everything was that it was hard to be happy.

Zero pulled up a chair. We had met in Paris on two previous weekends, and now he had travelled to see me in Épernay. We had spent most of it in bed but ventured out for food and drink.

"Who was that on the phone?"

"Oh, Lucy. She's getting married!"

"To the actor guy?"

"Yes, Hunter, to Mark Trevino, come on, are you telling me you don't know who he is?"

"You told me yourself you didn't know who he was when you met him."

"Yeah, I knew who Mark Trevino was. I just didn't match the two up in my brain."

He looked at me with a patronising expression and snorted. He held my hand and changed the subject; Zero always did this each time my friends came up in conversation. I looked down at his left hand; there was an indent left where his wedding ring used to be. He never mentioned his children or Alex. It was like his whole other life was a bad dream he was trying to forget. I didn't understand how you could have a gorgeous child and not want to spend every waking minute with them. I had no respect for Zero; using him like this didn't feel bad, it felt just.

"When do you finish here?" he asked.

"Oh, a few months to go yet."

"Shame you didn't land a job at Moët. That would have been something instead of this unknown Champagne house you've ended up in."

He pronounced Moët with a soft 'T,' and it fucking annoyed me.

"Yeah, not how you say it."

"Sorry? I think I know how to say Moët, Elle. I've drunk far more of it in my life than you have!"

"Well, sorry to burst your bubble there, Mr. Champagne consultant, but you are quite wrong! Claude Moët—the founder, was Dutch. It's his name, and it ends with a hard T."

"Um—well, I don't know about that. It's what it's called all over the world, and I've been to most places; I think you are incorrect. Anyway, I've been thinking, why don't we move into a place together when you're finished here? So, look, here's the thing: I've been talking to Simon from work, and he said you could get hired as a wine buyer for Harvey Nicks or somewhere like that," said Zero.

I laughed. I laughed so hard that I gave myself a stitch.

"Well, I'm the expert on this, so trust me when I say you are wrong. I don't tell you how to fly an A380, do I? You don't understand me, do you?"

He didn't reply but dropped my hand at the first sign of rejection.

"My dream, if you're interested, is to breathe in the aroma from those oak barrels every day of my life, walk between vines, care for and nurture them and create fabulous wines that give people joy. As for moving in with you. Ha. God no!" I said, drying my eyes.

"You're kidding yourself," said Zero, turning nasty as if he was some evil villain who had been disguising himself under a black cape all along. "You always have been. I don't know why I thought you'd changed. You'll come home and end up in some boring job, and all this will have been a folly."

His teeth gritted in an angry menace, spit flying out in all directions.

"You'll never pay off your apartment. You'll scrape by in life, just like your dad."

He waved away Épernay as if it was inconsequential. Little did he know it had risen from the ashes like my magnificent phoenix twin. He dismissed my dad, my degree, my career, and me in one shot.

I took my time to answer. Winemaking had given me patience.

"Oh, Zero, the UK isn't my home anymore. My home's in California where all the people I love live."

He turned a blotchy purple and scarlet red. Even his neck was red.

"As for my dad, he was the best I could have wished for. It was him who told me to try this new life. I owe all this to him. You'll never be half the dad he was to your kids; I pity them. Also, I don't have a mortgage anymore, thanks to Angus, another of the greatest men I know. So, I'll be OK, but thanks for the concern about my future. Your zeroes taught me phosphorous, and that is the one gift you have given me I'm grateful for."

"What are you talking about?"

"You should read more, Zero. A travelled man of the world like you."

"What was this, then?"

"I think it was what's called a karma fuck. A bit of fun, Zero, that's all. It was fun, but I've got all I needed from it."

Pecking him on the cheek like a stranger, I glanced over my shoulder as I walked away, savouring the moment as he googled zeros and phosphorus and a YouTube tutorial on pronouncing Moët correctly. He sank back into his chair, realising I had won a match.

Perusing pastries at a local patisserie, I decided on a silky chocolate éclair decorated in gold leaf to celebrate my victory. The park was alive with all sorts of people: lovers lying on picnic rugs, old men reading papers, children playing, and I felt like I belonged. I didn't need to lie on a picnic rug with a lover or push kids on a swing. Being me and living my life was enough. It had taken me over twenty years to figure that out.

My phone buzzed, and it was Angus.

"What are you eating? I'm so jealous."

"Go get one from that gorgeous bakery!"

"No way, I can't go there since you told me about Kyle, the cat hater."

The cream smudged on my nose as I tried to hold the phone and the eclair in the same hand.

"Oops."

"Haha, you fool, just eat it all at once!" he said. "What are you wearing? You're so chic! How about Lucy and Mark? It's going to be amazing! So, we need to organise a road trip for her hen party. Well, I'll organise it, but tell me when you will get back home before the wedding."

"Angus, I love how you say back home, like I live there. Should be able to make it back by the end of April, but I'll have to leave straight after the wedding. There's a job waiting for me in New Zealand."

"What?"

He clasped a hand over his eyes.

"Yes, with your friend Ken!"

"Why do you do this to us? You need to come back here. Jude won't wait forever."

"Wait? For me? I don't need this Jude drama. When I left, he was with Lara, and he hasn't been in touch with me since. I won't do that thing anymore where I bet my life on a guy. It ends up eating you alive."

I missed them all, but New Zealand was too good an opportunity to decline, and I didn't want to settle down with regrets. Afterwards, I could find any job I wanted in Napa or Sonoma.

"Oh, Angus, I miss you! It's not long till I come back for the wedding. Where are we going on this road trip?"

"Well, I thought we could go up the coast this time but fly back down, and I'll drive. I'm used to it now."

"Oh, exciting! Can we go to Seattle and see—"

"Grace Sloan Memorial!" said Angus.

He knew I was still a die-hard *Grey's Anatomy* fan. "Funny, but you know it's not an actual place, right?"

"Well, I gotta go—I've got to work tonight at a function."

I blew virtual kisses his way. The screen went black, and he was gone.

In the park, I was alone again. It was still the right move to bin Zero off; it gave me the closure I knew I needed. I had to see how bad of a man he was, and he had given me that to the nth degree with his last flurry of nastiness. I was sorry for his kids, and I was sorry for Alex, but I felt nothing for him—he was just a bit part.

Koshu

*L*ucy and Angus were waiting for me in arrivals when I walked through.

"Ooh, la la! You're almost French!" said Lucy.

Up from behind them popped Holly.

"Surprise!"

I burst into tears.

"Oh, I've missed you all so much."

"Hang on a minute," said Angus. "What have you got under your arm?"

"Oh, I almost forgot! You left some friends behind."

I passed the gnome riding the dachshund over to him, and he shrieked with laughter.

"Monty and Vinny! I've missed you guys!"

"I didn't know you'd named them," said Lucy.

"Yeah, Monty is the gnome because he's got white hair. We coloured it in with a red felt tip once, but the rain washed it away, and the dachshund is called Vinny because his parents kept riding him," said Angus.

"Funny story. I left these guys in the front seat of Dad's car with a seatbelt on, and Grey has been fostering them while I've been in Épernay. He sent them to me so I could bring them to their new home. I got some weird looks as I was getting off the flight."

On the drive to Sonoma, I asked Lucy how the wedding prep was going. It sounded like an extravagant celebrity wedding, and as I guessed, the venue would be Mark and Lucy's new vineyard, Castello di Amanté. Holly was catering for the entire event. Angus would oversee everything else, from invites to music, decoration, and security measures to keep the paparazzi out.

"Angus, how have you planned a whole road trip when you're doing all this, too?" I asked.

"Well, it's not like I have a social life, my friend."

"Hey Lucy, you said I can bring someone, right?" I said.

They all stared at me, and Angus squeezed between the front seats.

"What's that now? You're bringing a date?"

"Yep. If that's OK, Lucy?"

"Oh, course. So, who is the lucky guy?" she said.

"Oh, just someone I met."

The car fell silent, and everyone in it had eyes on me. Even Lucy was glancing sideways as she drove.

"Is that all you are going to say?" she said.

I gazed out the window, changed the subject, bit my lip, and asked about Jude.

Jude was taking a break from women after having a mini breakdown, they said.

"He never contacted me, you know," I said.

Angus changed the subject and talked about the road trip.

"We're going to drive to Yosemite!" he said. "It was too far to drive up to Seattle. It was like thirteen hours. I know you wanted to find 'Grace Sloane.' Sorry!"

I laughed and poked my tongue out at him.

"Holly is coming!" said Angus.

"Oh, yay! This is going to be fun," I said.

Holly stuck her hand through the seat and squeezed my arm.

"Lucy don't forget we have to stop at Taylor Street—well, the intersection of Taylor and Broadway," said Holly.

"What's going on there, Holly?" I asked.

"Oh, I found some sourdough starter on Facebook Marketplace. This lady has had it since nineteen sixty."

"Are we going to Barbary Lane?" I said. "Plenty of yeast action there, I'm sure."

Angus laughed as he had read the book series, too, on my insistence.

We headed up the ridiculously steep Russian hills, and all got out to stretch our legs when we reached the address. Angus and I looked at each other and began running around in circles.

"Elle, Elle, look where we are!"

I spun around.

"Oh, my god! It can't be!"

Angus knelt, and I picked up an imaginary sword.

"By the Genovian Order of the Rose, I knight you, Sir Angus."

Lucy and Holly looked puzzled.

"What is happening right now?" Holly asked Lucy.

"Don't you know?" asked Angus. "It's *The Princess Diaries.* Come on, you must have seen *The Princess Diaries?*"

"Oh my god, Angus, you've turned into me," I said.

I laughed, doubling over.

The seller of the bubbling sourdough popped her head out.

"Oh, more film buffs?" she asked. "I have to say the knighthood re-enactment scene is a fresh take on it."

⌘

At the white cottage, Walter and Nick came running out to meet the car, and not far behind, mewing, a much larger Luis. I was an emotional mess when I saw the little double act.

We caught up and played outside until I faded from the jet lag. Then Lucy took me to her vineyard as I would stay with Angus in his house on Lucy and Mark's grounds.

"This isn't the main house?" I said as we pulled up in the turning circle of the crunchy drive, past the lemon trees. A cherub-adorned water fountain bubbled in its centre. It reminded me of a Californian bungalow in *Home Again*—a Reese Witherspoon film, the first house that came to mind when I imagined L.A.—not a forty-million-dollar listing from *Selling Sunset,* but a home like this. Sadly, I imagined it didn't come with a young rock band in the pool house, and I wouldn't be able to have a cocktail with Candice Bergen.

Angus and Lucy showed me around, and I took my suitcase into the guest room and started unpacking. They sat on the bed, and we smiled at each other, none of us quite believing we were together again.

"Jeez," said Lucy, "you rob a bank? Where did you score all these beautiful clothes? Sugar daddy we should know about?"

"You know when I called you from the plane, Angus?"

"Yes, about the smuggled dog?"

Lucy looked confused.

"Well, I made friends with the owner; she's called Françoise. By the way, her dog was called Gatsby because he loves his new palatial home! Anyway, her family used to own one of the Champagne houses and—"

"Oh, stop," said Angus, "I can't listen—I knew this would happen—you've fallen in love with a French aristocrat, and now you won't move here. This will kill Jude."

❦

My nerves returned when I heard a car pull up. Mark and Jude had arrived, and after a few awkward hugs, we sat outside with icy glasses of La Limonar, and I recounted my experience in Épernay. Angus had made pizzas for everyone in the old oven in the garden and given us all woollen blankets. When the temperature dropped, we toasted marshmallows in the fire pit.

"Angus, why do you have so many blankets? Was there a big sale on at Williams Sonoma?"

He hit me with a cushion on the way by as he collected glasses.

I told them all about méthode traditionnelle, and Jude seemed transfixed. We sat poring over the pages of my notebook, and he asked me questions about each production stage. I relayed everything Monsieur Beaufoy had taught me.

"So, tell me about the yeast they use," he said.

I flipped to the page in the notebook, and the others drifted off into the kitchen.

"Can you make me a copy of this?" he asked.

"Um, sure, yeah. I can do that."

Angus, Mark, and Lucy had taken the dishes and glasses back in, and I followed them in with a few extra glasses they had missed. I caught the tail-end of their conversation.

"She's what? Man, that's going to be tough for Jude. I know he hoped they'd continue where they left off," Mark said.

Angus walked around in circles and pulled at his hair.

"Stop it, Angus," said Lucy.

"I knew she'd meet someone. Fucking typical. A bloody French aristocrat. We'll never see her. It's too awful. I'm happy for her, but it would have been perfect if she'd just come and lived out here," he said.

"Yeah," said Lucy, "But we can't live her life for her, Angus. She makes her own choices, and we have to support her."

"I know, OK, I won't say another word, but one of you needs to tell Jude, or he will be pretty upset when he sees her with someone else."

"That will be me, I suppose?" said Mark. "It's his fault. Why the fuck didn't he contact her?"

I wanted to interject, but I didn't know what to say. I made a few clatters with the glasses to announce my arrival and popped them on the countertop.

Back outside, I collapsed, sat back in my chair, and smiled at Jude.

"So why haven't you been in touch, stranger? I know you're not with Lara. What happened to us being friends?"

"You thought we were friends? You're so much more than that. Knowing what you've been through and how important finishing your degree and going to Épernay was to you, I thought it was better to let you finish it all. Maybe I was wrong."

"Has there been anyone else?"

"God, no. No. I'm in love with you. You are always on my mind. What about you?"

"Uh yeah, there's been someone else. I mean, I didn't know you still felt this way. What was I supposed to do?"

I might as well have pierced his heart with a red-hot poker. He looked like he was going to throw up.

"Fuck. I've messed this up. Shit, I'm sorry. I always handle this stuff wrong."

"Why didn't you talk to my sister, Lucy, or Angus? They'd have told you what you were doing was stupid."

"Well, you didn't contact me, Elle."

"Jude, when I left, you were having a baby; then I heard you were getting married. Do you think it was my place to call you? Oh, please!"

He got up and pushed his chair back. "I think I'd better go."

I sat still, shook my head, and knocked back more wine.

"Where's Jude?" asked Angus.

"I don't know. Something I said, I guess," I said.

"OK, well, that's our cue to leave. See you both tomorrow," said Lucy, kissing us both.

Angus was quiet. He grabbed me a blanket, and we sat, not talking for a while and looking up at the stars.

"So," I said, "let's change the subject, and you tell me about this road trip tomorrow."

❧❦❧

The following day, as the blankets of fog covering the vineyard in its slumber lifted, and moths gave way to bees, we packed the car, and Mark, Nick, and Walter waved us off. Jude was nowhere to be seen, and I was disappointed and wished I could stay on the off chance I might bump into him. I just wanted a chance to see him.

❧❦❧

"Road trip!" we all shouted as we drove out of Sonoma.

"Angus. You are going the wrong way," said Lucy.

"Am I, though, Lucy? Am I?" said Angus. "OK. OK, I'll come clean. We are not going to Yosemite."

"Thank fuck," I said.

They all turned to stare at me.

"What? Just it's so far, and I hate camping."

"Well," said Angus, "we are going to Santé, in Big Sur."

"Eh?" said Holly.

"Luxury spa for us, girls," said Angus.

"But you can drink there, right? I don't think I've got the right clothes for this," said Lucy. "Do they have a shop?"

We were silent when we pulled into the resort, perched in the redwoods above the Pacific.

"Three days of this I can manage," I said.

We dispersed into our rooms and agreed to meet in a restaurant where Angus had reserved a table.

I opened the door to my suite. The bed looked inviting, with a chunky knit throw on the end and linen covers. The interior was sophisticated yet cosy, with lots of bleached wood and marble. I contemplated never leaving. A welcoming stone bath was begging to be filled, and I headed straight for it. My back ached after the drive as I'd had to sit in the middle seat, and I groaned as I stepped in. I lay in the tub and admired the perfect view through the fir trees. It was faultless. Even though I was looking forward to hanging out with my friends, it would be great to retreat to this solitude later tonight. I laughed out loud, thinking of my tiny apartment in Épernay, the same size as the bathroom in this suite.

"Have you seen the menu and the cocktails?" asked Holly. "Unbelievable. Angus, as always, you have exceeded all expectations and the rooms! Don't get me started on the rooms!"

We worked our way through the cocktail list, and I waited for them to bring up the cocktail stick story. Holly finished it by telling them about Walter and him plonking the apple crumble on his eye. This was one of my favourite clumsy anecdotes. Getting a cocktail stick in the eye had been worth it.

Once we finished tasting every cocktail on the menu, Angus persuaded us to go back to his room for a joint he had brought with him.

Lucy had already pulled me to one side. She told me he had been to a micro-dosing conference at Esalen and had experimented with mushrooms.

❧

I sat next to him on his balcony, which was perched on a lower level of the building. We were right in the trees like a giant bird's nest.

"What's going on with you, Angus?"

"I'm good. I'm great."

"You never had a good poker face."

"It was OK being single when I was with you. We were in it together, but here, I'm always the third wheel."

I hugged him.

"Isn't there an abundance of Sonoma bachelors on tap?"

"Yeah, if you want a one-night stand. I even hooked up with Liam Golding. Remember the guy who lent you his waistcoat to go with your pizza slut knickers? Turns out he was trying to meet Mark. You know me, I want to meet someone and fall in love. It's why I went to Esalen. I heard some guys at yoga saying they were going. It wasn't what I expected. It's better than taking anti-depressants if you are feeling down."

"But Angus, we all feel down sometimes. It's the normal human condition," I said, taking a puff of Angus's joint as a gust of wind made it glow, and it took me by surprise. I dropped the joint through the balcony railings, and the grass below caught fire. It took off fast, and Lucy had seen it straight away and rushed to fill the ice bucket with water, throwing it on the blaze, but as soon as she dampened one spot, it took off again in another. Angus jumped over and stamped on it until it was a smouldering pile of damp black grass.

"I think I've hurt my ankle," he said, rolling around on the ground. "Darkling, trouble follows you. Someone find my shrooms."

The management at the resort evicted us the following morning. For smoking in our rooms, causing a fire hazard and taking drugs, although I suspected enforcing the last one would mean they'd have few guests left.

Angus was waiting for us next to the car when we meandered up with our cases.

"Well, that was short and sweet," said Holly.

"Not to worry," said Angus. "I had the best idea when you all went to bed last night. We're staying somewhere else for the next two nights."

"Where?" said Lucy.

"I'll give you a clue," he said. "A certain cat we all know and love shares the town's name."

"You have not?" I asked.

"Got to be kidding me," said Lucy.

"Err, what's going on?" said Holly.

"You've booked us in at The Madonna Inn, right?"

"I might have."

"Oh well, this is going to be different," said Lucy.

We explained to Holly about Angus wanting to stay there on our road trip, but we had both been wary, as it appeared to be a bit 'out there.'

Veering off at Morrow Bay, we headed to San Luis Obispo or SLO as the locals called it. We stopped at the bubble gum wall—for Holly's sake, Angus said. He was enjoying being an authority on the local attractions.

Holly was more interested to know why it was there, and we couldn't tell her because when we'd looked at it the first time, we weren't that interested in its history. After a Google search, we discovered it had been there since the fifties and may or may not have started as a rivalry between two schools.

"It's funny how one person can start something, isn't it," said Lucy. "You know it just takes one step, and sometimes you can leave a mark. You never really know what's going to stick, do you?"

I started to chuckle at Lucy. She made a lot of jokes that other people didn't seem to notice, but I always did.

We reversed most stopping points, like the lounging seals and the Bixby Bridge. I thought back the mad dash road trip we'd done last time, but now I stood on the cliff, calm and with nowhere else to be.

It was early, and we had the whole bridge to ourselves. We missed the sunrise, but it was still spectacular, and as I looked out at the Pacific, goosebumps ran up my arms. My heart and family were here, and this would be my home someday. It was where I belonged. Holly stood beside me and put her hand in mine.

"Come home soon," she said.

The Inn reminded me of a movie set. It could have been Hansel and Gretel's Cottage, part of which you could drive underneath.

Angus dashed off to speak to the reception, letting no one else go in, and when he returned, he had four cards, and on each, he had written the name of a room. 'Rock Bottom,' 'Merry,' 'Daisy Mae' and 'Yahoo.'

"What this?" asked Holly.

"These are the names of the rooms. It's your hen do. You get to choose everyone's room."

"OK," she said. "Angus–Rock Bottom, Elle–Merry, Holly–Daisy Mae, and me Yahoo. Can we have the keys now, you clown?"

I opened my door, scared to open my eyes, and was astonished to find a round room with pink glitter wallpaper to the ceiling, and it was a very tall room. The woodwork was all painted in bubble gum pink and two silver covered winged back chairs sat beside a small table. In the bathroom flowery, bright pink patterns covered two pedestal basins which matched the bedcovers, and I giggled. Then I noticed an enormous chandelier hanging from the circular wooden ceiling in the middle of the bedroom and two smaller ones over the bed. I wiggled my toes in the plush carpet that was bright pink. It was a kitsch paradise.

I texted the group chat and suggested a room tour because I needed to see Yahoo, Rock Bottom and Daisy Mae.

Daisy Mae was a fairy grotto with Christmas tree lights above the headboard and a stained-glass window depicting Daisy built into the rock walls. The shower, bathroom, and sink were all carved from granite.

Yahoo was a lot: crimson red carpet, glittering purple ceiling, bullhorns above the bed. The bed was a big cart on wheels with a seat at the end.

"This room must have seen some kinky shit. Lucy, this would make a great honeymoon suite! Mark could dress up as a cowboy. Maybe you should cancel the Farmhouse Inn."

I texted Mark a picture of Lucy posing on the seat of the cart sideways with her arms up, presenting the room as if she were a host on *Wheel of Fortune.*

Rock Bottom wasn't rock bottom. It was my favourite. It was a rock room with a cherub-stained glass window, a cute vintage couch, and a floor lamp light and upside-down candelabra.

"The universe is making a joke here," I said. "I love that you got the most normal room, Angus."

He looked very pleased with himself for finding this place and booking us in at the last minute.

"Love you so much," I said to him as I gave him a hug.

The Silver Bar Cocktail Lounge was another visual smorgasbord. There were too many things to look at, and I thought you might stay here a hundred times and notice something else on every visit.

Angus perched on a sturdy leather bubble gum pink bar stool with a gold ornate base, and as I turned around, I noticed groups sitting on winged leather armchairs in bright blue and two shades of pink in front of the bay windows. An ornate wood carving of bunches of grapes framed the bar, and I laughed at the appropriateness. The carpet was cerise with a flowered pattern that captured every accent colour in the room. It was crazy, and I loved it.

"This place is mad. What's everyone drinking?" asked Lucy.

We agreed on 'French eight zero fives' because they said I was French-ish and because it contained Champagne. It was a cocktail of gin, Limoncello, and Champagne.

I got up, approached Angus, and leaned on his pink barstool.

"Angus. You were right about this place. It's amazing. I mean, the last place was gorgeous, but this. It's quirky. I don't know why I don't trust you more; you are never wrong about anything. Hey, and I wanted to say don't worry about meeting someone. You never know when it could happen. I mean, it might happen today," I said, looking around at the women on hen weekends. "Well, maybe not today!"

I looked up as a server made the way to our group with a huge bright pink cake, and everyone crowded around.

"This is for you, Lucy," said Angus. I called and ordered it yesterday. It's the Madonna Inn's famous Pink Champagne cake."

"It's definitely pink!" I said.

The outside of the multi-layered cake comprised cerise chocolate flakes and topped off with a pile of bright pink chocolate swirls.

Lucy and I put our arms around Angus, and then Lucy cut the cake. The sponge was a bright yellow, and I caught a sublime scent of vanilla, jam, and champagne.

"It's a trial run for the wedding cake," she said.

Angus snapped photos of her pretending to cut the cake on her wedding day.

"You know, guys, I feel sad I missed your first road trip. You have so much fun and cake," said Holly. "I never had girlfriends before except you, Elle."

"Well, you are in the group now, Hol," I said.

We agreed to make this an annual event. We talked for hours about all the locations we could visit and agreed on Palm Springs for the next one.

Two days sped by. We hiked, swam, played tennis, and drank through the cocktail menu. On the second day, we sat by the pool with Moscow Mules, and I looked at a mother and daughter reading. I squinted and put my hand up to shield the sun.

"Hey, Holly, Isn't that Lara, the Instagram junkie?"

She was wearing a white string bikini with no baby in sight. I walked over to the bathroom and checked, dropping my sunglasses.

"Hi, Lara," I said.

I saw she was reading *Tales of the City*.

"Um, oh, hi," Lara looked vague. "Oh, it's you. Elle—the clumsy Brit! How are you?"

"Yeah, good. Just over for Lucy's wedding. So, you're reading a book?"

"Yeah. I took your advice. This is a great book series! Look, all that business with Jude. It wasn't my finest hour. I'm so sorry about it all. I'm taking English at Brown now. I owe it all to you. So, you don't live here? Thought you and Jude would have been married by now," she said.

"No, I'm not with Jude. So, did you have the baby?" I said, looking around.

"No, I lost the baby."

She looked down into her book, and I wanted to die.

I sat on the side of a pool bed and touched her shoulder.

"I'm so sorry, Lara. That's awful."

Lara introduced me to her mum, and we chatted about Brown, my experience in France and the upcoming wedding.

Lucy, Angus, and Holly came over, too; we ordered some more drinks, and by the end of the day, I had fallen backwards off the sunbed into the pool, and Lucy had invited Lara to the wedding.

Marsanne

J jumped out of the shower and wiped away the steam to check my face. Thanks to all the booze consumed in Big Sur and the Madonna cocktail lounge, a considerable pimple adorned my chin. Typical on this of all days, with all these beautiful people turning up. I would feel even more inferior. I looked at the blush silk Elie Saab gown hanging on the door. It was stunning. I picked up the hem and inspected the tiny stitches. Angus stuck his head in. He had started the day early, and he was buzzing.

"Oh my god, these celebs are painful! This one can't do this, eat that, sit by this person. It's exhausting. My phone has been ringing off the hook with assistants spelling out their demands. What the heck is that on your chin? This is a disaster. What time does your lover arrive?" he called back as he walked to his room.

"Eh, who? Lover? What are you on about? I keep trying to tell you—" I said as he walked out.

I dressed and left my hair and makeup until I got to Lucy's house.

"See you later, Angus," I called out.

When I entered Lucy's dressing room, the other bridesmaids and makeup artists crowded around me.

"This is a problem," said the makeup artist.

"Can't you just cover it up?" asked Lucy.

"You got a trowel?"

"Hey! I'm right here, guys—me and my pimple. Told you I had a plus one!"

"Looking forward to meeting the actual plus one. Be kind in front of Jude, though, OK? Mark said he'd taken the whole thing pretty bad."

"Taken what pretty bad?"

"You know the whole new boyfriend thing."

"I don't—" I said.

With that, someone whisked Lucy off to have her hair and makeup done, and an assistant worked on popping the pimple on my chin.

"Is it me, or are you enjoying this?"

"Yeah, I don't mind popping a zit or two," said the pierced girl. I could barely see any skin on her earlobes.

It exploded all over her black T-shirt.

"Elle, that's gross," said Claire, my old flying buddy, as she gagged.

"Ha! I know, right? Typical of it to pop up today, I guess."

The makeup artist worked miracles, and once she blended in the concealer, you wouldn't have known the zit was waiting underneath for another day.

"Wow," I said. "Who is that in the mirror?"

The makeup was heavy but looked flawless and tasteful. The top knot on my head finished the look, and I didn't think I looked half bad. Then I saw Lucy. Head-to-toe gorgeousness, also in Elie Saab. The dress was sleeveless, with two cupcake-shaped bralettes on the bodice, and then it gave way to a simple off-white skirt. It was modern yet classic, and it took me by surprise. I took a picture and texted it to Juliette.

"Oh, Lucy, that's the perfect dress."

I was on the verge of tears, and the makeup artist was stern.

"No fucking crying here," she said.

"OK, understood," I said, looking at the clock.

"Hey, I have to go meet my friend," I said, rushing out.

I walked down the aisle with my fellow bridesmaids and Angus, who looked handsome in a cream suit with a blush-pink pocket square. We stood under the trailing jasmine, facing the stunning celebrity crowd banked by the most impressive vineyard I had ever seen. I hadn't had a proper tour yet, but it was endless.

The music signalled Lucy was about to appear, and a hush descended upon the vineyard as if time stood still. Lucy appeared with tears running down her cheeks, and I could see Mark captivated; he wasn't looking at the dress but into Lucy's eyes.

The breeze from the Pacific whispered over my friend's perfect day.

I jumped back into a seat beside my date, grabbed his hand, and whispered something. Jude was behind me, and I sensed him stiffen in his chair. I didn't dare turn around.

The audience erupted once Mark and Lucy had said "I do," and the couple walked back down the aisle, stopping to hold hands and kiss and hug friends.

They paused by me, and I jumped out into the aisle and put my arm around them both. I noticed a small Times Roman tattoo on Lucy's wrist of an 'M,' which made me smile.

The marquee was vast, and it took my breath away. White and orange peonies with sprigs of eucalyptus filled the room like it might burst with flower petals at any minute. Twinkling fairy-lights twisted around the trunks of old olive trees in huge distressed concrete pots. A jazz band played "What a Wonderful World" in one corner, and smiling servers pushed through the crowd with delicate appetisers on pristine platters. Every place setting had a small white gift box tied with a tangerine-coloured organza ribbon. As I looked up, the whole canopy was alive with Chinese paper lanterns attached with invisible thread, so they appeared to float. The fragrance transported me to a surreal version of the cellars at Moët filled to the brim with peonies and candles.

Lucy and Mark jumped up behind me.

"So, this is your plus one? Aren't you going to introduce us then? You don't give off a French vibe," said Lucy.

"I think you'll find he's my plus one!" said Angus. "Elle, did I mention you are my favourite person in the entire world?"

"Well, you raged on at me about not having that dinner party and Grey and I have been in touch a bit because he sent your gnome over to France, and I suggested he come. I've been trying to figure out how to repay you for clearing my mortgage, so this is a start," I said.

"What about the French aristocrat?" said Lucy.

"Have you guys been smoking something? You've all been acting so weird. There is no French boyfriend, and I've been trying to tell you that all week," I said.

"So how can an intern afford a designer wardrobe because I've seen that gear," said Lucy, "and let me tell you, that's a wardrobe right out of the best Paris fashion houses."

"Yes. I've been trying to tell you! It's the lady with the dog Gatsby on the plane. Her daughter works for a fashion house in Paris. She's been dressing me head to toe for months. I think they felt sorry for me because my luggage was missing, and it became a hobby for them."

"Oh," they said.

"But you said you had met a guy," said Jude.

He looked around at the group as he realised he'd spoken out loud.

"Um, well, not someone new; I hooked up with Zero twice, no three times."

I looked down at my shoes.

"You did fucking what?" screamed Angus. "Elle Darkling, why in God's name would you go there?"

"I don't know. He kept calling me, and I was sad and broken-hearted. He's split up with Alex, and I thought, why not? We were both single. Then he started talking about me moving in with him, and I was like, dude, it's a fling."

Claire, who was standing nearby, interjected. "Elle, he never split up with Alex. I see them socially, and they have never split up."

"Ew, that's gross. What a dirty dog. Zero doesn't change!" I said. "Why am I not even surprised? Anyway, I reduced him to rubble. It made me feel better about the whole thing. Poor Alex—even she doesn't deserve the wanker. Right, you two, off to mingle with your guests. Crisis averted!"

Everyone drifted away except Jude, standing with a slim blonde lady with a kind face who smiled and looked away.

"Right, better go mingle too," I said.

I locked myself in the loo. Jude had told me he hadn't met anyone, and now he was with someone else. We would never get together, and I realised at that moment I had to let the idea of him go once and for all. I held onto my chest. It felt tight, and I wanted to call a Lyft and hightail it to the airport.

The pimple was still undetectable under the camouflage. I knew I had to go back and mingle, but all I wanted to do was cry in my bed.

I tried not to appear excited when I saw someone from a movie, but it got exhausting, and my only recourse was to get drunker and drunker as the night went on.

"Hey, slow down there, sailor," said Mark.

He sat down next to me at the bar.

"Oh, Mark, am I drunk?"

"Well, yeah, I'd say so, Darkling. That was a kind thing you did for Angus."

"Oh no, you know full well the extent of what he's done for me. I always feel like I'm in deficit—with all of you," I said. "So, how long has Jude had a new girlfriend?"

"Oh, is this why you are consoling yourself? Ha, well, that's my sis. She's known him since we were five, and when Lucy told me you were bringing a plus one, I suggested they come together, that's all. Sorry, Elle; knowing you, I should never have thought you'd be cruel. I know he's been distant, but you know all the crap with Lara and then his dad dying. Plus, he has some projects on the go that take up all his spare time. He wanted to give you space to finish what you had to do. Hey, changing the subject, but I swear I saw him talking to Lara earlier."

I put my hand over my glass when the bartender tried to pour another, kissed Mark, and left to find Holly in the kitchen. I watched her from the door, busying herself, wrapping up all the leftover food and putting things away.

"You don't stop, Hol. Can't someone else take over now? Come and have a drink."

We stepped outside and sat on a small stone wall, and I passed her a beer.

"So, when are you leaving?"

"I'm off tomorrow. I'm sorry I couldn't stay longer, but I had to take the opportunity when it came up. Will you guys come to visit me?"

"Tell you what, we won't make it to New Zealand, but can we meet back in the UK? I want to tie up all the loose ends I didn't get to last time."

We sat with our heads on each other's shoulders and breathed in the fragrant jasmine in the night air.

"Lucy looked amazing, didn't she?"

"Oh my god, yeah. That dress!" said Holly. "So, what are you doing about Jude?"

"Oh, nothing. I think it's best if we leave it there. I mean, I'm leaving. Jude seems super busy. Mark said he has other projects taking up his time."

"Yeah, he is busy working on a couple of things, but you have to know he's mad about you, don't you?"

"No one wishes more than me that the stars had aligned, but it's not meant to be. It's too hard. Like even being friends with him right now seems too hard."

We watched as Angus walked around the Marquee with Grey. They stopped and laughed together before disappearing off into the distance.

"You are a fixer, Elle Darkling. Look at him, drunk with happiness. Concentrate on fixing yourself up now, though, eh?"

She got up, brushed down her apron, and kissed me on the head. When the time came for Walter to leave home, it worried me how she would cope.

I returned to the cottage, had a hot shower, put on some comfy tracksuit pants and a sweatshirt, and packed my suitcases again. I had been packing suitcases for so long now I should have been better at it than I was. Years ago, I flew with a girl who knew how to pack a suitcase—she could have made a career out of it. You could turn up in her room for an impromptu catch-up, but her case sat on the unused twin bed as neat as when she'd first arrived. I hated the ritual because it always meant leaving someone I loved behind. I turned out the light and cried myself to sleep.

The next day, my eyes were bloodshot, and the pimple had made some friends.

After dotting Benzac all over my chin, I sat outside in the morning sun with my bare feet on the silver-weathered Adirondack chair, closed my eyes and tilted my face up. A shadow passed over me, and I opened one eye to see where the sun had gone, to be met with Jude standing over me.

"What's all over your face?"

"Oh god, don't, I woke up like this!"

"Well, you always look beautiful to me."

We sat silently until I offered him a coffee, which he refused.

"I looked for you last night, but you'd left. So, you are leaving again today? I thought you might stay?"

"Yep. New Zealand. I've got a job in Otago. Going to get my fix of pinot noir."

"Are you going to come back after you get your fix?"

"I don't know, Jude. I don't know what I'm going to do."

He knelt in front of me and took my hand.

"Please don't go. Please stay. I'm begging you to stay."

We both had tears in our eyes, and we hugged and cried.

"You know I love you, Jude. If you can wait for me, I'll come back, but part of me doesn't want you to wait for me because I love you so much. I want you to be happy. When I saw you with Mark's sister, I was heartbroken because I thought it was your girlfriend, but then in my heart, I felt good about it, you know, for you. After all, we have had this tortured, painful series of misunderstandings and mistiming."

"But you can do everything you want to do in New Zealand here. We have pinot coming out of our ears. Your friends and family are here. Why can't you stay?"

"It feels unfinished, you know. I feel like if I do this—"

Angus and Grey walked up towards us, and the conversation got cut short.

Later, I dropped by La Vallée to say goodbye to Holly. It had improved since I'd been away; it was a different space altogether.

Next to the tasting room was a farm shop. I popped my head in, and Nick was labelling goods with Walter's help. There were enormous baskets of bread, eggs, preserves made with Jude's wine, homemade biscuits, cakes, lemons, limes, and olives. I picked up a jar of marmalade which said 'Chardonnay and Lime—La Vallée Estate.'

"Holly!" I called out, walking into the barn kitchen. "Your farm shop is amazing; get me a basket so I can buy everything. You are so clever."

"Oh, it was Nick's idea. It's all online, too, and he's struck a deal with The Ox in Napa. They are giving him a spot. You know he's so good at all this stuff. When are you off?"

Looking out at the vines, I dreamed of staying and wandering between them and was mad at not having more time to stay here. Jude walked in and broke my daydream.

"Ready to go?"

"Yeah, soon. Just saying my goodbyes."

"Can I take you to the airport? We could chat on the way."

"Um, well, Angus was going to take me, but yeah, OK."

We chatted the whole way. My heart had wrenched as we'd left Sonoma, and now my stomach had butterflies as we neared the airport. Jude pulled off when we saw the sign, and then, instead of pulling into a bay outside the terminal, he pulled into a car park.

"Oh, Jude, you don't need to come in. Let's say goodbye out here."

"I need to come in, though, Elle."

He jumped out and went to the back of the truck.

I got out and sighed and looked at him as he took out my bags, then his own.

"Are you going somewhere?"

"Yeah, with you."

He grabbed me and pulled my head into his chest. "One of us has to make a move here."

M. J. PARFITT

Pinot Noir

$\mathcal{I}$t was bloody cold. The icy change hit us as we disembarked, even though we were still inside the jet bridge. I hadn't prepared myself for it. Jude pulled me close, and he rubbed my hands warm. It was the first time we had spent this much time together, and it didn't feel real. He seemed like an exciting stranger. I couldn't believe he had come with me; it was so out of character for him.

◦✧◦

I was staying on-site at the vineyard. Ken, the owner, used an apartment for seasonal workers, and he said I could stay in it as part of the contract.

I poked my head into the main office and asked for him. A tall, jovial man with crazy white hair and a red face emerged.

Looking around the office, I saw it was chaotic, with books and magazines stacked on every surface. He was Jude's polar opposite, but I kind of loved him from the outset. He was a loveable teddy bear.

"Elle! You made it!"

"So, I hope you don't mind, Ken, but this is my friend Jude. He's a vineyard owner like you from California, and he's tagging along for a bit. It was so last minute I forgot to contact you to check it was OK."

"Come on in out of the cold," he said.

He helped us with the bags, and we stashed them in his hallway. We walked through into a lounge room with a roaring log fire, and he came back a little while later with a giant wooden platter of cheeses and fruit and opened one of his pinot noirs. I had never felt so welcome in a place.

"You'll find it a little different here to California," he said. "A French migrant planted the first vines. The vineyards in Central Otago didn't get off the ground until the nineteen seventies. Some vineyards have wild thyme growing planted by gold miners in the eighteen hundreds. It's all a little accidental. I'll lend you some books. There's some interesting history of how pinot noir cultivation started here. You'll see most of the vines planted on hillsides and facing the sun because the winter climate is bloody tough, but you'll notice ours is flat. I've got a chopper, and I fly it over the vines to prevent the frost from settling. Then, in the summer, the weather is warm during the day and cooler at night, and that gives us this amazing intensity in our wines. The soils are mostly mica schist and greywacke and some clay and loam. It's quite diverse, but obviously low in organic matter and high in mineral content, so the vines aren't green like yours, but the berries are intense, and we get a great tannic structure."

I really wanted to see him flying that chopper and suck every piece of wine wisdom out of his brain.

As we were leaving to settle in the apartment, he handed Jude a pile of books for us to read.

"Now there's food in the fridge over there and some wine and plenty of wood for the fire. You won't need to worry about going out tonight. See you tomorrow."

We lit a crackling log fire at the apartment and drank more of the exceptional pinot noir from Ken's vineyard—Muselet Wines.

"Wow," I said. "This is good stuff. Jude, isn't it crazy that we are sitting right now in the world's most southern vineyards?"

I tasted layer upon layer of dark fruits, mixed rose petals, and a hint of violet.

"I'm glad I came. Seeing another vineyard in action will be interesting; I get so caught up back home I can't take time off. Having Holly and Nick there is amazing. I have you to thank for that."

"Yeah, everyone keeps telling me you've been working on several projects. What is it you're doing?"

"Ahh, you know, adding some more machinery. Boring stuff."

"How long can you stay?" I asked.

"Oh, a couple of weeks, then I have to get back—you know how it works. There's stuff I can't leave for Holly and Nick."

We were both too tired to go out and eat after the flight. In between making up for lost time in bed, we spent the night discussing what we should do when I wasn't working in the vineyard and agreed to visit some wineries, go skiing and head into Queenstown for a 'Fergburger' as Jude had read about them on the flight.

"I need to go shopping," I said. "My clothes aren't suitable for the climate, are they?"

Jude laughed at how I was so unprepared for life. I had got on a flight without even thinking about the weather. I would have to deck myself out in a new North Face wardrobe, and I knew it would cost a fortune in Queenstown.

"You know I rely on Angus for travel arrangements. I struggle when he's not involved in my plans!"

"So, when are you coming home for good?" he said.

"Give me a year."

"A year! What the fuck? It's been so long already. I'm sick of waiting for you. I want us to be together now."

"It will fly by. Meet me in the UK in six months. I'm meeting Holly to sort out the rest of the stuff in storage."

He ran his fingers through his hair.

"OK, but that's it. If you don't come back after a year, that's it— line in the sand."

Biting my nails and looking into my wine, I avoided eye contact; perhaps this was a huge mistake. It was risky; Jude was an eligible bachelor with a movie star for a best friend. He would have no shortage of women throwing themselves at him.

"Jude, can you understand I need to do this? Then I'm done, promise."

He had picked up a book on the coffee table.

"Are you even listening to me?"

"Oh god, sorry, but listen to this—someone smuggled a pinot noir cutting from Domaine de la Romanée-Conti vineyards in Burgundy in a gumboot! They intercepted it at customs, and this customs officer— Malcolm Abel, also a winemaker—sent it to be processed by the government. After they released it, he planted it. They cloned the vine, and it's the basis of many of New Zealand's highly regarded pinots! That's classic."

"I bet the guy that smuggled it got fined and missed out on the grapevine!" I said. My phone beeped just as Jude was coming back with some more wine when he looked down at the screen.

"Why do you call him Zero? I keep meaning to ask you that, and what does the asshole want, anyway?"

"I was reading some Dickinson poems when I found out about his thing with Alex, and I put him in my phone as Zero because of the phosphorus poem.

I stood on the sofa in Jude's green wool jumper and some fluffy socks and took a bow. "'The Zeroes taught us — Phosphorus' by Emily Dickinson."

We learned to like the Fire
By playing Glaciers when a Boy
And Tinder guessed by power
Of Opposite to balance
Odd If White a Red must be!
Paralysis our Primer dumb Unto Vitality!

"I saw something in the words that resonated with what he'd done to me, and I started my fire even in the nothingness he left me with. And now I have the spark. I value it more because I lived through all that awfulness with him, and I was silent and powerless for so long."

Jude laughed and stood up. He brushed the hair from my face and hugged me, staring right into my eyes.

"You have made phosphorus out of zeroes, and it's incredible. You should be proud of what you've done since then. Why's he calling you, though? Didn't you end it for good in Épernay—I still can't believe you slept with him again after everything."

"Don't remind me. We haven't spoken since then."

Then he sent a text which said: 'Call me now.' I deleted it.

Jude threw the phone on the chair and took me in his arms.

Jude hung around the vineyard most days, offering free labour or chatting with Ken. They became good friends, and I wished I could keep him there. We were so removed from all the old appendages, such as the Laras and Zeros of our previous lives. I didn't ask him to stay longer; I knew it was impossible.

It was hard for me to focus on my work. If I glimpsed him, I'd forget everything I was doing.

I was working in the shed one day, and he walked back into the yard after being gone for a few hours. He was carrying various shopping bags and a little striped paper bag.

"Where have you been all day? I missed you."

"Arrowtown. We should go tomorrow. It has some cute little shops and galleries you would like, and I found a sweet shop that sells British candy. I got you Pear Drops, Bonbons, and something called a Sherbet Dib Dab."

I hugged him, and I thought about Dad. Every Saturday when we were kids, he'd go to fetch the papers and buy Holly and me a bag of sweets each. Dad would have loved Jude, and then I thought back to what he'd said in the hospital about Holly standing in a vineyard and Pear Drops, and I sat down on a log seat and cried.

"What's wrong? What's wrong? Elle, talk to me."

"My dad said something before he died, and now it makes sense. Jude, you will wait for me, won't you?"

"You know I will. You are right to do this. The pinot noir—it's good, and it's your favourite wine. Let's be honest. You're not a chardonnay girl."

"If I'm only allowed one wine for the rest of my life, I'm choosing La Limonar," I said.

After Jude had left, I ate little for weeks. Every day, we'd text and FaceTime; it was as if we weren't apart. It was different this time because he could relate to the place where I was. He'd met the people I worked with and slept in my bed. It connected us. I'd put off washing my sheets for weeks because I became addicted to sniffing the scent he'd left on the pillow.

When I was in France, he didn't know my life, and I could tell he was jealous of the time I'd spent there with people he didn't know. He always asked me a million questions about the Champagne-making process but never about any of my friends.

I trusted him, and I knew I'd see him in six months, and then it wouldn't be long until we were together for good. I imagined a future where life was less emotional and on an even keel.

The phone rang. I beamed and dashed over to it, thinking it must be Jude because he'd been quiet for a few days. It had even crossed my mind that he was sick, but it was Angus.

"Hey, you! How's Grey? I think it's pretty ironic that you all live there without me."

"Can we talk?"

"Oh, fuck what's happened? Are you sick?"

"No, it's not about me. Damn you and your fucking love life, Elle Darkling. It's Jude. He's back with Lara. Never thought we'd be having this conversation again."

The words knocked me to the ground. They hung in the hair like the stalactites Jude and I had seen at Milford Sound, waiting to fall. It sliced me in two, and I sank onto the couch and stared at Angus, not crying, just saying, 'right, right.' Nothing was real. Jude had swept away all my hopes and dreams.

"Elle, I think the screen is stuck."

No, I'm stuck. Stuck trusting the wrong men. Stuck in a holding pattern where I fuck it up time and time again.

"Angus, I gotta go—I've got this work thing. I'll call you later."

I paced up and down the apartment. I had déjà vu. It was like putting on my old denim jacket with the gum still on it. I was too far away to have a heated row or deal with any of it. I lay on my bed, paralysed.

Holly and Lucy both called me that afternoon. He'd met up with Lara again at a friend's party.

"He's head over heels, Elle. I hate to say it, but this new Lara is the 'new, improved version.' It's odd he hasn't called you. What happened while he was there? Was it awful?" said Holly.

"That's just it, Hol. It was amazing. He told me he loved me. He was going to meet me in the UK. We agreed to be together. None of this is making sense to me."

Even though it was freezing, I'd wake in a cold sweat for nights on end, after dreaming something weird like Lara turning up in New

Zealand with two little kids in tow, and I'd be still working here, and she'd bought me Pear Drops to say sorry for stealing Jude away and breaking my heart. Then she would morph into Alex, and I'd wake with a blurry memory of everyone who'd contributed to the scars on my body from a thousand cuts, standing over me drinking La Limonar. I knew the way out was to find my phosphorus again.

I slouched through Ken's cellars, craving the familiar solace in the cool, dry air. Gone was Tay Tay's "Champagne Problems." My song du jour was "All Too Well"—Taylor's version. Ken was walking in as I was walking out one day.

"Elle, is everything OK? You don't seem yourself."

And that's what broke me. I was sitting in Ken's office with a whiskey, and he'd wrapped me in a tartan blanket. I blurted out the entire story right back to the beginning of everything with Jude.

"Something's not right here. I mean, Jude had the ring picked out and everything. He was going to propose to you in London."

"What? He told you that? Well, I guess he'll be giving it to someone else now. Not sure what I did to deserve this twice," I said.

Jude called and said I was right—it was too much—the distance, the not knowing. Why drag up the past like this? There was no apology; he seemed furious and didn't give me the opportunity of a rebuttal. I sat shell-shocked while he delivered the monologue. He was cruel, and

I had never imagined him as someone who would ever be mean. I put on a smile and told him it was OK. We could still be friends. While wishing him a painful death, I flipped him off under the screen of my phone. And then I walked into my bedroom, changed into the sexiest dress I owned and put on another fake smile.

I was at a tasting at the Skyline for another local vineyard. Drinking a lot presented itself as a good plan. I needed to burn bridges and make mistakes. I was going in for a refill when a ski instructor called Taj stood on my foot.

"Sorry," he said, "I was just trying to ditch this wine. I need to find a beer."

We flirted for the rest of the night. He had a shock of blonde hair and shiny white teeth. He looked like a catalogue model except for the large tattoo on his forearm depicting The Remarkables.

"Do you want to come home with me?" I said.

Gone was the scent of Jude in my bed. Now, it stank of booze and angry sex.

Taj stayed the night and woke up early to head off for work. He leaned in and kissed me. He was younger than me and eager to please. The change in dynamic was refreshing. I pulled him towards me and persuaded him to stay a while longer.

"That was so good. I wish I could stay here all day. Right, I'm going now! What time do you finish work? I want to take you to dinner," he said.

One dinner turned into a relationship. It wasn't deep and complicated. Taj liked me, and I liked him.

"Elle, why don't you stay here? I bet Ken would give you a job. We could move in together. I don't want you to leave."

"Taj. This has been amazing. I care so much about you and want to stay friends, but I don't want to lead you on. I mean, I hate skiing, and it's your life, and you hate wine, and that's mine."

"That's OK, though, Elle, to have different interests. We don't need to like the same things; we just need to like each other."

I'd already had a practice run of this break-up earlier that day with Angus, who'd been telling me to end it for weeks. He said Taj was too much of a pretty boy after stalking his socials. The reason I hadn't called it off was that the sex was amazing. It was carefree; without the weight of love, it could just be what it was.

"We should call it quits when I go back to the UK tomorrow. You're gorgeous. Forget about me. Find someone who loves skiing like you do. You're such a great guy."

He looked down at the floor, and I grabbed my bag as I left and questioned how men did this to women every day without feeling shit about it for the rest of their lives.

I landed at Heathrow, and it was sunny as I looked through the large windows to the planes lined up, waiting to turn around and go somewhere else. I imagined what a different place it would be if the weather were like this more often. Holly had arrived earlier and was waiting as I walked into arrivals.

"Friggin airports, Elle. Can we live in the same place? I'm over it."

"Me too. But right now, Sonoma might be awkward with Jude. I'm not sure what to do, but they offered me a job back in Épernay. I guess I may never live in California now."

"Fuck off. No, you can't do this to me. We moved there because of you. If you're not coming back, we'll move back here."

I looked at her in astonishment.

"Hol, I'm not being held to ransom over where I live and work. If you want to give all that up for what I don't know. I didn't promise you anything. Great to see you, by the way."

I saw that she had lost weight and was glowing despite the flight. California had been good for her in so many ways.

We made our way in awkward silence to the lock-up and pulled out everything of Dad's. We made piles of keep and donate like we were hoarders. Now and again, we stopped and reminisced about a photo or old book, which ended up taking us most of the day.

After dropping off the stuff for charity and a trip to the tip, it left us with what Holly would send back to California and a couple of boxes I would keep in my lock-up at the apartment.

"Don't know why I'm fucking bothering to send this, though,"

Holly said. "You're so selfish."

I ignored her and asked if we could go to the graveyard to check on Mum and Dad's graves.

As we pulled up, the old caretaker was pottering around.

"Hello again, miss."

Holly looked at me, but I ignored her, and we walked over to the graves. We both stood open-mouthed, and Holly gasped. The graves were both covered in an array of peach roses. I'd thought I'd find them half dead and was expecting to have to find another solution.

"Who did this?" asked Holly, looking at me.

The caretaker walked up behind us.

"They are coming along, aren't they? I've been pruning them for you, miss, but you did a great job digging them in; they love it here."

We walked back with him to the church gates.

"Is this your bike?" I asked.

"Yes, it is. I had a car, but my daughter got sick, and my wife's using it to take her in for the chemo now. I'm OK with this. It's excellent exercise."

"Thanks so much," I said, hugging him.

When we got back into the car, Holly was in pieces.

"I'm sorry, Elle. I'm the one being selfish. Here you are doing something like this, and I can only think about myself."

"It's OK. I know you must miss my scintillating company—one more stop. Let's take those boxes to my old apartment."

Grey had left the keys to the mini inside a key box in his lock-up. I knew he was selling the apartment soon, and I had to sort something out with the car.

"What will we do with it?" asked Holly.

"Come on, I know what Dad would have wanted," I said, and I drove it back to the church. Holly followed behind me in the rental car.

I handed the caretaker the keys and paperwork. I explained I was going back overseas, and the roses he was taking care of were sitting on our mum and dad's graves.

"This was our dad's car, George. This might sound strange, but I know you'll take care of it and put it to good use, and Dad would be so happy."

He stood looking bewildered, with tears streaming down his face as I hopped into the car with Holly, and we waved and said we'd see him again.

"What happened?" asked Holly. "It was like an episode of *Oprah.*"

"I dunno. Felt right, I guess."

We ordered steak and chips and sat in the beer garden drinking lager. I loved how it quenched my thirst, and I needed a break from wine. The problem was that everything about it reminded me of Jude, and even though I had it running through my veins, I needed a brief reprieve. I put my feet on the opposite bench and tilted my face to the sun.

Sitting back in our chairs, Holly and I appreciated the English pub garden; looking at it with fresh eyes, it was so different to our lives now. We had thrown ourselves into leaving the UK so fast we'd taken little time to stop and smell the roses. England had its merits on a glorious day like this.

We ordered a jug of Pimm's and talked for hours about everything.

"Jude seems happy, though," said Holly. "Lara is OK now; they're both sheepish about you."

Holly and I agreed I had to move on, and I was sick of giving Jude real estate in my head; he needed an eviction notice.

"What happened with Taj?"

"Oh god, it was awful. He wanted us to move in together. I felt like an asshole leaving him. He's great, but we had nothing in common. You know I've never enjoyed skiing, and he hates wine. He must despise me. That's why I've had so few relationships. I can't do this casual thing. It's too disingenuous."

Holly and I were spending a few days in London hanging out before we went our separate ways again.

We did everything we wanted to do while living there but needed more time and freedom to prioritise it. I could tell she was enjoying herself.

I told her about the items left on my 'Itch List' and one was a tattoo.

We stood outside the tattoo shop, Tattoo Inc.

"Well, go on then."

"No, you first," I said, pushing Holly towards the door.

"I'm not sure I can do it," Holly said.

I closed my eyes and pushed the door.

"Um, hi. Do you have time for a couple of small wrist tattoos?"

Holly's face was flushed, and she stood behind me.

"What were you thinking?" asked the man.

I knew it was a sign when I spied the tattoo of a calico cat eating sushi on his upper arm.

"We want a cat drinking a glass of wine," I said.

"Bloody love that!" he said. "Chris—guess what these two want? A cat drinking wine!" he shouted at his friend across the room.

The voice echoed through the warehouse-style shop in Camden, and everyone turned to look at us. I looked down at my Converse Hi-tops and wished I hadn't pushed the door open.

"Give me ten minutes, and I'll draw something up. How big? Just a small line tattoo? I'm Tony, by the way." He said as he swivelled on his leather stool.

Chris came over and showed us his own black and white tattoo of one cat painting stripes on another with a bottle of sake in the background.

When Tony returned, he'd come up with something different: a cat with its paws up on a ledge looking into a Champagne flute. Half its face reflected through the Champagne flute as though magnified.

M. J. PARFITT

"You look bloody familiar to me. Where do I know you from?" Tony asked.

The needle buzzed, and my stomach churned every time it touched my skin. I wanted to ask Tony to stop, knowing it was too late. I looked over at Holly; she was laughing and chatting with Chris.

"How are you doing this, Holly?"

"Childbirth," she said.

"TikTok," I said. "I'm La Fille Maladroit."

"No way? Do you mind if I add a beret and moustache to your cat?"

We sat on the tube, smiling at each other. In some weird way, living away from each other had brought us closer. We had a life woven together but stretched out across oceans.

We put our arms next to each other on the tube and compared our 'identical tattoos.' My cat had bigger eyes, and Holly's glass looked more like a wineglass than a Champagne flute.

A tall guy in a yellow puffer jacket, which was not warranted for the weather, pulled down his headphones and looked over at his friend.

"Look at these two. Girls, why did you get tattoos of cats? Evil creatures."

He wagged his finger at us and tried to encourage the rest of the compartment to agree with him.

"Hol, did you read that report that cat haters age three hundred and seven per cent faster than cat lovers?" I shouted.

"Yeah," she said. "I've noticed a correlation between untrustworthy people and cat haters."

People around started to snigger, and puffer coat got off at the next stop. He meowed as he jumped off and stared at us through the window as we moved past the platform.

"Hol, I don't miss this life, do you?"

"Sometimes I get nostalgic, but here we are, having a brief reality check, aren't we?"

"Imagine if you could immerse yourself into a virtual reality of your old life whenever you were having a bad day?"

"Which day would you pick?"

"Hmm—Zero telling me I was a terrible driver."

"You should suggest that to Lucy for a new app idea."

"I already have one about tagging Champagne bottles!" I said.

"Does your mind ever switch off?"

The plane descended into Queenstown, and I wondered if the actual love of my life was travelling. I needed it like air. Every place held different secrets and surprises. Here, the scenery was dramatic, and I lived each day in a scene from *Mission Impossible.* Queenstown airport had a view like no other. The backdrop of The Remarkables in the departure lounge was insane. I thought of Taj and hoped he wasn't planning on some dramatic gesture at the airport. The fact I hadn't heard from him was a good sign he'd moved on, but I was still apprehensive as I walked into arrivals.

M. J. PARFITT

When I arrived back at Muselet, my apartment was silent, like an old museum nobody visited.

The contents of my case were on the laundry floor, and as I went to sort through it all, I reached into the basket, seeing something dark, which I assumed I'd left when I rushed off to the UK. My emotion came bubbling to the surface as I pulled the garment out. I recoiled, recognising a pair of Jude's jeans. Then I collapsed on the floor, holding them next to my face and sobbing like a teenager. I was in pieces and checked the pockets like a crazed zombie. In one, there was a crumpled-up note which read: 'Blue Weber Agave, Phosphorus.' He had drawn a little plant at the end in black ink. I stared at his handwriting as if it would be the last time I might see it and pulled on the jeans. They were too big, but I thought I could make them work with a belt.

Ken put me straight back to work, and I threw myself into it with gusto because I wanted to block everything out and because it was so cold I could feel it in my bones.

I was working in the tasting room and chatting to people from all over the world. It was distracting until someone reminded me about a life I'd left behind, and the whole thing would rise to the surface like a fresh wound. I wondered when it might heal.

"Hey, you're La Fille Maladroit!" a group of women shouted at me as they walked in the door one afternoon on a later stage of the wine tour they were on.

It seemed there was no escaping from my alter ego, even though

Angus had stopped posting.

"That's me," I said. "I should get some T-shirts printed."

Emails continued to flood in from all over the world, addressed to La Fille Maladroit. If I needed a boost, I would open them up and reply to a few.

I sat down with the group of girls who told me all about their travelling adventures. I told them the entire story about Angus filming my accidents and monetising the TikTok account—it gushed out of me. Something about their warm demeanour and the Californian accents made me reminisce.

"Where can we buy a T-shirt?" said one of the group members. "That TikTok account is awesome. It was like a breath of fresh air, not to have perfection rammed down your throat from every direction."

As they were leaving, they asked me if I knew any ski instructors, and I gave them Taj's details. I hadn't called him back, even though he'd messaged me several times. I knew what would happen if I did. He was so easy to be with. It was tempting to stay in New Zealand, learn to love skiing and drown myself in pinot noir.

I could hear them laughing about him on their way out as they scoured his socials, realising I had gifted them the most good-looking instructor in Queenstown. It was a win for Taj, three beautiful women, some ski lessons, or both. It helped a little with the guilt I was feeling.

I met Ken one morning as I walked across the yard, still yawning and rubbing the frozen sleep from my eyes, my breath visible in the crisp frost and rubbing my hands together to get the blood flowing through them.

"Morning, Elle. How did you sleep? Listen, I keep meaning to ask if you'd like to stay here. There's a job for you. What will you do if you aren't going back to California? We could use you here as general manager."

This was tempting to me. It would be a significant step early in my career, but I knew I couldn't take it. New Zealand reminded me too much of Jude. It epitomised the best of times and then the absolute worst, and I didn't want to marry the two together in a life here.

"Oh Ken, this place is so fabulous, and it's a wonderful offer, but after what happened with Jude, I'm going back to France to figure things out. I'm so grateful to you for everything. Your wines are exquisite. If there's ever any way I can repay you for this opportunity, I will."

He nodded and stared at me through squinted eyes.

"Well, there's always a place for you if you change your mind."

He walked into the office, and I hated appearing ungrateful and perhaps a little stupid for giving up the opportunity. I knew it was the right thing to do.

With mixed emotions, I returned to the departure lounge at Queenstown Airport and took in the rocky vista for one last time. Who knew if or when I'd be back.

"Elle?"

I looked up, confused, trying to recollect where I had seen the face peering into mine. It was Monty Blake.

"Monty? How long has it been?"

"I'd have recognised you anywhere," he said. "I keep up with all your interesting stories through Alex."

"Alex?"

"Yes, she tells me you've made something of your life. You were lucky to escape Hunter, but I didn't say that—the poor girl. I'm glad I bumped into you like this. It's always played on my mind about our last meeting. You know how it is in these jobs, what I may or may not agree with. I had to toe the company line, but I started out pushing a cart myself and came across a few Philips.

"I always knew it wasn't you with the eye drops. You're an amazing friend to Angus, and how's Lucy? I heard she's been unwell. I'm sorry about that. Amazing what she's accomplished in life. I'm proud to have worked with all three of you. Also, you inspired me to retire and travel the world with Colin." He gestured over to his companion.

"I know you were just doing the job, Monty, and look how it all turned out, so don't even worry about any of it."

"If there is ever anything I can do to make it up to you, Elle, here's my email address."

He walked off, looking back over his shoulder, and I noticed he'd bitten the bullet and let his hair go white.

Marquis

*I*f I was a vampire, France was blood to me. And I came back to life. As I walked through arrivals at Charles de Gaulle, I knew I could survive and take another thousand cuts and more. I had been through many prototypes of myself, but this was to be the final version that would face the world.

❦

I hired a car and drove myself to Épernay. The old me would have caught the train or called Françoise, but I wanted to prove I could do it.

Stressed and sweaty, I made it in one piece to my tiny apartment, which was a step up from the first place I had lived. Juliette had gone to inspect it for me, and we had FaceTimed as she walked around pointing to the sash windows and original terracotta tiled floors. She led me into a kitchen with a wooden bench top. It blended old and new with a retro feel from the cigar-legged furniture and Formica table in the kitchen to the parquet floor in the lounge room. The clincher for me was the private rooftop terrace. One long terracotta wall held a multitude of small pots of herbs. I had already imagined looking out over Avenue de Champagne, sipping the golden nectar and people-watching. I could almost touch the fragrant rosemary, which I imagined snapping off for my occasional gin and tonic, which gave me pangs for Jude. She had me at rooftop terrace, and I'd signed a lease that day. Lucy's rooftop in Chelsea always made me envious, and although this one was a poor cousin, it would do.

When I stopped at a supermarket, I bought some bare essentials, but a chilled bottle of Champagne was at the top of my list.

This apartment was my French dream. I raced through the house, grabbed a Champagne flute from the kitchen, headed straight up to the rooftop, poured a glass and FaceTimed Holly.

"Look at my new home."

I held out the phone and swung it around so she could see the view of Épernay.

"Oh wow. Juliette did a great job of finding you that place. It's amazing."

"How are you all?" I said.

"Oh great. The restaurant is going well. Nick seems to run a lot of the vineyard these days. Jude is always so busy."

"What with? Everyone keeps saying he's busy, but what with?"

"Oh, this and that. I don't know."

Angus popped his head around the screen.

"Bonjour, La Fille Maladroit!"

"Angus! So good to see your face! How are you, and how's Grey?"

"I'm good," Grey said, coming into view on the screen.

"Ecstatically happy, thanks to you," said Angus.

"Not fair! You're all together. I'm jealous. You will never guess who I saw in Queenstown airport, Monty Blake!"

"No! It's a small world. Still a dickhead, is he?" said Angus.

"No, he was kind. He said he understood what happened that time with the passenger and the eye drops. He was doing his job, I guess. How are Lucy and Mark? I'll call her later."

"Don't call her tonight. It's a bit late, and she's exhausted."

"Oh, right, I'll wait and call tomorrow then. I need to figure the time difference out again."

"And don't forget, Elle, you can always just get on a plane and come back here. We miss you," said Holly.

"When it feels right, I'll be back."

My voice wavered, and I bit my lip as we ended the call, my finger hovering over the red phone symbol, not wanting to press it, and I was alone again.

Françoise and Juliette took their time to ask me about Jude and what had happened in New Zealand. I knew they had wanted to ask a million times but were waiting for the right moment as if I was teetering on the edge of a breakdown. I'd had my breakdown by that stage, and all that remained on the surface was a seething anger towards him.

"New Zealand was idyllic and romantic. We were making plans as though California would be home for me. Now he's back with his ex. Who knows what happened? How could I go back there? If I saw them together, it would finish me. Sucks for me when all my family is there now. If I didn't know better, I would think it was some grand practical joke I'm not in on. I couldn't stay in New Zealand after everything that happened, either. The place I've been most content is here with you and Juliette and working at the Champagne house. So here I am."

I told them about the wedding and the misunderstanding with Grey and then Jude and Mark's sister, and by the time I finished the entire story, they knew my family, too.

Françoise mulled it over as she picked raspberries off a bush in her garden and placed them in a basket. Juliette and I kept picking out the most enticing ones, and she slapped our hands away in jest. Jules and I sat back and licked our stained fingertips, and we plopped some raspberries into our Champagne flutes so they fizzed up.

"My goodness, what would I do without your stories? It's strange for a man to go to these lengths, to come to New Zealand with you then boom! — Meets someone else and doesn't even tell you straight away. You shouldn't have given him away so easily, Elle." Françoise tutted. "You should have gone straight back there and confronted him."

"Maman is right," said Juliette. "There's something off about all this."

"I don't even care anymore. I'm done with chasing men. But what about you, Françoise? I wanted to ask your friend's name—the one you fell out with. By any chance, was it Monsieur Beaufoy?"

Françoise blushed, and Jules coughed into her Champagne and made a neck-slashing signal from behind her back.

"Yes, that's him. Why do you ask?"

She looked down at her basket.

"It's that just I know him."

"From Châteaux Marguerite? Does he still work at his age? Oh, well, I'm not sure I want to stir up old memories. It was so long ago now. Some things are better left in the past. In fact, most things are best left in the past."

"Um, Françoise. Why do you have a vineyard here in your back garden?"

For the first time, I noticed row upon row of perfect vines stretched out in her expansive estate.

"They are some of the original vines from Hoffman. I look after them. It's not the perfect spot for them I know, but it was all I had left apart from this house. I wasn't interested in grapes like you, but I'm glad I held onto them. A local man comes by and tends to them, and in return, he gets the harvest for his boutique Champagne house."

"Are they pinot noir?"

"They are indeed."

I inspected the leaves and the stems and noticed a powdery white dust on some leaves. I ran my hand over the trunks.

"Tell your friend he needs to get this mildew off here, or you'll have a problem," I said. "Wow! It's like a mini vineyard. Why have you never mentioned this was out here?"

"I don't know. What was there to say? They are just some old vines. They are not up to your standards but produce beautiful grapes."

This time, I saw the complete cycle of Champagne production, from grape cultivation to the dark green bottles ageing in the cellars.

My work interested me, and it became my life. I often worked late or volunteered to help with projects.

As I was leaving late one Friday afternoon, Sebastian, a manager in the marketing team, called out to me and beckoned me into his office. He always wore a bow tie; today, I noticed it was green with pink dots. I could hardly see his desk because it had so many little notes and reminders plastered all over it, with no apparent system.

"Elle, I wanted to ask you something. An old friend from London is looking for a wine critic for *The Times*, and I thought of you. It's a—how you say? Side hustle arrangement, and they pay you per review. I hope you're interested because I gave him your number already," he said.

He laughed, scrunched up one note, and threw it into the waste-basket.

"Wow," I said. "That's incredible. I mean, it's scary, but I can figure it out. Have I got enough knowledge to do it, though?"

"Well, what else is there to know? You have mastered the complexities of wine tasting, and all that remains is a little prose and the actual drinking of the wine. I think you'll manage that, Elle."

I returned to my desk and dialled the number, expecting to leave a message, but Frank, the sub-editor, picked up.

"Oh hi, um—it's Elle Darkling here from Châteaux Marguerite in Épernay. My colleague Sebastian suggested I call you regarding the opening for a wine critic at *The Times*."

"Elle! Your ears must be burning. We were talking about you at our meeting earlier. Seb has given you a glowing reference. How are you fixed for a meetup next week in Paris? I'm there for the weekend."

We agreed to meet in Le Marais. Even if I didn't get the job, I was happy for the opportunity to walk around Le Marais, and I was sure Juliette would be OK with me staying at her place.

I bounced down the cobbled street, falling over and losing the contents of my Chanel handbag. There were no Jaffa Cakes in it this time. I was down to a strict item limit and a no-food rule in my handbags. I'd bought it with my first month's pay. I was La Fille Maladroit, but I tried to embrace it. After pulling myself together and straightening my black shift dress, I walked into a bar where I was meeting Juliette. I could hear the shouting and laughing before arriving at the little red door.

She entertained the group with a story about some starlet that had been causing havoc at a fashion house fitting. As I breathed in the wine and garlic aroma, it made me hungry and desperate for a drink. I walked up behind her and put my head on her shoulder. She turned and kissed me on both cheeks. Now, I was fluent in French; I had become part of her group of friends. This time, I was a local, and it opened literal doors into buildings I didn't know existed. Still mastering many of the nuances in conversation, I sometimes got confused, but day by day, I became French.

After telling my friends about the potential job at *The Times*, we toasted as we sipped a delicate rosé. The French way of living surpassed everything, and I was the happiest I had ever been. I knew that when I was eighty, perhaps sitting in a rocking chair next to Angus and Lucy, I would look back and mark this spot as the best time of my life. Everyone has one moment in time like that, and this was mine. I was young but independent, and I felt grown up for the first time in my twenties.

Partway through the night, I excused myself and called Holly to tell her the news. She was silent, then screamed into the phone, so I had to hold it away from my ear.

"You have to stop doing that. You are going to burst my flipping eardrum one of these days."

"Oh gosh. Such a great opportunity, and think of all the fabulous wine you will get to taste!"

"Well, nothing's certain yet. But you never know!"

Holly told me about Walter, making friends at school, and how Luis caught mice. She didn't mention Jude. We avoided the whole subject like he didn't exist. I didn't know if I'd ever be able to consider him a casual acquaintance who was in business with my sister. They had a formal partnership, and Holly and Nick had a share in the vineyard these days. What they had done creating all the little offshoots of the business for Jude had taken his vineyard to the next level, and it was becoming a well-known brand. I was looking forward to seeing it again someday when Jude was just someone I used to know.

I sat in a cafe in Le Marais, waiting for Frank. He was late; I studied the menu and looked at my phone until I fidgeted and contemplated ordering a massive lunch or leaving.

Then he turned up, flushed in the face, and I stood as he kissed me.

"Sorry, Elle! God, I'm so late," he said, looking at his watch. "Would you like a coffee? Or a wine, haha."

I looked at my watch.

"Frank, I'm a little nervous; it's been a while since I had a job interview."

"Oh, this isn't an interview. The gig's yours if you want it. I was in Paris anyway, and I thought we could go over the details. Well, more the logistics. I'll email you some past articles and all the contact details for submitting your copy, and it's up to you what you write about."

"Can you give me some tips? I mean, I'm not a writer. What makes you certain I can do it?"

"Be entertaining," he said, counting off items on his fingers. "Don't force humour, but write about something amusing, don't stick to wine—weave something else in there, know your facts, grammar, grammar and grammar, there's a book called *The Elements of Style*, that's your new bible, and kill your babies."

"Sorry, what?"

"You may write something and love the idea of it, but when you read it back, it just doesn't flow or work—kill it. Be ruthless. Right, I have to catch my flight. So, are you going to have a crack at it? Oh, and just one thing I should mention—the byline will be 'La Fille Maladroit.'"

And there it was, the reason he had been so keen to sign me up.

"Oh, right. Well, yes, I see why, I guess. Yes, OK," I said.

I shook his hand.

"Partners in wine?"

After about four hundred drafts, I had my first article and, keeping nepotism alive and kicking, I wrote it about Ken's pinot:

THE NEW ZEALAND PINOT NOIR, A HAPPY BY-PRODUCT OF THE ORIGINAL SIDE HUSTLE?

Side hustles—we all have them these days. Writing this is mine. We can credit the incredible pinot noirs coming out of New Zealand to a pioneer of the side hustle from the seventies.

The story goes that an errant rugby player returning from France attempted to smuggle cuttings from Domaine de la Romanée-Conti, Burgundy, in his gumboot.

In a twist of fate, the cuttings were confiscated at customs by a winemaker slash customs officer named Malcolm Abel. Abel paid for the cuttings to be processed by customs and planted them in his vineyard. Clive Paton bought three thousand cuttings from Abel and reaped the rewards. Abel died, never knowing how his actions would impact the revered pinot noirs of New Zealand.

When we conjure up our idea of a truly remarkable pinot noir, in our minds, we go straight to Burgundy, and with good reason. Unsurprisingly, the emergence of top-notch New Zealand pinots over the last ten years shares its lineage with those rolling hills of Burgundy.

One such pinot worthy of praise is the Cat's Pyjamas–Tisane pinot noir 2021 from Muselet Wines, Central Otago—£30.90.

I worked for a season at Muselet and saw first-hand that Ken Peterson has woven some magic with this vintage. My caveat is that if you push the boat out for a bottle of Tisane, it would be worth hanging onto it for a few years. If, on the other hand, you can buy a bucket load, fill your gumboots, cellar some and enjoy some. It's subtle and yet packs a punch with a complex structure. It has an outstanding palate weight to the finish. Roast chestnuts, dark maraschino cherry and subtle spices of thyme and vanilla dance on your tongue in this highly regarded pinot.

I promise future articles won't be as nepotistic. I want to recommend wines I love, and I know you, dear reader, will appreciate them too. Some may be wines from people I know. I'll work towards a review of a life-changing Californian chardonnay from an old lover who broke my heart. Stick with me; it will be worth the wait.

La Fille Maladroit

I walked past the shops and daydreamed, picturing Zero picking up *The Times*. Sitting at the kitchen table with a baby bouncing on one knee, spitting out his coffee when he saw my face beside my byline. Alex looking over his head, wishing the tables had turned.

Angus and Lucy running down to Holly's kitchen with a copy in hand, screaming on their way in and opening the page for her to see. Jude walking in and looking over their shoulders.

"Oh wow. That's cool. I mean, good for Elle," he'd say, not reading till the end, picking up some papers and rushing out again.

⁊⊙⊱

Mark sitting on a film set on a lot in LA, opening the page and saying, "That's our girl. Darkling strikes again."

⁊⊙⊱

And Françoise sat in her sublime French garden among the raspberry bushes and weird mini-vineyard, cutting out the article, which would be one of many she would add to her scrapbook.

⁊⊙⊱

A large grey poodle approached me, grabbed the ham and cheese baguette I planned to eat for lunch from my hand and ran off, dissipating my daydream back into the ether.

⁊⊙⊱

I was lounging around one rainy Saturday when Lucy called.

"You crack me up. I just finished reading your article. Is there nothing you can't turn your hand to? What you said about Jude at the end! I'm just waiting with bated breath for that review."

"What did he say? Not going to lie, it was touch and go whether I'd include it, but I feel like if I'm going to put myself out there like this, might as well let it all hang out."

"We haven't seen him for a couple of weeks. Been struck down with the flu for ages—can't seem to shake it."

"Get a check-up, won't you? Wish I were there to make you chicken soup."

"Anyway, enough doom and gloom. Any French lovers we need to know about?"

My winemaker and pseudo-wine reviewer achievements were stacking up, but love eluded me. However, wanting to forget the dream was one thing, but my DNA had other ideas, and a tiny part of me kept the flame alive. It wasn't as if I didn't go on dates, but no one could hold a candle to Jude, and each time they wanted to get serious, I'd make an excuse and break it off. Eligible bachelors in Épernay were getting scarce.

I was strict about not watching or reading anything in English except *The Times*. I was now completely fluent in French. Épernay became my home, and the idea of putting down roots in one place was growing on me. Life here was straightforward. You worked, had fun, dressed well, and ate well and all that equated to a happy and uncomplicated life.

Knowing I could live a whole life and not master all the intricacies of making Champagne, I thought that perhaps this was where I belonged. Telling Holly, Angus, and Lucy any of this scared me. It was a conversation I could see playing out in my mind. I knew they would be angry, and I thought they might let me go a little with each passing year until I wasn't in the club anymore—no more invitations on road trips. I would see the photos on Instagram and cry myself to sleep. One day, they wouldn't even wish me a happy birthday by phone. Then, it would slip to a text; then they might post on Facebook like an old friend you no longer knew, and even that would die off, and we'd lose touch altogether.

There was a Christmas party in London at *The Times* offices. Being remote, I ventured into the office only if I was in London for something else. I knew no one well, but I was there any way for a catch-up with Heidi and Vin, so I had little excuse not to go.

Vin had abandoned winemaking and was creating gin using water distilled from mist he'd collected on colossal plastic sheets in the Blue Mountains of New South Wales in Australia. He called it Mystic Moon, and Heidi had arranged a catch up with him in London, where he had meetings to get Mystic Moon into the international market. I wanted to write a review, but there was no way *The Times* would let me digress from wine. I intended to find someone else at the Christmas party to interview Vin and give him some free advertising, which was another reason for going.

My key contact was Lisa, the assistant to my editor, and I stuck to her like glue at the party, letting her introduce me to people. So, I was a little out on a limb when Lisa spotted a man in a strange tartan waistcoat she just had to talk to because she said he was 'the one fuckable man' there. I stood sipping my Champagne too fast and inspecting the baubles on the giant Christmas tree as I stuffed another sausage roll into my mouth.

"Any good?" said a deep voice behind me. I spun around and saw a dashing, fair-haired, Swedish-looking man. He was a dead ringer for

Alexander Skarsgård. I spilt some Champagne on my silk shirt and tried to chew and swallow the remaining sausage roll but choked on it and necked the Champagne.

"Oh god. I'm sorry to startle you. I recognised you from your column. Your photos don't do you justice. Pascal," he said, offering his hand, "I came here to make you a proposition."

I tilted my head at him and smirked.

"Well, um, no, not that kind of proposition," he said.

"I'm a TV producer. We're making a new wine show for the BBC, and well, after seeing you in the flesh—you'd be perfect. The camera would adore you, and we'd like to call it—"

"Let me guess—La Fille Maladroit?"

Pascal laughed with hesitation as if gauging my response.

"It's OK. I get it. It's a bankable brand thing. You should see the emails that keep streaming in. I can't make it stop."

"You have a dedicated email account? Interesting. It's a fair bit of travel if you'd be into that. I mean, it might not suit you."

"Oh, hell yeah, sounds amazing! It sounds perfect."

❧❦❧

It was painful to see Françoise and Juliette torn between sadness and happiness. They knew I wouldn't be back to live in Épernay. I promised that whatever happened, wherever I was, I would keep in touch, and I knew I'd be in France often.

They had shown me a level of kindness since we'd first met, which I had given up believing existed in people.

"Françoise, you have been a mentor and a mother to me. There's no gift I could give you to repay what you've done for me." I handed her a bottle of Châteaux Marguerite, Grand Dame.

"Drink this to welcome in 2024. It's great to drink now, but it'll be sublime by then. It's fresh with citrus and chamomile and has a complex texture. 2012 was an exceptional year! Also, I am hoping you can share it with someone."

I walked round to the side of her garden and pulled Monsieur Beaufoy into view. Françoise put her hand up to her throat, which was red, and tears formed at the corners of her pale blue eyes.

"Thomas?"

He held her frail hand and kissed her on both cheeks, and they stared into each other's eyes, unable to look away. Juliette and I stood nearby with our arms around each other. We had devised the plan a few weeks before and agreed that Françoise would never cause a scene when I was leaving.

❧

Two weeks before, I'd sat with Thomas Beaufoy at lunch and asked him about his life and how long he'd been at the châteaux, while waiting for the perfect moment to ask about Françoise. He had been avoiding me for weeks as if he knew I was stalking him. He sat back in his chair, rolled up his starched white shirt sleeves into neat little folds, straightened his light blue silk tie, removed his glasses, and rubbed his eyes.

"Why do you ask?"

"Well, I know we talked before about my friend Françoise. She used to be your friend too, didn't she? I'm leaving soon, as you know. I want you both to be happy, that's all. Isn't it time to forget the past?

You've taught me everything you know about Champagne, and she's taught me everything she knows about life. I see the two of you together instead of living in the same town streets apart but never meeting. It's such a waste. What happened? Why don't you speak?"

He tapped the wooden table and looked out of the iron-framed window onto the silver stones of Avenue de Champagne.

"Well. We were in love, and I was poor. Her family owned a Champagne house—Hoffman Estates—and I worked for them. I wanted to propose but didn't have enough money for the beautiful ring she deserved. Your first review hit me like a stone."

He paused as if he was willing the words to leave his mouth.

"I sold the cuttings that ended up in New Zealand. I stole them from Domaine de la Romanée–Conti, where I also worked extra hours to save for the ring. When I gave it to her, she wanted to know how I'd afforded it, and I couldn't lie. She broke it off then, and we haven't spoken since."

"What happened to the ring?"

He pulled out his worn black leather wallet, unzipped a compartment and passed me the diamond solitaire. I tilted it into the light, and it cast mini rainbows over the table.

"You still carry this around with you?"

"Yes. It reminds me every day not to take shortcuts in life."

I laughed.

"Jeez, I wish I'd known this when I wrote the article."

"You can't tell a soul about this."

"I'm joking, Thomas. I will never tell another living soul. Look, enough time has passed. She has a daughter, Juliette, and she agrees. This is hilarious, though. You are such a perfect gentleman. The thought of you stealing vines!"

"Shh, people are looking at us. Not another living soul."

Françoise handed me a small box and told me not to open it until I sat with a glass of Champagne on the Eurostar. I'd had enough of planes and imagined seeing many more of them, so I bought a train ticket at the last minute.

Françoise and Juliette hugged me, and we said our goodbyes. If there were a most used word of the year, like the most played song on my Apple Music account, it would have been 'goodbye' that year.

Sitting back in my seat, relaxing into my stress-free journey to Waterloo, I was excited but nervous about the show. The world of TV was alien to me; I'd never set foot in a TV studio, and it scared me it was happening for real in two days. Being thrown into the deep end wasn't what I'd expected, imagining there was a course I'd have to attend or at least some basic training in how to present on TV.

My phone lit up with Gerald's face.

"Morning, Elle. I've finalised your TV contract, but I wanted to double-check that you're OK with committing to two years. They can make you go wherever they want, and you don't have a lot of wiggle room in the terms."

"That's OK. What else am I going to do with myself?"

"Well, we would have all enjoyed seeing you return to California. Lucy puts on a brave face for you but misses you like crazy. Now no getting shit-faced on every flight with a stash of mini vodkas. You are going to be travelling a fair bit. I worry it's a lot for you. Anyway, see this contract out, and perhaps we can visit the idea of you producing the show down the line. I'd like to see you get some control over locations and timings, etc."

"Gerald, I don't say this often enough, but meeting you on that flight was one of the most fortuitous days of my life."

Gerald and Val had embraced the Californian life. He was CEO of Ignite now but still found time to take care of my petty legal issues. He was insistent, and I didn't want to trust anyone else. Besides, it gave me a good excuse to call him.

Angus and Holly had been happy for me, although I could see in their faces on the call that they were doing an excellent job of masking their disappointment.

"Oh, Elle, you are never coming back, are you?" said Holly.

Walter popped into view with a small plastic box.

"Hey, Walt. What you got there?"

"Aunty Elle. It's a lizard. He's sad because he can't have a birthday like me. He didn't have friends to play with. He doesn't have an aunt or anything like me, so I gave him a beetle, but they don't like each other. I'm both his daddys, like Angus and Grey."

"Angus, what does Walter mean?"

"He overheard us talking about a baby. We're getting a surrogate. I didn't want to do it without you here, but—"

I could tell he was tearing up, disappearing out of frame. All I could see was Grey looking down and Holly stretching her hand to Angus.

Lucy and Mark sighed when I told them, as if it was what they expected but were hoping for a different outcome.

I pulled the package from Françoise out of my bag, and the bouquet of Rive Gauche wafted into my face. I turned over the small card that was attached.

Dearest Elle,

My sadness did not end until we met on that plane, and you were gracious and kind. The depression had taken hold of me, which was why I was in London to see a hypnotherapist. I was desolate after my husband died, but you made me see it was possible to carry on living but have a different life. After hating that it took up so much of my family's life, you made me love Champagne again.

Juliette and I will miss you terribly, but we want you to know we are proud of you and the life you have built. You have shown Juliette how to be brave and strong, and I couldn't have asked for a better role model for her. Please keep in touch with all your news wherever you might be. If you are in France, we will visit you wherever you are—unless you are in Calais or somewhere equally awful! Please accept this small gift, which you can use on your show—we will watch every episode.

Bisous

Françoise x

I opened up the package and eased off the lid of the box. Sitting inside was an exquisite, handcrafted corkscrew. The box held a note from Laguiol. On the oak handle below the knife blade sat a bunch of grapes carved into the stainless steel, featuring a vine running down the handle. It reminded me of The Madonna Hotel. I'd always have to pack it in my suitcase, or I might lose it going through customs. That's how I lost my favourite Swiss army knife key ring when I was flying, and now it was in the hands of a Malcom Abel type.

Taking a sip of the Moët, I raised my glass to the passing French countryside, my friends, and my moment in time that would last in my memory as the best time of my life. Holding the corkscrew in my hand like a sword to conquer the world of television, I wondered what would happen next.

It was odd to be a passenger on a flight. Whenever a crew member told me what to do, I had to fight all urges to say, 'Yes, I know. I did your job for years; bother someone else.' As a passenger, I was always the kindest. I flew here, there, and everywhere, but now in business class. Being treated like crap myself had made me conscious of how not to treat people. I earned a reputation on Twitter for being one of the kindest celebrities people had bumped into. Well, B-list celebrity, anyway. I had the enviable perks of fame but could walk down a London street, and no one ever bothered me. It was an incredible life, but it was a solitary one. I reached into my bag, pulled out my laptop and emailed Angus.

"I'm so excited! It's twenty-three sleeps till we meet again, bestie. How are you and Grey? What's happening with the surrogate? I haven't heard from anyone in ages; no one is returning my calls. You've all forgotten me. So, I've been having a torrid affair with that TV chef, Damien Leven. I've put on a few pounds. He's always whipping up some delicious meal for me, and I can't say no. You'd like him. He's quite funny. Met his mum and dad a few weekends ago."

A reply landed in my inbox straight away:

"Just no! What is it with you and surnames? Eleven?"

"Eh?" I replied.

"You're Elle, and his surname is Leven,"

"Oh, right. Haha. Well, I wasn't planning on marriage. Just having fun."

"So, why did you meet the parents?"

"Uh. Dunno."

"Don't give up on love."

"I have, though. I'm going with the multiple cat option."

He sent me a cat emoji with love heart eyes, and I looked down at my table to see four empty bottles of Bombay Sapphire.

"Have you been hitting the bottle?"

"Yes. Two Bombay Sapphires."

"No, I mean in general."

"?"

"The latest review???"

I opened my laptop and pulled up the latest *Times* article.

'WHY DO WE LOVE TO HATE CHARDONNAY? IS IT ALL BS?'

In my first article, I alluded to a love affair with a divine Californian chardonnay. I refer to any period before I spent an idyllic autumn in California as BS—'Before Sonoma.'

I tried hard not to fall hook, line, and sinker, but I am imprisoned by its addictive palate, and you will be too.

During the eighties, a bottle of chardy was de rigueur and became mass-produced with careless winemaking; fast forward to the 2020s, and she has fallen from grace. It happens to us all. People called Karen come to mind as a current example. The difference with chardonnay is that unlike anyone named Karen—and I'm calling this naming of anything annoying 'Karen' out right now as mass bullying; stop it already—there might be a good reason you are not a fan.

If you know something about wine production, you'll know that we age wine in oak or steel—flashback to the eighties when they mostly aged chardonnay in oak barrels. If done in balance with the terroir, it can enhance chardonnay because it's a versatile grape heavily influenced by the region it's grown in. Oak barrels used aggressively to mask mistakes result in a wine that is an oak-infused, buttery mess you hate. What you hate is terrible wine, not chardonnay, per se. Invest in a cheap one, and you might as well go the whole hog, buy a box of wine, and put some popcorn in your glass.

Stainless steel barrels give us a crisp, clean finish so that all you can taste is the terroir, untainted. It's perfection in a glass. If you are a lover of an outstanding Chablis, you will also be a lover of an outstanding chardonnay—you just haven't tried one yet.

Sonoma is synonymous with outstanding wines, but no chardonnay in the region can match La Limonar 2016, La Vallée Estate £69.00.

From the first sip, I was forever in love with its simplicity, which delivers an outstanding balance of texture and acidity. La Limonar is a zesty fruit cocktail on a summer's day that's having a pool party in your mouth and tempting you with more and more until all you can do is submit and ask yourself why you ever thought chardonnay wasn't for you. Here, I must issue a warning—once you are under her spell, La Limonar will never let you go. On a hot summer night, your dreams will be of her lying silent in the cellars of La Vallée Estate, waiting for your return.

La Fille Maladroit

"I suppose it's a little obvious."

"Grey wants me to ask if you two got it on in the cellar. Oh, and is it really sixty-nine pounds or is that another double-entendre?"

"No comment."

I walked through the jet bridge into Barajas airport in Madrid, and my steps echoed on the thinly carpeted metal floor. I had a love-hate relationship with jet bridges. Heading onto the plane—anxiety at impending confinement. Away from the plane—excitement of being home or setting foot in a new place on an unknown adventure.

"Excuse me, Miss Darkling, may we have your autograph?"

A dark-haired teen rushed up to me with her friends as I walked through the gate into arrivals, and I obliged and tried to walk away before anyone else asked.

"You are so funny," she called out to me.

"I love how you pretend to make all those mistakes on your show."

Turning, I looked into her eyes. "Oh, it's not pretend. That's the real me. Remember, no one is perfect, and that's OK." I winked and walked off to collect my bags.

At the hotel, I walked up to the check-in desk and placed my purse on the counter with a thud. Yes, I would need one key. No, I didn't want a wake-up service. Yes, I would like breakfast and a newspaper. No, I would not like a free drink from the bar. Angus had now put thoughts in my mind that I needed to slow down on the drinking front. I couldn't recall much of writing the La Limonar review, which scared me.

I was here to film some shows, and then I'd meet Angus and Grey in Burgundy and I'd even slotted some time off to travel on with them to London. They were coming to a taping of the show along with Françoise, Thomas, and Juliette.

The dream of the same pillow each night was all-consuming. My life was a whirlwind of people and places. Dorothy in *The Wizard of Oz* had nothing on me, but I was ready for Kansas full-time.

There had been lots of the usual requests, such as *Dancing with the Stars* and the celebrity version of *The Great British Bake Off,* but I didn't want to be a media whore.

What I longed to do was buy a vineyard. I had to admit I was jealous of all my friends. They were living the life I wanted for myself.

So, this break would allow me to sit down, clear my thoughts, and plan the next stage of my life.

Gerald and Val were on a European tour, so they would stay at the hotel for a few nights, and we had locked in a meeting with the producers to work out an exit plan.

"Miss Darkling, um, Miss Darkling."

"Oh, sorry, I'm a little tired; what did you say?"

"I was explaining the pillow menu."

"I'll have a margarita with extra cheese."

"No, madam, I was explaining the pillow menu. Please consult the room service menu on your television to order a pizza."

"Haha, oh right, pillow menu. Yes, thank you. I'll do that."

I blushed and grabbed the room key and wished I could teleport myself into the lift so I didn't have to walk away, knowing that the reception staff would be having a good laugh about me.

I was taping a show in a state-of-the-art vineyard in La Mancha. It was over an hour's drive each day, which allowed me to catch up on emails my assistant had already filtered and consider my next wine review. I glanced at the passing scenery and wondered whether Jude or Lara had seen the article. I didn't know why I had written it that way. It was like a therapy session without the therapist. It surprised me they had even given it a thumbs up at *The Times*. I should have tried to slip in an article about Vin's gin. It was excellent, but I knew how hard it was to market even a superior product on a limited budget. I was sorry I hadn't secured a review with a colleague at *The Times*. I was a little worried about him. The current financial climate wasn't great, and it was the wrong time to launch a new business. I made a note to ask Angus if there was a place for him in California.

Sweet Jubilee

"Elle, you are so funny on screen. *Wine Adventures with La Fille Maladroit*, now there's a catchy title," said Angus. "Even I'm astonished about how many stuff-ups you make in one episode. But where's my commission cheque for the original idea?"

"Angus, when I think of how mad I was with you for the TikTok account and everything, look what it gave me. There would be no *Times* column or TV show without you, so name your price."

"Come home," he said.

I watched him looking down at the ground by the open door of their hire car. Grey hair speckled his hairline, and his gold wedding band caught my eye on his tanned hand. It was a rare moment of seriousness from him.

I was filming in Burgundy. Angus and Grey had already planned the trip back to Europe to launch Angus's book in London and sort out Grey's apartment. We thought this was the perfect excuse for them to see an episode of the show being filmed and for us to spend some time together.

He was right about me. I spilt wine, called people by the wrong name, forgot the country I was in, and once in Italy, I even tripped and head-butted a tree.

I filmed during the day and at night we spent hours eating long French meals with copious amounts of wine. Angus said it was a busman's holiday.

The evenings were cool, and the days were dry and glorious, and it edged its way up in the best moments of my life ratings.

We were all staying in a hotel in the centre of Beaune. I arrived the same day as Angus and Grey to catch up alone before the others came.

"Our room has a full-sized model of a brown sheep in it. When I think of the stick I got for booking The Madonna Inn," said Angus.

"Yeah, mine's pink and purple with a spiral staircase," I said. "My assistant booked it all. I told her to book the most expensive one."

The hotel was white with thin white shutters on every window. I fell in love with the internal fourteenth-century courtyard and restaurant in the cellar. The whole place creaked at the seams with antique furniture and huge oil paintings of French noblemen in dark wigs juxtaposed with a modern bar area.

"I feel like the interior designer was on acid," said Grey.

"Well, there is a twenty-four-hour bar and a Michelin-star restaurant. We'll survive," I said.

"Well, don't write any reviews while we're here. Next, you will review a Beaujolais and compare it with your tryst with young Taj," said Angus.

"Oh, don't. Did Jude read it?"

"Hmm, don't know. We're not talking much these days."

"Why?"

"He broke my best friend's heart. What more reason do I need? Write one about Zero and entitle it "So here's the thing about—"

I threw a cushion at him. I watched the pair, comfortable together, in tune with the other's movements and needs. They finished sentences and laughed at each other's jokes.

"Hey, get a room, you two! Maybe it was me who should have created the dating app. I seem to have a knack for it."

"I heard on the grapevine Zero and Alex got divorced this year," Angus said.

"Oh, good for her!" I said. "That asshole should be alone. I hope he burns in hell."

Françoise, Thomas, and Juliette turned up during a shoot at a local vineyard the next day, and Angus and Grey looked after them and introduced themselves.

"We are here in Burgundy in the most famous wine-growing region of Côte d'Or, home to one of the most well-known Burgundy vineyards, Domaine de la Romanée-Cont—" I stuttered, conscious of the fact that Thomas was there and even though we weren't at Domaine de la Romanée-Conti, I couldn't look up at him.

"Sorry, guys. I had a tickle in my throat," I said. "Can we start that again?"

I introduced Charles Duchamp, a local vineyard owner, who explained the difference between a claret and a Burgundy. We tasted some of his wines, and a waiter in a suit pushed out a trolley covered with a white tablecloth and on top of it was a plate of oysters for us to try. Laughing, I took a big swig of the nearby pinot noir, but it didn't help, and I had a laughing fit.

"Sorry, Charles. Are you a fan of James Bond? In *Diamonds Are Forever*, the baddies wheel a trolley just like that one to Sean Connery and his girlfriend with oysters on it and offer him a 'Nineteen-fifty-five Mouton Rothschild.' Bond sniffs the cork and says 'The wine is quite excellent. Although for such a grand meal I would have expected a claret.' The baddy makes an excuse about poorly stocked cellars and then Bond says, 'Mouton Rothschild *is* a claret and I've smelt that aftershave before and both times I've smelt a rat.' The claret, the trolley, and the waiter—oh, the whole thing came into my head. Sorry, Charles I digress!"

Charles started crying and laughing because I had butchered my way through a Sean Connery impression.

"Oh, just wait till they bring out the Bombe Surprise," he said.

The crew and audience cracked up, and I put my head on my knees. I was laughing so much my make-up was running down my face.

"That was hilarious, my friend. I loved it," said Angus. "While you were talking I remembered something I'd read about Champagne featuring in every Bond film. It used to be Taittinger because Ian Fleming included it in the books, but these days, it's Bollinger. I read they pay ten million per movie. You've got me thinking about wine placement for Castello di Amanté. After all, Mark has the contacts. Anyway, how do you know the words to a scene in *Diamonds Are Forever* off by heart?"

"Zero wouldn't let me watch much else for two years."

We dined in the hotel restaurant that night, and most of my favourite people were in one room. I sat at the head of the table, watched them all chatting and laughing, and knew this was what I needed back in my life, but I needed it every day.

"Elle, you are very entertaining. It would be a boring show without your funny little moments," said Françoise. She pushed her grey, immaculate hair to one side and smoothed her pleated skirt. I was stunned by how beautiful she looked. The only visible clue to her age was the grey hair and liver spots on the back of her hands.

"You're wearing the ring! Does this mean you are engaged?"

"No, but it's a symbol of forgiveness and commitment. I won't marry again, but I love Thomas, and in the end, what he did changed the wine world, and it was so long ago."

"Thank you so much for coming. It's been hard missing you all so much. Can you give me some advice about something? Travelling is doing my head in. Do you think moving to California and buying a vineyard is a sane plan?"

"That would be a wonderful idea. Your friends are so lovely, and you have your sister there. It's time, no?"

She placed a veined hand on mine, and my anxiety subsided.

"Will you promise me to keep in touch with Juliette? I have a feeling she might follow you when I pass away one of these days. She still hasn't fallen in love with anyone, and you know she considers you a sister."

"I think of her that way, too. I'll never lose touch with her, but you will live to be a hundred, Françoise. Your blood is just Champagne these days."

⚜

"Well, here we are again, dear old Heathrow," said Angus.

"I'm not experiencing the nostalgia like you," I said.

My heart raced a little as we walked from the gate to arrivals. Grey was striding along with his long legs, and Angus and I trailed behind like small children.

We caught an Air France flight the day before Angus's book launch and reserved rooms at a cute period hotel near the Barbican tube station in Clerkenwell.

⚜

My room was called The Rook's Nest, a quirky two-story penthouse with a huge round window encased with red brickwork and when I peered through, I could see St. Paul's. The bathroom had a Victorian bathing machine, according to the online review. It looked like a regular bath with glass screens and deep green brocade curtains matching the bedroom walls.

The big, hot, green bubble bath awaited me, and I poured a glass of Champagne, climbed in, and discovered it was too hot. I yelped and added cold water until it was less severe but nearly overflowing.

I was lying there trying not to flood the bathroom, and I thought I ought to wash my hair, so I submerged it to get it wet. As I sat up, my hair caught around a tap, trapping me. I pulled until it hurt and concluded I would have to break off an enormous chunk of hair to escape so I called Angus. My phone was on a stool next to the bath, along with the Champagne, and I kept my head still as I put him on loudspeaker. "You can say no, but I'm in a pickle."

"Oh god, what now?"

"I'm stuck in the bath. Go find a key and save me."

"While you are in the bath? Ew, Elle, I'm not sure I want to see your bits and bobs."

"Oh, it's OK. I know it's a lot to ask, but otherwise, I'll have to pull an enormous chunk of my hair out."

Angus and Grey let themselves in, and Grey waited in the bedroom. Angus held his stomach and had trouble breathing when he saw me all red-faced, up to my neck in bubbles in a vast green soup bath. He called to Grey, "It's OK, you can't see any minge—you can come in!"

"Hehe," said Grey. "It's *Pretty Woman*! Except you fell into a witch's cauldron."

"What's the plan?" said Angus.

"I don't know! Do something. It hurts."

He knelt behind the bath and eased the hair around the tap.

"What is this weird bath, anyway?"

"It's a Victorian bathing machine!"

"Oh, I read about them," said Grey. "Victorians used to carry them onto the beach to get changed."

"Bet they didn't get their flippin' hair stuck around a tap," said Angus.

When the hair was free, I raised my arms in a celebratory cheer and forgot I was naked as my boobs popped up, and Grey looked as if he might wet himself.

M. J. PARFITT

"Oh, Elle, you are the most hilarious girl I ever met. Please, please move back to California. Life is so dull without you!" said Angus.

Angus's book launch venue was a little event space with a library called Fidelio in Clerkenwell. It had three levels with a mezzanine restaurant area. The basement lounge had a bar. It was a light-filled building with odd-shaped windows and exposed bricks. People were already arriving when we got there. I was talking to old airline friends when I saw Monty Blake walk in and rushed over to greet him.

"Monty! This would not have happened without you. You got so many stories out of everyone. You're amazing."

"I have something for you," he said.

He handed me an envelope, and I opened it. Inside was a letter detailing how many miles I'd flown for Asana Air.

"Angus asked me to get it for you."

I hugged him and told him I would always hold it dear, and I meant it. I had found my own phosphorus, but flying had given me the greatest gift in my life—my two best friends.

I contacted Monty after he'd given me his card in Queenstown. As soon as Angus had started on the book, I'd called and asked him to email the crew for funny stories and anecdotes they wouldn't mind sharing. He had gone over and above, collecting over two hundred, many of them making it into the book. There was a special dedication inside the front cover to all the crew at Asana Air.

"Surprise!"

Lucy, Holly, and Nick jumped out in front of me. I broke down.

"You guys kept that a secret! You don't know how good it is to see you all! So that's why I hadn't heard from any of you."

"Oh, it's been so hard. In the end, I didn't call you back because I knew I would have caved and blurted it all out," said Holly.

"Well, the problem with this little huddle is now I know you will talk to no one else all night," said Angus.

"Isn't his book amazing?" I said to the group.

"I love it," said Lucy. "Did you see he put the eye drop story in there?"

The front cover had a beautiful picture of a cloud Angus had taken, and he'd called it *A Crack in the Clouds*, and as I looked closer up at the photo, I was sure it looked like the bum-shaped cloud.

"Angus! Is this the bottom cloud?"

"Oh my god, you are the only person in this room who noticed."

"Clever you, Elle!" said Holly.

"Oh, she's not clever," said Angus. "Tonight, Grey and I had a full frontal from her, and we saw her tape a show in France, and she failed at a Sean Connery impression. The whole thing was nuts."

Nick spat out his wine, and Angus recounted the bubble bath boob flash.

"Shush," I said, in a better Sean Connery accent since I had been practising. "I'm on the BBC, you know. It's a serious business, and you know what they say. What happens in a lady's bathing machine stays in a lady's bathing machine."

Holly and I revisited our parents' graves and saw Dad's old car parked outside. It was gleaming with a wax-shine, making us both smile.

"George?" I called out into the enormous workshop. "Are you here?"

He came out looking puzzled and beamed from ear to ear when he saw us.

"Ahh, my guardian angels!"

George was excited to tell me his family always watched my show. Since I had given him the car, his life had improved. Finding a second job was a tremendous help as his wife had to stop working to care full-time for their daughter.

At the grave, the roses were not in bloom but covered in buds; they were thriving.

"Oh, I forgot," he said. "Come back to the shed with me, will you?"

He opened a drawer and pulled out an envelope addressed to me in Brighton. It even had a stamp.

"I found it under the front seat of your dad's car; I was wondering how to get it to you."

We both stared at the familiar handwriting, much neater than ours:

Dear Elle,

I am so proud of you for changing your life. You are brave. Few people can pick themselves up and take a risk like you did.

Sorry for not listening when you keep telling me to go to the doctor. I've made an appointment for tomorrow. You're right about the check-up. Mum would have told me to stop being silly about it.

If anything happens to me, take care of Holly, won't you? She's let go of her dreams along the way. Help her find them again. I know you will. You are always thinking of everyone else. I hope you can look after yourself now too. I might plant the peach roses on Mum's grave this week. What do you think?

OK, well, over and out. See you when you come home next week-end. Can't wait! I'm sure Holly has a dessert planned! Also, there's something I need to talk to you both about.

Love, Dad

"Oh, Dad," I said, dropping the letter.

Holly hugged me.

"He was a wise man, wasn't he?" said Holly. "You did what he thought you'd do."

"You mean plant the roses?"

"Well, no. That was bizarre. I meant taking me along for the ride."

"We're sisters. You would have done the same for me, but what did he want to talk about?"

"Search me," said Holly, "And we will never know now, will we?"

George looked on misty-eyed and hugged us.

"Your dad did a fine job with you both."

We were filming in Argentina, but I had wrapped up my last episode, and now I was taking a break. My present to myself was a ten-day hike to a glacier, and then I'd head to San Francisco for my new life in Sonoma.

I'd been searching the internet for vineyards for sale for weeks, so much so that my wrist ached. The best part was that I had told none of them. I planned to drive up to Sonoma and surprise them all.

I was sitting on the edge of the hotel pool after a massage in my fluffy robe, daydreaming, when my mobile rang.

"Elle?"

I paused, not knowing how to respond. Jude's voice was silent on the other end of the line.

"Um, I drew the short straw in calling—It's Lucy. I'm so sorry, Elle. She's sick. Come home. It's bad. It's in the lymph nodes. There's nothing left to do. I'm so sorry, Elle. Elle, are you there?"

My hand relaxed, and my phone fell into the pool. I sat there staring at it, sinking to the bottom, and wanted to follow it.

Lucy had seemed so well in London. I thought about how radiant she looked.

A man swam up to me and handed me the wet phone. I didn't want it back. It was a newish phone, so it still worked. There was no getting away from reality.

My assistant sounded concerned when I asked him to change my flight to the next day. He said he would get onto it, and I sat there numb, waiting for him to reply, checking my phone every few minutes.

As the phone beeped with the updated tickets, I looked up and saw the pool was empty. My feet were white and wrinkled, and the sky was dark. Overcome by a sudden desire to drink myself into oblivion, I opened my contacts and called Angus.

"How bad is it?"

Looking out over Argentina as we took off, I knew I'd never return if Lucy died, but I'd be back if she lived. I would bring her along, and we'd trek to the glacier together.

The people behind me were chatting. "Who do you think you are,

Elle Darkling?" the lady scoffed at her husband as he gave her his tasting notes of the wine he was drinking.

It appeared I was a household name in Argentina, and I didn't give two fucks about any of it. This life had cost me valuable time with my friend.

My urge to vomit overcame me because of a headache that had come on since talking to Jude. It was moving into my face, and even my teeth hurt. Paracetamol was having no effect, so I ordered a scotch on the rocks, which did the trick, and I was out cold.

The plane lurched, and it woke me. Turbulence had always scared me; this was the worst I'd ever experienced. Overhead compartments burst open, spewing their contents on passengers, and carts escaped the galley. I wished I hadn't had the scotch as it gurgled around inside me. I looked at my fellow passengers, pale and frightened, and my mind turned to Lucy, and I imagined how she looked. Angus had told me it was desperate and that she had stopped the chemo. I was returning to say goodbye. It would take a miracle to save Lucy.

No one had my flight details in San Francisco. When Angus had asked, I'd been evasive. Before seeing them all, I wanted time to mull everything over, not just about Lucy but Jude and how a new life would work. The journey up to Sonoma was bittersweet. With Carly Simon to keep me company, I arrived at Castello di Amanté without knowing how but wondering if I'd been listening to one song on repeat—"California." I had chills as I passed over the Golden Gate Bridge, and my bones ached like a storm was coming.

M. J. PARFITT

Lucy, Mark, and Angus rushed to greet me at the door. My assistant had been so worried he'd called Angus with all the details. We sat outside on the patio, and Holly and Nick arrived with scones and jam. It was an awkward meeting. Lara was there with Jude, and she gave me a big hug. She was different without her phone as an extension of her hand. She had grown into a normal person as if the electronic appendage had stunted her emotional growth all this time.

We chatted a lot, but no one talked about cancer.

Lucy was thin. Even under her flowing kaftan, I saw she was all skin and bone. She had a silk scarf tied up on her head in a knot and a porcelain, airbrushed face. Her eyes gave the secret away. She caught me looking at her and smiled a tired 'C'est la vie' kind of smile. I moved beside her, holding her hand, and putting my head on her shoulder. I wanted to make use of every minute I had left with her.

"Oh, I forgot. I have something for you all in the car."

I came back with several bottles of wine I'd bought in Patagonia.

"Now, this will interest you all. It's a Domaine Nico Soeur et Freres, a pinot noir from Le Paradis, a small vineyard in Argentina. It reminds me of a Barolo. This amused me—the soil is heavy in lime and compacted. The locals call it Indian cement!"

I popped my hand in my bag for the corkscrew.

"Hang on, you've got a new fancy one," said Angus.

He took it and ran his hands over the engraved handle.

"Yeah, it was a present from Françoise when I left. I don't go anywhere without it."

I touched the necklace that Jude had given me, and we locked eyes."

"Cherry, floral and packed with fruit. It's quite austere, isn't it, Elle?" said Jude.

We all sat drinking. No one spoke. We didn't need to—the wine connected us. Even Lucy had a little sip, and I knew she wouldn't be able to taste much with all the drugs she was on, but she made a good show of saying how wonderful it was.

Everyone drifted off, and it was down to Lucy, me, and Angus; we helped her into her room, which was now off the main foyer. She padded on the travertine floor barefoot, her toenails still immaculate, but I observed a more subdued hue of tangerine. Angus and I glanced over her shoulders as she stooped, her fragile frame taking little effort to support. The Camilla kaftan with a print of the vibrant Amalfi Coast billowed behind her. I didn't think I'd be able to visit there ever again.

We eased Lucy onto the bed, exhausted from the social inter-actions of the afternoon. I turned to look at the room. Flatscreen TV on the wall, cut crystal vases overflowing with fresh flowers, a drip pushed off to one side. I watched the droplets inside the bag trickle down, mountains of pills, reading glasses I didn't know she wore, and next to the bed, piles of books: *Cancer Vixen, Beloved, As I Lay Dying—Slaughterhouse-Five*. Angus and I saw the book at the same time and exchanged a smile.

"Well, you two read it, didn't you? Right—" she said with a wheezy breath. "Now listen. This is what's going to happen. I don't want arguments or protests. I've thought about it, and Gerald and I have been over the legal stuff with a fine-toothed comb."

Angus started to interrupt her. "No, Angus! Let me finish. I'm outta here soon, but there's this whole vineyard to run. Mark can't do it. I imagine he'll make a new movie. I know he's always getting offered roles. Anyway, long, and short of it, we don't have kids, my mum's dead. You're it, folks. You are my remaining family. Mark and I've agreed to split the vineyard three ways between you two and him. Elle, I want you to run the place; Angus, keep working your magic on everything you do, which we know, my friend, is a lot. You may have to pull back on Jude's role or quit it, but it's up to you to figure out. In a nutshell, that's it. I've put aside a trust for Walter's college fees and bought Holly and Nick the cottage. Keep a good eye on Mark and Jude for me. Jude may appear happy now, but god knows how long it will last with that Lara. Elle, I'm not sure where you want to live. You might be a bit of a spare wheel at Angus and Grey's. You might like to convert one barn into a cottage, and I've also set aside some cash for that. Chat with Grey and see what he recommends. For now, you can stay here."

"But what about the T—" said Angus.

"Enough," said Lucy, holding up a hand. "Can you come back later, Angus, and we can chat?"

She flopped back on the pillow, exhausted from talking, and Angus and I stood open-mouthed. I walked up and stared close up at her face to make sure she was still breathing.

"Not again, weirdo," said Lucy. "I am still alive for now. Now, out of my face. And so it goes," she said.

Angus was silent. We closed the door as Lucy slept and stood unable to move our feet. I looked down to see a tear escape my eye and splash on the tiles. Angus saw it, too, and he closed his eyes and swallowed hard.

"How can we accept this?" asked Angus. "I mean, it's too much."

We walked back down to the cottage as Grey was pulling in.

"What's happened? Is it Lucy?" he said, jumping out and putting an arm around both of us.

"No. It's not that; it's the vineyard. Lucy's leaving it to us," I said.

We sat around the breakfast bar and contemplated the magnitude of the situation.

"Well, you don't have a choice, guys. It's a lot, true, but it's her dying wish. Talk about Champagne problems," said Grey.

He was right. It was a Champagne problem.

"Yeah, but shouldn't Mark have it all? I mean, they built this up together," I said. "I can't face him now. What if he's angry?"

"Mark?" said Angus. "Never seen Mark angry, and they've already sorted this out together. What will you do, Elle? How can you run this and do the TV show?"

"Oh, well, that was supposed to be a surprise. I already quit the show. I'm back here for good. It's time to be with all you guys."

Angus burst into tears as if a wave of built-up emotion after holding the fort at the vineyard on his own for months and losing Lucy was all rolled into one perfect storm, and he let go.

"You've made my year. Nothing is the same without you. Is it,

Grey? Tell her. We do all this stuff and then go, 'It's a shame Elle wasn't here.' It's been tragic. I can handle this now. I've been wondering if I would fall to pieces. I contemplated going back to Esalen and zoning out on shrooms to get through it all; seeing you today, I breathed a sigh of relief, and now—well, now I know I can deal with any old shite—and Holly, she's going to be on cloud nine. Did you tell her?"

"I haven't told anyone yet. I was going to surprise you all, then Jude called, and my phone fell in the pool, and I took it as a sign to wait until I got here."

Angus rolled his eyes.

We returned to see Lucy a few hours later, and she was sitting up in bed reading *The Picture of Dorian Gray*. Camomile tea wafted past my nose; her nurse walked past us in the doorway and touched my shoulder.

"OK, you caught me. I was trying to get through *A Hundred Books Before You Die*. The big question is, will I make it? I'm on twenty-five. Perhaps I should leave it there; it was my favourite age. Well, what's the decision, then?"

"We can do it if it's OK with Mark. I mean, shouldn't he have it all? We would work here for you," I said.

"No way! That doesn't work for me. That's the whole point. I'm leaving it to you, dumbo, because you're family, and it's my hard-earned coin sitting out there. Mark will remarry some young starlet, and why should she benefit from my fucking inheritance?"

"Hmm, fair point, I guess," said Angus.

"Elle, can you quit the TV show?"

"She already did," said Angus. "It was going to be a surprise."

"Surprise," I said.

Chardonnay

$\mathcal{I}$ was having tea with Holly, and I knew as Jude pulled up in his truck with Angus sitting beside him, they had news that would define the rest of our lives.

There had been occasional peaks, but life tumbled that September into a deep trough. I had known deep down there was a fault line running below us all, waiting to crack open and blast us with a tsunami of pain. We'd all had it too good, and now it was time to pay the piper. Lucy had been slipping from us day by day. It was as if her sorting things out had left her nothing to live for. Angus said she declined as soon as she had seen me and told us her plans. Every visit to her room, I lost more of her. She'd stopped eating and they had her pumped up with morphine to stop her screaming in pain. The vapour from toxic drugs, mixed with vomit, hung in the air each time I visited her room. It was awful enough that Lucy would die, and she had long since come to terms with it. Still, cancer was a cruel beast which took away the one thing she needed more than the air she needed to breathe—her independence. As soon as she lost that, she lost everything she was. Mark sat next to her bed most of each day, holding her hand. He was dying, too, in his way.

"She's gone, Elle. She's gone," said Angus.

I sat on the front step next to him and hugged my knees, rocking back and forth until Jude stopped pacing and sat by my side. We stayed like that, resting our heads on each other's shoulders for a long time, and when I surfaced into reality, the light had changed, and a bright, clear sky had become overcast.

Our worlds were never the same again. The planet kept spinning, but the fracture lines marked a spot of a significant loss that changed who we were forever.

The funeral was a celebration of Lucy. Her favourite flowers were the same as mine, peonies, and Mark had bought every single one in California. The church shone from a huge stained-glass window. It sang out in orange and red against the abundance of wood in the rafted ceiling. Flower arrangements with vast swathes of peonies sat at the end of every row of arched blonde wooden benches. The aroma hit you as soon as you walked through the doors, and to this day, I will never forget that divine fragrance when I'm reminded of Lucy.

Mark had created a day that epitomised her. This wasn't a day of darkness but one bursting with colour and life. He'd told us all to wear orange because it was her favourite colour, and it all fit together like a perfect ensemble with the stained-glass window as though he'd planned it that way.

The soundtrack to Lucy's farewell was a string quartet playing "Con Te Partirò," and despite being as sad as I'd ever been in my life, it gave me something memorable to hold on to: Lucy, head-to-toe in Camilla standing before a brilliant stained-glass window, barefoot with orange nail polish on her toes, surrounded by her favourite flowers.

People poured into the church until there were no more seats. I sat, eyes closed, tapping my foot, and scratching my head. Angus had to nudge me twice when Mark called out my name. Lingering, willing an overdue earthquake to arrive before my feet touched the pulpit steps. My mind was a dark void, and all that consumed it was thoughts of a glass of water or a shot of Tito's—either would do. Tapping my pocket for my speech, I found it wrapped around a mini–Grey Goose. With my hand in my pocket, it was a breeze to open the screw top after years of practice. Angus was always there for me, always thinking about what I'd need. The speech fluttered to the floor, and I bent to pick it up, swigged the vodka and stood up again with my placebo alcohol confidence, letting me become someone else altogether.

Looking up at the congregation, my eyes reflected a magnificent sunset. Every shade of orange imaginable and unimaginable combined to paint a nuanced masterpiece.

"Sorry about that. I dropped my speech. Lucy, um, Lucy. She was my best friend, along with you, Angus."

As I gestured to him, Angus swirled his finger at me above his head, and I carried on.

"I'm sorry, this is hard. You don't meet many people in life who are your soulmates. Your ride-or-die pack—the ones who know all your worst secrets but love you anyway."

My tears dripped onto the scrunched notepaper and made the blue ink run. It was illegible. I balled it up, threw it over my shoulder and went rogue as I was apt to do on every episode of my TV show. Life's scripts were guidelines to me. Lucy wouldn't be standing up here if I was dead, reading off a piece of paper in a wooden, contrived fashion.

"Um, Lucy was always the same from the day I met her living in a council house with her mum to the day she became a billionaire; she was always the same Lucy. She judged none of us, and if I'm honest, there were many times she might have judged me. We were all orbiting around her. She was like the moon and its gravitational pull on the oceans—she had it on all of us. Now we're lost, but she's still here. Something is still pulling me, unless it's like when you lose a limb, and it still feels attached."

The room erupted into laughter. I looked over at Angus as he put two hands over his face.

"Uh, sorry, that wasn't a joke, but I'll take the applause. I know Lucy is laughing somewhere! Anyway, a handful of people here know how our story started: how Lucy became the richest under thirty in the world, how I changed my life and became a winemaker and alter ego, La Fille Maladroit. How Angus published a book and now runs a thriving vineyard, how my sister and her family moved here to California and made La Vallée Estate a gastronomic success, how Grey moved to California and became an interior designer to the stars, how Jude and Mark have two of the most successful vineyards in Sonoma, how Gerald and Valerie invested in Ignite, and even how a street cat called Luis wound up at the most fabulous home a cat could wish for.

"It all started with a Philip, the cabin crew code for a passenger you'd like to punch in the face."

The congregation laughed again, and I blushed.

"All this is to say, don't discount the shitty moments life throws at you. Like this moment. Undoubtedly one of the shittiest moments we will have. You never know what might happen tomorrow because of this day. Lucy always said she owed her success in life to me, but that wasn't true. Something connected us, like mushroom mycelium, and we helped each other grow and manifest our dreams. Lucy achieved many great things but was brave and ingenious enough to create Ignite. Angus and I were her support team. And she was ours. Everyone needs one. I hope you all have one because it's been the greatest gift of my life.

"Anyway, now to the devastating task of moving forward without wonderful Lucy, but we have to. We have to wake up tomorrow and live life for her because it's what friends do.

"I can stand here and say I don't have many regrets about my friendship with Lucy. Perhaps that I didn't come home sooner and that I didn't say all this and more to her when she was here. Do that. Tell everyone you love what they mean to you today, and how they make you a better person, and then if you find yourself in my position, it'll be one regret you won't have," I said.

Then, there was no more to be done to stop myself crying, along with everyone in the church, and Jude rushed up and took me back to my seat. Angus looked into my eyes and held my hand.

"And so it goes," he said.

Mark walked into the office looking dishevelled, with a five o'clock shadow and dark patches under his bloodshot eyes. He hugged me and didn't seem to know how to let go. I'd read somewhere that you should never be the first to let go with kids, so I leaned into him and waited for him to make a natural break away from me. There was an awkward silence. The essence of hard booze was seeping out of his pores, and he no longer had the familiar scent of his aftershave.

"Um, you know, when Lucy explained she left you and Angus her share of the vineyard, she left something out. She thought it better that I tell you. It's easier if I show you," he said, standing and opening the door for me.

We got in his jeep and travelled on a dirt road about a mile off to the left of the main house.

"Where the heck are we going, Mark?"

"You'll see."

We parked by a dry-stone wall with two arched old wooden washed teal gates and a tarnished brass bullhead pull on each side. The sign on the front read Phosphorus Tequila, and a familiar tiny carved agave plant sat at its side as a logo. He opened the doors, and fields and fields of agave as far as the horizon went filled my field of vision. The frosted green tips of the agave contrasted against the sandy soil, creating a mirage. I thought I was in the Mojave Desert, not Sonoma.

Off to the right was another door with machine noise and chatter behind it, and Mark opened it. A guy I had seen walking around the estate held his hand up to us and continued talking to another worker.

"What is this, *Breaking Bad?*"

I saw Mark laugh for the first time since Lucy died.

"No, I'm not making meth, Darkling; this is our new tequila brand, Phosphorus. The whole thing was Jude's idea. We used Champagne yeast he had left over to ferment it; it's incredible. Better than we ever imagined. I'm going to Japan tomorrow to film a commercial for it. You, me, and Angus own a third of Castello di Amanté, but we all own a quarter of this brand, including Jude. Can you guys still work together? I mean, I am counting on it. It's looking a lot like we are going to be billionaires from it—I shit you not," he said. "Angus has been amazing dealing with all the distributor negotiations, and Gerald has been—well, you know Gerald. Nothing happens without Gerald."

I was silent.

"What the fuck? You're kidding? You've pulled a Clooney!"

"No, not kidding, but can you manage all this for me? Being here right now is killing me. Will you be OK working with Jude? We could ask Angus, but he doesn't know the technical stuff like you. Are you OK with handling it?" he said. "Sorry to drop this on you; it's a lot."

"Jeez, but tequila? Mark? What do I know about it?"

He passed me a shot glass, and we knocked back the tequila.

"Woah. That's so smooth. I can work with Jude. Water under the bridge and all that. Why didn't you tell me about all this?"

"We wanted it to be a surprise. Then Lucy got the cancer back, and shit, everything's been—I don't know how we even got to this point. Jude's been running it all. He said to wait to tell you because it might be too much to digest on top of losing your best friend. I mean, what it's worth. I know it seems unbelievable—but here it is." He waved his arm across the fields of agaves as though he couldn't care less about any of it.

I held up my hand over my eyes; it was staggering.

"Mark, this is impressive. You guys have been busy. I should be grateful you and Lucy have made me insanely rich, but you know I'd swap every dollar to have her back with us."

He looked proud and then broke down. I held him again, and we walked back to the car, and he leaned on the bonnet. I didn't know if he was fixable, but I owed it to Lucy to try.

"It's just—this was for Lucy so I could stop the movie stuff, and it was such a perfect solution, and now she's gone. I can't be here right now, Elle. Are you OK with giving up your TV job? It's a lot to ask."

"No, it's OK. Travelling and I are sick of each other. It's time to be here for all of you, Mark. It will be good to settle down. Why didn't I decide to do it when Lucy was still here? It will be my biggest regret in life. Plus, they want me to consider doing a show from here. It's all in negotiation. Gerald came to La Mancha, and we had a good meeting with the execs. We may do a wine spin-off show. Although looking at this, we should do one on tequila."

"She was proud of you and how you turned a shit show into an amazing life. We are all proud of you."

"So, Japan?"

"Hai! I've been trying to learn a bit of Japanese on Duolingo. It's been years since I was there. I have a film to work on after the commercial; I'll be there for a few months. Perhaps it'll help me heal— throwing myself back into work. I feel bad dropping you in it like this."

"Don't worry about it. Do whatever you need to do. Oh, I love Japan. Hey, I'll text you some places to go."

"Thanks, Elle. The last time, I just went snowboarding. It might be good to go incognito and check it out."

"You will be OK though, won't you? Lucy wanted you to move on and try to make a life without her. She loved you so much. I promised her I'd look out for you."

"Yeah, she made us all promise a lot of things, didn't she? I'll get there. I'll be OK at some point. And what about you? It's a shame Jude got back with Lara after all that business with the baby, but hey, it's his life. It never was the right time for you two. He was crazy about you, I know that."

"Yeah, that ship sailed a long time ago. Have you got any other perfect mates to hook me up with?"

"Like Jude? Nah, that would be tough. He's a good guy. Most dudes I know these days want hookups but no ties."

"How do you know that isn't what I need right now?" I said. "So, why Phosphorus?"

"Hey, I'm not sure; it was Jude's idea. Because there's phosphorus in agave plants? He was adamant it had to be the name, and he had the yeast and the idea. I wanted to call it Luce Juice."

"Yeah, she would never have let you call it that."

Fromenteau

S itting at Mark's desk, I slammed down the laptop screen and chucked my pen on the desk.

"Angus, I'm struggling with all this admin. I'm used to other people doing it all for me. I'm trying to understand the paperwork trail here, and I can't figure out why Jude buys grapes from Mark. What does he want with them? I mean, what's he using them for?"

"Hmm, not my area. You'll have to speak to Mark or Jude about it. I mean, does it even matter? We're making a profit, aren't we?" he said.

"I'm going out for a bit."

"OK. Bye," I said to the door.

Opening the laptop again, I pulled up all the transactions for the grape sales to La Vallée Estate. There were a ton. I called Mark, but he didn't answer, and I didn't even leave a message. Grabbing Lucy's car keys, I headed down to see Jude. She had even left me her fancy car, a Range Rover Sport, knowing I didn't have one here, and I kept her satsuma keyring on the car keys to remind me of her.

We'd bought it in Tokyo, wandering around the shop for at least half an hour. Both of us were struggling to choose one. We'd always joked about the realistic plastic food displayed in restaurant windows. We even tricked Angus once with a realistic bowl of katsu curry. Lucy had settled on a satsuma segment, and I had chosen a small melba toast with blue caviar spread over the top. The number of times I had to explain it wasn't a real melba toast was absurd. I would leave my car at the garage for a service, and when I returned, I'd be told at great length how my keyring was slowing down the mechanics' work as they took turns to inspect it. Sometimes, the cashier would ask me if it was actual food while I was at the checkout at the supermarket. Not choosing the orange had been a regret, but I didn't want to get it this way. Closing my eyes to the tears, I shoved Mark's chair under the desk.

❦

Jude was outside La Vallée. My heart still stopped whenever I saw him. Hesitation came over me after having set off with such confidence.

"Hey, Jude. How are you? I wondered if I could ask you something."

"Oh, hi, Elle. Yeah, all good. How can I help? Hey, are those my jeans?"

"Oops—yeah, you left them in New Zealand, finders keepers, plus I figured you owed me for breaking my heart. I wanted to ask you about the grapes you are buying from us. I'm trying to get my head around the admin side of the business. Sorry, I'm not used to this stuff anymore."

He looked confused. I wanted to hug him and breathe in his bergamot smell.

"Oh, it's a little sideline I've got going on."

"Will this be a permanent sideline? I mean, I have to manage the grape production, Jude. Will you need more or less for your 'sideline'?"

"OK, let me work it out and get back to you. Is that OK? It's great to have you here. I didn't know until now how much I'd missed you. Was it hard quitting the show and everything?"

"God, no. I was sick of travelling. This is home now, and I'm still writing the column for *The Times*. I'm keeping my hand in, and I'm enjoying doing some manual work. It's good for the soul. Hey, glad it all worked out with Lara."

"Thanks. Lara's great. Much improved from the train wreck when you worked here. It means a lot that you are OK with it. Gutted about how it ended with us, but I understand it."

"Understand what? Oh, well, that's water under the bridge now, isn't it? Tell me about this tequila brand. Mark's thrown me in at the deep end, and he's off soon. It would be good to know as much as possible about the technical side of production. He said you're using leftover Champagne yeast. How did you come up with the idea about the yeast?"

"It was your notebook. It fascinated me. I called your Champagne house and used their supplier, and then I had some leftovers."

"It's odd no one mentioned it to me."

"Yeah, I asked them not to. I didn't want you to think I was stepping on your toes. The Champagne yeast balances out the fruity flavour of the agave. We still use regular brewer's yeast, but we have an open-air fermentation tank. They sort of work synergistically with each other. We mustn't alter what we use now to keep the unique taste. Do you like it?"

"Oh my god, yes, it's smooth! I love it. Why Phosphorus?"

"You know the answer to that one, Darkling. Don't mention it to

Lara, though!"

I looked down at the shop and spied Lara looking out. I waved, and Jude waved, but she turned and didn't wave back.

"Hi, Nick. Was that Lara?" I said as I entered the shop door, and the bells clanged.

"Um. Yeah. Look, Lara's got the wrong idea about you two and got really mad and said he still loves you, and she didn't want to stand around watching him with you."

"No, I mean, I was asking him about grapes. It's hard. We have to work together. I don't know what else to do. There's nothing between us. It's over."

"Yeah, she wasn't listening to me. I tried to tell her. She told me to tell Jude she was leaving. Holly can do it."

At Angus's place, I slumped in the garden with a bottle of wine; over the drama—they seemed to overcomplicate everything. Then my phone rang, and it was Juliette.

"Bonjour! Oh, it's good to hear from you! Oh no—"

I saw Holly's car speeding by as if going up to Castello di Amanté and wondered where she was going in such a hurry.

Holly marched in through the garden gate, followed by Angus.

"What's going on, Holly?" he asked.

By this stage, I was in a fit of uncontrollable tears.

"What's happened? Have you seen Jude?" said Holly.

"Um, no. It's Françoise. She died. Juliette called."

Holly's anger dissipated, and she sat consoling me. Angus went inside and made me some lunch, sensing I needed food to soak up the wine.

Sometime later, Jude barrelled in through the back gate.

"Why are you crying? It's me who should be crying. Are you happy now? You've ruined everything. I wish I'd never met you," said Jude.

He stormed off, got back into his truck, and left in a cloud of dust.

"I don't understand. What have I done?"

Holly sat down and held my hand.

"Look, it's about the email. Jude says you dumped him over email after he left New Zealand. And now Lara saw you two talking earlier, and she's convinced he still loves you. Well, she packed a bag and left. I'm guessing by his mood now, he didn't make her change her mind."

"But what do you mean I sent him an email? He dumped me. Why would I do that? I'm confused. I'm too upset even to care. His relationship troubles are not my problem. I'm here living my life, and I'm not going anywhere. This is my home."

Holly left me to it as she had to pick up Walter from school, and I got stuck back into my bottle of wine. Angus said he had to go back to work too.

I called Juliette back and discovered that Françoise had died at home after a brief illness, and Juliette needed my contact information for something that had to be sent to me. She was insistent that I shouldn't travel out to France for the funeral, but of course, I would.

I called my assistant and asked him to arrange flights. "Any decision on moving out here, Ryan? I could use an assistant here, and I don't want to lose you."

"I don't think I can, Elle. My girlfriend says she doesn't want to leave London."

"That's a shame, but I understand. How about you keep working for me virtually until you find another job? I'll look for someone here when I return from France. Can you place an ad for me here?"

"Walter! Come on this way. Stop dawdling! Elle, Elle! Wake up! Wake up!" said Holly.

She shook my arm.

"What is it now? Can't you all go away and leave me alone? I'm sick of all this."

"No, listen," said Holly. "An email was sent from your account. I've seen it, but you didn't send it. Well, unless you went mental or something."

I pushed myself up on my elbows and looked at Holly.

"Aunty Elle. You're bleeding," said Walter.

I looked down at my top, and I'd spilt a whole glass of pinot noir on myself.

"Oh no, Walter, it's wine. It's OK."

"You can borrow my old bib if you like, Aunty Elle. I don't need it anymore, do I, Mum?"

Holly and I laughed.

"There was no email. Not from me. I loved Jude, and I'm still in love with him. It's why I'm still single. Every time I meet someone, they don't stack up to him. He was the love of my life. All I thought about was coming home and settling here. I was even going to leave New Zealand. Then, I had to make a whole new life alone without him. Now I have to see him every day with someone else. It's like torture."

"Yeah, well, there was something in the email I remembered. Did you change all your passwords after you split up with Zero? Elle, tell me you changed all your passwords?"

"Nah, I didn't. But wait, you think Zero sent Jude an email pretending to be me?"

"When you think of the phrase 'Look, here's the thing,' what does that do to you?"

"No?!" I shivered like someone had scraped nails on a chalkboard. "Was that in the email? Oh god, yeah, then he sent it for sure. But why?—Oh, Claire, at the wedding, remember? We talked about Zero coming to France, and she said they'd hadn't split up. Well, I've heard they got divorced now. So, this is payback? Ruining my life again?"

I dialled Zero's number and put him on loudspeaker.

"Elle?"

"You bet it's me, dickhead. Have you been sending emails from my email account? Did you send Jude an email from me?"

"Oh, for god's sake, Elle, that was bloody years ago. Get over yourself. You fucked up my marriage, so I thought I'd give you a taste of your own medicine. Also, I saw the list of all the things you hate about me in your drafts. You're a really mean bitch. Looks like I did you a favour, anyway. Let's look at the facts. I cheated on you, and you got a degree and a new career. I dumped your boyfriend over email, and you somehow became a wine critic and TV star. If not for me, you'd still be a trolley dolly pushing a cart. Your life was pathetic. Where's the gratitude?"

Jude had turned up and had been listening from the point I had said I loved him, and at Zero's speech, we all replied in chorus, "Oh, fuck off, Zero!" I covered Walter's little ears. "Excuse me? I ruined your marriage. The one you told me was over—that one? Funny, Zero, I didn't see you attending my classes, sitting exams, travelling around the world, meeting with TV executives, and presenting and producing a TV show. All you did was stick your limp dick into someone. I'm not sure how that was incentivising me to change my life. You are hands-down the most awful human being I've ever met, and now you dare to say my success is all because of you? Please! You are completely fucking delusional."

"Prick. Fucking gonna kill you, man," said Jude, lunging at the phone on the table. Standing, I pushed him away, and he stumbled backwards and sat down, sweeping back his hair, and grabbing the back of his neck.

"Who was that? Where are you?" asked Zero.

"Oh, Zero—it's the sound of me making phosphorus from all your zeroes, buddy. Duck you!" I said, releasing Walter's ears as he wriggled away.

"What does that mean, Aunty Elle?" asked Walter. "What are you making?"

"She's making something amazing out of nothing as usual," said

Jude. "That's why we love her so much."

As I ended the call, Angus walked into the garden and heard the last exchange.

"Oh my god, I got that, because you bought me Dickinson. That was a real literary burn, Elle. Still, I must confess my favourite part was the limp dick bit," he said, waving a piece of soggy celery he had in the bloody Mary he was carrying from the kitchen.

"You two need some time," said Holly. "Come on, Angus, let's find you another Bloody Mary and some fresh celery."

She kissed Jude and me on the cheek and gathered up Walter, who was looking at us all with wide-eyed curiosity.

Standing, I tried to straighten up my white linen shirt but saw it was all buttoned up wrong, the wine stain making it look worse, so I tried to rub it off. Jude laughed, shook his head, and pulled me close.

"Jude, we missed the boat. Go back and salvage your relationship with Lara. You can do it. It's so important to me."

"Well, if my happiness is important to you, you'll come here," he said, pulling me close again. "Lara and I had a chat, and it ended well. I think we can even be friends at some point. She pointed out to me— a love like this, you don't ignore it; you don't take it for granted because most people never have it. She said I had to accept that you're my soul mate, Elle Darkling."

"But how do I know you won't run off at the first sign of trouble, Jude? You didn't even fight for us when you thought I'd emailed you. Why didn't you call me and say what the fuck? Or speak to Angus,

Lucy, or Holly—even Mark would have told you it was insane. All this would never have happened. I need to know this is for good."

He paused and looked off into the distance.

"I can prove it to you."

He grabbed my hand and pulled me outside.

Outside La Vallée, the bougainvillaea was blooming and had doubled in size from when I'd seen it years before. Angus and Holly sat out front, entertaining Walter and sipping chilled La Limonar.

"Have we made up?" asked Angus.

"It's time to show her the good stuff," said Jude.

He threw his arms up in the air, and I stood by, watching them all as if they were in some bizarre play they had rehearsed for years without me.

Holly and Angus shrieked, and so did Walter, and they called out for Nick to close the shop. He came running over, beaming from ear to ear. I looked at each of them.

"What's going on here?"

Luis let out a big mew and jumped out of Walter's rucksack. He ran over to me, and I picked him up for a cuddle. "Are you in on this too, Luis?"

We all headed to the iron gates that led the way to the path to the cellars. My face burned, recalling the last time I had been here, and I looked down in case anyone saw me.

As Jude pushed open the oak doors, the freshness hit us as we ventured deeper and deeper through each tiled tunnel. I loved any cellar. I loved their stark, minimalist nature. They had one job, and there were no extra furniture additions or anything non-functional to distract from the primary job of ageing and storing wine. The simplicity of that captivated me.

After a fast-paced march down one tunnel, we stopped in front of rows and rows of dark green bottles. It was like bumping into an old friend on the other side of the world, which had happened to me several times.

I knew the shape, but nothing matched with La Vallée Estate. The bottles were too big and too dark. Jude turned around and lifted a bottle, which he presented to me. He looked into my eyes, searching for my response.

"Elle, we love you but disagreed with your speech at Lucy's funeral. You are the catalyst for everything that's happened to us over the last few years. You connect us all. What Zero said back there made me mad because you didn't need him or any of us; you changed your life, and this incredible story grew, and because of you, wonderful things have happened to us all."

"Aw, stop. That's what life is about—the connections between us all. I didn't say it well when I talked about the mushrooms. I had it all written down, but then I cried on the speech and couldn't read it anyway.

"What I was trying to say is that it's like cells. One on its own is nothing. There's a reason we are comprised of over thirty trillion of them. We're nothing without each other. It's not my actions that make your life a success; it's the connection of all our lives. Holly telling me to quit flying, Angus inventing my alter ego, Lucy starting Ignite, you giving me a job here, Grey being kind when I was low, even fucking

Zero sleeping with Alex. A series of connections led us to this cellar right now. What are we doing in it, anyway? What's going on?"

"Read the label, Darkling."

They all crowded around me. Holly was bawling, and even Nick had to pinch back the tears. Angus put an arm around me. My heart was full of love as I studied my perfect, imperfect family. I looked down at the bottle in my hand. Here was the unmistakable mushroom cork in its wire muselet. The bottle was heavy, and I pushed my hand into the deep concave, twisted the bottle up to a small shaft of light and read the label: Méthode Traditionnelle, La Fille Maladroit, La Vallée Estate, 2022.

fini